KRIS LONGKNIFE: STALWART

MIKE SHEPHERD

COPYRIGHT INFORMATION

Published by KL & MM Books
December 2019
Copyright © 2019 by Mike Moscoe

All rights reserved. No part of this book may be reproduced or transmitted in any form or by any electronic or mechanical means, including photocopying, recording or any other information storage and retrieval system, without the written permission of the publisher.

This book is a work of fiction set 400 years in humanity's future. Any similarity between present people, places or events would be spectacularly unlikely and is purely coincidental.

This book is written and published by the author. Please don't pirate it. I'm self-employed. The money I earn from the sales of these books allows me to produce more stories to entertain you. I'd hate to have to get a day job again. If this book comes into your hands free, please consider going to your favorite e-book provider and investing in a copy so I can continue to earn a living at this wonderful art.

I would like to thank my wonderful cover artist, Lee Moyer. His skill created our cover illustration and design. I also am grateful for the editing skills of Lisa Müller, Edee Lemonier, David Vernon Houston, and as ever, my wife Ellen Moscoe.

Rev 1.0

Cover Illustration and Design © Lee Moyer

Ebook ISBN-13: 978-1-64211-0333
Print ISBN-13: 978-1-64211-0340

PRAISE FOR THE KRIS LONGKNIFE NOVELS

"A whopping good read . . . Fast-paced, exciting, nicely detailed, with some innovative touches." - Elisabeth Moon, Nebula Award-winning author of Crown Renewal

"Shepherd delivers no shortage of military action, in space and on the ground. It's cinematic, dramatic, and dynamic . . . [He also] demonstrates a knack for characterization, balancing serious moments with dry humor . . . A thoroughly enjoyable adventure featuring one of science fiction's most interesting recurring heroines." - Tor.com

"A tightly written, action-packed adventure from start to finish . . . Heart-thumping action will keep the reader engrossed and emotionally involved. It will be hard waiting for the next in the series." - Fresh Fiction

"[Daring] will elate fans of the series . . . The story line is faster than the speed of light." - Alternative Worlds

"[Kris Longknife] will remind readers of David Weber's Honor

Harrington with her strength and intelligence. Mike Shepherd provides an exciting military science fiction thriller." -Genre Go Round Reviews

"'I'm a woman of very few words, but lots of action': so said Mae West, but it might just as well have been Lieutenant Kris Longknife, princess of the one hundred worlds of Wardhaven. Kris can kick, shoot, and punch her way out of any dangerous situation, and she can do it while wearing stilettos and a tight cocktail dress. She's all business, with a Hell's Angel handshake and a 'get out of my face' attitude. But her hair always looks good . . . Kris Longknife is funny and she entertains us." - SciFi Weekly

"[A] fast-paced, exciting military SF series . . . Mike Shepherd has a great ear for dialogue and talent for injecting dry humor into things at just the right moment . . . The characters are engaging, and the plot is full of twists and peppered liberally with sharply described action. I always look forward to installments in the Kris Longknife series because I know I'm guaranteed a good time with plenty of adventure." -SF Site

In the New York Times bestselling Kris Longknife novels, "Fans of the Honor Harrington escapades will welcome the adventures of another strong female in outer space starring in a thrill-a-page military space opera." - Alternative Worlds

"Military SF fans are bound to get a kick out of the series as a whole." - SF Site

AUTHOR'S SPECIAL NOTE TO READER

Acknowledgement

I'd like to thank you for waiting patiently for this book. It took off with a mind of it's own and is chock full of action and adventure.

I know we missed our usual November 1 deadline, but it couldn't be helped. As you know, I've been searching for illustrators and finally found one! Lee Moyer is a local, Pacific Northwest artist with has many skills, the least of which is creating and designing book covers. I am so grateful for his skills and attention to detail and of making my dream of Kris in a kimono come true.

I'd like to thank my senior editor, Lisa Müller, for all the work of getting this manuscript into the pleasant format you're reading. Edee Lemonier, David Vernon Houston, and Gwen Moscoe deserve credit for spotting my usual swarm of nits. We do try.

Next year, 2020 will be an adventure! I'm anticipating another Kris novel, a Vicky novel, and perhaps a book involving Sandy Santiago or Grandma Rita, and or interim novella or two. For updates, do follow my Facebook page, Mike Shepherd.

Enjoy the read and thank you for all your kind words of encouragement!

Happy Holidays,

Mike

1

Grand Admiral Kris Longknife, first Human ambassador to the Imperial Iteeche Court stood on the observation deck of her new embassy in the Imperial Capital. A soft breeze blew through her hair. The air at this height was cool and crisp and clear of the pollution at street level. The view was incredible.

"Nelly, Abby, you have really outdone yourselves this time."

"I'm so glad you like it," Abby drawled, drolly. "I half-expected you to want us to do it over again."

Abby might no longer be Kris's maid, but she hadn't lost any of the attitude she reserved for her employer.

"What changes might you want?" the Magnificent Nelly asked from around Kris's neck. "I can have it done in five minutes. Less if I don't have to involve too many humans."

Kris's personal computer, her sidekick from her first day at school, had often been upgraded. The last upgrade involved adding a chip from a planet that aliens had turned into one super, computer-based, adult learning center. After that, Nelly became even more sentient, and had started telling atrocious jokes and giving Kris a lot of backtalk.

There was, however, no device in the entire galaxy to rival the lively and magnificent Nelly.

"I think I'll just enjoy what you've done for a while," Kris said, cautiously. Sometimes she had to be very careful what she asked Nelly for. She might deliver it.

"It's beautiful up here," Jack Montoya, Kris's husband, and father of her two children said into her ear. He stood behind her, holding her tight in a hug. "You have truly made a silk purse out of a sow's ear again."

They stood 800 meters high above the endless city. The Imperial Palace grounds was a splotch of green in one direction. The rest of the capital sprawled out before them, stretching away to the horizon in all directions.

That Nelly and Abby had been able to design and build this massive new embassy in less than a month was a testimony to Nelly's capability, Abby's street smarts, and the wondrous phenomenon of Smart Metal™. A month ago, the structure that was now the embassy had been part of six battlecruisers, starships capable of crossing the galaxy and fighting their way out of just about any tough spot Kris might get them into.

Now they were all part of a vast building standing on an 800 meter-square block in the closest ring of avenues circling the Imperial Palace.

Until a month ago, the previous owners of this large swatch of valuable real estate had been one of the five most ancient and largest clans ruling the Iteeche Empire. These same clans pulled the strings on the "all powerful" puppet of an Emperor. The Domm Clan made the mistake of starting a rebellion, grasping for more control over those strings.

Then they made an even worse mistake. The Domm Clan tried to bury Grand Admiral, Her Royal Highness Princess Kris Longknife under six fifteen-story apartment complexes.

That had been a bad mistake.

By the time the sun rose the next day, that clan's palace was a smoking hole in the ground, in bad need of redevelopment. Kris had persuaded the young Emperor to grant her that hole in the ground, and now the wreckage of the Domm Clan Palace was 500 kilometers to the west awaiting the return of how ever many members of the clan survived this civil war.

They were no longer one of the five most powerful clans and not likely to be so ever again.

There was a lesson in that: *Don't mess with Kris Longknife.*

Kris hoped she didn't have to teach too many more Iteeche that lesson, but some of the four-eyed, four-armed, four-legged aliens could be very poor students.

The civil war was still raging out among the nearly 3,000 planets of the Iteeche Empire. Pretty soon, Kris would have to get back to that. However, for now, she could enjoy Jack's arms around her and the view from her Embassy.

"Kris," Nelly announced, "General Konga of the Imperial Guard would like to talk with you."

"General," Kris immediately said, "What can I do for you?"

"I would very much like to meet with you. Are you busy?"

"At the moment, I'm relaxing on the observation deck of the Embassy. Is this business or pleasure, General?"

"More likely pleasure than business, but do the likes of you and I ever get to do just one or the other of those?"

"I can't remember the last time I did," she said, squeezing Jack's hand to let him know she did, indeed, remember when it had been just pleasure for them.

"May I join you? I imagine that you must have quite a view from up there."

"Most assuredly. I will meet you at the elevator below."

"You don't need to bother yourself. I imagine someone can guide me up."

"Oh, you will definitely need an officer guide to get you up here, even as far as the elevator. However, the exit terminates into our battle station. I'd very much enjoy showing you just how we defend this embassy. Now, with your Imperial Guard quarters located so close to us, you will come under our umbrella if someone is so foolish as to make another attempt that involves slinging rockets at us."

"I would very much like to see what you call your battle station. I have had several enlightening conversations with the admiral responsible for defense of the airspace above the Imperial capital. He was quite impressed with the defense of your previous embassy. That only involved two starships worth of your magic metal. I can only imagine what you must be capable of now that you have added six more."

"Yes, and these came equipped with 24-inch lasers," Kris added, diffidently. Still, she doubted her light comment was lost on the general.

"Yes. I would like to know which direction those lasers are pointed."

"I can understand your interest, General. I will meet you at the elevator in my battle station."

With that, Kris cut the connection. "Well folks, fun's over."

"Back to work for us galley slaves," Abby said.

"Nope. I'd very much like you to be at my elbow when we talk to the general. Nelly, I don't usually ask you to do this, but could you use Smart Metal to weave all three of us a set of full-dress uniforms with all the gee gaws?"

Without even replying, Smart Metal flowed up from the deck to clothe Jack in the dress red and blues of a full general of the Royal US Marines. Abby's uniform was the dress whites of an Army brigadier with a full chest of medals. Kris's uniform was also dress whites with a ton of fruit salad that she had somehow managed to survive earning.

Kris didn't often come a Grand Admiral with intent, but this seemed like a good day to do it.

Nelly even put a Grand Admiral's baton in Kris's hand.

"My, aren't you being fancy," Kris observed.

"You're the one that asked for all the gee gaws," Nelly snapped back.

Prepared to impress, Grand Admiral Kris Longknife went to meet the commander of the Iteeche Imperial Guard.

2

Kris led her tiny leadership team downstairs and out of the fresh air, through the heavy armored hatch, and into the secure battle station. The air took on the familiar scent of ozone, light machine oil, sweat, and canned air familiar to all places where people made deadly decisions or waited, expectantly, hoping today would not be that day.

"Admiral on deck," the Marine colonel commanding the watch announced as Kris entered his domain.

"As you were, Colonel," Kris said, glancing around the dimly lit room with all its luminous gear. Readouts displayed information across the full spectrum of the rainbow. They told Kris little, except that there was nothing hooting or blinking red. Those attending each set of instruments were highly trained to comprehend and interpret the future that all the colors augured.

Those standing, who had gone to attention, relaxed. Those seated at their stations may have sat more attentively, but none had stood. They had a job to do.

"Colonel, General Konga of the Imperial Guard will be arriving shortly. He's just passing through to the observation deck, but he may benefit from a quick orientation on what we do here."

"How much of an orientation?" the colonel asked.

"Unclassified only. No Foreign Eyes."

"Understood, Admiral. All hands, attention to orders. US eyes only, no alien eyes. Gear is to be turned to neutral. Set alarms, but no readouts. Understood?"

"Aye, aye, sir," answered him and about a fifth of the screens in the battle station turned to something else. They still looked like they were reporting something important, but it wasn't what they'd been showing a moment before.

Doubtlessly, they'd been tracking comm traffic. The Humans now had full access to the entire Iteeche net, including the private and encoded personal message traffic. Likely, the general had his suspicions that the Humans had gone past just using the Imperial net and had penetrated it for their own purposes.

It was obvious to any astute observer that Kris had come from Human space with some aces up her sleeves. Otherwise, how could she have pulled off the force deployment that had stopped two major clans in their tracks when they made a grab for the young Emperor?

Still, there was no need to confirm the suspicion.

The elevator dinged its arrival.

Kris and her team turned toward the doors as they slid open. There stood an Iteeche, General Konga of the Imperial Guard. Beside him was a Marine captain, calm as if every day he escorted generals with way too many eyes, elbows, and knees around the Human embassy.

General Konga raised both his top hands to shade his eyes, the Iteeche salute. Kris and her team raised their right hand, returning the honor.

"Oh," Kris said, "you're not in formal dress."

The Iteeche raised all four of his eyebrows. "Did I miss something? Is there a parade today?"

Kris chuckled. "No, General, no parade. I should have checked in with your escort to learn what your uniform of the day was. I take what you're wearing is an undress uniform?"

"My everyday uniform. Yes."

"Nelly, change Abby and I to undress whites and Jack to undress khaki."

In a moment, the spare Smart Metal™ was flowing off Kris and her team to merge back into the deck. In the place of full dress uniforms, the three Humans now stood in undress uniform shirts and trousers.

The Imperial Guard general shook his head. Because the Iteeche had a backbone that was just two long bones, a head shake had to start at the hips, so his entire body ended up twisting slowly back and forth.

"I wish you Humans would stop doing things like that with your magic metal." He seemed to frown, something not easy with the hard beak for a nose and mouth that evolution had given the Iteeche as well as a few facial muscles. However, Kris was getting better at reading Iteeche faces.

He was definitely frowning.

"You do so many things with your magic metal. Did your computer just weave cloth out of it and duplicate all your medals?"

"I'm afraid that you found us relaxing on the observation deck in very informal clothes, General," Kris admitted. "Rather than delay our meeting until we could return to our quarters and dress properly, yes, I asked Nelly to program us up some uniforms of Smart Metal."

"I could understand you using the magic metal to create armor for you Humans, but simple cloth? How is that possible?"

"Actually, General," Nelly said from Kris's neck, "it's no harder to spin cloth out of Smart Metal than it is to create ceramic armor. It all depends on the way I program it. The bed I sleep on, the pillow I lay my head on, and the fluffy towel that I dry myself on after I take a shower are all made of the exact same stuff as these instruments are made from, or the thick armor that protects this battle station."

"Magic," the Iteeche spat. "Magic. And the Nelly computer around your neck is just more of the magic. How did we people ever think we could defeat you aliens?"

"Neither of our people intended or wanted to fight each other," Kris pointed out, referring to the Iteeche-Human War of ninety years past. "Your masterless men and our pirates stumbled into each other and started the fight. I'm just glad my Chooser of many generations, Grampa to me and King Raymond I to everyone else, could resolve the war before it became too bitter to end."

"I as well. Speaking of now," the general said, his eyes roving over the battle station, "is one of these devices your people attend to the one that lets you keep track of all the messages we commit to our net?"

Kris hadn't expected a question that blunt. She'd have to dance around it carefully. She didn't want to actually lie to someone she needed to work with.

"What makes you think we can do that?" she asked.

The Iteeche's four eyes continued to rove the battle station. "I have talked with the battle leaders of both the We and Quo Clans. They told me how aware you were of the treacherous plans of the Wo and Domm Clans. You knew down to almost the exact moment when they would move to capture the Emperor. How, but with access to our comm lines, could you have known that?"

"Actually, it was easy. There was way too much easy talk among the middle grade officers in the armories. After you hear the forty-eleventh say how excited he is and that his men are ready to move out at o-dark-early, you know something's afoot. The JOs called it pretty close to when they got their move-out orders. Meanwhile, I had deployed my troops in innocent-looking trucks of Smart Metal based on the loose talk among those junior clan lordlings."

"Oh yes," the Imperial Guard General mused. "you do have those tiny dust motes with eyes and ears. Still, how did you come to be right there, ready to block the attacks on the entrances to the Imperial Precincts by what looked like just random civilians?"

"General, that was just using our head," Kris said. "Anyone who wanted to seize the Emperor would have to breach the Imperial grounds. I didn't know how or when they would do that, but I positioned myself and some of my forces to be there, waiting for them to make their move. When the so called 'rabble' began to tramp toward your gate guards, I moved to block their way."

"With armored gun trucks," the general pointed out. "Armored gun trucks that close to the Imperial Palace." He gave Kris the sternest look she'd ever seen from an Iteeche. "That is forbidden."

Kris had to squelch a grin as she said, "Yes, I parked *armored trucks* nearby where they could slide in between your guards and the rabble. Only when your guards asked for our active help did the *armored trucks* become *armored gun trucks*."

"There you go, using that magic metal again," the general growled as he filled in for himself how armored trucks suddenly became armored *gun* trucks.

"Yes. When we needed guns, we spun them out of our Smart Metal. We had propellent for the autocannons, but until your officer asked for our help in defending the Emperor, there were no guns."

"You Humans are sly creatures."

"Say, rather, that we have technology that allows us to meet our duty to your Emperor without violating the laws of your Empire."

The Guard General shook his head. "You think of so many ways to use that magic metal. We make the battlecruisers or tanks or wheeled gun trucks that you have shown us how to make, but we can't seem to think of ways to program new uses like you do."

"If you will permit me to speak truth as it is known to me," Kris said slowly, "the Iteeche Empire puts a lot of effort into doing things the way it has always been done. Your clan leaders send runners to carry messages from one clan to another. That must slow the business of the day down very much."

"You get on the commlink and talk all the time," the general said. "There are those who do not wish to live at the end of a red-hot wire stuck up their butts."

Kris and the humans around her chuckled. "Yes. There are a lot of Humans who would agree with you on that. Still, we have bureaucracies where different people are responsible for different things, much like you Iteeche. Minor problems are solved by minor officials. Only the most difficult problems should show up on the senior people's desks."

"Does it work out well that way?" General Konga asked.

Kris looked at her team.

"Not even close," Abby drawled ruefully. "Still, you bop someone on the head, and he knows not to send the easy stuff up to his boss the next time. You bop him enough, and he learns . . . or you get someone else who will."

The general slowly shook his head. "I wonder if we could learn things like that."

"That's what kids are for," Kris said. "Each generation starts the struggle all over again."

"And the older generation complains about them all the time," Abby said, with a chuckle.

"You Humans and your affection for those you spawn. . . is it wrong to say you Chose them?" General Konga said.

"We women produce them from our own bodies, or vessels we call uterine replicators," Kris said. "Yes, we know they are flesh of our flesh and we raise them up to be as full of piss and virtue as we can."

"Hmm, we should talk more about that another time. Now, could we go up to your observation deck? I have some concerns that we must resolve."

Kris raised an inquiring eyebrow, but the Iteeche likely didn't understand the gesture . . . or ignored it.

Since he said no more, Kris led the way to the secure hatch and up to the observation deck.

She allowed herself a sigh of relief. The general hadn't asked again about where the 24-inch lasers that had armed the battle-cruisers were aimed. She hadn't let him see that they covered a 360 degree circle around the embassy. A circle that included aiming huge battle lasers in the direction of the Imperial Palace.

Kris didn't expect an attack from the Palace. She did expect that an attack could be mounted from the mountains 50 kilometers in the distance. Yes, her embassy was ready to apply heavy laser power in every direction.

3

At the top of the stairs, the four of them paused to take in the rare view of the Iteeche Capital from 450 meters up.

"You can see everything from up here," Imperial Guard General Konga said after doing a slow walk around the perimeter of the observation deck.

"Yes, we can," Kris answered.

He paused facing the tree-covered precincts of the Imperial Palace. It was surrounded by a flooded moat of gray stone etched in the green of what the Iteeche no doubt called moss.

Looking hard at over 60 square kilometers of trees, lakes, and buildings, the general asked, "Which one of those devices above our head is the spy glass you use to watch on Imperial Precincts?"

"I have no optics focused on the Imperial Palace grounds," Kris answered, careful to be honest.

"No, nothing so prosaic. I imagine you use those dust motes with eyes and ears. Tell me, do they drift around the palace or do they stick to the trees and flowers?"

"Likely a little of both," Kris admitted.

"Well, that's honest of you."

"Would you rather we be taken by surprise when the next treachery occurs?"

The Imperial Guard General, charged with protecting the physical person of the young Emperor, turned from the view. "No. The times are strange when my most trusted ally in the protection of the Emperor's life is a hated Human."

"I hope that if I earn your trust, I will no longer be hated," Kris said.

"But most of the Iteeche in this city were taught to hate you Humans from the moment we were Chosen and passed into the Palace of Learning."

"Can hate be unlearned?" Kris asked.

"Let us hope so," the general said, turning from the view of the Imperial Palace. He glanced down at the Embassy Palace beneath him. "I see that you have not repeated your cold and threatening image of a dagger in the heart of our capital."

"Dagger?" Kris asked.

"That gleaming monstrosity you hung in the sky over your last palace."

"I'd intended it to look like a starship," Kris said.

"That's not what it looked like to us."

"Hmm. Nelly, why did you choose this architectural form for my new embassy?"

"The embassy is in the shape of a U with the open end pointed out from the palace toward the rest of the city. This reflects the structures regularly repeated in the Iteeche apartments. Some are U's. Others are in the form of E's. All use the space between wings for greenery or pools of water," Nelly replied.

"So, you are trying to do something like we Iteeche do," the general said.

"Yes, only much bigger. We need more space, so I built a much taller version of the standard U.

"But you aimed the U toward the city," the general pointed out.

"Yes. I thought it would be better if the average Iteeche saw us as more like them," Nelly said,

"You've also softened the surface of your building. It's not so much dazzling chrome and glass."

"I made it to look more like stone," Nelly answered. "I also broke up the hard lines of the building with balconies of different sizes."

"And bought up about all the available greenery within a thousand lu of the palace," the general said.

"Some of those will be gardens for growing Human produce," Nelly answered. "We hope to grow many fruit trees, our own grapes, and some of the heartier perennial grains."

"We Humans," Kris said, stepping back into the conversation, "have an ancient story about the hanging gardens of Babylon. We are hoping that we can present a green and fresh face to the Iteeche, both those in the palace and those who work for them."

The general nodded. "And that place down there that looks like an entire floor or more?"

At about the fiftieth floor, far below them, the entire U was filled with a large open-air space.

Kris chuckled. "That, good general, is a playground. It has a huge swimming pool, a water park, exercise space, and room for our children to run and scream and grow their small muscles into larger ones."

"A playground for children? That large?"

"We have a lot of children in the embassy, General. But it's not just the children's play area. A lot of their parents love to play with them. My own children were complaining about not getting out into the open air. Now they and their friends can. We're also shipping air from up here to down there. Along with the scent of growing things, it should make for a very good experience."

"You Humans never cease to amaze me," General Konga said as he turned back to face the Imperial Palace grounds. However, it wasn't the green space he focused on but something closer.

"Do you know how many interesting things your taking possession of the Domm Clan's district is making possible?"

Kris shook her head.

"Your gift of the apartments next to the palace in your borough is giving my officers and men chances to express themselves as never before."

Kris listened intently, waiting for the general to go on.

"Privacy is something rare for an Iteeche, but much sought after. For want of space, my Guardsmen and even officers live in barracks. The females we associate with live in harems. They aren't restricted to them, but still. Men sleep in one part of the barracks, women in another. They may spend time with each other over meals or at entertaining sing-alongs, but still, they go their separate ways."

"I had heard that," Kris said.

"Now, we have space to spread out. We have six apartment buildings that are ours. Can you imagine what that is like?"

"No, I can't," Kris admitted. "Even our warships can expand to give people space. Then, come a battle, we shrink them down into fighting ships."

"Well, you have done something to my Guardsmen and their women. To the sailors and their women. Taking this space away from the Domm Clan and giving it to us, the lowest of the low, is changing things. For us. For them. Maybe for the Iteeche Empire."

"My father warned me that we rarely do just one thing," Kris said. "I wanted to take the space away from the Domm Clan. They'd lost and I wanted them to appear to all as having lost. I also thought that your Guardsmen and the sailors deserved more respect."

"Oh, we are getting respect," General Konga said. "Respect that we are feeling. Space like we never would have expected. You have to understand, we soldiers, sailors, and Marines are the leftovers. We weren't good enough to be selected by the Choosers. Still, we were good enough not to be flushed through the grinder and turned into fish food for the next pool full of fingerlings. We were plucked out to namelessly serve the Empire. Members of the clans have long names that identify their pedigree. We have a name that they can use to holler at us."

Kris had never detected this taste of bitterness from an Iteeche officer. Was it universal or just something that was stuck in this general's craw? It was hard to tell. She'd need to have this talk with Admiral Tong when she found time.

"Yesterday," the general went on, "I was inspecting living spaces. In the apartment of one of my junior officers, I found a woman. I asked him if he had chosen her for a concubine. He said that she had chosen him. He had the silliest grin on his face, but he made it worse. The two of them had a ... I guess you Humans would call it an aquarium. He had been granted permission to be a Chooser after his gallantry in the defense of the Emperor. The two of them had mated and brought the fruit of their mating home to watch them grow. They know they can choose only one, but they are watching them all."

The general turned to glare at Kris with all four of his eyes. "The two of them looked at those tadpoles just as smitten as I see you Humans with your children."

"Hmm," Kris said. "That is ... interesting."

"Is that what you call it? Interesting? I call it shocking."

"I call it change," Kris said.

"Yes. Change. Change such as this old Empire has not seen in several eons."

"Maybe the young Iteeche they raise will be the seeds that flower with the sort of change we were talking about earlier," Kris pointed out.

"It is still frightening to an old man like me."

"Do you have a woman friend?" Kris asked.

"Yes," he snarled. "And she says she is tired of living in a harem with the other women and would very much like to share my quarters."

Kris said nothing. Not a word.

The silence between them stretched out and began to bend in the middle. Before long, it would be a pretzel if someone didn't talk.

Kris kept her silence.

"Worse, several of the woman are asking their men for arms training. Just yesterday, I came across a class in the exercise room. An old Marine sergeant was teaching twenty women how to fight, hand-to-hand. I am scheduled to visit our firing range. I must requalify on my sidearms every half year. I have been warned that I may see many Guardsmen there, training their women how to shoot. It seems that some of the women shoot better than the men."

"We have found that female snipers can be deadlier than the men," Kris noted.

The general turned to eye the embassy that lay at his feet. "I thought that when we sent you off to build your new embassy that we had you well away from our sandy beach, busy chasing after wild gossips and anticipated that we would not see you again for a long time. Instead, you conjure this out of nothing and have thrown a snowball off of a snow-covered mountain."

"A small snowball can create an avalanche," Kris remarked.

"And you, Human Princess, seem to know exactly where to throw snowballs."

"I have been told that trouble follows in my footsteps."

"And here I thought we'd brought you here to solve our troubles."

"Yes. Speaking of which, I will soon be leaving. I have a few more planets to conquer."

"I had heard that you were going to take matters more slowly."

"Yes, I had heard that, too. However, I think I need to kick some rebels a few more times in their shins before I offer them an olive branch."

"Well, at least you are talking about that olive branch. I suspect that the Domm Clan will not be happy to speak of peace with you."

"Yes, but the lesson I taught the Domm Clan here may create opportunities with others. If not for profit, then to avoid further losses."

"I can only wish you a quick departure. I wonder what our fine capital will look like when we next see you."

"We have a saying. 'Rome was not built in a day.' "

The general looked nonplussed.

"Great cities are not built in a day," Kris amended. "Change has to be built slowly."

"You have not seen what I have," General Konga said. "At least among the fleet and Guard, they like the change they see."

"Until we meet again?" Kris said.

"Yes," the general answered.

With that, the general left, leaving Kris with her husband and Abby.

"That was interesting," Abby drawled. "Kind of surprising, but interesting."

Jack shook his head. "It is stupid for an Empire to separate itself from those who defend its existence. No ruling class should treat its defenders like second-class citizens."

"More like dirt," Kris said. "The clans have first- and second-class citizens. The Navy, Marines, and Guardsmen are not even in a track for citizenship."

"So, you treat them decently," Abby said, "and they'll be eating out of your hand in no time."

"Or eat your hand off up to the elbow," Jack added.

Kris mused for a moment on both their thoughts, then said, "You both seem to have the proper take on it."

For a moment longer, Kris enjoyed the air and the view from up here, then she shook herself. "Okay, team, we've had enough fun for the day, let's get back to work. I got a war to win."

"But win slowly," Abby said.

"Yeah, very slowly," Jack added.

Kris said nothing as she lead them out of the sunlight and down the stairs.

4

It had been a while since Kris held a staff meeting. She'd talked almost daily with each member of her staff but hadn't had time to talk to them all together. Now it was past time.

While the embassy was very imposing from the outside, much of the inside was vast volumes of empty space. It had to be that way. If all that space had been divided up among those still in the embassy, each man, woman, and child would have a hectare of deck to call their own. It would take half an hour for anyone to get to breakfast.

Most of the humans were crammed into the top twenty stories.

Thus, to find room for Kris's meeting, Nelly had bulged her day quarters out onto the balcony. It provided for a nice view of the Imperial precincts.

At Kris's elbows sat Jack and Abby, then Abby's husband, Lieutenant General Bruce RUSMC. He'd commanded the defense of the embassy during the rocket attack.

Next to him were Gramma and Grampa Trouble, temporarily borrowed from riding herd on Kris's two kids. The two of them were Kris's great-grandparents and veterans of the Iteeche War. There, both of them, first Grampa, then Gramma, had earned their name. It was no longer a nickname. Grampa was trouble to his enemies, trouble to his superiors, and very often just too much trouble to have around. Still, he'd earned four stars. Gramma had only won a single star, but any Marine in Human space braced when she came in sight.

Amanda and Jacques were next, representing Kris's brain trust. Amanda was a brilliant economist who, at last report, was still trying to figure out the Iteeche economic system, if what they did followed any sort of system. Jacques was a sociologist and fascinated by the structures and strictures of Iteeche society. Like everyone else on staff, the more he learned about the Iteeche, the more puzzled he became.

Admiral Tong provided the Iteeche voice on Kris' staff. He commanded the Iteeche Battle Fleet swinging around the station well over their head. He had escorted Kris back to the capital and his fleet Marine Force had provided Kris with the fire power to resolve the recent unpleasantness before it got out of hand.

He was now her right-hand Iteeche.

At his elbow was his own right-hand man. Admiral Ulan was acting Chief of Staff for the Combined Fleets. He'd stayed back at headquarters in the capital, holding down the fort, while Kris and Admirals Coth and Tong were out winning battles. Still, Ulan was the man to go to if you wanted to know where the most recent skeletons had been interred around the capital.

Both had served well in the recent imbroglio.

Coming back around the table was Ambassador Kawaguchi. He represented not only Musashi and Yamato but several other small associations. He had also been the sole ambassador not to run for the exit when things got hot. While the rest of the trade delegations from Human space, even old Earth, had failed to find anything to trade with the Iteeche, he had. Today, he had a man at his elbow who also had the lean and hungry look of a diplomat. No doubt, the ambassador would introduce his guest.

Which brought Kris's gaze to Lieutenant Megan Longknife, Kris's young cousin and *aide de camp*. The young woman was about due for a promotion. Time in grade didn't mean that much to Kris. A year around her passed quicker, like dog years.

Next to Amanda was Jack.

Kris started with Abby. In theory, she was the contract boss supporting all administrative needs for the embassy. If you needed anything, from an ice cream sundae to a large ballroom for a diplomatic reception, or a nice huge hall to throw a beer bash for a victorious army, Abby supplied it.

"Anything we need to know about the workings of the embassy?" Kris asked.

Abby shook her head. "I've just about polished off the long list of grumbles about the new spaces in the tower. I don't expect any more," she said, scowling around the table.

Kris doubted anyone would dare.

"We've refilled our pantry and freezers now that no one's protesting around us and keeping folks from running up and down the beanstalk. I got a few replacements in this week for those that ran when things got a little hot. My staff is at full strength. We're having no problems quartering that brigade of Marines you've got down here. How long they gonna stay?" Abby queried.

"I haven't decided yet," Kris said. "Depends on when I sail the fleet out of here."

"Any idea when that will be?" Jack asked.

"I'm still thinking about it as I watch the clans shake out their new pecking order. Trust me, General, you'll be the first to know."

"Hmm," her husband and the head of her security force muttered.

Kris ignored any vague question buried in that response and went on, "General Bruce?"

"The embassy defenses are fully online, ship shape and Bristol fashion. We can protect the embassy from everything from rioters to rockets. We've also taken over security for six blocks around the embassy. Iteeche MPs are walking the beat in this district you 'inherited.' It seems that law enforcement as well as the fire department is part of the clan's power in its own enclave. The MPs are keeping an eye on strangers who wander in. Some we bust for spying on us. Some we let outsmart us. It's better to have a few tame spies than not know who is in the business around you. Thanks for giving me Agent Foile. He really understands how this game is played."

"Is he having any trouble tracking our spies back to their clients?" Kris asked.

"We're bugging them and tracing them when they wander home," Steve said, then shrugged. "Usually they take steam baths as soon as they get back from their foray into our space. That washes off the bugs, but by then we know which clan they moseyed back to."

"Don't you just hate it when the bad guys learn the dirty tricks you're playing on them?" Abby drawled, ruefully.

Sadly, Kris agreed with Abby, but she had more to do. "Who's spying on us?"

"Everyone, I think," Bruce said, with a lopsided grin. "Our friends like the We and Quo Clans are keeping an eye on us. Same for the clans that sat out the last shoot-out. Of course, those clans that don't like us are doing their best to watch from behind the curtains. There hasn't been a twitch from the clans who went to war with us last month, but then, there isn't a lot of them left."

That got a snicker from most of those around the table. The two diplomats stayed diplomatically straight-faced.

"Five will get you ten," Jack said, "that some enterprising Iteeche opens a public steam bath a block or two from our district so the spies can wash off sooner."

Kris shook her head. So did everyone else around the table.

"No takers, huh?" Jack muttered.

"Bruce," Kris said, "I got a nice, friendly visit from General Konga today. I walked him through the battle station, and we hung around the viewing deck for a bit. I'm pretty sure he was looking for the 24-inch lasers we took off the battlecruisers that we made the embassy out of. Where are you storing those lasers?"

"I figured you wouldn't want them aimed at anything unless and until we needed them. Abby gave me space from the twentieth to the fortieth floors to store the lasers, their reactors, and their capacitors. I figured you'd want them handy if we needed them, but not threatening anyone if we didn't need to."

"Good thinking, General. Yes, I don't want to look too paranoid, but my mom didn't raise any stupid children."

"There are times when I wonder about that," Jack muttered.

"Down, husband. This is official business and you must not give away state secrets."

That drew chuckles again from around the table. Even the diplomats cracked smiles.

Kris figured she'd heard all there was to hear from her defense chief. She passed on to her historical advisors.

"Gramma, Grampa, can you add anything to help us figure out the enigma of the Iteeche Empire?"

"It is interesting that they are allowing you to set up shop so much closer to the Emperor and violate their building height limits around the palace," Gramma Trouble opened with. "Back in the day, every Iteeche POW we had did the same thing every day. They followed the orders of superior clan lordlings we captured and kind of set up their own demi-clan in our POW camps. You earned a lot of good karma when you saved the Emperor and they're letting you break rules they wouldn't let anyone else break."

"There's more to it," Kris said, then filled them in on what she'd learned from General Konga about couples sharing the new and larger quarters Kris had gotten for them.

"My lord," Gramma Trouble said, "even in the POW camps, the females and males stayed separate. The women even asked for blankets so they could set up their own purdah. If you've got them mixing, you've got a revolution on your hands, Kris."

"Will the clans put the entire Navy in purdah to keep this from spreading?" Jack asked.

"Hard to say, old horse," Grampa Trouble answered. "I don't think the Empire has faced anything like this in several thousand years."

Jacques was quick to jump in with the views of a sociologist. "I don't think they are equipped to protect themselves from this or any other human sociological viruses. They've worked hard to pretty much keep in coventry our Human engineers who helped them build the Smart Metal battlecruisers. Still, everyone knows we Humans are running around doing things different. Or winning battles against impossible odds. All I can say is that it will be interesting to watch this."

Kris glanced at her two Iteeche admirals. They sat with all four hands folded in front of them and their faces blank. Since Iteeche had so few face muscles, that wasn't hard for them to do.

"May I add," Nelly put in, "that Agent Foile has monitored the presence of Navy couples in the bazaars. It's not unusual for a half-dozen sailors to cruise the bazaars or a dozen women to come as a group to shop. However, couples, especially a lot of couples together and separately, have been remarked upon by those who saw them. There is now a buzz in the bazaars about the new Navy ways. No doubt what is talked about in the bazaar is talked about at home. At work. Wherever. This new thing is no longer a secret."

"Congratulations, Princess Kristine," Ambassador Kawaguchi said. "You have once more set an Empire on a new course. Hopefully you will be just as successful at keeping your head this time as well."

The good ambassador, as Kris's lawyer in a capital trial that could have ended with her meeting the axe-wielding head executioner of the Musashi Emperor, would notice that.

"Thank you, counselor, I'll try to remember that," Kris said, dryly. "Amanda, are you having any success in figuring out the Empire's economy?"

"I've got something, but I don't believe it," the lovely economist said.

"You don't believe it?" Kris said, her interest piqued.

"Everything I can figure out tells me that this entire three thousand planet Empire is operating on a feudal economy. They have no central bank. As best I can tell, the clans use fiat money within the clan and gold or a barter system if they have to trade anything across clan boundaries. According to what all human economists hold good, holy, and economical, there is no way that something this big can do this, but I can't find any strings to pull that will unravel this picture."

"Feudal?" Jack asked, incredulous.

"Yes, General. Feudal all the way down, and I do mean down. The

Middle Ages on Earth averaged five levels of fealty. The king was at the top. A duke or something like it was next. Below him might be another level of barons. Then you got to the local knight ruling over his peasants. The basic coin of the realm was men-at-arms available to fight for the king."

Amanda glanced around the table. The humans nodded understanding, the two Iteeche admirals stayed motionless.

"You know the old saying, 'It's turtles all the way down'?"

Nods again from the humans. No response from the Iteeche.

"Well, it's feudalism all the way down. It crosses and criss-crosses here at the capital and out among the planets. The old Scottish clans had septs, cadet branches, extended families, and dependents. These clans have those and a couple of dozen layers below them, all connected in a web as much as a ladder, and all denoting a whole host of obligations and privileges reaching out in at least three dimensions, if not four. I've got my computer trying to map it all, but the picture makes a star map of this arm of the galaxy look simple."

Kris raised her eyebrows; she'd circumnavigated the galaxy. She'd seen some pretty intimidating star maps.

"What I cannot find," Amanda went on, "is what powers the relationship between all these groups caught in the web. A colony world may have three power districts, each under a different clan's control: A, B, and C. A swaps power with B when needed. B does the same with C. However, A and C refuse to have anything to do with each other. How does B handle power it has borrowed from the other two when one calls up to borrow a gigawatt on a hot day?"

She shook her head in dismay. "Here on the capital, we know that clans handle fire and police. Way down the pecking order, though, one sub-sub-sub-sept may be providing one or the other to five or six groups from other clans, and not all of them might be connected on the ground, either. I have no idea how they pay for this or otherwise handle the swap. I'm at my wit's end."

"We do have experts on the Iteeche now in our midst," Ambassador Kawaguchi said.

Kris turned her focus on the two Iteeche admirals.

Admiral Tong said one word. It involved two clicks of his beak and a sound like he'd swallowed his tongue, then coughed it up again.

Nelly did not translate it.

"Nelly?" Kris asked.

"Yes, Kris."

"What does that word mean?"

"Kris, I have been trying to translate it since I first encountered it. It seems to represent values such as debt and honor, but with strong hints of karma and just plain luck. The debt aspect certainly carries no hint of a monetary debt. The entire mixture of meanings cannot be translated into Standard or any other tongue spoken in Human space."

The room filled with silence as a breached hull filled with vacuum.

"I think we have finally found an example where our and their differences in evolution smack right up against each other," Jacques finally said.

"Can you fill the rest of us in on this?" Kris asked.

"This is all guesswork, but I've been mulling this over since Amanda brought this to me a couple of nights ago. Okay, we humans were, in ancient times, born into a family or small hunter-gatherer group where every man is the father and every woman the mother of every child, okay? That is the basis of almost all human relationships. The group has a leader who may have this or that level of authority, but we would not survive to adulthood if we didn't have this group to nurture us. Got it?"

"Yes," Kris said.

"Later, the group gets larger. Families coalesce into groups, then groups gather in villages, and so forth. Exchanges take place between groups, like barter and what have you. We got through feudal to more advanced stages of cultural development until you have the mature economic and social structures of the modern world. Still, drop us down on a fresh new world and we're back to family, friends, and barter. Okay?"

"Where is this going?" Jack asked.

"Have you ever studied a goldfish bowl?"

"I've spent time staring at a few when I needed to relax," Jack admitted.

"Now, fill it full of primal Iteeche. Or take a look at a breeding pond. Every one of them is chow for every other one of them. It's a zero-sum game of the worst order. Then someone gets Chosen, hauled out of that hellish rat race, and sent off to school. They owe everything to their Chooser. Add to that how much of your status depends on who your Chooser is and the order of your choosing. I seriously suspect this caste system starts the first day of school. What you get out the other end is someone acculturated to looking at everything up, down, and sideways, all while looking over his or her shoulder for the bigger fish looking to chow down on the smaller fish."

Jacques paused. "I know I'm not supposed to say this, folks, because aliens have a right to be alien, but brother, they're all crazy. The system they're born into, raised in, and live in, is bound to make them crazy. At least from a human viewpoint. Sorry if I offend, Admiral."

Admiral Tong bowed his body gently from the waist. "No offense is taken. Indeed, I find myself filled with amazement now as I look at my peoples' ways as seen from the outside such as you have just given me. It is something that I think can be thought about for a thousand years before every last drop is squeezed from it."

The Iteeche admiral turned to Kris. "It also makes the change you are bringing to my men and women very interesting. I find myself wondering how a child raised up in one of your 'fishbowls' with food provided would behave. Would he thrive in our society or be unable to fit in? Or worse, would he become a rebel against not just his Emperor, but our entire social structure?"

Kris knew the admiral had several very good points. She also knew that there was no way to answer his questions. Mathematical simulations would be less than worthless. No one had any basis for the simulations, and worse, some people might mistake the results for reliable predictions.

Finally, Kris voiced her limits. "Admiral, I have no idea what this might mean. We Humans learned long ago that you cannot change just one thing. You may or may not get your intended consequences, but you will certainly get unintended consequences. Maybe a few. Maybe a lot. You never can tell. What I *can* tell you is that we Humans have fought wars for thousands of years. The last eighty years have been the longest length of time for us Humans when we were not trying to kill one another. If you change enough, you can find that sweet spot that you and your people can enjoy."

"It took thousands of years to get where you Humans are?" the Iteeche said.

"Thousands," Kris agreed sadly.

The Iteeche actually managed a sigh. "At least we can enjoy it for now. I know that my woman friend and I are finding our shared quarters very comforting and relaxing. I had no idea that areas of my skin so enjoyed being touched. However, that woman has discovered such places. And I find that we share many of those places. This is most anti-social of me, but I would rather enjoy this than worry about what my Chosen, or my Chosen's Chosen faces. They will be sailors, anyway. We sailors of the Imperial fleet have a more simplified structure of, what did you call it, fealty?"

"Yes," Jacques said.

"You obey your commander and those beneath you, obey you," Kris said.

"Yes, all in the name of the Emperor, poor youngling."

Kris nodded. There was no doubt in her mind that this would be a topic of conversation among a lot of people, Human and Iteeche, for a long time to come. Still, there was no need to tie up any more of her staff meeting with it.

"Ambassador Kawaguchi, I see that you have brought a friend. He appears to be suffering from the same mortal disease you are."

"Disease, Admiral?"

"The diplomatic disease. It almost killed all of us just recently."

"Oh, yes, Kris. Indeed, he is a diplomat. May I introduce you to Ambassador Kopp."

He bowed his head stiffly to Kris; she gave him a medium nod in return.

"Ambassador Ulrich Kopp comes to us from the Helvetican Confederacy. He has heard of my poor efforts to begin trade between the Empire and Musashi and our associates. He believes that similar trades can be worked out between their planets and the Empire."

"How are our trade contacts going, Ambassador? I hope our move from the Pink Coral Palace has not interfered with them."

"Oh, far less than those hooligans protesting around the old palace. I have not only met with all my former clients, but they have referred several more to me. I doubt that I and Ambassador Kopp need squabble over who gets to talk to whom."

"You are most gracious," the new ambassador said to his senior.

"Let me or one of my staff know if there is anything we can do to help you," Kris said. "I know that trade is an essential part of my mission. I also know that it is not easy to find what the Empire has and is willing to exchange. Even if none of the Iteeche have read of the Opium Wars, and I suspect several know of them, I will not stand for any such unequal and destructive trade."

"Nor would I, Your Royal Highness."

The meeting was rapidly reaching the limit that Kris had mentally set for it. She turned to Meg. "Do you have anything I should know?" contained a heavy load of DON'T.

"Regretfully, Admiral, I come bearing a problem which only you can resolve."

Kris gave her *aide de camp* a doubting look.

Innocent as any child, or maybe dumb as any Longknife, Meg forged forward. "All these buildings we inherited from the Domm Clan, ma'am."

"Yes?" Kris asked, letting her disinterest show.

"They could blow down in a strong wind."

5

"What?" came from several humans around the table. Out of the corner of her eye, Kris noticed that the two Iteeche admirals seemed unfazed by the statement. That, more than anything, told Kris that Megan might well be on to something.

"Talk to me," Kris snapped.

"Walt was wiring the new buildings for electronics. While doing that, he noticed how scanty the steel was under the brick and stone facades of the buildings."

"I thought there was a lot of steel beams in the rock pile you dug me out from under," Kris said.

"So it seemed that day. Every time we came across a steel beam, it slowed us down. However, the apartment buildings were down, and I wasn't concerned with what kept them up before the bomb took them down. However, when Walt and I started studying the apartment buildings in our district, we didn't much care for what we found."

A hologram of one of the many ten story apartment buildings in the former Domm, now Navy District, appeared. It showed a facade of stone, wood, and brick with a skeleton of steel to support it.

"This is what it would look like if it was built to Wardhaven building codes," Megan said.

A second hologram appeared. Where the Iteeche had steel, these structures had thicker beams. There was also a lot more steel spread out, adding support to the structure.

"If these buildings were hit with a Category 3 or 4 hurricane or F3 tornado, they'd be reduced to kindling."

Kris turned from Megan to her two Iteeche admirals. They'd been sitting very quietly while the construction practices in the Iteeche Empire were reviewed and found wanting.

Admiral Tong shrugged. He put both of his shoulders into the motion. "If one is fated to die when the wind blows, that is your fate."

Kris found that much fatalism more than unsettling.

"Now I see," said Ambassador Kawaguchi. "The Empire's mandarins are quick to nix any trade in metals. If they have such a small amount of steel available to keep their buildings up, no wonder they do not want to trade any out of the Empire."

"We fought thousands of starships in the Iteeche War," Grampa Trouble said. "I figured that they had metal to throw away, but I begin to see how heavy a tax on their resources those warships were."

There was a lot of nodding from the Humans around the table.

"I wonder what goes into their production of Smart Metal?" Jack asked no one in particular.

"The basic component of Smart Metal," Nelly informed them, "is huge molecules composed of many atoms, iron, chromium, magnesium, copper, boron, carbon, oxygen, hydrogen, and quite a few other elements. They are formed into huge molecules in the Smart Metal foundries. Each molecule is then attached to its neighbor using the same powerful bonds that hold different atoms in the molecule together."

"So, you had to have some sort of metal resources to feed into the foundry," Jack observed.

"What exactly goes into Iteeche Smart Metal?" General Trouble asked.

"I'm not aware that any Human lab has examined the Iteeche

product," Kris said. "I just keep the Human and Iteeche metal segregated from each other. Maybe we need to run some tests."

The two Iteeche admirals at the other end of the round table were fidgeting. There was nothing to be gained from making them uncomfortable. They had no control of the use of the resources of the Empire. No, Kris needed a solution to her present problem.

"Do you and Walt have any suggestions for how we keep our buildings from falling down around the heads of our sailors and their women?" Kris asked Megan.

"I've talked with the engineers, both Human and Iteeche. The Iteeche verified that the situation is as precarious as I feared. The Human engineers said that there had been efforts to strengthen buildings when new earthquake zones were identified late in a city planning stage. Unfortunately, it usually meant tearing the buildings up to slip additional steel into them."

Megan paused. "We don't want to tear the buildings up. Besides, we don't have any more steel to slip into them."

"Please tell me that you have some ideas, Lieutenant, of how to solve this problem. I really don't want to look out my window after a storm to see all my apartments turned into rock piles," Kris said. Maybe her *aide de camp* wasn't ready to be a lieutenant commander.

"Smart Metal, Admiral. We drill a few holes around the outside and inside of the buildings and feed the metal in. That strengthens the buildings' supports. We should be able to do that without having to empty out any apartment while we work."

"Any idea how much Smart Metal we'll need and where we can get it?" Kris asked.

Megan appeared to swallow hard. "We'll need about a hundred thousand tons, ma'am. Our rough estimate is that you can get it by taking the embassy down forty or fifty stories. You might not lose too much height if you raised the ceilings by 300 millimeters. Most of the metal is in the floors."

Kris did like the view from the observation deck atop her embassy.

On the other side of Kris, Abby cleared her throat, soft as thunder.

"Yes, Abby."

"Admiral, we must have browned off some of the shipping companies when we got blockaded by our protestors. Lots of ships arrived from the human side, but no ships got emptied, so they kind of stayed up there, swinging around the hook. There was hollering that if we didn't cut loose of some of those fast attack transports, they were gonna quit sending us anymore."

"I can just hear Grampa Al screaming something like that," Kris agreed.

"Anyhow, we off loaded the backlog and shipped the empties back home. Interesting thing, though, the two freighters that just arrived yesterday left before any of the offloaded ones got back to human space."

"Oh?"

"Yeah, Kris, and funny thing about those freighters."

"Funny strange, or funny ha-ha?"

"Funny interesting," Abby said. "Both of those freighters were from the very first batch of Smart Metal freighters that Grampa Al ever spun out. They were under-powered, intended to ply the secure and established routes inside human space."

"And they came out here?" Jack asked.

"Yep. It took them about an extra week to get here, what with their weaker reactors."

"Are you thinking that Grampa Al would like to have something faster on his established routes?"

"Some of my sources say so," Abby said, glancing at Grampa Trouble. Initially, Abby had been hired as an intelligence and security agent for some organization that Grampa Trouble still had his fingers in. Kris suspected she was telling her old boss that just because the two of them were way out here, that didn't mean that she didn't still have her fingers in the right pies.

"So, are you suggesting that we might abscond with another

hundred thousand tons of Grampa Al's Smart Metal?" Kris said, grinning.

"The thought did cross my mind."

"What about metal fatigue?" Jack asked.

On Alwa Station, Kris had discovered that the Smart Metal™ in her battlecruisers developed metal fatigue. Every six months or so, the metal of the ships needed to be combed through to isolate molecules of Smart Metal™ that had lost their effectiveness and needed to be pulled out of the matrix.

"Abby?"

"I was worried about having these ten-year-old ships plying our long trade route, so I had one of the repair ships topside do a check on one. They found very little metal fatigue. I guess if you aren't forming and reforming the metal all that much, you don't get that much fatigue."

"Are the reactors powerful enough for us to bring them in deadstick?" Kris asked Nelly.

"If we bring them both in as one structure, I can land them both at once on top of our embassy and flow most of the Smart Metal out of it, then lower the reactors by elevator to the bottom of the building. Although, Kris, I would hope that Abby would have all of the metal checked for fatigue. I'd hate to have some of the outriggers with rotary wing blades fold on me during final approach," Nelly replied.

"Abby?"

"I'll have Admiral Kitano take personal responsibility for quality control of the metal, Kris."

Kris turned in her chair to look out the window at the apartments far below her. The more she won, the more she found ducks trying to peck her to death.

"I think I better go have another talk with General Konga. Let him know we'll be landing another rotary wing craft on our embassy."

"Why tell him?" Jack asked.

"We'll be bringing down a hundred thousand tons of Smart Metal even closer to the palace than the last two times. He should be the first to know. With any luck, he'll offer to talk to that admiral in charge of securing the airspace over the capital. If I had to talk to the two of them, I prefer Konga," Kris answered.

"Any other matters?" Kris asked, standing up.

No one replied. Everyone stood. Kris stepped off the last few meters to the outside window as the room emptied. Jack came to stand beside her. The two of them gazed down on the six blocks of drab apartments ringing the embassy.

"Who would have thought they housed their senior Iteeche clan officials in such death traps?" Kris mused.

"Certainly not us."

"I should have thought about that, Jack. Fifty billion people living here. Ten thousand years of blowing ships to atoms. They must be scraping the bottom of their resource barrel. I should have thought about it."

"How could you have? No one else did. You've got Amanda chasing down the Iteeche economy and she didn't spot a metal crunch."

"No, she didn't," Kris agreed. "I did notice how little gold was in the braid the admirals wore."

"Yeah, but you and I both figured that was just because the clans had no respect for the Navy."

"Yeah," Kris admitted, then changed the subject. "Jack, do you think Megan is ready for a promotion?"

"She hasn't been a lieutenant for five years."

"No, but she has been my dog robber. Doesn't time served close to me deserve to count double?"

"She did do a great job with that taking down the Planetary Overlord on Zargoth," Jack said. "She also used exemplary initiative to keep the utilities working for one major city."

"And she's not a bad *aid de camp,*" Kris pointed out.

"So, you want to deep select her?"

"More like double deep select," Kris said. "Nelly, any reason why I can't or shouldn't do it?"

"You can certainly do it, Grand Admiral. I don't think there would be any complaining about it from the fleet."

"My opinion," Kris said. "Nelly, cut the papers and give it to me."

"They're on the table," Nelly said, and a full set of promotion papers rose out of the table.

Kris strode over, looked them over, then signed them. "Now I just have to figure out when to give these to her."

Then she turned to Jack. "Now, you need to get me an escort, Jack. I'm off to see the Guard."

"Yeah," Kris admitted. "Well, get me an escort, Jack, I'm off to see the Guard."

"I'll go with you."

"I'm not so sure that both of us ought to be in the same car from now on, Jack," Kris said. As a mother, she couldn't make herself say just how shaken she'd been when both she and Jack ended up under that rock pile together.

"They didn't get us both last time and they won't get us both next time."

"Would you stay behind if I gave a direct order?" Kris asked.

"Obviously, but it would take one of those."

Kris headed for the elevator.

Jack followed.

6

From Nelly, Kris found that General Konga was working from home. She soon had an invitation. The walk to his quarters was an exercise in change.

She took the elevator down to the fiftieth floor of her own embassy, then the skybridge across to Main Navy. A moving sidewalk made that quick.

Once in the new offices for the Iteeche Navy, the Minister of the Navy, Navy Chief of Staff, and Staff of the Combined Fleets, Kris found another elevator to take her to the bottom floor. All around her, Iteeche Navy and Marine officers and men moved quickly about their business.

Some stared in shock at seeing their Human commander moving among them, but after a moment to recover, all gave Kris and Jack smart salutes.

There had been whispers of riots as she began the transfer of all three staffs to the same building. They hadn't developed. Still, the three levels of the Navy's command structure eyed each other cautiously, jealous of their prerogatives.

So far, sharing the same wardroom, mess hall, and snack bars had not killed anyone, but quite a few of the senior admirals in all three headquarters were not yet persuaded that it wasn't a likely outcome of this crazy Human experiment.

Once on the ground floor, Kris stepped out into the bright Iteeche sunlight. She also got a whiff of the usual aroma of the Iteeche capital. It was not overwhelming. In a few moments, Kris's nose adjusted and it disappeared into the background. Still, it was there.

The odor of the capital was a delicate blend of machine and Iteeche with hints of the stone dust that still lingered in the air after Kris's recent effort at urban renewal. Of anything natural, there was not a hint. Even out in the open, the air smelled stale, as if it hadn't been through air scrubbers recently.

When Kris could get her hands on more greenery, she'd have to add a hanging garden to Main Navy.

Ahead of her was the first of several rows of apartments that stood between her and the Imperial Precincts. There was stone on the lower three or four levels, then brick above that. Windows were many, though they looked out onto only a small plaza of green speckled with bubbling fountains.

She entered the foyer of the first apartment building. One of the eight Marines Jack had assigned to her security detail stepped ahead to open the door. They were under arms, but at least Jack let their sidearms stay holstered. Still, all eight of them had their weapons free to draw.

The inside of the apartment building was pleasant. The floor was hardwood; the tiled walls were green and blue, with mosaics of underwater and beach scenes.

The Iteeche did like their oceans, lakes, and rivers. Too bad so many of them were so badly polluted. Kris would not dare let the children have a day at any Iteeche beach.

She passed through garden areas with their fountains, then more buildings, all with the sameness that seemed the norm for the Iteeche. When you have to produce accommodations for fifty billion people while keeping as much arable land in cultivation, your buildings were mass produced and tall.

When Kris reached the final line of apartments that abutted the perimeter avenue that encompassed the Imperial Palace, she got a surprise.

She'd known that the general had taken an apartment on the top floor. What she didn't know was that it was a ten-story walk up.

Come to think of it, she hadn't noticed elevators in any of the Iteeche quarters.

With a wry glance at Jack, Kris began to climb.

Kris had been meeting surprised Iteeche since she began this walk: men, women, and younglings. The elders had managed their dismay at seeing both a Human, and a very senior one at that.

The younglings gawked at her. Likely, none of them had seen something on two legs during their short lives.

In the stairwell, Kris found herself passing startled women and men, and gaining a tail of children. The stairwell was not that spacious and Human and Iteeche had to give each other room to pass. Some of the Guardsmen recognized Kris from the recent problem. Though dismayed, they saluted, bringing both hands up to their forehead. Kris returned it with her one hand.

There was much muttering after the Human admiral had passed.

"How am I doing?" Kris asked Nelly.

"They're shocked you are not in a sedan chair," she quickly replied. "That the admiral commanding the Combined Fleets is walking their own halls and stairwells shocks some, but others kind of like the idea that someone with your seniority is walking around just like them."

"That's interesting," Kris said.

"I wonder if there isn't more willingness to change in the common Iteeche than any of those in the sedan chairs and fancy palanquins think there is," Jack said.

"That is something we should think about," Kris said.

By the tenth floor, Kris was thinking that she needed to either spend more time swimming or join the Marines for their early morning jogs. Still, she caught her breath before the Gunny Sergeant leading her detail rapped on the desired door.

It was quickly opened by a female Iteeche. She was only slightly taller than Kris and wore a simple green shift made of something like cotton. The dress looked like it was cut more for comfort than allure. She gave a shallow bow as she opened the door and backed away.

Kris entered to find General Konga seated on cushions with a low table before him. He sat beside a picture window that overlooked the palace grounds. Quickly, he stood to greet Kris and offered her and Jack cushions of their own to settle in. He sat only after she had.

The woman approached them. "May I offer you water? I do not know what other types of our liquids you Humans enjoy."

"Water will be fine," Kris said.

The woman, likely the one General Konga had chosen to share his quarters with, retired to return a moment later with a tray of glasses filled with a clear liquid. Kris tasted hers.

The drink was cool, but, like all water that wasn't filtered through the embassy, it tasted flat and stale with a hint of something Kris really didn't like to think of.

After a sip, Kris held the glass in both her hands and joined the general gazing at the Imperial Precincts.

"You have a lovely view," Kris said.

"My previous quarters were underground," he said, dryly. "Yes, I am enjoying the view. Though it is not as lovely as the view you have."

"Do you want to move into Main Navy?" Kris asked. "I could probably stretch out another floor for you and your senior staff without getting too many beaks out of joint."

The Iteeche general laughed, which sounded much like he was hacking up a hair ball. This was impossible, since Iteeche had no body hair.

"Yes, that would be a sudden low tide for those space-less spacers. Still, I enjoy being close to the Emperor. It is a short dash for me to join my Guardsmen at the gate."

He paused, then fixed Kris with all four of his eyes. "Now, how is it that you come to see me not three hours after I went to see you?"

So, Kris told him about her discovery of the flimsy construction of the apartment buildings, ending with, "Do you know how much damage a wind or rainstorm could do to your buildings?"

He fixed Kris with a frown. "Of course. We all know about how violent weather can leave death and wreckage in its wake. It is merely the fate of those who die. It takes a while to rebuild, but for those who were displaced from clan housing, it is merely an inconvenience. They pay rent and don't care where they live."

"What about those that aren't in clan housing?" Kris asked.

The Iteeche shrugged, this time using only his topmost shoulder. "It was their fate and misfortune to be chosen by someone who owed no allegiance to the most highly chosen. They will just have to swim as they can until the Most Worshipful Emperor deigns to build housing for the loyal masterless. That may take a while."

Kris thought of the many artisans she had seen in the bazaars. Their handiwork added a dash of color to an otherwise drab palate. The reality that they were just one natural disaster away from being left homeless saddened her deeply.

She sighed. There was only so much that a lone human could do for an Empire of three thousand planets.

"Well," Kris said, "I will not have the quarters I house my troops in reduced to jackstraws. I intend to reinforce their construction with Smart Metal. A hundred thousand tons of Smart Metal."

The general rolled his eyes. "Let me guess. For that you need to land another hundred thousand tons of your magic metal right in the middle of the capital, within a stone's throw of the Imperial Palace."

"Of course," Kris said, cheerfully.

"If I hadn't seen you do this twice before, I would not believe it possible, but since you have turned this wild and crazy hi-jinks into something to be celebrated, I guess I had better get used to this."

"I am doing this for you and your men," Kris pointed out.

"Yes," General Konga said, then seemed to let out a sigh. "Many a clan lord has skimped on the costly steel that is needed to put strong backbones into the buildings his people live in. You, a hated Human, are bringing down more of your magic metal to buck up the quarters for Iteeche sailors, Marines, and Guardsmen. A song should be sung in the marketplace of your deeds. It would have to be one of those ditties where every second line is preposterous, but the people enjoy a hearty laugh at those songs."

"So, I am a joke?" Kris asked.

"Oh, no. You are just impossible to believe. I am studying you Humans, trying to understand you. Recently, I stumbled across some stories of a Paul Bunyan from your planet of origin, Earth. If I read it right, the entire thing was a long stretch."

"We call them tall tales," Kris said.

"An even better name. So, tell me, when do you intend to treat us to another one of *your* tall tales?"

Now it was Kris's turn to shrug. "We want to look the ships over carefully. These are not from my fleet but old freighters from my grandfather's shipping lines. Once we are sure they are trustworthy, I will go up the beanstalk and ride it down."

"You do not have to accept that personal risk," the Imperial Guard general said. "You have proven it can be done safely for all concerned."

"Sorry, General, there are just some risks that can't be delegated. Those will be my kids at the bottom of the landing drop."

The general shook his head, which started from his hips. "Of course, you so highly value your Chosen ones. May I offer something to you for your children?"

"I would be very happy to accept it, General," Kris said.

"I don't know if I heard you say it, or maybe one of your officers mentioned it to one of your Iteeche Navy officers, but I understand that your children love to swim but have had no chance to get out and enjoy themselves in water not confined to your embassy pool."

"I have heard that complaint from my children," Kris admitted.

"During the recent emergency, we were forced to open the Imperial Precincts to those fleeing the violence. Violence and the battlecruisers you were about to land right in front of the gates to the Imperial Palace," the general said, giving Kris the fisheye.

"Ah, yes. Sorry about that," Kris said.

"What you proposed was a logical conclusion. You did something no one would ever have considered doing and I found myself allowing something I never thought would happen in my life." The general chuckled, a very unique hacking sound.

"We are still trying to restore order to the grounds, replant bushes, even trees. However, I found myself standing on the sandy beach of a lake we have on this side of the grounds. It is well away from the official residence, but it does have clear running water. The thought struck me that your people and your children might enjoy an afternoon frolicking in the Emperor's lake."

Kris paused for a long moment to consider all that the Guard general was offering. It was not a small gift.

"I would be very grateful for such an opportunity. I know that the fleet must sail for battle soon and I must leave my children behind, once again," she said, tasting the sadness. "I think we would all relish such memories during the long absence."

"I suspect that there was no greater gift that I could offer you in thanks for saving my Emperor from his own clan chiefs. It is possible that you may find a young Iteeche joining you for your beach party."

Kris did her best not to show shock. "Can he slip the leash his servants keep him on so tightly?"

"Let us say that he intends to do that, and if they try to stop him, they may discover new backbone in that young man."

"That alone would be worth the beach party," Kris said, and allowed herself a chuckle.

"Now, I will have a guard detail of fifty Guardsmen to assure your safety, and that of my Emperor. I imagine that you would want to have some of your own Marines at the ready standby. Would forty meet your needs?"

Kris did not let her eyeballs roll, not even a little bit. He was offering her four of hers for five of his. She would have expected the ratio to be closer to one to two.

"I will make sure they are my best," she told the Guard general.

"I know I can count on them to defend my Emperor as courageously as my own Guardsmen."

"I hope that no one will have to defend anyone and we can

exhaust our children so thoroughly that they are taken home asleep and in their father's arms."

"Two days from now? At the noon hour?"

"A beach party usually includes a barbecue," Kris said. "Can we have a fire on the beach, or should we bring large cooker grills?"

The question seemed to puzzle the general.

Kris quickly added. "We will bring grills so as not to leave anything but footprints in the beach sand."

That seemed to settle everything Kris had come for, and more. She stood. The general stood. With a nod, Kris left and returned to the comforts of her own quarters with its sparkling, distilled, and aerated water.

She spread the word quickly about the coming beach party. It was the main topic of conversation at supper that night.

7

The next day was busy. That was the night of the diplomatic soiree, or sing-along. The last time Kris invited the local powers that be to a Human Embassy Party, it had crashed and burned. Few of those invited bothered to show up.

Kris would not repeat that mistake.

Weeks before, she challenged the staff of the Navy Ministry, the staff of the chief of staff of the Imperial Naval General Staff, and the staff of the Combined Fleets, to each contract for a different choir. After the Combined Fleet chief of staff pointed out that the fleet had its own award-winning choir, they were added to the promised list of entertainers. A few hours later, both the Navy Minister and the Navy General Staff added their own choir.

This time, Kris would have six choirs, competing for an Admiral's Cup.

"Nelly, get me Admiral Tong."

"Yes, My Most Eminent Admiral," the Iteeche admiral answered a moment later.

"We're going to have a sing-along in two weeks," Kris said. "Have any songs been written about the fleet's recent battles or the dust-up we had earlier this month?"

"As a matter of fact, they have. The Combined Fleet's Choir has been practicing them, as well as one Guard group General Konga sent over."

"I know that these sing-alongs are supposed to feature the oldest of oldies, but do you think you could slip those into the repertoire?"

"I already have," the admiral said, his face pulling back into the best example of a grin Kris had ever seen on an Iteeche.

"Very well, Admiral. Very well."

"Trust us, My Most Eminent Admiral, this one will be a night long remembered."

Abby did her own thing as well. The three ballrooms could be expanded as the need developed, including four more grand halls. There was space for every soldier as befit their rank.

The guards that escorted the high muckety-mucks usually just stood around in the courtyard, waiting the pleasure of their lords. This time, they were invited to beer bashes put on by the enlisted, petty officers, and junior officers of the Combined Fleets. Each three levels of uniformed personnel headed off to lift an unlimited number of beers with their Navy comrades and discuss the realities of life in the service.

Even the slaves found that space had been set aside in a dry and pleasant basement for them to find food and drink well above the quality that they usually ate. There were singers to entertain them as well.

At all halls, Military Police were a visual presence that their hostess expected good behavior should be returned for good food and drink. Kris need not have worried. Seniors leaned on juniors properly before the MPs had to intervene. It is also possible that Kris's Combined Fleet MPs used their earbud com links to whisper preemptive action before anything escalated.

Upon review of the audio, even the poor slaves hunched down in their corners and constantly looking over their shoulders, were very well pleased and behaved.

Thus, with skittles and beer did Kris continue the seduction of the Iteeche Empire.

Meanwhile, the party on the fourth floor was just getting started.

Kris had intended to greet her guests in the foyer as they exited the elevators before they headed into the ballrooms. The job of initially greeting them as they descended from their palanquins in the courtyard was assigned to Admirals Kitano and Tong, although Ulan soon had to be dragooned into helping them as the flow of arrivals exceeded Kris's wildest dream.

For tonight's party, Kris had no problem filling up her ballrooms. Indeed, Abby and Mata Hari had to do a fast job of rearranging the right wing of the Embassy to find more parking spots for all the fancy walking palanquins.

The early rush of clan lords and lordlings included the senior lord of the Abba Clan. He latched onto Kris's elbow. Apparently, it was advantageous for him to be seen greeting her guests while standing close to the Ever Victorious Admiral's right hand. When the senior lord of the Quo Clan arrived, he smoothly inserted himself between Kris and the Abba Clan lord. There may have been a bit of shoving and a few elbows thrown, but the Quo Clan had fought with Kris and the Abba Clan had not.

That arrangement didn't last very long. Roth, senior lord of the We Clan, arrived five minutes later and pushed the other two down the line to make room for himself beside Kris. Thus, the next hour went with the three most senior clan lords holding court right beside the Human emissary.

Kris got quite an education.

Honestly, it wasn't that different from the catty whispered conversations at one of Mother's afternoon teas or the equally catty comments whispered behind fans or hands at the political balls her father had insisted she attend while a junior officer.

Kris couldn't keep track of all the clans mentioned, but she knew Nelly was. Tomorrow or the next day, what with the beach party planned, she and Nelly would have to go over a three-dimensional chart of all these clans that were visiting her tonight.

When the tide of guests slowed down, Kris paid a visit to her three salons. The one with the professionals that the three different

Navies had hired was singing right along. The songs were kind of laid back with all sorts of harmonics that Kris would never have thought a throat could make. The Iteeche seemed to relish the voice extremes. Many paused in their singing to enjoy those solos. Others who had the vocal cords to do it joined in as well. Everyone was enjoying themselves.

The ballroom with the three Navy choirs was very different. The songs here were loud and boisterous. Some were even bawdy. Everyone in that salon sang along lustily, enjoying themselves and the songs.

When Kris ambled in with Roth on her elbow, a song was just finishing. Nods passed from front to back and the choir director seemed to shuffle his music, then pointed at an able sailor.

He stepped forward and in a clear, ringing voice began to sing of victories won among the stars by the Combined Fleet. The stanzas were new, but the refrain was a catchy ditty. It quickly caught on with the audience. The soloist would sing his story, and everyone would come in on the refrain. Even Roth joined it.

"That's a song they'll be singing in the bazaars tomorrow," he told Kris, nudging her in the side.

That was what Kris hoped.

A different soloist introduced a second new song. This one recounted the recently attempted putsch by the Domm and Wo Clans. It also had a snappy refrain that the audience quickly joined in.

"Do I smell some fish stranded at high tide?" Roth asked Kris.

"If it's fresh, why not eat it?" Kris answered.

Roth guffawed.

Before he could finish, Nelly reported, "Kris, we have an unexpected guest arriving."

"Who?" Kris asked.

"The Worshipful Emperor."

8

"He can't come here!" yelped Roth, denying that the young Emperor had slipped his strings and was doing something a good puppet would never do.

"Apparently, he is," Kris muttered as she turned her full attention to this new challenge.

From below came the sound of Ruffles and Flourishes from the Royal US Marine Corps band. The bandmaster then hoofed it brilliantly by breaking into a song Kris had last heard for the entrance of her grampa, King Ray I of United Society, Here Comes the Chief.

The bandmaster and the entire band deserved a bonus for being this fast on their feet, though Kris pitied the poor tuba player.

"Jack, I need Marines in dress uniforms in the ballrooms, STAT. The Emperor has come to call. I want security jacked up a dozen notches."

"It was already plenty high, but I'll make it tighter. I've got a platoon of Marines moving in your direction. Do we surround the Emperor?"

"No. He has his Imperial Guard for that. I want your guys guarding doors and any place else you can put them to look decorative but at the ready for anything."

"I'm on it."

With the greeting music in the background, Kris and Roth hurried back to the foyer. Several other major clan lords were also rushing in that direction. They hardly had time to arrange themselves in some sort of order before the largest elevator opened.

There stood the young Emperor. His robes were cloth of gold embedded with jewels, but it seemed to have only two or three layers. No heavier a burden of fancy dress than Roth, clan chief of the senior We Clan, wore. Beside the Emperor stood Guard General Konga. Around them were a small phalanx of guardsmen in dress uniforms . . . weapons at the ready.

Thank heavens he'd left the headsmen and the snake wranglers at home, Kris thought as her stomach was grateful it would not have to face that bunch tonight. Those symbols of Imperial authority gave her the willies.

Kris smiled at the young Emperor as he strolled from the elevator. The Imperial Guards opened their front to allow him to pass toward the clan lords and greet Kris.

She bowed from the waist, forty-five degrees exactly, as the Emperor said, "I am so glad that you are throwing such a lovely party. I could hear the music from the palace. General Konga assured me that you would have room for me if I chose to come calling."

"The Emperor is always welcome at the Embassy of the Human Race, Your Imperial Majesty," Kris said as she rose from her bow.

Around her, confusion reigned among the clan lords. Some were ready to go down on elbows and knees, as they would at court. Others seemed ready to follow Kris's lead, although their bows went down a full ninety degrees. Still others seemed in too much shock to make any call.

A Marine Staff Sergeant with a tray of drinks wound his way through the Iteeche lords and lordlings to stand at Kris's elbow.

"May I offer you a drink?" Kris asked.

"I would very much like one," the Emperor answered.

While they talked, General Konga nodded at an NCO who produced a cool bottle from somewhere, and in less time than it took to bat an eye, the bottle stood among the drinks being offered by the Human sergeant.

The Emperor took it.

"Oh, you have my favorite soft drink," he said. "I'm so glad you have some."

There was no way the young Iteeche hadn't seen the sleight of hand that got him what he wanted, but Kris had to respect his grace and wisdom at praising his hostess.

"Your Imperial Majesty, we have several choirs to sing along with tonight. In the first salon I am told are some of the best choirs singing songs that were ancient when the Empire was new." Kris said that with a smile and got something like it from the young Emperor.

"We have in the opposite salon, choirs from the Navy, including one from the Combined Fleets. They are singing some very new songs celebrating the victories of the fleet both in space and the recent trouble in the capital."

"Oh, that sounds very interesting. I would very much like to hear those new songs."

Kris aimed the Emperor and his party to the right. Ahead of her, smooth as silk, Human Marines in dress red and blues slipped into place, guarding the entrance to the salon. No doubt, others were striding in a back way. If the door wasn't there a moment ago, it certainly was now.

The Iteeche choir master for the Combined Fleet's choir didn't fail to notice the commotion in the back of the ballroom. He turned, and may or may not have recognized the Emperor, but did know Kris.

WHAT SHOULD I TELL HIM TO DO?, General Bruce asked on Nelly Net.

THE EMPEROR WANTS TO HEAR THE NEW SONGS, Kris answered.

GOT IT.

The Human Marine general stepped up to the choir master. A moment later, the Iteeche directed the first soloist to take his place and they began again the victory song for the battles among the stars.

This might have been a repeat for those in the room, but it was fresh for the Emperor. How many of those in the room knew they were seeing their Emperor for the first time was hard to tell. Neither the Emperor, nor his portrait, was ubiquitous among his people.

Still, everyone seemed to know that something different and unique was happening. The presence of so many Imperial Guardsmen had to mean something. The ranks and file of Iteeche opened up and Kris led the young Iteeche forward until he stood right before the choir. Kris couldn't call it the best seat in the house, because no one was sitting.

The choir went through all four of the new songs, including one about Kris getting buried under a falling apartment, how she broke all her fingernails digging her way out and then brought down a few apartments of her own by huffing and puffing and blowing them down (there was no mention of high explosive). It ended with her bringing starships down out of the sky to land on her embassy and using the metal to strengthen the apartments of humble sailors, Marines, and Guardsmen.

"Are you really going to do that?" the Emperor asked.

"Day after tomorrow, very likely."

He frowned. "I seem to remember hearing whispers that you did that before."

"Twice," Kris said. "Then we also landed six battlecruisers to defend the gates to your palace. We're getting quite good at this, I hope."

"I certainly hope, also. You piloted the first two and will do the same for this one?"

"Yes, Your Imperial Majesty. I and my computer."

There was a "harrumph" from Kris's neck.

"Well, actually my computer will do most of the flying. My main duty is to be there and make fewer people panic."

"I do not think that I will panic when you do this again."

The Emperor enjoyed his time. He'd had another bottle of his favorite drink. He'd also enjoyed several of the hors d'oeuvres, always taken from a tray that was half-eaten.

Kris had set a rule before the party started. Servers kept their eyes on the trays. If they had any reason to think that their drinks or tidbits had been compromised, the food went back to the larder. The was a lab checking on each questionable tray. So far, Nelly reported no poisons had been found.

The night was going well when Kris noticed something strange out of her peripheral vision. She could not have rationally said what it was, but she reacted nonetheless. One step forward put her between that itch and the Emperor.

She felt the small dart take her on the shoulder. Four centimeters higher and it would have hit her neck above her body armor.

"Assassin!" Kris shouted in her command voice. "That man is an assassin! Grab him! Purple cloak over black tunic!"

The assassin had stepped right up to the Imperial Guard to get off his blow dart. Now he was doing his best to merge back into the crowd. Too many of the Iteeche around him were reacting too slowly.

Kris might have given chase, but she had a dart in her uniform, likely poisonous, and could not risk it ending up in anyone else.

She need not have worried. Four Royal US Marines converged on the Iteeche's escape route. He tried to dodge; Kris hadn't seen such good broken field running since the last Army-Navy game she'd watched.

The assassin faked out the first Marine, but dodged right into the next Human in red and blue. He knocked the Marine down, but the Human latched onto one of his four legs and held him long enough for two more to connect. The Iteeche went down under a pile of Marines.

Kris dearly hoped the fellow was out of ammunition.

Now four Imperial Guardsmen had a chance to catch up. Two pummeled the assassin. At least Kris hoped those punches were going into an Iteeche and not her Marines. Quickly, the Marines jumped to their feet and withdrew, letting the Guardsmen haul the offender up from the deck.

Manacles extruded themselves from the Smart Metal™ deck to wrap themselves around his feet, hobbling him to a shuffle. More snaked out from the floor to tie his right and left arms together, then back until they were painfully restrained behind him.

That was one assassin who was not getting away.

He was also not going to suicide. A third lump of Smart Metal™ had crawled into his mouth and forced it wide open. No way could he follow the honorable assassin's path of crunching down on a fake tooth containing poison and taking his story to the grave.

At the moment, he looked like an advertisement for some sort of BDSM club. No doubt his Iteeche interrogators would be happy to supply the sadism for him.

Meanwhile, Abby and the Human Fleet's Chief Surgeon appeared at Kris's elbow.

"What you got there, baby duck?" Abby asked.

"A blow dart, or the likes of one," Kris admitted.

The doctor studied the problem. The dart hung on Kris's white dinner jacket. The question was, how far had the dart had gotten into her spidersilk armor? Clearly, it had not pierced through the tight weave. If it had, Kris would likely be dead. Humans had found out during the Iteeche the war, much to their sorrow, that most poisons that killed Iteeche, also killed Humans, and vice versa.

The fleet surgeon frowned at the dart. "I could take it out now. However, the slightest twitch might drive it just that tiny bit deeper. Alternately, I can rush you to the Embassy clinic and stabilize both you and the dart before drawing it out."

"That sounds like a good idea," Kris said.

"That assumes that you walking from here to there doesn't joggle the damn thing and poison you," the doc added.

Now it was Kris's turn to scowl.

"May I offer a suggestion?" came from Kris's neck.

"Go ahead, Nelly."

"Abby, could you pick up a small device next to the toe of your right shoe?"

Abby glanced down, then stooped to pick up a small, circular device. It looked like a thick ring.

"Doctor, if you will hold the ring around the dart," Nelly said.

The surgeon took the device from Abby, and, looking it over said, "I take it that I am talking to that magnificent computer of yours, Admiral?"

"Yes, that is Nelly," Kris answered.

"And she spun this contrivance out of the Smart Metal of the deck?"

"It was easy," Nelly said.

"Is it sterile?"

"Very likely, but for this use, Doctor, it doesn't need to be. Just center it over the dart and slip it down to her shoulder. As the iris closes, keep the ring as close to center over the dart as you can. The ring will then remove the dart."

"How?"

"I will slowly extend the ring, extracting the dart."

"None of which I will be able to observe," the doc grumbled.

The device in his hand turned transparent.

His body shook in surprise.

"Be careful doing things like that, Nelly," Kris said. "It's hard on older hearts."

"Umm," the surgeon said, but he was centering the ring over the dart. Nelly slowly closed an iris from the inside the ring. The doctor adjusted its centering.

"It's centered," he said

"And the iris is closed," Nelly said.

At that point, the ring grew longer, raising the needle slowly from Kris's uniform dinner jacket.

"Done," the surgeon announced.

"Very good," Kris said, finally glancing over her shoulder at the place where the poisoned dart had been.

She was now in a dilemma. Did she continue to host her party? No doubt there was some residual poison on her jacket, likely in the spider silk shirt beneath it. Possibly on the outside of the spidersilk armor.

Inside, Kris could feel herself trembling like a rung bell. Still, she swallowed hard, plastered a smile on her face and said, "Shall we listen to the rest of this song, Your Imperial Majesty? I understand there is another new song you have yet to hear."

"Are you well?" the Emperor asked.

"It's been a while since someone attempted to assassinate me, but I'm not out of practice at dodging them," she said lightly.

It took the lad a few seconds to process that Kris was accepting, indeed was claiming, this assassin for her own. Maybe it was best that way. People should not be trying to assassinate the Emperor.

"Yes. Yes, I would enjoy hearing the rest of this song."

Thus, the cheerful party began again. The young Emperor enjoyed singing along with the refrains and eyed Kris with wide eyes as he heard the ballads of her space battles, planetary seizures, and recent defense of his own body.

Once the Combined Fleet's choir had finished its new repertoire, the choir of the Chief of Staff of the Imperial Navy took the stage. They offered rollicking songs and ditties that were likely old when ancient Iteeche sailors traded sail for steam. They were new to the Emperor, but he quickly caught on.

Kris had the advantage that Nelly had heard them during practice and could feed Kris the words, though it was Nelly singing at Kris's neck that the Iteeche heard.

The night held no more surprises. It couldn't. Not only did the Imperial Guard close in tight around their Emperor, but a hard-faced bunch of Humans, clearly MPs and Special Forces in mufti, provided a second outer ring just as tight. Beyond that, there was a wide empty space with no one save the occasional server with a platter of drinks or snacks.

The Iteeche clan lords and lordlings were keeping their distance. It was hard to tell if this was to avoid the next near miss of a dart or to sidestep any hint that they might be considering something so unthinkable toward the Emperor. Whatever the reason, stay back they did. Even Roth kept his distance.

That left Kris with a very curious young lad who found the stories praised in ballad and song to be very exciting. He had question after question to ask Kris and she gave him honest answers.

Hopefully not too honest for his young ears.

Their conversation went long until Nelly took an opportunity to interrupt.

"Kris, we had thought the party would have begun to break up half an hour ago, but no one has left."

"No one?"

"Nope, not a single person."

"Why would everyone stay so long?" the Emperor asked.

"I think, Your Imperial Majesty, that they are unwilling to leave before you do. No doubt they wish to give you open space to get safely back to your palace without being caught in the press of everyone leaving."

"Oh," the lad looked crestfallen. "I had not thought of that."

"May I escort you to your palanquin, sir?"

"I guess you must," he said, turning toward the elevator.

"Nelly, get his ride ready."

"Doing it. They will be ready for him. We may have a major traffic jam when it comes to the rest leaving."

"Invite them to leave by order of seniority but hold the elevators until after His Imperial Majesty is away.

The Imperial Palanquin looked rich and ancient, clearly not Smart Metal™. At the steps, the young Emperor turned back to Kris. "I hope you have more parties like this one."

"I intend to, though I and my fleet may need to sail soon enough for action."

"Please do be careful."

"I always am," Kris said.

The Emperor suddenly looked burdened by the weight of an Empire of three thousand or more planets. He turned and went up the stairs. Several Guard officers followed him.

General Konga held back. "You did well. I think this is the most fun this poor lad has had since his Chooser died. Maybe since he was Chosen."

"I am glad to have been of service."

"By the way, I would not mind if some men in civvies, much like those who surrounded His Worshipfulness tonight, came with you to the beach party tomorrow."

"Thank you. I will have them there."

"Good. Now I bid you good night."

The Imperial Palanquin had hardly cleared the gates of the embassy before fancy rides were rolling out for the chiefs of the three most powerful clans. Kris bid them all a good evening.

They assured her they had greatly enjoyed the party as they quickly left. More rides, these smaller, hurried out right behind them from the right wing of the Embassy. They had hardly been set down before their lords were piling aboard and ordering them home. Few bothered to say good night to their hostess.

Kris didn't have all that much need to say goodbye to them. She had poison from a dart in the right shoulder of her uniform and she wanted to get out of it before something evil happened.

An elevator appeared on the side of the embassy and quickly whisked her to her quarters. No doubt, she faced more safety measures as she undressed tonight.

Kris hoped matters would go quickly. She was very tired.

9

Jack was waiting for her in her quarters as the elevator door opened. Behind him were both of her bat women, Alice and Jane. However, it was the figures a few steps farther back that told Kris how her night would go.

There was the fleet surgeon as well as a chief that Kris didn't recognize, but he held a large kit at his side. Likely he was her chemical honcho. Behind them were three people in full environmental suits, complete with their own air supply. They also carried several large cases.

Kris held her hands up. "Jack, if someone thinks I'm dangerous, all you not in an E suit step back and let's go a round or five with them. Okay?"

Jack backed up as Kris carefully strolled to the center of her day quarters.

"Nelly, do we have a tight filter on this room's vents?"

"Yes, Kris. We know the molecular size of the poison and have adjusted the filters for this room. The poison is similar to the puffer fish from old Earth. No doubt, the intent was for the Emperor to die and you to be held responsible for serving bad fish."

"That sounds like something the rebels might pull," Kris admitted.

Meanwhile, one of the people in an E-suit was fitting a plastic bag over the shoulder, sleeve, and chest of Kris's dinner jacket. A moment later, one associate cut the jacket off Kris. It slid off her and right into the plastic sack waiting for it. The hazmat tech quickly sealed the cut garment away.

Once the jacket was sealed in and the bag put aside, they repeated the process, cutting Kris's silk shirt off her body. That left her nearly fully dressed most places, but down to her spidersilk under armor around her right side.

"Can we cut that body stocking off?" a filtered voice asked.

"They haven't invented a pair of scissors that can cut this stuff," Kris replied. "Someone has to peel me out of the rest of this monkey suit."

A patch went over the place where the armor had stopped the dart. Then one of the three in an E-suit tried to undress Kris. Their thick gloves were never intended to support fine motor skills.

Next, one of the heavily protected safety folks produced a small and well-protected hand circular saw. He placed it carefully under the spidersilk at Kris's neck and turned it on. Diamond dust flew from the blade, but the spidersilk showed not a scratch.

More pressure on the neckline only produced a screech from the saw and the engine seized up.

"That saw can cut anything!" its startled wielder remarked.

"Not processed spidersilk," Kris said. She felt where the saw had tried to make a cut. "You also activated the second layer of armor. I don't know of anything that has managed to chew its way through both."

Without being summoned, Alice and Jane stepped forward and began to strip or cut Kris out of her formal dinner dress uniform. While they worked, Kris did her best to stand still as a statue.

She spent the time thinking through how she could get out of this tight body armor without doing her usual wiggle and waggle. She not only had too much of an audience at the moment, but the more she moved, the more likely poison was to flake off into the air of her quarters. In theory, the patch would hold in the poison.

Once Kris's shoulder was clear, the environmental people pulled a plastic over-sleeve up her arm and sealed it to her shoulder

The moment of truth came finally. Kris was down to bare feet and one body stocking. Very slowly, so as not to activate the armor, Alice and Jane began to peel Kris out of her armor. As usual, they began from the top. This time, though, Kris held as still as she could, wiggling as little as possible.

They started with her left sleeve and soon had her out of it. The right sleeve proved to be a sticking point. The plastic over-sleeve's seal made her shoulder too rigid to work with. The hazmat team gave up and removed the bag on Kris's arm.

With extra care by both Kris and her two body servants, the spidersilk began to slide off Kris. That is, right up until they hit the patch; it was too rigid.

"That's gonna have to come off," Alice said.

That led to more debate about safety that ended with the fleet surgeon providing Alice with medical gloves that she wore as she removed the patch. Then gloves, patch, and all went into its very own containment bag.

The Hazmat people wanted to paint the spot where the dart had hit, but no one at this point was very sure exactly where that was.

"Get me out of this thing," Kris grumbled. "I really need to pee."

Three minutes later, Kris was out of her body armor and headed for the head. She walked with Jack's arms around her. She closed out the noise from behind her and concentrated on feeling Jack's warmth.

In the head, Nelly was already filling a bathtub large enough for two. Jack shucked out of his dress uniform while Kris relaxed on the toilet for as long as she could remember. Done, she joined Jack in the tub.

"Do you want the jets on?" Nelly asked.

"Not now. Not just yet. Jack, please hold me."

"That's what I'm here for."

They lay, side by side in the water, his arms around her, her head rested on his strong chest. He stroked her back, helping her to calm. She felt the vibration, likely of her soul, slowly calm, suppressed by Jack's gentle touch.

Finally, she let out a deep breath.

"You better?" Jack asked.

"Much better," Kris admitted with a sigh.

"It was a crazy night," Jack commiserated.

Again, Kris let out a deep sigh. "Who would have thought the young Emperor would slip the leash of his guards and escape to my party?"

"Yeah."

"I was worried enough that I'd have another flop on my hands," Kris said, letting the words rush out of her. "You could have blown me over with a feather when we got hit with the first wave of lordlings. And then the clan chiefs!"

Kris paused to catch her breath and heave another deep sigh.

"When the Abba clan chief turned my lone greeting post into a receiving line, you could have blown me over with a feather. Then the Quo clan chief elbowed his way between me and the other clan chief. I felt fantastic. I haven't felt that good since I first got asked to dance."

"You never told me about that," Jack said, nuzzling that delicious spot on her neck.

"It wasn't much really. I found out later that the boy had done it to win a bet. Did he dare dance with the Prime Minister's daughter? You know, that kind of thing."

"I wish I'd been on your Secret Service detail. I would have boxed his ears back," Jack muttered into her ear.

"You would not have. Why do you think the boys were so scared of approaching me? What with the hulking big guys in dark glasses lurking around the gym, it's amazing that any boy worked up the courage."

"Are you feeling better?" Jack asked.

"Much better. Nelly, turn on the jets."

Water jets began to massage Kris and Jack's back and shoulders.

Two other jets did wonderful things for her tired feet. Nelly kept the jets moving up and down, then sideways, taking full advantage of the Smart Metal™ to reach exactly where Kris needed it.

Maybe the Iteeche had it right. It was magic metal, at least in Nelly's capable, ah, hands?

10

Rank does indeed have a few privileges. Kris and Jack slept in and barely made it to the final seating for breakfast.

Gramma and Grampa Trouble had gotten the kids off to school. They had wisely chosen to absent themselves from last night's festivities. Human and Iteeche relations needed to look to a bright future. They didn't need ghosts - even if they were legendary - at the feast.

When Kris did get to work, there was a bill for the last night's food and drink. Even for a Longknife, there were a lot of zeros and commas at the bottom of the annotated bill.

"Problem?" Jack asked.

"No. I'm just glad I've got all those captured rebel battlecruisers. I'm going to have to sell one of them to the Imperium to pay this bill."

"You're kidding."

"Nope, look at this. I knew we were going lavish on the food and drink, but there were a lot of troops in the honor guards and even more slaves carrying those fancy palanquins around."

"I can't really begrudge what the slaves got," Jack said.

"Me either. I doubt if I'll get anything back from giving them a good evening. They are about as powerless as they come. Maybe it will just add a drop of good karma to my tiny bucket. The bad karma needs an eighteen-wheeler tanker truck to hold all that."

"That's strange, Admiral. I would have reversed those two."

"Sometimes I really like the way you see me, Jack. Now, the EMs, NCOs and JOs ate us out of a good chunk of a battlecruiser."

"The chiefs, lords, lordlings, and hangers-on didn't go light on the chow, either."

"The Emperor told me that he wished I'd have these parties more often. If we're gonna do that, I've got to go capture another rebel fleet."

"You've got plenty of prize ships," Jack pointed out. "Hundreds at last count."

"Yeah, but I may need them if we can figure out where the rebels are and bring their fleet to battle."

"They have been kind of running away from you of late," Jack admitted.

Buried among all the other bills was an order to resupply the battle squadron that had brought her here. They'd been eating from day-to-day, never ordering more than two or three days' worth of food at the most. Admiral Tong wanted to take on a full month's worth of supplies.

"Does he know something we don't?" Jack asked.

"Would you want your fleet tied to such a short string? We could end up with demonstrators blockading us in the embassy again," Kris pointed out.

"It would be kind of hard now that we've got an entire district to call our own, with it extending to say, seven or eight blocks on any side."

"Yeah," Kris admitted, but she signed the requisition anyway. At least this money would come out of the accounts for the Combined Fleets, not her Human embassy purse.

Below that were three more requisitions. One for reaction mass, one for fuel for the reactors and a last one for spare parts for the lasers and any other ship parts that were not Smart Metal™.

Jack looked at them over her shoulder. "Maybe he does know something we don't."

"He hasn't told me," Kris said. "Nelly, get me Admiral Tong."

"Yes, My Most Eminent Admiral," the Iteeche said a moment later from Kris's neck.

"Admiral, I'm looking at the recent requisitions you just sent in to outfit the fleet and resupply it. Do you know something I don't?"

"No, ma'am. But I would like to be ready if matters change. I have served around you long enough to know that this has been the quietest stretch since you took command."

"You are learning what it's like to serve with one of those Longknifes."

"Yes, My Most Eminent of Admirals. Something is bound to happen soon."

"I, for one, hope you are wrong," Kris said.

"It would not break my heart if I was."

Kris signed off and signed the requisitions. Kris found that she was adopting some Iteeche ways. Where anyone at Wardhaven Navy headquarters would text, email, or fax a packet to someone down the hall or on the next floor, she was now using Iteeche runners for priority mail. It moved faster than the interoffice mail and met with approval from the receiving Iteeche officers.

When in Rome, it's best to grow a Roman nose.

11

Kris continued to conn her desk until two squealing short people invaded her space.

"Mother!" Ruth leaned her elbows onto Kris's desk then bent her arms and put her chin onto her cupped hands, "Remember? We're having a beach party today!"

"Today?" Kris said, looking puzzled. "I thought it was yesterday and nobody came."

"Mommy," Johnnie said in a voice too high pitched, "It's today! It's today! It's today!" He, too, had rested his elbows on her desk, the spitting image of his sister, if a bit too short to pull it all off just right. However, the excitement took him as it can only take a five-year-old, and he jumped up and down with each exclamation.

"Okay, okay," Kris said, standing, "maybe it is today. Shall we go see if they'll let us onto the palace grounds?"

"They'll just have to. The Emperor promised," Johnnie insisted.

"The Emperor's Guard general said we could. There's a big difference between a general and an Emperor," Kris said as her two children towed her out of her day quarters and toward the elevator. Abby was holding the door. Cara and a half-dozen other kids, some of which were Abby's, some were borrowed, raced after each other, shrieking with joy.

It was going to be a noisy afternoon.

Jack joined Kris, and Johnnie grabbed his hands and made to pull his father along faster. Neither Kris nor Jack could fail to laugh at the sheer joy surrounding them.

The elevator took them down to the fiftieth floor where more parents and kids were waiting for them. There were also some men and women with no kids attached and eyes that never stopped roving.

Kris had gotten a call from General Konga earlier in the morning. He had matched each of his Guardsmen with one of Kris's Marines. The two were making a good pair. "Can you send me over another ten so I can pair up all fifty of my lookouts?"

"I'll have them on their way, General."

The kids and parents would be well protected. Kris wondered if the protection was just for them. Might there be one more person at the beach party?

Once everyone agreed that the partiers were all present, Kris led them across the sky bridge to Iteeche Main Navy then down another elevator ride to the bottom. A long line of happy kids began to hike to the pond by walking across streets and through foyers of apartment buildings.

This was a risk that Kris chose to take. There was always a chance that the more exposed they were, the more chances someone had to take a shot at them. However, this was an embassy, the first Human embassy to the Iteeche Empire. The Iteeche needed to see Humans. They needed to become familiar with having Humans around them.

Kris knew she was risking children. *Her own children!* Still, she was willing to take that risk to close the chasm between the two former warring races. She'd done everything she could to reduce the risk. The only safer thing she could have done was move the kids to the Imperial palace in armored cars.

That was something she refused to do.

The excitement was contagious. Iteeche younglings ended up

walking and skipping alongside the Human youth. Until you've seen a half-grown Iteeche skip along on four legs, you have no idea what coordination is.

The kids quickly raised the question, could their new Iteeche friends join them at the party? Kris had considered this as a low possibility, but still a possibility. Ruth and Johnnie, however, latched on to kids their own age and begged for them to be allowed to play with them.

Kris paused her parade just short of the Imperial Guard Barrack apartments. "They can come if their mommy or daddy says they can come. Okay?"

That got high pitched squeals.

"But their mommy or daddy has to come with them."

Many of the Iteeche kids had a little trouble understanding the concept of "Mommy or Daddy," but they raced off and over the next few minutes, Iteeche sailors, Marines, and Guardsmen were dragged out by children that really were telling the truth.

There was a lot of culture shock in the courtyard of those apartments, but soon the beach party had twice as many kids celebrating the bright sun and blue sky.

General Konga appeared at Kris's elbow.

"More of your sedition?"

"Please. I had nothing to do with this. This is kid-to-kid diplomacy. Besides, kids having fun want more kids to have fun. Isn't that universal?"

"Would you believe that this is the first beach party this planet has ever known?"

"But you have a lake with a sandy beach," Kris answered.

"Yes. For poetry competitions by adults," the general said. "If your kids are still laughing as they enter the Palace Precincts, that may be the first laughter there in ten thousand years."

"Will you excuse me if I say then that the palace grounds need some laughter?"

"I have been thinking on that since I first offered you the opportunity to hold your beach party. Tell me, did you expect that your youth would sweep in to include our younglings?"

Kris shook her head. "I thought your younglings were still housed at the Palace of Learning?"

"Um," the general said. "Strange that. Being a Chooser is a major honor. After watching you humans and your kids, a lot of our people and their companions wanted to take a try at having kids in their quarters. I now have two. They'll be along shortly with my companion. It's an... experience."

"I would imagine so," Kris admitted. "You've got kids around your homes and my kids want to play with them. That's the way of it in Human space. If I'm honest, my kids do a lot to keep me human. They drive me insane," Kris added through a wide grin directed at her two kids, "but they keep me human."

"And now we will see what they do for us," the Iteeche general said.

"Yes, let us see what happens today at the lake... and through the years to come."

The parade was now a mixed bag of Human adults and kids, as well as Iteeche adults and kids. When the parade came out of the Guard quarters, they found Iteeche and Marines MPs ready to direct them as well as more MPs to act as road guards. Each Iteeche Guardsman was paired with a Human Marine.

This was likely the most combined troop movement in the long history of either the Iteeche Empire or the Human race.

Traffic stopped to let them pass. Drivers gawked at the strange sight of young and old, Iteeche and Human. There was an Iteeche there taking pictures, while another filmed the entire thing. Kris pointed that out to the general.

"Ah, yes. We do not have anything like your media. However, in between songs, our TV stations have been known to carry matters of interest to all proper thinking Iteeche. The Emperor commissioning a new ship, a clan lord opening a new apartment complex. This or that."

"So, this may be seen by more than just the drivers here on the perimeter avenue," Kris said.

"Yes."

"I like that. Who arranged for the photographers?" Kris asked.

"The media is free to float on the waves," the general said. "Someone may have made a call to them suggesting there was something happening near the palace that they might be able to sell to their media outlets. Thus, the waves washed them up on our beach."

"Ah, yes. I have helped land just such fish," Kris admitted.

The parade of excited kids of both species and the parents who were dividing their attention between the hijinks of their offspring and the other adults they now shared childcare with, reached the crosswalk to the Palace gate.

MPs took their lives in their hands to step out and stop traffic. Apparently traffic lights had not been invented in the Empire. Only when all lanes ground to a halt did the senior Iteeche MP wave for the kids to cross.

To shouts of "Walk, don't run!" both in Standard and Iteeche, the kids launched themselves in one huge wave for the other side of the broad avenue and the wide gate into the palace grounds.

There was a broad bridge across the moat. It had to be that wide to accommodate the palanquins that clan lords rode through it. The kids spread out, wanting to see over the bridge at what was in the water. There were whispered shouts that monsters with huge teeth lived in the moat. One Iteeche lad claimed to have spotted one, but it was gone before anyone else did.

He got a lot of joshing from both Iteeche and Human kids, but it was in good humor. Kris suspected they all wished they'd been the one to spot the elusive legend.

Once the last kids had toddled across the street, the road guards recovered, and traffic resumed whizzing around the avenue.

Kris was glad to be safe on palace grounds and out of that potential shooting gallery on the streets, but Ruth and Johnnie were not satisfied with her progress. Once they had finished looking over the low stone walls on the side of the bridge, they headed for her. Johnnie was so excited that he was hopping in her direction.

"Mommy! Mommy, hurry up!" the two insisted as each of them took a hand and began to pull her faster up the tree shaded lane.

Behind her, Kris heard General Konga do that strange Iteeche laugh. Apparently he thought it very funny that the commander of the victorious Combined Fleet could not resist two humans half her size.

Kris didn't mind. She let herself be towed along until she'd caught up with the two tutors that had the duty for this outing. They laughed, too, as the kids hurried her past them.

Soon, the lake came in sight.

It was quite lovely. The waters were mirror smooth and pale green, reflecting trees that shaded the banks. There was a large sandy beach, white and sparkling in the sun. It, too, might have been smooth, but now it showed plenty of footsteps. From Kris's left wafted the delicious aromas of wood burning grills and the first of the hamburgers and hot dogs, as well as barbecued brisket, pork ribs, and chicken.

Kris had to smile at the thought of the many light years that the food had come so it could feed humans in the center of the Iteeche Empire.

However, her kids had other ideas. They'd seen the water. They dropped her hands and took off running, hopping, and dancing - whatever it took to shed their clothes. As a mother, Kris checked to see that lifeguards were on duty. They were.

A reasonably large area off the beach had been roped off with floats for the kids to romp in. Outside that, there were several floating platforms for swimmers to rest on. Beyond them was a marked off area, complete with goals for water polo.

A game was just starting.

Good. It looked like someone had everything in hand. So, of course, she spotted just who that someone was.

"Hi, Abby, you keeping busy?" Kris called.

"No rest for us wicked."

"Where's Cara?"

"Getting the third field set up for polo. You wouldn't believe how many fools signed up for that game. Oh, and we're getting Iteeche who want to play, too. You think anyone would mind if we had twice as many people on a team, half Human, half Iteeche?"

"I won't tell the Olympic committee if you don't," Kris said.

"Good. I will not let them have a Human against the Iteeche. We don't need to start another war over polo."

"Yeah. We got enough working on that outside of the water."

There were screams of "Mommy, Mommy!" from where her kids were splashing around in the shallows.

"I better go spend some time with the kids."

"It don't look like anyone has a gun to your head," Abby said, dryly.

"Nope, just pudgy little fingers wrapped around my heart."

Now it was Kris's turn to shed her clothes and join the kids. There was splashing and swimming and all kinds of jumping up and down. It seemed that just adding water to kids made for a mix of delightful fun.

If Kris had thought to wear them out, it worked the other way around. She finally had to wave for one of the nanny/tutors to step in and she trudged across the sand to where a row of pavilions stood for those wanting a place to rest out of the sun. General Konga had saved a low chair for her and found a comfortable bunch of pillows for himself.

She joined him.

"I'd never seen one of you Humans without your clothes," he said in greetings. "You have a lot more bumps and stuff," he said, waving his hands, two in her direction, two at the crowd in general. "It is strange. You treat men and women equal in status, but you are much different."

The general was still in his undress uniform, but Kris had seen Ron the Iteeche naked one night when she was recovering from battle wounds and could not sleep. She'd wandered down by the pool just before he chose to take a moonlight swim.

Seated in the shadows, she had gotten her first glimpse of a bare Iteeche. They were smooth down there as well as everywhere else. Both male and female had a small cloaca, an orifice they used for everything. While the general found the Human anatomy interesting, Kris found theirs strange as well.

Both Iteeche sexes look pretty much the same unclothed. So, why did the Iteeche treat their females to purdah and keep them out of the workforce?

The two species were certainly alien to each other.

"We like the way we are just as much as you like the way you are."

"Yes," the general said, musing. "Yes, but the way you play with your children, and they with you. I wonder. If I and my woman were to mate in our small pond and chose from the best of the fingerlings, could the three of us enjoy each other as much as you enjoy your children? Oh, where is your husband?"

"Checking on security. We need to get permission to fly a helicopter over the pond."

"A helicopter? Why?"

"Do you like the small white fish?" Kris asked in return

"Of course. Every Iteeche does. There isn't a planet in the Empire where we don't have free or farmed white fish."

"Well, I don't think you'll want any of our barbecue."

The Iteeche Guard general glanced at the smoking grills and shook his head. "No. Definitely not. You don't even have fish on the grills."

"Yes. So, what would happen if a helicopter made a low pass over the pond and dumped several tons of living white fish into the water?"

The general made a loud coughing sound, "Our younglings would be diving and snapping the fish up in their beaks. It would be . . ." suddenly he got serious. "It would be the most fun. Yes, I think I would actually understand what you mean by fun. Wildly doing something for the pure joy of it. Nothing required. No propriety. Just good food caught like our ancestors did it before we came out of the water. You would do that?"

"I will if we can get permission from the admiral controlling airspace over the Capital, yes."

The Iteeche general made a face. As much as an Iteeche could. "Admiral, can your marvelous computer connect me with Capital Airspace Defense?"

"Yes, I can," Nelly answered immediately.

"Please do," the Guard general said, then added softly to Kris. "I can't believe I just asked a computer to please do something."

"It's always a shock the first time," Kris whispered back.

"Capital Airspace Defense," instantly came from Kris's neck.

"This is the Commanding General of the Imperial Guard. Put Admiral Fanz on the line."

"One moment, sir. He is on another line."

"I am on the Imperial grounds. Is there anything more important than the defense of the Palace?"

"N- n- no, sir. One moment, sir."

"Nelly, is Jack on the other line?"

"Yes, Kris."

"What is it, Konga?" an irritated Iteeche admiral snapped, a moment later. "I've got enough problems from those denizens of chaos-from-the-deep Humans."

"That is the matter on which I must talk to you."

"Don't tell me that you have a Human badgering your ear as well."

"As a matter of fact, I do have the Imperial Admiral of the First Order of Steel seated next to me. I am watching Iteeche and Humans swimming together in a most proper and fitting way. I think all our Iteeche younglings and even their Choosers would find the dropping of white fish into the palace pond a pleasant reminder of how our ancient ancestors fed themselves from the sea. Please grant the Humans the brief use of the airspace between their palace and this lake."

"General, you want me to give in to the Humans?"

That was no question. The admiral was asking the Imperial Guard general to accept responsibility for any risk attached to this wild Human carrying on.

"Yes, Admiral, I will cosign any order you wish to write that will give the Humans the use of the palace airspace for . . ." the general turned to Kris. "When do you want to do this?"

"Between the second and third hours after midday," Kris answered.

"So be it upon your head," the admiral said, and cut the call.

"Well, I hope you will not do anything too improper," General Konga told Kris. "How do you Humans call it? My neck is out a mile."

"We will be very careful," Kris assured him. "I'll make sure the first drop isn't too large. Nelly, can you get me Jack please?"

"Of course, Kris."

"Hi, honey. How's the swim party?"

"Can't you hear the squeals in the background?" Kris asked right back.

"I do think I hear some small riot going on. Or is it a large riot by small people? I can never get those two right."

"Nope, you got it right both ways today. Listen, General Konga called the Capital Airspace Defense admiral. We've got permission to run choppers between the embassy and this pond between fourteen and fifteen hundred hours. Can we use smaller skitter choppers and have more runs with smaller loads?"

"Sure," Jack said. "It will make for a better lunch for the kids. I'll break the fish into six or eight loads and space them out every eight or ten minutes."

"I think that might be better," Kris said.

"Ah, admiral," interrupted in the voice of a very nervous Human. It came from Kris's neck also.

"Yes," Kris said.

"Ah. Sorry to disturb you, ma'am. This is staff sergeant Munez. I'm covering the road and I think the Emperor is coming to our party."

"Are you sure?" General Konga asked, directing his voice at Nelly.

"No, Sir. Neither is the Iteeche sergeant with me. He's never seen the Emperor before. Neither have I."

"He should be in pretty fancy clothes," Kris put in, "and have half his court with him."

"Yeah, Admiral. That's what we expected, but this Iteeche is just wearing a singlet and he's only got a half-dozen guys in fancy clothes all arguing with him, telling him to get back in the palace."

"That sounds like my Emperor," General Konga said.

"Make sure he is safe, but take no action, sergeant."

"Yes, ma'am."

"Jack?"

"I heard. Nelly cut me in. I'll tighten up surveillance in the airspace over the pond. I've got a nano spy over that group. You want to see its take?"

"Please," General Konga said.

A moment later, a holograph appeared in front of them. Sadly, Kris still had trouble telling Iteeche apart. Of course, the problem was returned. Iteeche couldn't tell Humans apart. Still, even Kris could tell that the young Iteeche in the simple purple singlet, surrounded by a half-dozen fussbudgets in many-layered formal court clothing was indeed the Emperor she'd seen several times over the last month.

The Emperor was coming and she had nothing to wear. She glanced around the beach. Some nice person had collected all the clothes that had littered the sand an hour ago and put them somewhere.

"Nelly, how close is the Emperor?"

The holograph swapped for a map. The Emperor and his entourage weren't more than two hundred meters away.

Well, this is a swim party.

Kris and General Konga went to meet his Emperor.

12

The Imperial Household Staff was busy arguing with the young Emperor They didn't notice the approach of the Guard general in undress uniform and the Human in little more than a smile. A smile which she struggled mightily to keep friendly and not nervous.

NELLY, WHAT ARE THEY SAYING?

PRETTY MUCH WHAT YOU'D EXPECT. 'YOU CAN'T DO THIS,' 'THIS IS NOT PROPER.' THAT KIND OF STUFF. YOU DON'T NEED ME TO TRANSLATE.

NOPE, Kris admitted.

The Emperor noticed Kris and Konga and turned to them, ignoring his harridans. Kris bowed. Konga bowed deeper.

The kid was loose and ready for play in the Emperor's voice, "Please see me today as Tranna. I heard that you were having a swim party," he said. "May I attend?"

"Of course, Your Imperial Majesty," Kris quickly answered. "After all, we are borrowing your pond. There is always a place for you whenever we Humans throw a party."

From the water polo field, a shout rose up. One team had scored a point.

That drew the eyes of the Emperor. "What are they playing?" he asked.

Kris gave him a bare outline of the rules and strategy of water polo.

"Oh, I must play."

"They are starting up a new game," Kris said as they anchored the third field in place. "I'm sure you could join."

The Emperor glanced around. Within his view, all the Iteeche and Humans in the water were unclothed. In a moment he pulled his singlet over his head, tossed it aside and dashed for the water, letting out a whop of pure joy.

Did General Konga actually grin at Kris as he went to collect the purple singlet?

"Jack," Kris called on net, "I need more lifeguards and safety boats. Include diving gear. I've got an Emperor to take care of."

"You're kidding me."

"No joke. It's his pond. He's come out to play."

"I bet he's got some minders that are upset."

"Yep, and they're glaring at me. Fortunately, I have General Konga to hide behind."

"Oh no you don't," Konga said, making that weird Iteeche laugh. "If they come at you, I'm running. Oh, and I heard about tripping people in case of an event called the Zombie apocalypse. The fiction of you Humans makes me wonder what actually goes around in your brains."

Kris laughed. "Sometimes we don't have brains."

The Emperor, or should she say Tranna, dashed through the shallows, sending spray scattering before him, then dove in and swam for the third game that was just forming up.

"Nelly, get some drifters or tiny skeeters over the Emperor. Nothing obvious, but don't let him out of your sight."

"Doing it, Kris. Kris, we need more lifeboats and crews. There's only one boat at that new field.

"I know. Jack?"

"I've got a fast skitter headed your way with a dozen strong swimmers," Jack reported.

"Good," Kris said. For the moment, she and Konga strode toward where the water lapped on the sand. Konga had been talking into the commlink Kris had given him. Now, a dozen Iteeche Guardsmen raced from the gate guardhouse; they were tossing off their formal dress uniforms. They were down to the buff by the time they reached General Konga.

"The Emperor is swimming in that game over there. Examine the other two games. Physical contact is allowed by all players. Do not interfere in the game unless you truly see that the Emperor is hurt. Bleeding, maybe. Not surfacing, definitely."

The senior NCO in the group took his ambiguous instructions in without so much as a blink. "Yes, General."

"Some Human lifeguards will be joining you with boats. You will be able better to see what's going on from one of those boats."

"Yes, sir."

"Now get out there."

Twelve Iteeche charged into the water and threw themselves into racing dives. Kris was amazed at how well their four legs and four arms worked in the water.

A moment later, a large four-engine skeeter raced up the path they had walked an hour ago. It went straight for the playing fields. A dozen strong swimmers dropped from the air vehicle before it settled to the water and divided itself into six boats.

These were well-balanced catamarans, stable, as well as a good platform for viewing the events around them. Each had a ladder at its stern and the Human swimmers were soon hauling themselves aboard, two to a boat. They offered the Iteeche swimmers a hand up the ladder as well.

One of the catamarans took station at each corner of the field the Emperor's game was being played on. The other two hovered in the middle between the first two fields. After a few moments, the catamarans sprouted a high chair that offered a Human swimmer a good view all around. Meanwhile, an awning unfurled itself to shade the three other swimmers, Human and Iteeche, without interfering with their watch. Soon, chairs for Humans and stools for the Iteeche appeared to make it easier to stand their watch at either corner of the bow and one at the stern.

"Nelly, could you walk one of those pavilions over here?" Kris asked.

"Of course," Nelly said with a laugh.

A moment later, one of the pavilions began a stiff-legged walk on its four corner poles toward where Kris and Konga stood.

"Magic," Konga said, shaking his head.

"I can almost agree with you," Kris admitted as the ungainly thing did a slow waddle up to them. Covering them, it settled into place around them, then spat up some pillows for the Iteeche and a lounger for Kris.

Kris was glad she'd divided the Iteeche and Humans equally between the sides. This kept the cheering equal for both teams, and the foul calls came out about even as well. Fortunately, the Human refs covered Humans and the Iteeche did the same for their own. Thus, most penalties tended to be called on a Human fouling a Human and Iteeche fouling Iteeche.

The refs were going easy on the rules. Few of the players appeared to know anything about the limits on who was supposed to be in the zones in front of the goals. The refs just let them play and stood back, calling fouls only when two players got to boisterous.

There seemed to be as much laughing on the fields as among the spectators.

The games went on; no one seemed to be keeping score or track of the time. Kris didn't realize it was two o'clock until a skeeter with a big belly arrived and circled the pond.

Nelly amplified General Konga's announcement that lunch for the Iteeche had arrived. "White fish will soon drop from the Human device circling the pond. Every half hour for the next two hours, a new load of fish will arrive, so enjoy and happy eating."

The skeeter began dropping water and fish in a long line right down the middle of the water polo fields. In a second, the game ended as Iteeche players and onlookers dove into the water. Many surfaced with fish in their beaks. They tossed the fish in the air and caught it again, maybe several times, before they caught the fish head or tail first, and it slipped right down their gullet.

The kids in the wading and swimming areas weren't forgotten. The skeeter held back enough for a small drop over them. The young Iteeche attacked the fish with the enthusiasm and gusto of their few years. There was no question, Iteeche were still very happy to dive for their dinner.

This was all an education for Kris.

"You want to dive in?" Kris asked General Konga.

"I'll wait for a later delivery. I'm not sure there's a fish left in the pond at the moment."

"You may be right."

A runner double-timed it up the wide, stone path. He looked around, hurried and worried, then jogged over to General Konga and saluted.

"I have a message for Admiral Longknife," he said.

Kris eyed him. He was about the same rank as a Navy lieutenant commander. Too senior to be running message traffic.

Kris had a bad feeling in the pit of her stomach that normal had just ended.

"This is Admiral Longknife," Konga said, introducing Kris.

If the Iteeche was embarrassed to be addressing his admiral out of uniform, or anything else, or maybe embarrassed that he'd been found out as unable to tell one Human from another, he didn't flinch. He offered Kris one of the electronic boards she was getting the Combined Fleets to adopt for running message traffic around the headquarters.

At the moment, the board showed red with a white diagonal slash from one corner to the other. In that slash usually were the words Top Secret.

Today the white line held **Most Secret. Eyes Only.**

Kris applied her thumbprint to the proper place, then looked into the camera and let it get a picture of her right eye. A moment later, the red screen changed to red letters against a white background.

FROM: COTH, ADMIRAL OF THE SECOND ORDER OF STEEL

TO: LONGKNIFE, IMPERIAL ADMIRAL OF THE FIRST ORDER OF STEEL.

REPORT JUST ARRIVED THAT PLANET ARTECCIA HAS BEEN RETAKEN BY A FLEET OF TEN THOUSAND BATTLECRUISERS. MORE TO FOLLOW. YOUR INSTRUCTIONS?

Kris handed the message board to General Konga. "Apparently, either someone didn't get the word that the coup here in the capital had failed or this is their answer to it."

The Guard general scanned the message. "Impossible to tell."

Kris turned to the messenger and asked, "Did the planet fall without a fight? Has it been destroyed?"

"Our understanding is that the clan lord ruling the planet evacuated by battleship ahead of the assault. There were only a hundred thousand troops on the planet. They got away in what transports were available or were crammed into the few battlecruisers available."

"Very good, commander. Send my complements to Admirals Tong and Ulan. I will meet with them tomorrow morning. They should begin to make ready for the fleet to sortie. We will need at least a million troops plus enough clan lords to run two planets. Maybe three."

The Iteeche Navy field officer raised his hands in salute to Kris, as he said "Aye, aye, Admiral. It will be done."

He was off at a quick jog the next moment.

"Ah, so you intend to finish a game of bowls before turning your attention to battle," General Konga remarked.

"Oh, so you know that old story," Kris said, delighted that her Iteeche friend was interested in such minor bits of Human history.

"How could I not like a man who insisted on finishing his game even with the Great Spanish Armada bearing down on his England. Great story. Is it true?"

Kris shrugged. "There's a saying, 'If it isn't true, it should be'."

"Oh, yes, I found that quote most interesting. You Humans are a slippery lot."

Kris eyed the general. "And you Iteeche are not?" she said, raising an eyebrow.

"Hmm," was all the reply she got.

"So, tell me, how are you finding out so much about my species when we know so little about yours?"

"Actually, you are. I guess you haven't gotten the book yet."

"Book?"

"Your Ron the Iteeche wrote several reports for his Chooser," the general said. "They were distributed to all the clans. In your embassy are several historians as well as many learned men. We have assigned our own librarians to work with them. There is a kind of trade going on. We share with one historian while another of your historians talks with our people. Every couple of days the two groups get together to make sure the trade is going equally well for each side. It is working out very well. I spend my evenings reading the latest reports. You do have a bloody history."

"And you have too large a fleet and army to claim to be peaceful," Kris shot back.

"So obvious. Now, I am hungry, and I can hear the third skeeter approaching," Konga said as he tossed off his uniform. A moment later, he raised a great foam of water as he charged into the water and did a lovely racing dive. Before the food skitter arrived, he was out among the hungry throngs of Iteeche.

Many of the Humans were taking this opportunity to come ashore and follow the delicious smells the grills were producing. Kris found her own two short people among the others, thanks to Nelly's help, and joined them getting food and finding a place to sit down and enjoy it.

Now that she knew her time was short, she stayed close to the kids.

After eating, she joined them in a tug-of-war, or at least they tugged and she shouted encouragement. Other games now started ashore, all by age groups. The three-legged and wheelbarrow races had more people on the sand than near the finish line. The egg toss and water balloon throws were, as usual, hilarious. The younger kids loved the blanket race with mommy or daddy hauling them along on a blanket toward the finish line. The bigger kids thought the Watch Your Step was great, with everyone trying to pop two balloons around everyone's ankles.

Kris got dragged into that game with Ruth and Johnnie and kids of their age group. She and several other parents only managed to survive half the game before both their balloons got popped. The kids loved it. None of them noticed that the adult players hadn't popped anyone's balloons.

Around five in the afternoon, there were more fish drops for the Iteeche and a second round of food was ready at the grills for the Humans. This time, large buckets of beans, potato salad, and ears of corn were provided.

Soon, the younger kids were happily full and thoroughly tired. The guards arranged for a quiet parade back to the Human Embassy, Navy, and Guard housing for the parents and their smaller children. Kris walked home with a wonderful bundle. Johnnie was asleep on her shoulder. It had been years since he'd been that tuckered out. Ruth sleepwalked along, holding on to Kris's free hand.

Kris got the kids back to their quarters where she helped the nannies put them to bed. Then she took a shower and changed into undress whites before she went to the command center. There, Jack was alert to the safety of everyone from the boundaries of the Embassy quarter to the far side of the Imperial Precincts.

"Any problems?" she asked.

"Not a squeak."

"How's the Emperor doing?"

"I have a good visual on him. He's back to playing water polo. I don't think Iteeche ever get tired of swimming. Most of the Humans have joined the spectators. Now it's just Iteeche playing."

"That doesn't surprise me."

Kris watched the screen that stayed with the young man who carried the burden of an Empire. He was splashing around and being splashed, making that strange hacking laugh, as were those around him. If any of the other players thought of the youngling they were dunking and who was dunking them, they did not let on. Likely a lot of teenage Iteeche would be shocked when their folks told them as they walked home who they had played with or against.

"Have you heard the word?" Jack asked Kris.

"About Arteccia?"

"Yes."

"Yeah," Kris said. "I got the message flimsy. It said that our ships and troops left as they came in. Is that right?"

"Yep."

"So the planet wasn't turned into a waste land."

"That's the word that we have. A flotilla held back at the jump to report what it could of the new occupation. While an army landed, there was no fighting. Not so much as a peep."

"Good. I was afraid that Arteccia was at risk when we moved most of the fleet to the Glorious Golden Eel system. Coth is strong enough to hold that system against ten thousand."

"So, what do you have in mind?"

"I want to get a good night sleep. The kids are tuckered out and so is their mom. Tomorrow, we go to war, but, as General Konga said, there is still time to finish a game of bowls."

"So, now they're quoting our own history back at us."

"I hope that helps."

Two hours later, the swim party was over, and Kris saw to it that Jack was relieved of the watch. Together, they headed for bed. Tomorrow was going to be busy.

13

At 0800 the next morning, Kris faced her key battle staff at the conference table in her day quarters. On her right, Jack and Admiral Kitano represented the Human fighters. Iteeche Admirals Tong and Ulan sat in stools on her left. At the foot of the table, Jacques sat ready to provide sociologic input to the conversation. Grampa Trouble was the last to arrive. He would provide sage advice and hard-won experience while Gramma Trouble kept her two kiddos busy.

"Do we know anything more about the situation on Arteccia?" Kris asked the Iteeche admirals.

Both shrugged; that involved all four shoulders and most definitely got the point across. "The rebels entered the system and demanded the surrender of all loyalist ships. Instead, before crossing spears, our ships loaded the army and withdrew in good order. One thousand battlecruisers do not take on ten thousand."

"Previously, would they have surrendered?" Kris asked. The Iteeche considered it appropriate for a fleet outnumbered two-to-one to surrender. Kris had fought outnumbered four-to-one and won. Of course, she had tricks up her sleeve.

"Yes. From of old, in the Iteeche way, it is dishonorable to run away," Tong said. "They would have attacked and surrendered when honor was served."

"Well, at least they've learned to run away and live to fight another day," Jack said.

"It is not a doctrine that is easy to learn," Admiral Tong said. "Admiral Sim sincerely regretted not being able to hold the planet."

"Ulan, send Admiral Sim my strongest well done." Kris thought for a moment then added. "Also, establish a medal for something like Outstanding Fighting Withdrawal."

"But there was no fighting," Admiral Tong put in.

"Okay, Outstanding Orderly Withdrawal Against Overwhelming Odds," Kris proposed. "And don't make it a somber ribbon. Bright and colorful. I suspect before this war is over, we'll be issuing a lot of them."

"Maybe if you affix the first letter of the planet's name," Grampa Trouble said, "everyone can know which withdrawal they were in."

"Can they wear two or three letters?" Admiral Tong asked.

"Yes. We issue stars for medals that have been awarded twice," Jack said. "No reason why they can't do the same with planetary letters."

"This may make it easier for the officers and men to accept that they have run away from a fight. Still, fighting is something every sailor, Marine, and soldier is trained to do. Running is not."

"Tong," Kris said, "if Admiral Sim had done it the traditional Iteeche way, his ships would now be fighting against the Emperor and the soldiers and sailors would be doing the same. Likely a lot of clan lords would have been executed and many of the cities reduced to rubble as battles raged through them. Now, I get the ships and men back and I can use them to my purpose. Do we know where Admiral Sim is withdrawing to?"

"Yes, Zargoth."

"Good. That will make him available quickly. Now, the next question for you, Admiral Tong. According to the Iteeche way, what would honor require me to do next?"

"Their capture of Arteccia dishonors you. For your honor, you would be required to attack the planet that was taken from you."

"I figured as much," Kris drawled softly. "Nelly, let's see a map of the Iteeche Empire. Show the planets by productivity."

A holographic map of the Empire quickly appeared above the table. Most planets sparkled red or yellow, depending on their loyalty. They likely had fifty billion Iteeche on them eking out barely a survivable living. As a whole, they contributed nothing to the Empire. However, for the clan lords on the planet, their huge number of loyal clan members was a status symbol of honor and power.

Some of planets had recently swapped hands, mainly so clan lords could earn the medals Kris was handing out for capturing one. She, however, dismissed most of the planets with a shrug.

One or two rings circled the more productive planets. The planets with two rings were the most industrialized systems in the Empire. They were few, about fifty in number, and split thirty-twenty in favor of the Emperor.

The planets with one ring around them had productivity somewhere between planets with two rings and those with none.

Kris concentrated on the double-ringed planetary systems.

"Nelly, show me how many jumps from here to the double-ringed planets."

"All of them, Kris?"

"Yes."

"Standard jumps or fuzzy jumps?" Kris's computer asked. The fuzzy jumps were harder to find and usually required the new Mark XII fire control systems on the Human battlecruisers. The Iteeche knew the Humans used the jumps and were most anxious to figure out how they did it.

Numbers began to appear above the most productive systems. First a green number for standard jumps, then a slash followed by a brown number for the fuzzy jumps. The brown number was always smaller than the green.

There were two productive rebel planets just four jumps from the

Capital Planet. However, there were six potential targets five fuzzy jumps away.

"Nelly, please add the number of jumps from any of the planets with two rings."

Below the planets, numbers began to appear.

"What do you have in mind?" Jack asked.

"Ever played checkers?" Kris asked.

"I prefer chess," Jack admitted.

"I do too, but for now, it's still checkers for Johnnie. Chess only allows you to take a single piece at a time, checkers permits a double or even triple jump."

"Are you thinking a double or triple jump here?"

"I'm considering it. Admiral Tong, how many battlecruisers, assault transports, or anything else that carries soldiers can you lay your hands on?"

"How soon?"

"In the next five days," Kris answered.

The admiral commanding the task force that brought Kris back to the capital looked straight ahead, all four of his eyes going unfocused as he thought.

"There are one hundred and sixty Human battlecruisers," he muttered.

"Excuse me for interrupting," Admiral Kitano said, "but we're expected a flotilla each from Savannah and Pittshope in the next few days. We'll have two hundred and twenty-four battlecruisers very soon."

"Thank you, Excellent Admiral," Tong said, then went on. "I commanded fifteen flotillas that held four hundred and eighty Iteeche battlecruisers. Also, two flotillas of the Wo Clan tied up at the space station attempted to sortie when it was clear the assault on the Emperor had miscarried. My Marines encouraged them to stay put. We can add them."

"Can we get anything from the 'loyal' clans?" Kris asked.

"You have a right to make that request. They should each provide at least five flotillas more, say four hundred and eighty more. That would give us a total of a bit over a thousand battlecruisers available."

"Can you make the request for the ships or must I?" Kris asked.

"They are much less likely to give you the run-around," Tong answered. "While they may owe us the ships, there are many ways to delay making them ready such that, in effect, they don't give us the ships that they, by rights, must."

Kris frowned, even as she sighed. "So, I have to go begging."

"The Admiral Commanding the Combined Fleets never begs, Most Excellent Admiral. One asks respectfully and firmly."

"Yes," Kris said. "Jacques, you have any suggestions on how I go about being respectful but firm?"

"You're going to have to go visit them."

"Can't I invite them to visit me?"

"No, no, no," Admiral Tong put in, quickly. "That would never do for an admiral to command a clan lord to visit them."

Kris's frown deepened. More evidence of the fleet's second-class status.

"Could I politely invite them to maybe smell my rose garden?" Kris growled.

Both Iteeche Admirals shook their heads.

With a sigh that was awful close to a growl, Kris said, "Nelly, can you get me Ron the Iteeche?"

A moment later, an image of Ron floated above the table. It looked like he was in a library. Next to him were the two Iteeche called Fred and Shorty that the Quo and Abba Clan had sent to Ron so they could study the strange ways of Humans. No doubt, Kris was about to give them an entirely new lesson to examine.

"How may I help you, Most Excellent Admiral?" Ron asked. Interesting, he didn't call her Princess, or Emissary. Someone was expecting a call from the admiral side of Kris's mission.

"Greetings, wise Imperial Advisor." Kris could go formal, too. "I find that I need again to visit with your most Eminent Chooser. How are the flowers of his garden?"

"Most lovely in their color. Magnificent as they scent the breeze."

"Very good, then he will enjoy sharing them with me."

"He would be most honored. Would you like to visit him in one of your fortnights?"

"I would prefer this afternoon. Say, the first hour of the afternoon," Kris said, removing the velvet glove and showing the steel underneath.

"But he often dozes in his garden after his noonday meal."

"Would the second hour be better?" Kris asked, most solicitously.

"Are you available that hour a week from now?" Ron countered.

"Ron, can't we cut out the bullshit? You know as well as I do that we have lost a planet. I need battlecruisers, and I need them now, not next week. I wish to talk to your clan lord about seconding several dozen flotillas to the Combined Fleets. Freddy, Shorty, I will need to talk to your clan chiefs later this evening about the same matter."

"Admiral," Ron began, "you know that the forces defending the Capital Planet are still recovering from the terrible losses in the recent attack on the Capital. You ask for far too many ships."

"Yes, I do. However, ships that sail with me win victories. Captains and Admirals gain prize money. Executive officers quickly get their own commands among the captured ships. Division heads get promoted. Have you ever considered how many ships you would have left in orbit if I merely gave permission for anyone to join my battle fleet?"

"No Admiral Commanding the Combined Fleets has ever done that," Freddy said, cutting in.

"No, but a Human has never commanded the Combined Fleets," Kris countered. "Nor has an admiral run up my string of victories. Now, can you arrange an invitation for me at the second hour after noon today or do I go recruiting around the stations?"

The three Iteeche turned to look at each other. Their beaks were wide open, and likely out of joint, since Iteeche used their beaks as both mouths and noses.

"We will arrange the visit for you," Ron said, sounding very much exasperated.

"Very well. In addition to ships, I will need enough junior clan lordlings to rule two or three planets. Can you ask your clan lords to begin arranging for them?"

That was greeted with much more enthusiasm from the three junior clan lordlings.

Kris let them enjoy that thought, before going on. "I will see you soon. Freddy, Shorty, you may message my computer with the time your clan lords can extend me an invitation. Please assure that they are today and do not conflict."

"They will not conflict," Freddy spat.

The connection to them was then cut at the other end.

"You play a risky game," Admiral Tong said.

"If I don't get more ships, I'll have to play an even riskier game. Now, Nelly, I keep hearing that some of our admirals are seizing rebel planets. Have any of them captured a planet that we have designated with one or two rings?"

"No Kris. We have taken an even dozen subsistence planets. The rebel commanders have also joined the fray. So far, they have taken five of the loyalist's minor planets.

"Have the rebels counter-attacked to retake any of the planets they have lost?"

"No, Kris. Seventeen planets have changed hands. No one has tried to retake a planet."

"So, Admiral Tong, why has the honor of neither the rebels or the loyalist admirals or clans compelled them to retake the planets they lost?"

"I expected you to ask me that, Most Excellent Admiral. While some of the task forces were small forces from the Combined Fleets, most were from minor clans or septs. The planets lost were not theirs, so they lost no honor. Those whose honor was besmirched have not responded. Maybe they are gathering forces. Maybe they lack the forces to attempt a counter-attack. It is hard to tell."

"Hmm," Kris said. "Is this the Iteeche way, or have my victories inspired my junior commanders to get into the fray? Admiral Tong, you are the historian among us."

"I think this is more of your influence," he replied. "As I said, we usually build up our forces and attack the most recently seized planet, or the most recent planet that has raised the banner of rebellion."

"I imagine that makes it easy for everyone to mass their fleets for a battle, or steer clear of the invasion fleet and keep their honor intact."

"Yes."

"Are you thinking something, Admiral?" Jack asked. He was clearly all business.

"Yes. Back in the Age of Sail on old Earth, when you couldn't see farther than the man in your foretops, and message traffic was no faster than a frigate or sloop could sail, finding the fleet you wanted to fight was a bit difficult. Nelly, what was that battle?"

"The British Admiral Nelson wanted to fight the French and Spanish fleets even though they outnumbered him. The French admiral sailed his entire fleet across the ocean, some twenty-five hundred miles, and then sailed them back again the selfsame twenty-five hundred miles. The Royal Navy chased the hostile fleet across the ocean, then back again without the two fleets catching sight of each other. The only reason Nelson caught them was that the French and Spanish fleet were too big for most ports. He guessed right, and found them holed up in Cadiz, Spain. When the French tried to slip away to a different harbor, Nelson managed to catch them and fight a decisive battle. The Royal Navy had only twenty-seven ships of the line. The Franco-Spanish fleet of thirty-three lost twenty-two ships. The Royal Navy lost none."

"So," Jack said, added things up, "they had to chase them all over the place, but when they finally caught them, one side lost two-thirds and the other lost nothing."

Admirals Tong and Ulan exchanged glances. "A victory much like you have been fighting, Admiral, although they were only outnumbered less than three-to-four."

"Do you think we could fight outnumbered three-to-four and not lose any ships?" Kris asked.

"Definitely."

"Okay, enough ancient history," Kris said. "Admirals Tong and

Katano, prepare the fleet to sail. Admiral Ulan, find out where we can scrounge up enough troop ships to lift a million soldiers. Also, order food and expendables for three dozen more flotillas. I may not get all that I want, but then again, I may."

Kris paused, then frowned a moment. "Admiral Tong. I'm going to the biggest clans. What about the smaller clans? Do they have flotillas?"

"Yes. If you can get the large clans seconding your ships, the lesser clans should be standing in line to join you for gold and glory."

"Is there any way to get those lesser clans joining us between now and fourteen hundred hours?"

"I have some admirals and captains in my fleet who know their counterparts in those flotillas," Admiral Tong said slowly. "I could ask them to see if those officers could get their clans to second them to the Combined Fleets. You have a reputation for victory. Being part of your victory might well raise their status."

Jacques cleared his throat. "You might suggest that clan lordlings from those minor septs and families provide lordlings for the Battleships of State. There's no reason why they shouldn't have some of the spoils from our victories."

"Will they be rich planets?" Tong asked.

"When have I ever messed with poor ones?" Kris answered.

"Mmm."

"Now, I have a visit to prepare for and I'm sure you have many things you want to do," Kris said.

The three admirals around Kris's table took their dismissal and hurried from the room.

Kris waited until the door closed. "Nelly, can you shrink this table?"

In a moment, it was a small round table with just Jack, Grampa Trouble, and Jacques around it. "Jacques," Kris asked, "did I screw anything up?"

"Bear with me for a moment," the sociologist said. "I'm arriving at some conclusions about these people. First off, it's top-down. Everyone does what they're told. That works fine for those at the top of the totem pole. Or, at least it's supposed to. I read Megan's report on working with the technicians of Zargoth to get water and power back online after a clan lordling took it upon himself to sabotage half that city. I think the folks well-down the pole care more about survival and their families than they do clan politics. Notice how many of the Wo and Domm class soldiers threw down their weapons when you had them outgunned, or at least they thought you did."

"Yeah, I noticed that," Jack said. "No one was really much interested in dying for anything, but they all wanted to move up the totem pole."

"Right," Jacques said. "If you're tight in a clan orbit, you play the clan game. Now that brings us to the head of the clans. I imagine they play a pretty cutthroat game among themselves. However, they like the game. It's rewarded them with power and pleasure. The reason this Empire hasn't changed in three to five thousand years is because those guys don't want any change. Knife me in the back? Fine, that's part of the power game. Change the game in any way? Suddenly you have all of them down on you like a pack of rabid dogs."

"So," Jack said, "do they find this Human emissary and Admiral Commanding the Combined Fleets as an agent of change, or an agent to keep them safely tucked away at the top of the power pyramid?"

Now it was a very human shrug that came back at Kris. "I don't know. Likely, we won't know until something very bad happens to you, Kris."

"Worse than dropping a couple of high-rise apartments on my head?"

Jack snorted.

Jacques shrugged. "Obviously, they'll have to come up with something worse. That pile of rubble did not succeed in killing you."

"Umm," Kris answered, then changed her focus. "Grampa?"

"All I learned in the war, sweetheart, was to keep kicking them in the balls until they hollered uncle. I never found an Iteeche that would surrender to me while they still had a bullet or a grenade."

The general made a face and shook his head. "No, that's not

exactly right. At the level where your Grampa Ray was negotiating, that's the way it was. Down at my level, those four-eyed hulks fought me hard and heavy. However, once they saw they were defeated, they surrendered pretty fast. Both officers and men."

"So, those down the totem pole can be reasoned with. If they are in an impossible situation, they'll throw in the towel."

"Yeah. Most clan lords will fight to the last drop of some other clan's blood before they call it quits."

Kris nodded. She wasn't sure how much of this she could apply to the coming series of meetings, but it was all nice to know.

She closed down the meeting. Alone, she stared out the window, deep in thought.

Then Nelly reminded her that there was a fast attack transport leaving for Human space. Kris spent the rest of the morning preparing a report for King Raymond and a quick letter to her brother, Hanovi. He'd pass the news along to Father.

She had a working lunch with Abby and Ambassador Kawaguchi. Megan and Cara sat in. It was fascinating to see the gleam in their eyes as they listened to all the planning necessary to keep a diplomatic mission going hundreds of light years from the nearest Human planet. It went the same for the trade reports from Kawaguchi. Clearly, Cara would be in great demand when this mission finished. Maybe sooner if some of the great interplanetary corporations knew what was good for them.

Then it was thirteen hundred hours and it was time for Kris to risk another walk in the park with her Iteeche friends.

14

For this visit with Roth, Kris did not attempt to conceal the power of her escort. Since the entire drive would be along city streets, there was little gained by tracked vehicles and the ride on tires was smoother.

Two battalions, each with 54 gun trucks, provided a vanguard and rear guard. Another battalion of 54 infantry fighting trucks was mixed in with the gun trucks. Interspersed among them were a dozen scout trucks maintaining the drones and popping any nano spies that the situation might call for.

Today, each gun truck had a crew of five. There was the standard commander, gunner, and driver. Seated behind them were two sensor operators. One kept a careful eye on the radar feed from the battle station above the embassy as well as the close-in situation. The other maintained downlinks with all the drones in their area, including a full picture of the situation around the parade.

Kris deployed three different variations of gun trucks. Forty had a 50mm anti-armor laser that could be quickly converted to anti-air. Forty had a 50mm anti-air laser that could quickly convert to anti-armor. If they were in anti-armor mode, the gunner had control. Let it switch to Anti-Air, and the radar operator took over. He also controlled a 12mm laser that would respond to any rocket attack.

Any rocket launched from a building's window along the line of march would be drilled and exploded well before it was halfway to its target.

The remaining 28 gun trucks were pure psychology. Each mounted a 12-inch howitzer. The guns were not in train, but cut loose to point forward as well as to the right, left, and rear. Any Iteeche who got a look down one of those barrels would walk away with a serious case of respect.

The gun trucks themselves were big. Each truck carried three times the armor of the ones that had been buried under rubble. This time, if someone dumped bricks on Kris, the troops would not be crammed into survival bunkers gasping for breath. Each vehicle carried oxygen and a kit to scrub CO_2.

Once burned, twice shy.

The same went for Kris's palatial palanquin. It was just as huge as her last one, but it needed a lot more wheels to support it. The twenty-four Marines marching along each side of it still had a wing providing protective shade. Now, however, there was a winglet spreading out farther.

If they had to snatch the two Gunnies from their positions, the winglet would pull them in even as the wings swept up their Marines. Kris would still have a bunch of people in her survival bunker, but this time they'd have room for some bridge, chess, and poker games.

Even the three-wheeled motorcycles fore and aft of the parade now sported four big wheels. If they had to duck from flying bricks and stones, they'd be covered.

Kris looked at all Jack had done, and found it good. Unfortunately, it felt like she was locking the door after someone stole the barn. Still, no matter what surprise someone threw her way, she had more resources to handle it this time.

Riding the edges of the palanquin, Kris has female Marines with many bags of candy. She'd considered using Iteeche for that job, but she wanted the kids to remember that it was Humans that fed their sweet tooth.

Maybe female Marines weren't the best representatives of humanity's softer, gentler side, but it was the best Kris could come up with in the time available.

Thus, Kris paraded down the wide avenue that was the inner circling road. The ride was short; there was only one other palace between her embassy and the We Clan palace.

Since she was traveling through the main district of the Abba Clan, she should not run into any trouble. Despite all her preparations, or maybe because of them, Kris had no trouble at all this trip.

The Admiral Commanding the Imperial Combined Fleet arrived at exactly two hours after midday. The gates to the We Clan palace were wide open. There were honor guards both outside the gates, lining the block the palace occupied, as well also inside, drawn up in order.

As her gun trucks and infantry fight trucks rolled in, they folded themselves back into large blocks of Smart Metal™ that rolled over to be absorbed into a huge and growing cube of the stuff.

Kris's personnel slid out of their rigs and trotted over to their place in formation where they quickly dressed right and checked their interval. In less than five minutes, the Commanding Admiral of the Combined Fleets had an honor guard of Human and Iteeche standing in ranks across from three differently uniformed formations.

Drone feed had warned Kris what to expect, but she eyed the Iteeche Honor Guard waiting for her as her palanquin stretched out and lowered itself to squeeze through gates never intended for Kris's over-the-top display of Iteeche pomp.

Waiting for her were three battalions. One clearly wore the colors of the We clan: magenta and cream. Another of the other formations wore burgundy and tan uniforms. The last was in turquoise and white.

CLAN COLORS? Kris asked on Nelly net.

THOSE ARE THE CLAN COLORS OF THE QUO AND ABBA CLANS, KRIS.

I THOUGHT SO. JACK, THERE MAY BE A PRIZE HIDDEN IN PLAIN SIGHT.

KRIS, YOU THINK YOU MAY BE FACING ALL THREE CLAN LORDS AT ONCE?

WOULD YOU TAKE THAT BET?

NOPE.

Kris let Jacques and Jack dismount first. Grampa Trouble, or rather General Tordon, Hammerer of the Iteeche, preceded Kris. Normally, she kept Grampa Trouble in the nursery. After all, he and Gramma had only come along to help with Ruth and Johnnie when she and Jack were off blowing things up.

Today, however, she was hauling in the big guns.

Kris was last to let the palanquin's elevator take her to the ground. She marched to the head of her guard even as more of it rolled into the palace and folded its armor away.

In front of her, Ron and his two friends Freddy and Shorty, bowed to Kris. She saluted them.

"May we offer you refreshments?" Ron said, most obsequiously even for an Iteeche.

"Thank you, Ron, but I would prefer to share refreshments with your clan lords."

"Of course. Let me lead you to them."

"By a direct route?" Kris asked, raising an eyebrow.

"Most certainly," he said. A magic metal elevator slowly grew along the outside of the palace. By the time the small group got there, it reached to the top.

Kris's four and the three Iteeche stepped inside and were quickly whisked to the garden on the roof. Ron led them through a jungle of blossoming flowers, past a goldfish pond, and into an open space.

There, three Iteeche in the heavy robes of state lounged on pillows and cushions. With the Iteeche four legs and congested hip bone, chairs were out of the question. Kris was quick to provide stools for her Iteeche Navy officers, or cushions as the situation demanded.

These three clan lords felt no need to provide the same accommodation to their Human guests.

NELLY.

KRIS, YOUR CHAIRS ARE ALREADY ON THEIR WAY. JUST SIT DOWN.

Kris reached behind herself for the arms of a chair; they were there. She kept sitting down; the rest of the chair formed itself out of tiny drones as she settled into it. As she got comfortable, more small drones formed chairs to her right and left for her three staff.

Other Smart Metal™ drones added to Kris's seat until it was a throne fit for a king.

Across from her, the Iteeche clan lords did their best to keep their faces impassive but didn't quite succeed. The three lordlings advising their chiefs did a worse job of taking in the evidence of just what the Humans could do.

However, the Iteeche Kris called Roth, clan chief of the Chap'-sum'We did not take long to recover. His response was almost Human in its directness.

"Good afternoon, Admiral Commanding the Imperial Combined Fleets. What do you intend to do about the affront to the Emperor's honor?"

"Which affront to his honor are we talking about today?" Kris answered back. She refused to be knocked off balance by the clear slap at her own honor. Nor did she want to wander off into some wild rabbit chase after something she had no interest in.

"The assault on the Imperial planet Arteccia, of course."

"Oh, that assault on the Emperor's honor. Very likely I will do nothing about it."

"Why not?" demanded one of the other clan chiefs.

"Because responding to their initiative is exactly what they want me to do."

"There are ten thousand rebel ships at Arteccia. Don't you intend to destroy them?" said the other clan chief.

"In order to mount an attack on Arteccia, I would have to pull in the battle fleet presently guarding the Glorious Golden Eel system. That is one of the richest systems in the Empire."

Kris studied the three Iteeche. Were they really that dumb? "That would lead to two possible outcomes. I could arrive at the Arteccia system with enough ships to defeat ten thousand rebel battlecruisers only to discover myself facing twenty thousand . . . or none."

"Why twenty thousand?" the other of the clan lords asked.

At least Kris had gotten them past demanding. That was worth one point in this game they were playing.

"They know that the traditional Iteeche Way would require me to assault that system immediately. They know that we know they have ten thousand battlecruisers there. Of course, they would prepare a trap for us by doubling their strength."

"And none?" Roth asked. His big head was leaning to the right as if he might actually be thinking about Kris's words. She sincerely hoped he was.

"In order to launch an attack on the Arteccia system, I would have to strip the Glorious Golden Eel system of the battle fleet now defending it. If I was them, at just the right moment, I'd take the fleet from Arteccia and jump it over to the Glorious Golden Eel star and snap it up while it was undefended."

Kris shook her head. "No, I will not be going anywhere close to the Arteccia system for a while."

She glanced at each of the Iteeche clan chiefs. "The smart move for them would be to hit the Glorious Golden Eel system while we were concentrated somewhere else." Kris let that point hang for a moment until she had all the Iteeche nodding agreement.

"The smart move for me would be to hit them when they are elsewhere. They have taken one of the Emperor's planets. I will take two of theirs. For that, I need ships, soldiers, and junior lordlings to run those planets. How many ships can you give me? There are ten Battleships of State at the space station above us. How many of them can I have?"

Now the clan chiefs found themselves having to pull their beaks closed again. They eyed each other for a moment. Then Roth turned to Ron.

"Why don't you take our guests to enjoy the flowers?"

"Of course, My Most Eminent Chooser," Ron said, jumping to his feet.

Kris did not get up.

"You know I have dust motes listening to every word we say here. Do you really think I won't be listening to your discussions even if Ron walks me to the opposite wing to enjoy the flowers?"

It was blunt of Kris to slap the clan lords with Human capabilities. Still, they were the ones who had installed the new shower and steam room in the basement to keep their secret talks from the Humans.

Kris went on into the silence. "We have a saying among my people. 'Open covenants, openly arrived at.' Shall we try that this time?"

"Openly arrived at?" Roth echoed.

"You tell me your concerns," Kris said, "and I do my best to answer them. I tell you how many battlecruisers you have swinging around the space station and you tell me why I can't have them all. Then, we reach an agreement. Is there anything else we need to include in today's discussions?"

Again, the three eyed each other. That was not so easy with the two other clan chiefs seated slightly to the rear of Roth, the senior clan chief.

"You might find it easier to take each other's measure if you moved the cushions of the other two clan chiefs forward. Again, it is our custom that the head and the foot of the table often times have the most power. Usually because the two most powerful at the table refuse to admit who is sitting at the foot."

Several Iteeche nodded their heads. Likely they did not consider it a joke, but funny or not, it got the meaning across.

The two other clan lords rose to their feet. Freddy and Shorty rushed to move the pillows and cushions around to the front at Roth's right and left hands.

Without looking at Roth, the two clan chiefs sat down, then they looked around the circle.

"Gentlemen," Kris said.

Jack got up and his chair slid over to Kris's right. Grampa Trouble and Jacques rose, and their chairs did the same. With a quick bow to Roth and a deeper bow to Kris, the men settled back into their chairs.

"Now," Kris said, "As Admiral Commanding the Imperial Combined Fleets, I am authorized to speak in the Emperor's voice to request and require the clans to make flotillas available to the Combined Fleets. I have placed before you a request for sixty flotillas of battlecruisers from each of your clans. How soon can you provide them to me? I intend to sail in five days."

"We cannot provide any ships to the Combined Fleets," Roth said, curtly.

"Roth," Kris said, and paused while Nelly added all the fancy words to Roth's names and titles, "why do you say no to the voice of the Emperor? Are you prepared to offer an apology?"

Kris was careful to make that a lower grade apology that didn't involve snakes and axes.

"I cannot provide any ships to you because I have already provided every available ship to the Emperor's defense."

"Roth, you have nearly a hundred flotillas, some three thousand ships at the different space stations in this system and the next. So do both the Quo and Abba clans."

"Yes, we have those ships, but they are all assigned in the name of the Emperor to his defense. Maybe you do not remember, but in that victory you won in the Imperial Guard System and this, the Capital System, we lost nearly every ship we had defending the Emperor. We are a long way from replacing those losses. Had you not been off chasing around the Empire and come quicker to the battle, you might have won a quicker victory. We might not be in this situation. However, we are. The rebels have shown that they can amass ten thousand battlecruisers. You fear they may attack your most recent conquest. We fear they may attack us here."

Roth took a moment to glance at his two fellow clan leaders. The

Iteeche turned back to Kris. "Until the clans can defend the Emperor, we can second no ships to the Combined Fleets."

"I was asked to defend a planet strongly staffed by the We Clan," Kris growled.

"That does not matter. The rebels played you. We lost many ships. Until we have replaced those dedicated to the defense of the Imperial Person, we can give you no ships."

Kris leaned back in her chair, not breaking eye contact with Roth. Was it possible for an Iteeche to squirm? If so, it sure looked like Roth was struggling not to.

Grampa Trouble leaned forward in his chair, but Kris rested a restraining hand.

NELLY, GET ME ADMIRAL TONG.

YES, MY MOST EMINENT ADMIRAL.

HOW MANY SHIPS HAVE WE RECRUITED FROM THE MINOR CLANS?

THREE FLOTILLAS. ONE FROM THE HAR'SUM'KEY CLAN AND TWO DRAWN FROM ONE SHIP HERE, THREE SHIPS FROM SMALLER CLANS.

THANK YOU, TONG. KEEP ME UPDATED EVERY TIME YOU RAISE A NEW FLOTILLA. NEGOTIATIONS HERE ARE TOUGH.

AM I TO TAKE IT THAT THE MAJOR CLANS ARE LESS THAN FORTHCOMING WITH SHIPS?

YOU CAN.

OH, THIS WILL AID MY RECRUITMENT. IF THE LARGER CLANS ARE NOT GOING TO HOG ALL THE MOST SENIOR LEADERSHIP POSITIONS, I CAN GET A LOT MORE ALLIES.

DO IT, TONG.

UNDERSTOOD.

Kris allowed herself a moment to compose herself. "Fine, then. If your clans will not assist the Combined Fleets, I will make up the shortfall in battlecruisers from smaller clans."

"Small clans?" the Abba clan chief barked.

"Yes. I am told that the Har'sum'Key Clan has made a flotilla available to my fleet. We have formed two flotillas using ships from other smaller clans, septs, cadets, and families."

"They cannot give you much of anything.

MY ADMIRAL, WE NOW HAVE FIVE FLOTILLAS.

"I have five flotillas," Kris said.

"You said you only had three," Roth snapped.

"That was then. Now I have five.

SEVEN.

"Make that seven."

Seven in what? Half a minute?"

"Twenty-two seconds," Nelly contributed. Then added. "Oh, Kris three clans just jumped in with five flotillas. They also control a Battleship of State. It's not a big one, but it will do."

"Give us a moment to talk among ourselves," the clan chiefs said, hefting their bulks from the cushions.

"Four more," Nelly said. "Kris, this is snowballing."

Kris made no response as the three powerful Iteeche stomped away, signaling their three advisors on Human affairs to follow them.

ADMIRAL TONG, IS THE COUNT REALLY UP TO ELEVEN?

YES, MY MOST EMINENT ADMIRAL.

CAN YOU TELL ME WHY EVERYONE IS GETTING ON MY BAND WAGON?

CERTAINLY, MY MOST EMINENT ADMIRAL. IT IS BECAUSE THE SENIOR CLANS ARE NOT GETTING ON IT. THIS IS THE FIRST TIME THE MINOR CLANS HAVE HAD A CHANCE LIKE THIS SINCE, WELL, FOREVER. THEY KNOW YOU WILL GO FOR ONE OF THE LARGEST, MOST PRODUCTIVE SYSTEMS AND THEY WILL ALL GET A MUCH BIGGER CUT OF THE PIE THAN THEY WOULD IF ROTH AND HIS THIEVES WERE DIVIDING UP THE PURSE.

HOW MANY DO YOU THINK WE COULD GET IF WE COLD-SHOULDERED THE BIG BOYS?

I COULD HAVE YOU TWO HUNDRED FLOTILLAS, MAYBE MORE, IN THE NEXT THREE HOURS.

THANK YOU, TONG. NOW, ANY SUGGESTIONS ON HOW

PISSED THE THREE DUDES FROM THE LARGE CLANS WILL BE AT ALL OF US IF WE CUT THEM OUT OF THIS GAME?

THEY WILL NOT LIKE IT.

BUT CAN THEY LAND ON ALL THE MINOR CLANS?

NO, BUT THEY CAN LAND ON YOU WHILE YOU ARE OUT WINNING BATTLES FOR OUR MOST WORSHIPFUL EMPEROR.

HAVE THE REST OF YOU BEEN FOLLOWING THIS?

YES. YEAH. OH, SHIT.

On Nelly Net, Kris wasn't sure which of the three men around her had said what, but she figured they all three agreed with all three answers.

"Any suggestions?"

Grampa Trouble just grinned. "Couldn't happen to a nicer bunch of assholes."

"Jack?"

"What Grampa Trouble said." Like Kris, Jack was trying to keep a clean mouth since you could never tell when the kids might be listening. Maybe she didn't need to protect them from their Mom and Dad so much as their Grampa and Gramma Trouble.

"Jacques?"

He was not so quick to respond. After three sighs, each deeper than the other he said. "This is risky. The major clans are used to holding almost all the cards. However, the huge number of volunteers you're getting tells me the underlings are not at all happy with the status quo. You've already defeated two clans by street fighting. Now you have the Imperial Guard allied with you. This could get very interesting. Very interesting. What do you plan to do?"

"Walk out," Kris said simply.

"Walk out on them while they're out talking?" Jacques said in shock.

"That's what they're doing at this moment and this is the moment I feel like taking a walk. Any problems?"

"You know, Princess," Grampa Trouble said, "kicking them in the cojones doesn't work here. They don't have any."

"So it won't hurt them so much," Kris said, standing. Her seat immediately converted back to micro-quadcopters.

Beside Kris, Jack was whispering softly to the air. Down in the courtyard, officers and sergeants shouted orders. That was immediately followed by the slapping of boots on ancient cobblestones and the squeak of tires as gun trucks and infantry assault vehicles moved out.

Kris lead her team toward the elevator.

"What are you doing?" Roth shouted when they came in sight of his six Iteeche squabbling among themselves.

"Leaving. We are done here. We asked. You refused. We have no further business."

"You can't."

"I believe I am doing it." Kris said. "Nelly, can you get the elevator to open its doors?"

"No problem," and the doors opened.

"You are taking your fate in your own hands," one clan chief shouted.

"That is where my fate always has been," Kris answered.

"You will find it shattered to pieces," the other added.

"We shall see whose fate shatters," Kris replied, as she entered the elevator.

"You won't get enough ships from those minor clans," Roth shouted.

"Want to place a bet?" Kris shouted, but the elevator door was closing.

A Human and Iteeche Marine honor guard waited for them at the elevator gates opening to the courtyard. They marched Kris to her waiting palanquin, fancy as it was, and stood by while the escalator raised them up.

Per protocol, Kris was the last to step onto the escalator. As she rose higher Roth shouted, "We will destroy you!"

Kris knew she should not give in to certain urges. After all, she was a diplomat on a diplomatic mission. She was also a princess. Yet, she was also a sailor.

She casually raised her right hand, then extended the middle finger.

There was a lot of questioning among the three clan chiefs. Freddy and Shorty stepped way back. Unfortunately, Ron couldn't get away with feigning ignorance. He whispered into his Chooser's auditory orifices what the hand motion meant.

The Iteeche Lord exploded.

"What's he saying?" Kris asked.

"I don't know, Kris," Nelly answered, "but I've only heard these words on the street. I must do further research."

"So, likely he is cussing me out."

"I think so, Kris."

Kris stood in the armored bubble of her fancy walking shed. From here, she had a good view of three clan chiefs who were not at all happy with her.

Beside her, Grampa Trouble was chuckling.

Kris turned to eye him.

"I'm not saying a word," the old general said. "However, if I did it would be something like 'It's so much fun to see those bastards get back some of the hell they've dished out'."

Jack had nothing to add to the silence.

Jacques looked around, studying the looks on all the Iteeche present. Their clan chief and the admiral had just exchanged major disparaging remarks. There should have been some reaction.

There was none. Not so much as a twitch. Still, he was glad Kris's fancy ride was hardened against every weapon in the Iteeche inventory.

For the ride home, Nelly had a counter on the window, keeping track of the number of flotillas Admiral Tong had recruited. It hit 152 before they returned to the embassy.

15

Three days later, Kris was back aboard her flagship the *Princess Royal*. Today, she'd brought both Ruth and Johnnie aboard with her; the kids were so excited she felt she should have brought along strong string to wrap around their little toes. They were high as kites.

The *Princess Royal* was far past the showboat size of Condition Able, but well short of Imperial Barge. For the moment, the Forward Lounge was just below the quarter deck, amidships, and laid out to support a huge meeting.

Every admiral and ship captain of the two hundred flotillas that had volunteered to join Kris's Combined Fleet, all 6,400 of them, were on one side of the lounge or the balcony above. They gathered around tables on aisles that slowly stair-stepped up to give everyone a good view of the stage. The largest formations took over the front rows. The small division and single ships were in the back. Some were stuck in back areas of the balcony.

Half the space on the other side of the main aisle on the lower deck held well over a thousand chiefs of small clans, large septs, cadets, and families. Being politicians, they'd brought along deputy lords and staff. Again, the larger clans and septs among them managed to get the tables closest to the stage. The lesser cadet branches and families took the more distant tables.

Beyond them, the overflow of captains filled up the nose bleed tables.

All were drinking Kris's beer, or the Iteeche equivalent. Kris had to mobilize a regiment of US Marines to keep the drinks coming. Fortunately, Each level of balconies had at least one bar.

While the Iteeche drank and talked, most stared down at the two huge rotating drums. As best as they could, Ruth and Johnnie stood quietly and very officially beside the two slowly spinning cylindrical cages. Keeping Johnnie still required a small bag of cookies doled out by Abby's niece, Cara. Usually, the boy wanted a cookie in each hand, but Cara had him down to one.

Kris stepped forward. She was in full dress whites with a ton of ribbons, sashes, and medals glittering in the floodlights aimed at the stage. She raised her hands and the noise subsided a bit.

"First, I want to thank all of you for coming today. I also want to thank all of the chiefs of the clans, septs, cadets, and families who have contributed ships to the Combined Fleet for the next year. I hope to return your ships in less time. I also intend to return them to you as stronger fighting vessels with trained, victorious crews."

That got a cheer from both sides of the room. Kris let it go for a minute, then raised her hands again.

"We are gathered together today to divide up the spoils. Admittedly, we have yet to capture anything, so some might consider this optimistic. However, the last time I sailed from the Imperial Capital, I captured three planets and quite a few prize ships."

A loud and more raucous celebration of expectations interrupted Kris. She let it go on for a long minute, then cut it off.

"We will do this is by pulling chips from these two drums. In one drum we have put a collection of chips with the name of each clan that is loaning us a ship. For example, if you assigned a flotilla of thirty-two battlecruisers to the Combined Fleet, you have thirty-two chips in the huge right-hand drum. If your family or cadet has given us the use of one ship, you have one. Since we have a total of sixty-four hundred ships, there are a lot of chips in that one."

That got a laugh.

"The smaller drum is filled with chips that have the name of major and middle administrative jobs that need doing for a planet or a city. There is one with the title of Planetary Overlord on it. There are also chips with the titles of ministers of power, security, water, population, and housing; all the major and minor leadership positions needed to run a planet. We'll be assigning city positions, even though we don't know how many cities any particular planet will have. On average, you have about a hundred cities per planet, from large to average size. Any questions?"

"Who's gonna pull these chips out?" came from somewhere in the middle of the clan chiefs.

"How about me?" Kris offered.

Kris knew that the Iteeche equivalent of a boo was close to a Bronx cheer. The room rocked with them.

"You don't trust me?" Kris sniffed.

The "No!" came from both sides of the lounge and just about blew her back against the bulkhead.

When it quieted down again, Kris said, "Admiral Tong told me that you might react that way."

The admiral jumped to his feet and let everyone know, "I sure did."

There was more happy laughing.

Kris knelt down, and invited Ruth and Johnnie forward. They came to stand, one hugged to her right breast, the other to her left.

"I'd like to offer these two younglings for this job. Ruth, how old are you?"

"Seven," she shouted out through missing front teeth.

"Johnnie, how old are you?"

"Five," he announced, holding up a cookie-crumbed hand with all five fingers spread.

"Ruth, has anyone told you to pick a particular chip out of the drum?"

The seven-year-old turned in Kris's arms to look back at the huge drum. "How could I do that? They're all mixed up in there. I just reach in and pull one out. I'm even supposed to look the other way."

"Johnnie?"

"I do what Ruthie tells me to."

"Does anyone doubt that these kids are innocent of guile or instructions?"

The room was quiet.

"Now, since they're small, and this could go a long time, I'd like to offer you two other youngsters. Aroha and Asher."

Cara urged two more kids onto the stage.

"They're both ten and the children of some support staff at our embassy. Will you kids play fair picking out the chips?"

"Yes, ma'am," came from two nervous kids.

"Okay, shall we start?"

"Yeah." "Go." "You bet." And "Don't take all day," came back at Kris.

Marines helped the kids to the top of several steps until they were at a level where they could reach in. The large drum quit spinning. Ruth slid the door aside, looked away, scrunched up her eyes to keep them shut and then reached into the drum. She handed the chip to Kris.

Kris announced a clan. It was one of the minor ones that had provided two flotillas. There was no surprise that they'd come up.

Meanwhile, Johnnie had done his very best to do the same and provided Kris with a job. It was a minor office, sewers for a city, and it drew groans from some parts of the room and hilarity from other corners.

A clan lord made his way down the aisle. He took both chips, raised them high for everyone to see, then walked down the front row of clan chiefs so they could verify that what Kris had called was correct.

Kris was taking no chances that the Imperial Capital planet had a conspiracy clique.

"If anyone wants to take a look later at how many and what names are on the chips in the big drum, you're welcome to come up here and count all sixty-four hundred of them."

"I got a week I ain't doing nothin'," someone shouted.

The kids got back to choosing chips.

After thirty minutes, Johnnie was tired, so Aroha and Asher replaced him and Ruth for a break. Johnnie dashed off to find a bathroom with Cara right on his heels.

That set the pattern for the rest of the day.

There were some interesting surprises. Some of the minor clans won major fiefdoms. Of course, the larger clans with the most ships won most jobs. However, the biggest surprise of the day was when Ruth drew the chip for a minor family that had provided only one ship.

Then Johnnie drew the big one: Planetary Overlord.

There was dead silence as one rather unimpressive Iteeche made his way down the aisle from well in the back. He looked like he was in shock as he took both chips.

Then he turned to Kris. "My clan can't provide a Planetary Overlord. The other clans would walk all over us. What do I do with this?"

"First, may I suggest you take it over to the clan lords in the front row and show them that you actually won? Then come back to me."

He did. From the looks of avarice on the chieftain's faces, they all looked like they were about to come out of their seats and grab the job chit. Clearly, the fellow knew what would happen if his clan tried to rule any planets.

He returned to Kris.

"Now, this is no business of mine," Kris said. That got a laugh. "However, my father is a politician back on Wardhaven. He would tell you that what you have there is trading stock. What kind of job do you think your clan could handle well? How much gold or battlecruisers do you think you could swap that for? Are there any small families or cadet branches that might want to join with you to make a minor clan? You have all sorts of possibilities with that chip. I'd suggest you sit on it and see what other clans are willing to offer you for that chip. You might get two or three jobs you can do. You might get some other Iteeche to join with you in doing those jobs and crewing those new battlecruisers."

Kris paused for a moment, then asked, "Chiefs, would you like to make a place for this lord at your table?"

They quickly did, and the horse trading began. His wasn't the only minor group that drew a larger job than they could handle. They were quickly invited to the front tables and wined and dined.

However, when lunchtime came, Kris noticed that the lucky minor families slipped back to talk to those that they'd shared the distant seats with. Clearly, none of them wanted to be overwhelmed and swallowed up by the big fish.

The drawings went on through the afternoon and well into the evening. They went through the job drum three times. The clan chiefs clearly thought Kris was biting off more than she could chew, but if she was handing out jobs, they wanted them. The thought of capturing three large planets and taking them over for the smaller clans to manage had every one of them salivating.

It wasn't just that they'd have a new planet to rule. It also meant that they'd be tossing out the lords and lordlings of the defeated senior clans to make way for their own men. If they did manage to capture these planets it wouldn't be the larger clans replacing lordlings from one of their septs with someone from another one. No. This would be a major turnover.

Just as importantly, these minor clans would now have the wealth and industry from those planets to use in the search for and colonization of a new planet. They could fill that fresh planet up with their own chosen. If what Kris was offering them worked out, their future could be quite a bit different from their past.

Kris kept tabs on the small fish as he negotiated with the bigger fish. He did swap the Planetary Overlord chip. He got the Ministry of Power and several city positions for that one chip. In addition, he got three ships, complete with crews. That allowed him to promote his captain to commodore of a division. In addition to gold, he found himself lord of a very minor clan. Now he had the right to his own coat of arms.

Around midnight, he stood a lot taller. He'd not only had cadet branches and independent families join him, but two small septs broke away from their minor clans and attached themselves to him.

Two other tiny clans with big chips swapped them around for more minor jobs and ships and grew themselves.

Admiral Tong came up beside Kris as Abby brought up a new bunch of four Human kids from the embassy. They were the fourth bunch of the day. As they began pulling chips, Jack relieved Kris of calling the names. Her voice was beginning to get raspy.

Now, she listened to Tong.

"You do know that here you have subverted the Iteeche Way even more than you have at any other time since you arrived."

"Subverted?" Kris echoed, the sweet innocence in her voice reflected on her face.

"These clans will never be the same if you can indeed give them control over two or three planets."

"I went to the old clans first," Kris pointed out. "If they'd given me the ships they owed the Combined Fleets, this meeting would never have happened."

"What is it you Humans say? 'Give them enough rope to hang themselves.' They are very much hanging themselves."

"Oh, I think there's a better one. Have you heard about 'hoisted on your own petard?'"

"I've heard it, but I don't understand it."

"Before the cannon really got its act together, the best way to blow up a gate was to run up, hammer a nail in the door, hoist up a petard, or small keg, full of black powder then run away."

"But," Admiral Tong took over, "if someone were to hoist you up and hook you on the nail with your own sack of explosives..."

"Yep. You got blown up while you were trying to blow up the gate."

"Since the major clans refused to cooperate, you are hoisting them up by giving the smaller clans what you would have given the larger ones if they'd cooperated."

"You got it. They are blowing themselves up. Now, speaking of blowing things up, how are we doing recruiting soldiers and troopships to carry them?"

"The last hundred thousand were pledged today along with another quarter million yesterday. If I can find the troopships, you will sail with one and a quarter million soldiers."

"That might well let us garrison three planets. What about Battleships of State? What do we have, two? We need at least three."

"You good friend General Konga slipped an Imperial Rescript to our young Emperor. He was most happy to sign four of the largest Battleships of State over to the Combined Fleet for use in the coming year. For once, some clans are going to discover that the Emperor really does own those plush tubs, not them."

Clan lords from the wealthiest satraps competed in building the most luxurious and fancy Battleships of State. This, despite the battlecruiser having very much rendered them obsolete as fighting vessels. Still, all were "owned" by the Emperor. It had been a while since those clan lords had had their noses rubbed into that ownership. They were very much in for a surprise during the next week.

It was well after midnight when some very sleepy kids drew the last pair of chits. Kris expected horse trading to go late into the night. She'd arranged for Admiral Kitano to take over for her, watching to make sure there was no chicanery. Admiral Ulan replaced Admiral Tong. Knowing she and Jack could be woken on a moment's notice, they made their way to their quarters on the *P Royal.*

16

In the morning, a call from Abby awoke Kris. There were half a dozen requests for appointments from major clan lords, starting with Roth and going quite a way down the clan pecking order.

Kris was not surprised.

Her plan for today was to take the fleet out on maneuvers. This would not only introduce these new ships and admirals to Kris's way of fighting, but also give Nelly's kids a chance to sneak around inside the new battlecruisers and tweak a few things that were wrong in all the Iteeche made warships.

The Iteeche fire control computers were more Iteeche than Human. The changes made to provide an Iteeche interface added significantly to the time needed to come up with a firing solution. Nelly had found a way to keep the needed interface that didn't slow down the fire control computers.

Also, Kris had long ago found that the lasers never came from the yards ready for fighting. Loose lasers meant wider salvo spreads and very few hits. Tightening the guns down as well as changing the fire control computers made her ships of the Combined Fleet equal to two or three of the rebel ships.

Kris arranged to have Nelly and her kids make these adjustments quietly, with no fanfare. That way, since no Iteeche knew about them, there was no way it could leak it to the rebels.

Now, with 6,400 ships to modify, Kris faced a major challenge. Rather, with her going dirtside, it would be up to Admirals Kitano and Tong to put the fleet through major fleet exercises while, all the same time, Nelly and her kids tinkered with their weapons systems.

Kris did a quick nose count of Nelly's children. Both Admiral Kitano and her wife were paired with one of Nelly's kids. All seven of the admirals commanding Human flotillas, as well as several admirals commanding their task forces, now had them.

Kris ordered Lieutenant Megan Longknife, her *aide de camp*, to bring her Lily up here. Ruth and Johnnie now also had a pair of Nelly's kids for their computers. The education of the two kids was hardly scratching the surfaces of what their computers could do. The attack on the embassy, however, had shown that the kids and their computers could be quite helpful. That also left retired Gunny Gabby Arvind, the senior Nanny. She could not only use her computer to help with the modifications, but also coordinate the kids' computers in the background.

That gave them fifteen of Nelly's kids to handle 6,400 ships. One computer for every 430 ships was going to be a bit of a stretch. They'd need more than a day. If Kris knew Johnnie, one day of excitement while the ships sailed around them would be about all he'd take before he wanted his mommy.

Clearly, this would take several days, and they'd have fewer assets for it as each day passed.

Kris called Admiral Kitano to give her a heads up about what was coming her way. She didn't seem surprised.

"Could I have Jack?" Amber shot back. "It will let him spend more time with the kids," she added, sugar coating her theft of Kris's husband.

Kris really wanted Jack at her elbow with these negotiations, but Amber had several good points. She needed all of Nelly's kids that she could get, and Ruth and Johnnie would consider this more of a fun time if they had their Dad along.

With a deep sigh, Kris gave in, then hurried to catch the next ferry to the surface.

As much as she despised the very thought of it, Kris spent the drop down to the planet thinking about what to wear. She really didn't have a thing to wear to an informal get-together with a dozen or so very snobbish clan chiefs. They'd be in several layers of fancy robes, sashes, and gold cloth.

The clan chiefs had seen her come formally as the Grand Admiral. She'd shown up to meet the Emperor in full and dirty battle armor. If this was a ball, she wouldn't mind wearing a lovely gown, either a slinky one that clung to her or that ballooned out like something from the court of the Sun King.

Declining all those options, Kris was left with nothing to wear.

She could make it very informal, hold it poolside, and show up with just a smile, but she'd done that at the beach party by the lake.

No, this required something totally new. Something breathtakingly lovely, yet something very much Human.

"Nelly, I have an idea. Do you think you could patch this together out of Smart Metal?"

A few minutes later, Kris was smiling at just what her computer had come up with.

"Get me Abby," she ordered

A moment later, Kris was talking with her embassy's administrative chief. "Girl, have I got an idea for you. Old Roth has met me in his gardens. Could you arrange for us to view the flowers on a balcony somewhere around the hundred and fortieth floor facing the Imperial Precincts?"

"I'm suspecting that you want me and Mata Hari to see that every flowering plant in the embassy is out on that balcony."

"Yep. Oh, and plenty of water. Waterfalls. Ponds. Running brooks."

"Oh, my! Girl, you really are going all out."

"Yep. Oh, and I'd like to have you and Amanda as my ladies in waiting. You'll get to be just as fancily dressed as I am. Well, not quite, but close enough."

"Oh, this is going to be so much fun!"

17

The elevator opened at the one hundred and fortieth floor. Twelve clan chiefs with three young advisors found themselves gazing out at something they had never seen before in their long lives.

If they'd had the references, they would know it was a blend between a formal garden such as one might see at Versailles or Blenheim Palace. Blended into it were rock gardens in the best Buddhist style with the sand raked into waves and circles. Interspaced with the verdant plants or bushes were water displays: bubbling brooks, shooting fountains, and ponds with schools of Koi fish, both large and small. Meanwhile, the entire balcony had the fresh scent of water. This came from a ten-story waterfall that ended in a mist where rainbows danced on a pond before the white water rolled down over rocks, through a curling watercourse of smooth ponds.

The Iteeche might not know the name for what they saw, but they clearly saw it and were taken aback with the view. All of them had gardens on the roofs of their palaces. Still, their eyes grew wide as they gazed around in awe at what the Humans had done.

Two Human females greeted them, draped in the most unusual

clothing that they had ever seen. That they were colorful was beyond a doubt. One used different shades of green, the other blue. Somehow the long flowing sleeves and floor length skirts were iridescent in scenes of strange buildings, forests, and mountains, all sewn with threads of silver and gold. Jewels fit perfectly into the art as eyes, or pebbles in bird's beaks.

Roth knew the Human Amanda Kutter the best. This Human was always asking questions about how services and goods were exchanged among the clans. Today, she swung a graceful arm to point them deeper into the balcony. Cloth hung from the arm to just past her knees. The scenes on it were of flying, swimming, and fluttering creatures from the Humans' worlds.

Roth and the other eleven Iteeche followed the two Human women down a winding path. They paused to gaze into a small pond here, a calm pool there. In each swam fish of many varieties and so very many colors, each one of them unique to themselves. There were so many different patterns of whites, golds, silvers, reds, and oranges. Also, along the stone path were those strange stretches of sand, marked by different patterns that whispered gently of calm and harmony.

Meanwhile, everywhere, there were greens of many different shades from dark trees with needles for leaves to delicate things where the green was almost overcome by yellow. Throughout the stroll, flowers bloomed, scenting the air.

Often, Roth went to his own garden to calm himself after a long day of dealing with the other clans. Of course, he also made sure that his garden was very capable of impressing. Every clan chief spent much time and effort on their garden, competing to have the most impressive backdrop for any meetings between them and their clan chief associates.

The Humans, once more, had taken an Iteeche idea and run with it until they had enough speed to leap off the planet and into space. Part of Roth's mind raged at being outdone, even as most of Roth was calmed and soothed by this unique display of delicate beauty.

Despite himself, Roth was impressed. He found himself going

within, finding his center, and calming. The Humans had done the Iteeche Way very well.

Finally, the twelve were ushered into the presence of the Human they had come to meet. Never had Roth seen such a display by the Human, Kris Longknife. Never.

18

Kris Longknife relished the looks of surprise on the faces of the twelve Iteeche clan chiefs as they followed Abby and Amanda into her presence. She watched them, however, through lowered lashes, keeping her head down. At the moment, they seemed too awestruck to bow. She certainly wasn't going to go first.

On the drop from the space station, she had considered all sorts of different clothing options for this meeting. She'd thought back to all the various styles that Humans had used to dress and impress. Clearly, the robes these clan chiefs would be wearing to meet her would be fancy with the intent to impress upon her just how important they were.

She doubted that they'd drag out their formal court dress. No. That was worn to impress each other while they made their show of subservience to the Emperor. It might be a sham, but it was a very fancy sham.

After reviewing all that she'd seen Roth wear in his garden and what all of them wore when attending her reception, she had thought long and hard. Then she remembered the 600 year old kimono that she had warn to attend the Tea Ceremony the Emperor of Musashi had invited her to. Being an unmarried woman at the time, Kris had not worn an actual kimono.

No. What women wore was divided by their wedding date. After marrying, women wore more traditional kimonos. Before the big day, young women had to wear a furisode. They were kimonos, but with a lot more artistry.

A furisode not only had extraordinary art on it, there was more cloth to put it on. Their sleeves were long, reaching past their knees. With an apology to Japanese tradition, Kris decided to dress herself and her ladies in waiting in furisodes even if they were all married women with kids.

Now, Abby and Amanda came to stand to Kris's right and left. They opened their arms, all three of them, to greet their guests. The spectacular artwork that the Iteeche clan chiefs saw began on the left sleeve of Abby's furisode and swept across the skirt to her right sleeve. There, it was picked up by Kris's gown and from there, it went on to finish on the right sleeve of Amanda's.

The picture the Iteeche saw was both colorful and delicate. Fish and birds shared the tableau with butterflies and flowers. It was a lovely landscape of old Earth, executed to perfection as only Nelly could do it. The feathers of the birds and the fins of the fish shimmered iridescent in the sunlight as if the dust of diamonds, rubies, and emeralds had been sown into the cloth. Where the artwork didn't take precedence, the cloth sparkled with threads of gold and silver.

Kris was used to carrying thirty kilos of weapons and armor. Today, this outfit was heavier.

The motif of the furisode was carried over to the pavilion Kris had erected to give them some shade from the afternoon sun. The sides and backs of the tent-like arrangement were broken into strips that flowed and curved in the gentle breeze. Those along the back were transparent so that the Clan Lords could look past the left of Abby's opened hands to take in the view of the Imperial Palace.

Kris suppressed a smile at the Iteeche clan chiefs. Most of them were dressed in bold colors in robes that might fit somewhere in an ancient Asian court of one sort or another. There was artwork also displayed on their robes, but it was much simpler than what she wore. It was almost stylized. It left Kris wondering if Nelly's artwork was breaking new ground or resurrecting an out-of-fashion art form.

Now that all twelve Clan Chiefs and their three aides had arrived, Kris gave her two friends a three-count, then they all knelt on the brightly colored, brocade cushion laid out before them. Down on their knees, they rearranged all the layers of their furisode using video feed from one of Nelly's microdrone cameras.

Satisfied, the three of them rested back on their heels and continued to keep a meditative silence, their eyes downcast.

In front of them, the twelve Iteeche clan chiefs found themselves confronted with two rows of six small cushions suitable for them to kneel on. There were no lounging cushions or pillows as they preferred, and, unlike Kris, none of them traveled with their own supply of the magic metal. Even if they did, they had no one to program it into serving their purposes.

Several tried to kick one of the rear cushions up to the front row. However, it turned out that the cushions were not going to move. Indeed, if kicked too hard, they melted into the floor. While the Iteeche stared at the vacant spot where it had been, it slowly rose again from the floor in its original space.

No one bothered to kick a cushion after that.

The clan chiefs finally shook themselves out according to their own pecking order and knelt. The cushions were small, fit for a Human's two knees or the front two knees of an Iteeche. As soon as they knelt, the cushions grew to a U shape that supported all four knees of an Iteeche.

Roth kept Ron at his elbow as did the other two major clan chiefs who had advisors on Human matters.

Done, they found themselves joining the Humans in gazing down. Only then did they hear the growing roar of waves on a beach and songbirds trilling in the bushes. Despite the driving intent that brought them here, they found themselves taking long, deep breaths. Strange, none of them felt compelled to break the quiet to give the Human admiral the angry words they'd come to burn her with.

It was a long five minutes before Kris raised her gaze to the clan chiefs. "You wished to have a meeting with me. I apologize for having time for only a single meeting. I suspect you all wish to discuss the same things. If I am wrong, feel free to remain after the others leave and I will listen to your concern."

"Yes, wise and victorious Admiral Commanding the Imperial Combined Fleets," Roth began for them, "we wish to offer you ships for your fleet."

"And we want first pick of the plumb positions on the planets our ships take for you," added someone from the second row.

Kris didn't recognize the Clan Chief with the bad manners, but she didn't much care.

"This is so very embarrassing," Kris said, finding that wearing the furisode was infecting her thoughts and language. Or maybe it was the calming effects of the garden. Whatever it was, she continued smoothly, "The fleet presently exercising today between the Capital Planet and its most distant moon are all that I can command effectively. It totals some seven thousand Iteeche and Human battlecruisers. Any larger will make the formation most ungainly."

"We can match the sixty-four hundred raised by the minor clans that now show pretensions that are unbecoming people of their low rank," Roth snapped.

"Yes, Most Eminent Chooser," Kris said, "but these ships are available today. Today they are training with my experienced ships and learning my ways of war. I do not wish to delay. The recent disagreeable state here in the capital has given the rebels a vacation they do not deserve. We must end it before they get too complacent. After all, as you mentioned to me yesterday, they have already had the gall to take back what we took from them fair and square."

Kris was not surprised that her humor went straight past the clan chiefs.

"We could have the fleet available tomorrow. Maybe later this evening," Roth offered.

"That is very good of you," Kris said, again wondering who she was channeling. "May I suggest that you guard the Imperial Capital System as you proposed yesterday?"

Roth glanced to both sides, then behind him at the six Clan Chief kneeling there. "We want to conquer planets, not sit on our duffs."

Kris let Roth's demand hang in the air while the birds chirped their song. Finally, she said, "Might you have one of your admirals take command of your fleet and strike out to capture one or two other planets? I showed you several pairs or trios that I could think of to attack and capture. If you will pick one of them, I will pick my own from the others."

"Which ones were they, again?" Roth asked.

Some of the murmuring behind him showed division among the clan chiefs. Some wanted to continue pushing to replace Kris's present fleet. Others were interested in getting their hands on spoils whichever way they could.

The Iteeche Empire appeared in a holograph between them. The capital glowed golden on one side of the collection of over 3,000 planets. Few, however, were circled in gold to show that they produced more than their people needed to survive at the hideous population levels the Iteeche quickly filled up a planet with.

A few more were surrounded by two circles. They were the most productive planets in the Empire. It was their shipyards that spun out most of the tens of thousands of battlecruisers that fought this war. The two groups were divided by colors. Blue for the loyalists. Red showed the planets the rebels held.

The split was close to 60/40 for the Emperor. However, that could change quickly.

Above the closest productive planets, numbers began to appear. For the moment, they showed only the number of jumps needed to leap from the capital to them. A moment later, numbers also appeared below them. They showed the number of jumps from that plant to the nearest industrial one.

"If you will pick the one pair you want to assault, I will choose from the others," Kris offered calmly.

A debate immediately broke out. Kris knew that each clan had septs and cadet branches on either side of the rebellion. What she didn't know was that if a planet was captured, the clans replaced their people on a one-for-one basis. Thus, if Abba had the Planetary Overlord, they got to swap the bad rebel one with a nice loyal one.

Certain clans wanted certain planets attacked.

The parties in favor of this or that planet formed, grew, shrank and shifted as the Clan Lords horse traded for the best result for them. In the course of the eager deliberation, the Clan Lords stood up to make their point more strongly.

Kris was not about to stay kneeling while those guys towered over her. She and her handmaidens rose. Indeed, Nelly raised a platform for them, then, as the talking went on and on, she raised two more steps and made it a dais.

Kris ordered up chairs. She got an extra step to put hers higher than Abby or Amanda and the three of them sat down together.

ANYBODY FOR A GAME OF BRIDGE? Kris asked.

I'D SAY CHESS, BUT ONE OF US WOULD GET STUCK PLAYING AGAINST NELLY," Abby said.

OKAY, ANYONE GOT A REPORT FOR ME? ABBY?

SORRY, KRIS, BUT THINGS ARE HUMMING ALONG AS WELL AS CAN BE EXPECTED. NO MORE THAN THE USUAL SURPRISES. INTEL TELLS ME THAT THE CHATTER SHOWS A LOT OF THE CLAN LORDS AND LORDLINGS DON'T MUCH CARE FOR US, BUT THE FOLKS ON THE STREET ARE ENJOYING THE SONGS ABOUT YOUR EXPLOITS. IF THEY ACTUALLY LET THE COMMON FOLKS VOTE ON ANYTHING, YOU'D LIKELY WIN.

SADLY, ONLY THE VOTES OF THE CLAN LORDS GET COUNTED, Kris muttered in her head. AMANDA, HOW'S THE INVESTIGATION OF THE EMPIRE'S ECONOMICS GOING?

NOT BAD, KRIS. WE STILL THINK THE TRADE AT THE CLAN LORDS LEVEL IS BARTER AND HORSE TRADING. JUST LOOK AT THIS SHOW! HOWEVER, WE'RE BEGINNING TO DISCOVER A MONETARY SYSTEM AT THE LEVEL OF THE COMMON PEOPLE. THEY GET PAID IN PAPER MONEY. THEY

USE THAT TO BUY FOOD AND PAY THE RENT. IF SOMEONE WANTS TO BUILD AN APARTMENT COMPLEX, THERE MAY BE HORSE TRADING TO GET SOME LAND TO BUILD ON. THE CAPITAL DOESN'T HAVE ANY UNUSED LAND. IF YOU WANT TO BUILD SOMETHING, YOU HAVE TO TEAR SOMETHING DOWN AND THAT'S USUALLY SOMEWHERE ON THE BORDER IN A CLAN DISTRICT. THE BORDERS BETWEEN CLAN DISTRICTS IS WHERE A LOT OF THE MINOR FAMILIES SURVIVE.

Amanda went on. Kris found the unique process the Iteeche had developed to husband and divide up scarce resources very interesting. She'd learned basic economics at her father's knee, listening in on the discussions he had with other politicians, labor leaders, and industrialists. She knew the process was critical to success.

The Iteeche emphasis on expanding their population without reference to the resources available was crippling the empire. Planets that were barely getting by on a subsistence level might have a rich asteroid belt they could exploit, but there was nothing left over after feeding the last mouth to do anything about it.

This conversation could have gone on for several hours, but the Iteeche clan chiefs were finishing up their pissing contests and horse trades. Kris had to focus on them.

They chose a large and productive system, the Golden Flying Fish. It was only four jumps from the Capital. They intended to grab it and dash to the Golden Giant Squid System. It was only of middling production. It showed one ring, but it was only three jumps away.

"This will be our chosen strike," Roth said, speaking for all. "What set of planets will you attack?"

"I haven't made up my mind," Kris said, refusing to give up operational security in a room full of Iteeche that would likely sell her out if offered the position of dog catcher on a subsistence planet.

Okay. The Iteeche didn't have dogs. They couldn't afford the lost calories. Maybe an offer of Chief of the Sewage Plant would suffice. *Now that might get her battle plan handed over to anyone asking for it.*

"Then it is agreed," Kris said. "Your fleet will attack those two planets and my fleets will leave as soon as possible to attack a different planet."

"I have spent much time with my chosen one, Ron," Roth said. "He has told me that you can make our ships more destructive. One of yours can fight three rebel ships and destroy them all."

"That has happened several times," Kris admitted.

"Would you please do whatever it is that you do for our fleet before we sail?"

At least the "please" was present even if it was mighty weak.

"I am so sorry, Roth, but I fear I must decline. Such changes to ships are not done easily and they require that I draw from limited resources. Ron's flotillas have already been brought up to my standards, but I do not see a way that I could do that for any more ships before I depart."

Which was not a total lie. She wanted to sortie soon and all of Nelly's kids were concentrating on her own fleet.

"I am told," Ron said, cautiously "that it just involves tightening down the lasers in the cradles the builders left them loose in."

"Yes, you are right, Ron," Kris said, still letting the kimono bind her to a gentler way. More harmony. "I fear that the rebels have used the time I've been involved here to have programmers tightening down the guns on their ships. You should have no problem doing the same."

"Our programmers are not able to make the necessary adjustments to the guns," Ron spat.

That left Kris puzzled. "Ron, now that the programmers know about the problem, they should have no problem correcting them."

Ron turned to his Chooser, as if passing the question along to Roth.

The eminent Imperial Counselor shrugged both shoulders. "As you have shown, our computers are not as fast as yours and they process data differently."

Kris nodded.

"Your Human programmers took their computers with them

when they left. We can spin out ships exactly the way we have built them. We just can't make anything but the most routine changes in them after they are commissioned."

Kris gave her Iteeche guests the most puzzled look. "The Human programmers have left?"

"Yes," Roth answered for all.

"When?" Kris asked. How could all of the Humans scattered throughout the Empire have picked up their computers and gone home without her hearing about it?

"Two or three months ago," Ron answered. "We canceled their visas and they left on the first available ship. We also ordered our power plant engineers to return from Human space."

Kris had only a moment to consider the question that flashed across her mind. *How did Grampa Alex take to losing those engineers?* No doubt, his spies provided him with all he needed to know about building the unique power plants that produced many times the power that they'd gotten from the previous Human design.

There was something seriously wrong between the Empire and Human space. All the bridges that they'd built between their worlds were down now. The sole Human presence in the Empire was Kris's embassy. How long would that last?

"Excuse me, Most Eminent Roth," Kris said slowly, "can you tell me why all the Human ship spinners were exiled from the Empire?"

The Iteeche Clan Chief dismissed Kris's question with a little shrug. "Both we and the rebels determined that we had no further need of the Human ship spinners. We could spin out the battlecruisers just as easily ourselves without their disruptive presence."

Kris glanced around at the other eleven clan chiefs and the three advisors that stood beside them. Their faces were as blank as stone statues.

"Does it seem now that you might need the Human programmers back?" Kris asked, probing gently.

"If you had not sold us a design with a basic flaw in it, we would not have this problem at all."

"It is a flaw I have tried to get corrected," Kris said, softly. "However, when a quality standard makes its way into a contract, it takes the devil's own whip to get it beaten out. I've found it easier just to make the change when the ships join the fleet."

"Still, you sold us a defective design," Roth snapped.

"Yes," Kris agreed. "If you hadn't sent the Human workers with their Human computers packing, you might be in a position to correct this minor problem. Tell me Ron, didn't you and I upgrade the guns on your battlecruiser squadron on the way out here? You have known about this flaw for much more than two or three months. Roth, did you dismiss the Human programmers knowing your ships had a flaw in them?"

Kris was met by silence.

She examined the conversation for its most salient points. Roth had gamed the rebels to dismiss their Human shipbuilders, knowing the Iteeche design had a flaw in it. Second, he had expected Kris to rework the gun cradles on his fleet and that of the other major clans. Then they had tossed a banana peel in front of Kris, but it was they who had taken the pratfall.

Why the devil had they refused to give her the ships they owed her?

Once again, Kris was reminded that the Iteeche were aliens. Of course, Human governments through the ages had done stuff just as stupid.

Their chestnuts were now in the fire. There was no way Kris was pulling them out.

Kris examined her options and chose the hard-nosed one.

"Roth and clan chiefs, I am sorry that your fleet is less than perfect. However, you were the ones that refused to contribute ships to the Imperial Combined Fleet. Faced with that refusal, I have recruited a fleet of ships from other sources. I will sail with them. I strongly recommend that you sail for your own targets."

"This is wrong!" came from someone in the back row.

"This is the way it is," Kris said, putting her foot down. She'd had enough of all the polite dancing the furisode was encouraging her to do. "I would suggest that the next time the Commanding Admiral of the Imperial Combined Fleets comes calling, you immediately provide the ships that are her due."

"You haven't heard the last of this," was again from the back.

Kris eyed Roth, but the We Clan Chief had nothing more to say. He collected Ron and the other two clans with young Human advisors, and they turned to go.

Abby lead them to the elevator.

Kris turned to Amanda and they went to the edge of the balcony and gazed out over the palace.

"What do you think Jacques will have to say about our little meeting?"

"No doubt he'll be here in a moment to tell us."

"He was watching it?"

"Wild horses couldn't have dragged him away from the monitors."

Kris waited to see if the professor would give her a passing grade. She was pretty sure the Iteeche clan chiefs would flunk her if they could.

19

Abby returned from the elevator with both Jacques the sociologist and Ambassador Kawaguchi.

"Nelly, get us a table. It's too nice to go back inside."

"Kris," Abby asked, "Have you ever thought about keeping these fancy digs? I've got some flower seeds and seedlings that came in on the last ship. I can put together a mix and match of Human and Iteeche flowers."

"Do we need this space?" Kris asked.

"Baby duck, over half of this building is empty and people are rattling around in the quarters they have like peas in a tin can."

"Let's do it then," Kris said. "If the kids can have their water park and fancy playground, we adults can have a quiet place to help us keep our sanity."

"Gee, Kris," Abby said dryly, "I thought your sanity had gotten up and walked away long ago."

"Abby, dear, I'm a Longknife. We're born without any sanity and rarely acquire any along the way."

"Can't disagree with you on that," Amanda said, arranging the long sleeves of her furisode on the table. "What you just did with those clan chiefs sure looked insane to me."

"Dear wife," Jacques said, "maybe she wasn't quite as insane as you might think."

"Oh, wise sociologist," Amanda shot back. "Did you see something that I missed?"

"I doubt it. It was all out there for everyone to see. However, I'd say Kris wasn't crazy, unless we include crazy like a fox."

"Are you calling her foxy?" Amanda huffed at her husband.

"You're all middle-aged women with growing kids," Jacques said, then ducked as several women had Nelly manufacture snowballs right out of the table.

"Okay, I surrender! I surrender! You're all foxy ladies, okay?"

Amanda's last snowball hit him right on the nose. "Okay," she sniffed.

"Okay. What I was trying to say is that the clan chiefs tried to play Kris. By withholding their ships, they expected her to come begging again. Or maybe come twice more, hat in hand. I doubt if any of them ever thought that Kris could raise a fleet from among the smaller and minor clans, septs, and junior parties."

He paused to glance around at the women at the table.

"I think you're right," Abby said. "The major clans ignore the lesser ones. It's as if they don't exist."

"Yet their stiff necks," Kawaguchi said, "blinds them to what is possible. They ignore the trade channels we have established with the minor players, and they ignored the idea that those same players might rally to Kris's flag and give her a fleet without a single ship from them."

"This is not the way it's supposed to go," Jacques said, "and they don't know how to adjust to a society taking off for trails they haven't trodden."

"How are they going to respond to all that is going on?" Kris asked.

"I'd suspect you should get ready to quickly erect a wall around the embassy and Navy quarter," Kawaguchi replied. "If you thought the protests we faced the last time Kris was out fighting rebels was bad, you have no idea how crazy it's going to get this next time."

"That was what I was afraid of," Kris said. She swiveled her chair around to face the Palace. "I'm torn. Half of me wants to fold this embassy up and ship it with you and the kids home where you'll be safe."

"Yeah," Jacques said, "but with the programmers expelled, we're the only Humans in the Empire. So long as you're winning victories and the folks in the marketplace are hearing songs about them, you are the only Navy game in town."

"But what happens when the war ends?" Kris asked. "What if the major clans make common purpose to close down the war, get rid of this troublesome Human, and force everything back into a small tin can?"

There was a long silence. It was Abby who stepped in to break it.

"First, folks, let's remember that we're right next door to the palace. If anyone takes a swing at taking that kid Emperor hostage again, we're in a good place to back up the Imperial Guard. I don't see your General Konga being bought out by any of the big clans. If someone tries to storm his gates, he's gonna fight to hold them and fight to the last Iteeche standing."

Kris nodded.

"Now, Baby Duck," Abby said, reminding Kris that she got no respect from this escapee from the depths of the slums on New Eden. "I don't know if you've forgotten, but you brought down six divisions on those six battlecruisers you landed on the palace door. Ain't nobody bothered to count noses lately, but I see their food bill, and we've got some eighty thousand troopers on our ration count. That's over and above the extra division or two that you had before those ships did their belly flop right in the middle of the plaza in front of each of the gates to the Imperial Precincts."

She paused for a second, making sure the civilians at the table were keeping up with all this military stuff.

"Steve and I have been wasting a lot of our pillow talk at night going over how he'd defend the embassy, starting at the gates to what's being called the Navy quarter. We figure we can lock the Imperial district down solid. He's also thinking that we might want to donate some Smart Metal to the Imperial Guard to give them some shelter from the sun. You know, nothing to block the gates. We don't want nobody looking at the gates and thinking we don't trust them. Still, what's shade today could be an armored gun truck a second later."

"Maybe you could add some flowerpots along the bridge over the moat," Amanda added with a lovely grin. *Who would have thought such ideas could come from a nice civilian?*

"The more the merrier," Abby said. "I'm just saying, we can rig this place so we can go into lock down in the blink of an eye. Tomorrow, we're due to dock the Fast Attack Transport *Sirius*. Even with our extra Human Marines, the sides of beef on that trooper will feed us for a month, and we still have six months left of frozen food and vegetables. With what we're growing, I don't see us having to touch the rice and beans for at least half a year. You gonna be gone that long?"

"Not bloody likely," Kris said. "I figure we can take down three highly productive planets in two, maybe three months. Four at the most"

"Well, I can hold out that long standing on my head," Abby said with the confident and hungry grin of a tigress.

"Have you got enough computing power?" Kris asked.

"Strange thing about that," Abby said, sounding kind of dodgy.

"Yes?" Kris said, not liking dodgy.

"Well, I kind of put in a request for some more self-organizing matrix. Paid for it out of my administrative funds."

"How much matrix?" Kris asked, cautiously. "I know the size of your budget and I also know what one of Nelly's kids costs. It wouldn't take much to drain every last penny in all your accounts to fund two or three."

"Well, there may have been a special grant from Grampa Ray and maybe your Da tossed in a few coins."

"How many?"

Abby held her secret.

"Nelly?"

"Ten, Kris. It seems to me that Megan's friend might need some help, so I would recommend that Walt Vilmus get one of them. It will help greatly with our connectivity. Then there's Leslie Chu."

"My number one fan?" Kris asked.

"Yep. She's still sending reports to your fan club. I think Special Agent in Charge Foile would like some extra help keeping track of what things the clans are doing to each other and plan to do to us. Then there's Grampa and Gramma Trouble. I'd love to add them to my family."

Kris noticed the precise wording. Add Grampa and Gramma Trouble to *her* family. *Exactly what did this network of relationships look like from Nelly's end? What was going on deep inside her electronics?*

Kris would have to check on that . . . when she got the spare time. Or maybe not. Maybe it was better not to look this gift horse too much in the mouth.

"How could you buy that much matrix?" Kris asked.

"Your family managed to raise enough funds for ten more children," Nelly answered. "I think even your Grampa Alex chipped in."

"Al chipped in without trying to sneak one of Nelly's kids for himself?" That totally astounded Kris.

"He now has a computer around his neck that uses the exact same self-organizing matrix as I have," Nelly replied. "It will never wake up. It lacks my kernel to build its personality around. Even if it did have that, so long as he keeps hollering, "Hey, you, computer," it's not going to wake up."

"Nelly, I'm glad you woke up," Kris said.

"Kris, despite you almost getting me killed too many times to count, I'm glad I woke up around your neck, too."

Taking a moment to let those feelings work their way through her, and maybe Nelly, Kris then continued.

"By my count, that's four. What are your plans for the other six?"

"Grampa Ray was in a very generous mood," Abby told the surprised people seated with her around the table. "He sent along two more flotillas of battlecruisers. I assume that you will want to give each admiral commanding a flotilla one of Nelly's kids to help them fight their ships."

"Nelly?" Kris asked. They were her kids. She always had the say so in what Human got to be the consort of one of her kids. Without her kernel, there was no kid.

"Of course." Nelly said.

Kris swiveled her chair around again to face the palace, the green of its grounds, and the moat surrounding it. Once, thousands of years ago, that wall and moat would have held back an army. Now, it was hardly an inconvenience.

She would need to talk to General Konga about doing something about the defense of his responsibilities.

Speak of the devil.

"Kris," Nelly said, "General Konga would appreciate a chance to talk with you."

"Tell him I'll be ready in just a second. I need time to . . . no, Nelly, don't tell him I need time to change. Invite him up here immediately." With hardly a pause she went on.

"Are we done here?"

Everyone nodded.

"Abby, stay. The rest of you are dismissed. Abby, I want General Bruce here immediately. Nelly, could you get Gramma and Grampa Trouble up here?"

"You're going to receive him in the garden?" Ambassador Kawaguchi asked.

"Yes," Kris said with a gentle smile.

"Dressed as you are?"

"Do you think he's ever seen a Human in fancy dress?" Kris asked.

"Except for a few of us who occasionally wear diplomatic uniforms, no. I don't think he has.

"Then this should be fun."

"No doubt it will be," Jacques said as he bowed to Kris and made his way through the garden with his wife, Amanda. *What did the two of them laugh so uproariously at just after they got out of earshot?*

"Nelly, make the table disappear. It's time for those kneelers. Can you make them more comfortable?"

"I'll try, Kris. I'll try.

20

"Kris, they're on their way up the elevator. All four of them are on the same one."

"Thanks, Nelly," Kris said. "Abby, you want to give them the full treatment?"

"I'm all dressed up like a china doll. Why not?"

Kris did not remark out loud just how long it had been since Abby, Kris's former maid, had been so accommodating to her old employer. Born poor, she enjoyed reminding Kris that she did not own her.

Kris never had thought that she "owned" her good friend.

Waiting with her eyes unfocused on the lovely flowers surrounding her, Kris enjoyed the moments of quiet. They were so few.

The elevator came to a halt with a distinct knock, and the doors slid open just as obviously. Normally, Nelly assured that there was no noise in the things she built. A smooth, quiet machine was an efficient machine.

Today, Nelly chose to give the General Commanding the Imperial Guard tactile and audio references to track. At least Kris knew when the door opened and the newly invited guests to Kris's garden were admitted to the restful space. She followed the low murmur of Abby talking to her husband, the Iteeche general of the Imperial Guard and the two retired warhorses.

NELLY, TELL ME HOW LONG IT TAKES ABBY TO GET HERE.

YES, KRIS.

The stroll was a good four minutes long. Yes, Abby took them on the scenic route. While General Bruce looked alert, eyes darting around for the surprise, Gramma Trouble had let the beauty and order of the gardens relax her. She walked slowly, meditatively.

Grampa Trouble was somewhere between the two generals, his wife, and Abby's husband. His eyes flitted from side to side, missing nothing, but he also was breathing slowly, matching his wife's pattern of breathing.

Interesting.

The Iteeche Guard general was an entirely different case. The two center eyes on his face were downcast, enjoying the garden and relaxing. His two outer eyes were darting about, checking every corner for danger.

I guess having four eyes has its advantages.

Kris rose from her knees with as much grace as her human body allowed. She spread her arms as Abby did, showing the new arrivals two thirds of the art the clan chiefs had enjoyed.

"I hope you have enjoyed your walk through my restful garden," Kris said, then knelt on her cushion. She and Abby artfully arranged their furisode and fell back into a meditative silence.

The other four spotted their own cushions and knelt on them. For General Konga, the cushion quickly changed, forming a U to fit his four knees. The Iteeche general knelt next to Kris. General Bruce was next to his wife. The two Troubles knelt across from Kris and Abby.

Kris let the quiet grow for five minutes. When the Guard general did not interrupt it, she said, "You asked to see me?"

"Yes, Your Highness," General Konga replied. "I appreciate you honoring me with the greetings you gave the clan chiefs and their young advisors. However, I enjoy sitting at one of your conference tables much more. I find it encourages productive talk and conclusions. Could we please have a table and comfortable stools?"

Kris allowed herself a chuckle. "I do appreciate your honor and your honesty, General Konga. Yes, let this silliness end."

Nelly raised up a table with five chairs. The Iteeche general found himself perched on a stool.

"Very good. Please don't abandon that lovely regalia you are wearing on my part," the general said quickly. "It is the first time I have seen you Humans come fully and artistically dressed for court life. I think you may have outdone the clan chiefs."

"Thank you. I usually prefer my uniform. It announces the seriousness of our situation," Kris admitted. "However, today was not meant for productive consultation or reasonable conclusions. I take it that you have already been briefed on the results of our great clan chief confab?"

"Actually, I have not," the Iteeche Guard general admitted. "We lack the gadgets that you use to listen in on our conversations. I am told that less and less meetings are taking place on clan palace rooftops. I can tell you that I knew as soon as they stormed out of here that the meeting was over and many of them did not care for the fish that they had been fed. My defense center now has feed from your cameras. I am grateful that I can see what your General Bruce watches," he said with a bow toward the Human general.

"We're both on the same side here," Steve answered. "You want to keep the Emperor safe. I want to keep this district secure and my wife and kids safe."

"As well as my companion and the swimmers that we hope to choose a youngling from in a bit. Yes. We are in this together. So, what are you willing to tell me about your meeting with the clan chiefs? Did it go well?"

"From their point of view, I do not think so," Kris said. "They came insisting that I back away from the many minor clans that had volunteered battlecruisers to fight with me in the Combined Fleet. That is something that I would not do. They finally agreed to conduct their own operations, seizing one or two good planets while I would take the Combined Fleet out to capture two or three more."

"That was what I expected would happen. You have helped me win a bet with a subordinate. He expected you to cave to the clans."

"Longknifes do not cave," Kris said, stating the obvious for anyone who knew her way of doing business.

"So, you will be departing in the next week or less," the general stated.

"Yes, and that is why I need to discuss matters with you. I remember when I last returned that protests had surrounded and blocked off my embassy from food and other services. What will happen this time while I am gone?"

Kris let the rhetorical question hang in the air for a moment before going on.

"It is tempting to pack up the embassy and my children and send them back to the safety of Human space. However, I just learned that we are the only Human presence in the Iteeche Empire. The programmers that have been assisting Iteeche shipyards to spin out battlecruisers have been sent packing. I cannot allow all the bridges that we have built between our two people to be demolished. We must hold our position here in the Imperial Capital."

"What help can the Imperial Guard give you?" the general asked.

Kris had not expected her plea to be met so quickly.

"The last time I sailed, I left behind the Pink Coral Palace, and that was all we had to defend. I have no more Human defenders, but now I am responsible for an entire district of nearly forty square blocks of housing, shops, and small craftsman's workshops."

"Yes, Your Highness," the Iteeche Guard general said, "but most of the housing in your quarter is filled with soldiers, sailors, and Marines of the Combined Fleet and Navy Headquarters, as well as my Guardsmen, in addition to the consorts many of them are choosing to share their quarters with. I do not think any of them would like to see their apartments cut out from the Embassy Quarter and taken over by some clan, no matter how senior or powerful it is."

"We intend to defend the legation, General. We think we can hold the line at the major boulevards and avenues. I have General Bruce here, and you. Do I need to add any more to this conversation before we draw up a plan to defend the Embassy Quarter's boundaries? Defend them while feeding everyone who lives within its limits. Provide them with power, water, and waste removal. Hold a patch of land deep in the middle of an immense city, and hold it while also defending the person of the Emperor."

"Thank you for adding defense of the Emperor. For me, of course, that is the first priority. However, it might be one of the avenues that open up our chances of avoiding blockade."

"That is something I want to talk about, but do we have the right people for now?"

"Your Admiral Ulan, Number One of the Combined Fleet Staff should be at this table," General Konga said. "It will be his sailors and Marines that defend the Embassy Quarter because they will be defending their right to keep the apartments you gave them. You have much loyalty among the sailors and even the old chiefs. They like the way you treat them."

"Nelly, could you ask Admiral Ulan to meet with us? Tell him that you will provide a bridge and elevator car to hurry him to my garden."

"He just closed down a meeting and is on his way. I will save him the time of going down, across the bridge, and up."

"This should be fun to watch," Grampa Trouble said, happy as a kid with a new gadget. He led the others to gather at the edge of the balcony as the Magnificent Nelly put on quite a show.

A moment ago, there had been nothing. Now, an elevator hung on the side of Main Navy near the thirtieth floor. It flowed up the building, then slid across the space between the Iteeche Main Navy tower to the Embassy tower by riding a rail that suddenly appeared along the top of the walkway at the fiftieth floor. As soon as it touched the side of the Embassy, it began to rise again until it came to rest right next to the garden.

Abby just had enough time to get there and greet him. They hurried through the garden. Still, Ulan was impressed with just the glances he got of the beauty around him.

"Quite a ride you had there," General Konga said to Admiral Ulan.

"I take it that I was in the reliable hands of Your Highness's brilliant computer?"

"My reliable computer who loves to show off?" Kris asked.

"Yes, Kris, I do like to make sure that people know what I can do," Nelly replied.

"Just keep your head small enough that you don't need to buy an entire new set of cover and hats," Gramma Trouble said.

"I know that is metaphorical, Brigadier General Trouble, but when you are the best, you just have to suffer the problems it brings."

"Oh, love, I think she just burned you," Grampa Trouble said.

"I accept the burn," his wife answered.

"How was the ride?" Kris asked, trying to get her meeting back on track.

"Other than the way that my elevator car slid at crazy angles over walls and windows, it was quite pleasant. I assume that I would not have been hurried here if it weren't for a serious need."

"Yes," Kris said, and ushered everyone back to the table. It was interesting how they arranged themselves. General Konga sat at Kris's right elbow, with Admiral Ulan at his right. Grampa Trouble sat next with General Bruce at his elbow. That brought the table around to Gramma Trouble and Abby who sat at Kris's left.

While putting the combat flag officers together, the women had ended up in a single lump. Since Nelly had turned the table into a circle for the seven of them, it really didn't much matter.

Kris quickly explained to Admiral Ulan the question before them. Could the Embassy Quarter be defended if enclosed by an armed barricade?

"Strange, that," Admiral Ulan said, "I have just come from a meeting on the very same topic. Tell me first. There are approximately eight Iteeche divisions in the compound. I think you have at least eight brigades of US Marines. They are all comfortably billeted, and we are having no problems providing them decent and diverse rations. I believe the Human story is, 'They followed me home. Can I keep them?' "

"A joke from an Iteeche flag officer," Kris said, feigning amazement at the startling turn of events. Then she got serious; her lips disappeared into a concerned line.

"For now, let's assume they are available to defend the quarter. I've been promised a million and a quarter soldiers to support my planetary assault effort. However, riddle me this. Can we maintain a force of ten divisions this close to the Imperial Palace without the clan chiefs having a cow?"

"I like that one," General Konga said. "Once you realize the size of the orifice you Humans have to birth a child, birthing a cow becomes quite funny."

"Since all the women at this table have birthed children, we can tell you that even a six- or seven-pound Human is not something that our men would want to birth."

The Human males at the table had the good sense to agree. That balcony was quite close, and the rail wasn't nearly tall enough. Maybe they could learn to fly. Or maybe the Magnificent Nelly could spin out a butterfly net before they reached the bottom.

None wanted to test their luck.

"Getting back to the matter at hand, General," Kris said. "How do we persuade the clans that more than eight divisions are not a threat to the Emperor?"

"There are two avenues into the heart of the Imperial Precincts. We could block them off. Indeed, it would be very nice if we got several large boulders and placed them in the center of the approach to the bridge. Maybe even add three staggered rows so that a vehicle would have to slowly wind its way through them."

Nelly quickly produced a hologram. The entrance from the circular avenue was blocked in most places by rough boulders, cut from the same rock as the moats blocks. However, they were not the only blockage. Just as you got to the bridge across the moat were two more lines of large stones that would require any vehicle trying to enter the Palace Grounds to first zig right, then do a hairpin turn to pass between the first and second row of boulders before doing another hairpin turn to pass down the second and third rows of standing stones.

Stonehenge it wasn't, but it would drastically slow down any armored vehicle attempting to charge into the Imperial Precincts. This would also fragment any attempt by a larger force. A tidal wave of armor would be reduced to a trickle. A trickle that any anti-tank weapons could ratchet down to a halt by destroying a single tank at the entrance.

"We could also add a coating of Smart Metal," Nelly went on to suggest, "to all of the guard houses and barracks at the bridges."

Kris nodded.

"One question," the Iteeche Guard general asked. "How do we make all this happen without every great Clan Chief knowing we did it when you have the key that can not only make the boulders disappear but reappear as tanks and gun trucks?"

"Who controls the quarry where the stones are cut?" Grampa Trouble asked.

"The Imperial Guard, Most Eminent General," the Iteeche answered.

"I may be an old soldier," Grampa Trouble said, "but couldn't you have a few explosions out there to show you're blasting the raw face to create some new rocks? Meanwhile, we pull small flitters off our building and hustle them out to your quarry. Your flatbed trucks pick up the Smart Metal boulders the next morning and haul them in, wench them into place, and there you have it. A defense no one can squawk about."

Kris eyed the Iteeche Guard general.

"We can do that," he said. "I imagine that you would fly the same small flitters and wrap them around our Guard buildings. Not many would notice a few centimeters of extra rock."

"That closes down the approach from our Human Embassy. Can you do anything with the other four?" Kris asked.

"We could use the same type of boulders to block the avenues, limiting access to a single-wide opening in the standing stones," the

Iteeche general said. "You could thicken up our buildings. The only thing we wouldn't do is the stony zig-zag."

"You can work out with General Bruce various code words that could get you immediate standardized reactions," Kris said. "If things develop that require a measured response, he and his computer can do anything you need."

"Very well. Now, if someone attempts to shut your embassy up like a clam, we can bring food in at night to keep the garrison going. For myself, I have a hard time believing that they will attempt that again. After all, you are also quartering the Navy Headquarters and all the sailors that work there. Then there are my Guard battalions. I think they are much more likely to try to level the embassy with rockets, or maybe a truck bomb."

"We will need to search trucks traveling through the avenues that drive by us," Kris said.

"That's a very busy avenue," General Bruce observed.

"Nelly, can you set up sensors?" Kris asked.

"Kris I can have warning sensors set up several blocks out in any direction. If a vehicle smells of explosives, both refined and raw, I can spot it and blow out its tires. With any luck, your "helpful" guards should be able to separate the driver from his load and maybe close down the explosives before they get a chance to harm us."

"It's going to be a tough time," Kris said. "We'll have to keep a step ahead of them."

"You have your snoops," the Iteeche Guard general said. "Can't they keep you safe?"

"General," Kris said, and allowed herself a deep sigh. "I don't know how things are with the Iteeche intelligence services, but usually it's the tiny bit of data that you failed to notice or refused to believe that gets you every time."

The examination of different options for the defense of the embassy continued for the rest of the morning. Kris had lunch brought in, a nice picnic for both the Humans and the Iteeche. The garden allowed for the occasional pleasant break for coffee or its equivalent for the Iteeche. Several times they all gathered at the terrace rail to eyeball parts of the Imperial Precincts, looking for ways to move food or troops.

The meeting ended shortly after Jack and the kids got down the beanstalk from the fleet exercise and updating. Kris gathered her kids and together they went to the water park. Aware of the coming separation, the kids stayed close; Kris was glad for that.

That night, she held Jack close. Their pillow talk involved holographs created by Nelly as she brought him up to date on their efforts. One thing led to another, and it was quite late when Kris finally drifted off to sleep.

21

A week later, Kris led a fleet of some 7,000 ships drawn from clans, septs, cadets, and families that had never before formed a fighting force. Exactly where they were headed, no one knew, but they were eager to follow Her Royal Highness, Grand Admiral Kris Longknife, Imperial Admiral of the First Order of Steel.

Kris, back on the *Princess Royal* for this operation, was not impressed. Each of the 7,000 battlecruisers had been upgraded to her standards: new fire control computers, and lasers tightened in their cradles. However, the crews were slow. Reloading the lasers on those 6,400 new ships took almost twice as much time as it did on the 640 ships that had fought with her before.

Admittedly, the 64 new Human battlecruisers weren't as bad as the Iteeche, but even they had some hard work ahead of them.

During the run out of the Capital System, Kris had her ships at a modified Condition Baker. She wanted the crews to get comfortable at something less than the pleasant Condition Able before they went to Condition Zed. The drills getting the new battlecruisers into their tight fighting shape had not gone well. Many of these ships and their crews had never been at anything but Condition Able.

Too many of the crews had never really expected to have to fight.

This explained why Kris's first fight in the Imperial Capital Defense System had been a slaughter before she showed up. Most of the ships fighting had never done anything but swing around the space station.

Now Kris had the ships at a Modified Condition Baker. It was still tight for the crews, but the ships were bloated with extra tanks of reaction mass. Kris did not want to run out of fuel as she drilled the crews constantly.

Some battlecruisers showed improvement. Some didn't. Some showed major improvement. Hard-to-believe improvement.

Assuming they were cheating, Kris cheated, too.

Nelly used the backdoors that she or her kids had created and went inside the Iteeche ships' computers, checking their actual time. Her reports were interesting.

Almost all of the ships that showed little improvement hadn't bothered to drill very often; possibly half of what Kris ordered. The major problem was that Nelly found that ships that showed vast improvement had done no more drilling than the first bunch.

No surprise, it was the ships that had drilled by Kris's schedule who showed the smaller increments but earned hard-won improvements in gunnery.

Kris needed to make changes.

She promoted the XOs on her experienced Iteeche battlecruisers and dispatched them, with a Marine platoon, to relieve the skippers that were the most lazy or biggest liars. In the case of another thousand, she fired the captain and promoted the XO with orders to follow the book or they, too, would end up on the beach.

The drills had shown one battlecruiser to be in unacceptable material condition. How it got away from the pier without killing its crew was a minor miracle. Kris dumped her failed captains on it, then made an announcement to the entire fleet.

"I want a fast ship and a willing crew for I intend to go in harm's way. If your ship is not fast enough or you are not willing, please request a transfer. The *Emperor Urg 273* will be returning to the

Capital with officers I have relieved of command. Anyone reluctant to follow me into battle should immediately put in for a transfer to the *Urg*. Alternatively, any of the crew of the *Urg* may request a transfer to the remaining ships of the fleet. Admiral Longknife sends."

Twelve hours later, the *Emperor Urg 273* fell out of line and proceeded to the nearest space station in the Guard System. Nelly set the *Urg* to Condition Able+. She had to, it carried over 3,000 officers and barely enough chiefs and ratings to get the ship there.

However, the *Urg* was replaced when 33 ships began boosting from the four fortresses in the Guard System eager to join Kris's Combined Fleet.

Not bad for a culling of deadwood officers.

With matters better in hand, and drills going twelve hours a day, Kris set a course at one gee for the improved jump out, one of Nelly's fuzzy jumps, with more ships than she had when she entered the system.

Kris intended to use the improved jumps to get her to three highly productive planets that had not been on any of the options she had offered the clan chiefs to choose from. There was no doubt in her mind that the list she showed them had been passed along to the rebels before the sunset that day.

Obviously, Kris needed to be somewhere else.

To do that, without taking forever to get there, she needed to use the shortcuts the three alien races who created the jump points added just before they gave up traveling the stars and vanished. Kris thought of it as a highspeed highway connecting two cities that saved you the time of driving through all the other towns and villages in between.

However, that created a problem. Only the Human's latest Mark XII fire control sensors could spot these new jumps. The Iteeche were blind to them. Having watched Human ships disappear into them, they knew they were out there. However, their fire control system could not find one with all four of their hands.

As much as Kris hated to, she would have to break up her Human battlecruisers and assign one of them to each Iteeche flotilla. While the improved jump points were nice, they still orbited four or six other suns. This gravitational pull caused them to move at irregular times and disappear.

Kris had once had half her fleet jump into a raging battle when a jump point took it in its mind to ramble off. It took the rest of the fleet a while, but they spotted it thousands of klicks away from where it had been. Half of her fleet had to reform, get themselves lined up for the new jump, and then hurry through it to arrive, like the cavalry in some old-time movie, their armored cars rolling in to save the civilians from the evil Iteeche.

Kris had 224 Human battlecruisers. She had 216 Iteeche flotillas. If she assigned each of her Iteeche flotillas one Human ship, she'd have eight left over to shepherd the one hundred and twenty-five troopships loaded down with a 100,000 Iteeche soldiers each, and the nine Battleships of State as well as one or two to assign as a rear guard to help any Iteeche ships that missed the jump.

Kris also intended to adopt an idea that Admiral Kitano brought from the Alwa Station. The rabid alien raiders had come up with a method for invading a system much faster. They'd bind six ships or more together and charge the gate as one.

It was embarrassing that those bastards had come up with the idea before Humans, but they had. Humans had brought space stations and beam battleships that weighed in at over a million tons through the jumps. Humans should have realized that eight or twelve battlecruiser-sized ships could make the jump as a single unit.

Now that it had been done safely, it was easy using Smart Metal™ to bind several ships together and split them apart quickly and smoothly. For the vicious alien raiders, it was much harder and required more hands-on experience that usually ended up with space-suited aliens floating alone in space, waiting for their air to run out, or popping open their helmets after they had sawed the cabling through that bound the ships together.

The aliens were crazy suicidal in their commitment to destroy all intelligent life in the galaxy . . . except their own. Almost their entire species had also been genetically modified a hundred thousand years ago to slavishly obey any order.

The problem was the "almost." For a few, the modification hadn't taken. Those few were now in charge leading all of them in a genocidal rage against all intelligent life not their own.

It was not a good combination.

Still, Alwa Station was holding their attention all the way on the other side of the galaxy. There had been no sightings of the aliens near Iteeche space for seven years or more. The two species had time to prepare.

Time that was, unfortunately, being used up as the Iteeche Empire tore itself apart. Kris needed to end this insane rebellion before the alien raiders stumbled into them again and found a species spread across over three thousand planets and ripe for the plucking.

Kris held the fleet at one gee as they decelerated toward the improved jump point. For the Humans, that was comfortable. For the Iteeche, it was closer to 1.25 gees. Unpleasant, but not uncomfortable.

Intending to take this jump easy, Kris decelerated the fleet down to 40,000 klicks per hour and organized the fleet into a single column. Even at a two second interval, it would take the nearly 7,300 ships over four hours to pass through the jump. With the flotillas formed by squadrons into eight ship clusters, and the troopships in divisions of six, the fleet might complete the jump in half an hour.

It was definitely worth the risk of a ship pranging into another if Kris could cut the vulnerability to the fleet being defeated in detail by 88%.

Kris was also taking the fuzzy jumps because most of the systems she'd be passing through should be empty of hostile ships . . . or ships of any type. The systems her fleet would be traversing were off the Iteeche map or unoccupied or just well off the main shipping lanes.

Since the first jump was a safe one, Kris let the fleet go through in single file, even if it did take four hours. Nobody wandered off and missed the jump, nor did the jump do any wandering.

On the other side of the jump, Kris increased the fleet speed to 1.5

gees. It was still easy on the humans, but for the Iteeche it was double their usual acceleration and left every one of them carrying double their usual weight. As much time as the sailors could manage was spent laying on well-cushioned high gee couches.

The Humans had brought target drones for practice. They expanded them to full battlecruiser size and turned them over to Nelly. She increased the maneuvering jets until the targets were as jumpy as one of Kris's battlecruisers, and the live fire drill began.

The Iteeche ships were firing full broadsides at targets executing Nelly Evasion Plan 6. Kris didn't expect a lot of hits. She mainly wanted to see how fast the ships could fire. In that respect, she was not disappointed.

Admiral Kris Longknife watched 6,400 of her volunteered warships plunk away at their dancing targets. There were few hits. Worse, the speed at which ships produced broadsides was dismaying.

She let them spend thirty minutes struggling to get off as many broadsides as they could. The best managed battlecruiser managed 48 salvos. Several hundred, however, were in the single digits.

After calling a ceasefire, Kris ordered Admiral Tong to assign one of his battlecruiser flotillas to take four of the targets under fire.

"Pick one of your flotillas whose shooting is somewhere in the middle of your force and turn them loose on four drones. That's one per squadron," Kris ordered on a live line to every ship in the fleet.

Flotilla 12 took its 32 ships out of the line. The flotilla went to full battle stations. The outer hull of the ships began to spin at 60 revolutions a minute, the best rate to distribute hits and avoid burn-through. The ships also executed their own Evasion Plan 6.

Organized into four squadrons of eight, aligned one on top of the other, they turned their bows toward the targets.

"You may open fire when ready," Kris ordered.

The battlecruisers opened up with each of the twelve 24-inch lasers in their bow battery. Six seconds later, with capacitors empty, the battlecruisers flipped ship and fired their eight aft lasers before flipping their nose back to the enemy.

Reloading the forward battery began the instant their capacitors ran dry. Twenty seconds after the first blast, the entire flotilla executed that same drill, dancing like a corps of ballerinas. They did this in just over four times a minute, then ceased firing.

There was nothing left of the four target drones.

Flotilla 12 holed them so badly the fake battlecruisers could not hold together. In one case, they hit the anti-matter power plant and the entire target vanished. In others, they shot up the maneuvering jets so badly they failed entirely, making the drones much easier targets. What was left of the three surviving targets were holed so badly, portions of the outer hull were bent and tore off to drift away.

"Well done Flot 12," Kris said. "I think all your ships have qualified for a Gunnery E. For the rest of you, I hope you now know what I expect of you. You will recharge the capacitors for your lasers as fast as their specs allow. Your firing control teams will develop solutions quickly and accurately. Guns will be ready to bear on the target and laid quickly. You have a lot of work ahead of you. I want you to drill until you can do this in your sleep. Admiral Longknife sends."

The Human ships recovered their drones that hadn't been shot to pieces. The fleet went back to drilling with breaks only for chow and sleep.

Kris remembered days like the ones she was inflicting on her fleet. As a boot ensign, she'd been put through them, numerous and repetitive by her skipper on the old *Typhon*. Then, it had been intended to get her ready for a fight . . . and to dull her mind until she could do no more than obey orders.

Then Captain Thorp ordered them to attack the Earth squadrons that had come to celebrate the devolution of power from the Society of Humanity. Hundreds of Human planets had been demanding freedom from the taxes and policies they complained were restrictive or unnecessary, and they were about to get it.

However, someone intended to start a war between Earth and the Rim Worlds; Kris found herself right smack dab in the middle of it. Even as they closed on the Earth battleships, Kris had somehow managed to raise a mutiny against Thorpe and Nelly had helped them smash through the jamming to receive a frantic message from Grampa Ray to abort the attack. It was not authorized.

Strange that the memory of that mutiny should be forever attached to the deadening mindlessness of hour after hours of drill.

At least the Humans and Iteeche under Kris's command could rest assured that she was out to end a war, not start one. It had been a long time since she had given any thought to that callow young woman.

As they drew closer to the jump, Kris turned the fleet over to Admiral Tong to organize the battlecruisers into clusters by eight by squadrons. The troopships were edged together into groups of six by divisions. The Battleships of State were huge and built of traditional materials. They would go through alone.

It was no easy job to bring ships together without smash-ups. Indeed, it was probably impossible by Human or Iteeche standards. However, Nelly and her children had seeded each of the near 7,300 ship's computers with automatic routines that, when activated, would do all the work for them.

By the time they reached the improved jump, the fleet had reduced its deceleration and was traveling at only 40,000 kilometers an hour. Kris and Admiral Tong had placed their flagships in groups well to the rear of the column. The fleet took this jump with more distance between formations. There were four-second intervals between each squadron or division. Admittedly, this would double the jump time to an hour, but Kris wanted as few banged up ships as possible.

Nelly might be able to take most of the dings out of the hulls, but the sound of ships grinding together was not something a skipper or sailor liked to hear.

Admiral Kitano in the *Resolute* led the first flotilla through. Her sensors took an immediate snapshot of the system and beamed it back to the last battlecruiser coming through. That ship shot a small message beacon through that gave Kris a good look at their destination system. It allowed her to decide to abort the jump or go through with it.

As planned, the *Resolute* jumped a mere two hundred light years to an uninhabited system. It was empty; Kris ordered the ships to continue with the jump.

This fleet evolution proceeded as planned. The jump was gracious enough to stay put. Each flotilla followed its assigned Human battlecruiser through that same point in space without a hitch, except for those captains who panicked and hit the abort switch.

Kris had detached the *Intrepid* to shepherd those formations back to the jump and lined them up to go through. They arrived late and under the watchful eyes of their fellow captains in the squadron who had kept their nerve.

It was very embarrassing.

Kris congratulated the skippers and their crews for a job well done and gave them four hours to call their own while the ships detached and reformed into flotillas.

This time, while the fleet accelerated at 1.5 gees toward the next improved jump point, the flotillas organized themselves into wings.

The standard battle formation was a cross, with five equal wings. A vanguard, center, and rear guard were strung out in line ahead. Above and below the center wing was a top and bottom wing. For Kris's fleet, each wing held 45 flotillas, or 1,440 ships. Standard doctrine in both the Human and Iteeche Navy would array the flotillas in five files of nine flotillas following in line ahead.

The wing could be ordered to cover more space by stretching out and going to seven or eight files with fewer flotillas in line ahead. It all depended on the situation.

Now Kris began drilling the ships in performing those changes. First, they performed a uniform turn to the right.

And the formation went to hell.

"Admiral Tong, didn't you practice these drills?"

"Yes, my Most Eminent Admiral, we did."

"And?"

"What you see here is the best I got from them. You would not believe what happened the first time we tried this drill."

"Somehow, I think I would. Okay. Admiral Tong, please take up where you left off. We need this fleet to be able to maneuver under fire."

"Yes, My Most Eminent Admiral."

Since most of Kris's Navy responsibilities had been delegated, she switched to her political hat and checked in with the Battleships of State.

She wished she hadn't.

If she thought the people in the senior clans had long names, those in the junior clans frequently had to include at least a major clan somewhere in their last name, and likely two before they got down to what made them a distant sapling of that august and mighty oak. Once again, Kris resorted to short names she could remember and left it to Nelly to say whatever the etiquette of the present situation required.

Sam was the name Kris called the future Planetary Overlord of the first planet they would retake for the Empire. None of his clan had ever served the Emperor as a Planetary Overlord and he was very excited.

And also full of himself.

"Do you have to race around the stars at an acceleration that leaves us flat on our backs?" He was speaking from one of the improved Iteeche high-gee stations Nelly made for them out of Smart Metal.

"Most Eminent Clan Leader," Kris said, "I am moving quickly so that I can surprise the rebels and seize three planets out from under their noses before they know I am no longer sitting on my rear at the Capital."

"But this confounded weight," he grumbled.

So, Kris did her best to slowly and simply explain about the short cuts she was taking and how she needed to hit the jumps at a much faster velocity than usual. "That requires high accelerations and decelerations."

"I still think this is a poor way to travel."

"Do you think I should offer all those on a Battleship of State an opportunity to go back, now that they understand the price to be paid for their new positions of eminence?" Kris asked, diffidently.

"No, no, no. Others might, but I would never call it quits over a minor thing like temporary weight."

"Okay, but I thought I should ask."

"No, no. No problem."

Kris checked in with the other two future Planetary Overlords and got the same whines which she answered with the same potential offer. Both shut up.

If only all of Kris's problems could be solved so easily.

22

After many exhausting hours of drilling, and not a few hours of the fleet jinking around at first Evasion Plan 1 and slowly working their way up to Plan 5, Kris was reaching a new understanding of how the Iteeche Empire ran.

There was no way that they could have almost wiped out humanity in the War.

Kris had held her fleet to a gentle 1.5 gee acceleration, then deceleration.

The crews and officers of the Human battlecruisers were chosen from the younger up-and-comers. The Iteeche on Admiral Tong's ships were also experienced and often young.

However, it was not the same on the newly contributed Clan battlecruisers. By the time they were ready to take the next jump at 250,000 klicks and twelve revolutions on the boat, there was a crisis of leadership on many of those new battlecruisers.

Far too many of the officers and senior chiefs of the Iteeche Navy were superannuated barnacles that should have been left ashore. Time after time, a skipper had to be relieved after he wrenched his back. This was usually followed by his XO and even senior division heads ending up in sick bay for any of a number of reasons, including heart attacks as well as all sorts of sprains and broken bones.

Old chiefs were falling like flies as well.

After Kris's twelve tiny forces of fast attack mosquito boats saved Wardhaven by blowing six super battleships out of space, she'd been assigned to teach other planets how to develop a swarm of these self-same mosquito boats. This had been her first use of the jinking pattern to save ships by not being where the next salvo was aimed.

It also had ended up with a lot of older officers on the disability retirement list.

Wardhaven had collected a bunch of misfits much like Kris and turned them loose to develop their own doctrine. Without even meaning to, they had taken in stride the demanding physical needs of the fast attack boats.

Kris couldn't be too hard on the Iteeche. Several Human Navies had to get past the idea that these tiny boats might be a good command for the officers who had been passed over once and desperately wanted to catch that next promotion.

Now, these ships from the minor clans were discovering that if they actually intended to use those warships for like war, they needed officers who could conn them and men who could crew them under high gee and jinking.

Most of the ships managed to find in their crew the hidden skills needed among their junior officers and sailors. In a few cases, Kris had to order some of Admiral Tong's new XOs to take command of a ship that just couldn't get its act together.

For once, Kris was glad that the Iteeche crews were numbered 1,000 strong for a battlecruiser that the Humans usually had less than 400 aboard.

It was a tighter fleet . . . with very full sickbays . . . that headed for the next jump. This jump would not only be taken faster, but at three-second intervals between formations.

Again, the ships came together with no major dings to their hulls. Unfortunately, at this velocity, it required the finest navigation. Several of them missed the jump, often by only a few hundred meters, but the jumps were that small. These usually involved screaming debates between three or four ships that the other three or four were off course with each group, or several groups riding their steering jets trying to "correct" the course.

Again, Kris assigned a Human battlecruiser, this time the *Audacious* to round them up and shepherd them back to try the jump again. This time, however, it took them a lot more time to shed 250,000 klicks per hour, get back around to the front of the jump, build up its velocity to 250,000 klicks again, and hit the jump just right.

The *Audacious* was the flagship of one of the Human flotillas. Her admiral had one of Nelly's kids. She slaved all five of the groups to her helm and went through last.

They were very late to the party, but at least they were in the right system.

While the *Audacious* was playing sheepdog to a bunch of Iteeche, Kris was using the next system to slow down. She intended to take the next jump at 250,000 klicks an hour. That would put her fleet just one jump out from the target system of Balan.

Despite Kris's wish to get there as fast as possible, she slowed the acceleration and deceleration in this system to a mere 1.25 gees for Humans and closer to 1.5 gees for the Iteeche.

There was less complaining, but there were still admissions to sickbay. With sickbay overflowing, Kris detached a few pinnaces from her Human battlecruisers and sent them around the fleet picking up those too sick or who just wanted off their ship. Some found it hard to face their shipmates from beds where sprains and broken bones had made them unfit for duty.

The Battleships of State took on some more passengers. Kris's fleet, however, increased in combat effectiveness.

Her ships went back to drilling. They zoomed over an asteroid belt; it made for a lot of target practice. Admittedly, asteroids didn't make for rambunctious targets. Still, it started as an asteroid belt and finished, as they drew out of range, as a gravel belt.

Her gunners had a lot to be proud of.

The *Audacious* and her strays were just rejoining the fleet as they drew to the jump out of the system. Again, they'd be going at it at 250,000 klicks an hour. Hopefully, by now, the skippers knew to trust their computers.

As Kris tallied up her ships after that jump; they were all present.

There was a single jump between them and Balan. The system they were in was worthless. Traffic through it was so rare that the Iteeche didn't bother to keep a jump buoy system in place at the jump Kris aimed her fleet toward. She ordered them back to drill.

Halfway through the drill, Kris gave them a few hours for maintenance, then once more tossed out the target drones. This time, each flotilla had a target. The gunnery practice was short.

There wasn't a target drone in operational order after the first minute was up.

"Well Done. Admiral Longknife sends."

Her fleet was as ready for battle as she could make it in the time allowed.

23

The Balan system was a busy one. Freighters came and left from three main jumps. The system had a productive asteroid belt as well as mining concerns on the hot third planet. Balan 4 was where most of the population and industry was. It had four space stations in stationary orbit and two space elevators. There were also factories on the large moon.

The forty billion Iteeche on this planet were all gainfully employed in serious industry. They produced at least a hundred battlecruisers every month.

As soon as the planet had time to discover that a hostile force had entered the system, the radio net shut down, with emergency communications only.

Whatever faced Kris, the rebels were giving her no hints.

"Sensors, what kind of ships do we have in the system?" Kris asked.

"The usual freighter traffic, shipping colonists off-planet. There are a few of the poop freighters lugging sewage over to the third planet."

"I thought that planet was too hot to do much on," Kris commented to Admiral Tong.

"I know nothing of this, My Most Eminent Admiral."

"I may have an answer," Sensors offered.

"Run with it."

"There seems to be a huge shade, or something, being constructed in orbit around the third planet. Could they be trying to cool the planet to make it more habitable?"

"Nelly? Has anyone tried anything like that?"

"Not that I am aware of, Kris. Venus, the second planet from old Sol was converted from a runaway hot house to a livable planet, but they seeded its atmosphere and slowly used biologicals to take the carbon out of the atmosphere and clean it up."

"Oh, that's lovely," Sensors observed.

"What?"

"A comet just impacted on the third planet. No, actually, it grazed the planet so that all of it evaporated into the atmosphere. Good shooting."

Kris checked the system map. The nearest ice giant was well out from the star. If someone was lobbing ice at the third planet, they were tossing it from quite a distance.

Kris found herself liking this planet's management. They were investing in their system. They'd managed to hold their population at forty billion rather than the usual Iteeche tendency to push it up to fifty billion before leveling out.

"I've got to make sure the new kids on the Battleships of State that we'll be turning this planet over to understand that I want it given back to the present management after this rebellion is over in the same shape it is now. No messing with what isn't broke."

"Do you think those jumped up junior clans will listen to you?" Jack asked from her elbow.

Kris shook her head. "No. More likely as not they'll act like juvenile delinquents turned loose in the liquor store with a prepaid charge chit."

"You think it will be that bad, huh?" Jack said with a raised eyebrow

"I can't say that I really doubt it." Kris paused. Quickly, she reviewed all her options and found them wanting. She expanded the list from usual to different through wild and crazy. After a moment's thought, she picked the most outlandish of the bunch which, just possibly might have a chance.

"Comm, get me a channel to Balan."

"You've got it, ma'am."

"Greetings to the Planetary Overlord of Balan 4 from Admiral Kris Longknife, commanding the fleet that has just entered your system. If you are like all the other planets I have conquered in my effort to put an end to this unhelpful and inharmonious war, you are packing your bags and getting ready to flee. That is the usual reaction of the planetary leadership when a large force threatens their planet and a stronger force is not at hand.

"However, I would like to offer you a second alternative.

"I see that you are investing in increasing the productivity of your system. You have active industry in your asteroid belt. You are terraforming the third planet from the sun. I see that you're constructing a shade to reduce the extreme sunlight baking that planet. My sensors just recently observed a ball of ice boil off in the planet's atmosphere.

"I imagine you would hate to see your efforts taken over by a less interested party. Therefore, I would like to offer you the chance to stay. Under supervision, you would still run the planet with your management team. You could continue to work on developing the third planet. In return, I would require you not to destroy the battle-cruisers now under construction in your yards.

"What does that amount to, three hundred warships? As soon as I have control over your planet, I will have construction resume, and in two months, your yards will again be turning out ships for my fleet. This strikes me as a small price to pay to save your investment in infrastructure.

"I will, of course, require supplies for my ships and soldiers while we are in your orbit. The sooner you submit to the Emperor, the sooner I will be on my way. Admiral Longknife sends."

Kris knew she'd have a long wait to get an answer. However, a base in the asteroid belt must have gotten her message first. Someone there very quickly fired off a request for clarification.

"Are you the Longknife that slaughtered our soldiers in the Human Wars nearly a hundred years ago?"

"Oops," Jack said.

"Yeah. Oops," Kris said.

"Well, what do you have to say to that fellow?" Jack asked.

Kris sighed. There was no way to get out of this but go straight through.

"Comm send to whoever sent that last inquiry. 'I am Grand Admiral, Her Royal Highness, Princess Kristine of Wardhaven, Imperial Admiral of the First Order of Steel and Commanding Admiral, Imperial Combined Fleets. I hold my commission direct from the Emperor's hand and he has commanded me in his name to restore tranquility to the Empire and bring justice and peace to those in rebellion. I also have the honor of being the daughter of William Longknife, Prime Minister of Wardhaven, granddaughter of Alexander Longknife, a man of industry and resources in Human Space, and great-granddaughter of His Royal Majesty, Raymond the First, King of the United Society, who entered into the Treaty of the Orange Nebula that brought peace between Human Space and the Iteeche Empire.

Kris paused for a moment to organize her final thoughts. "I have entered the Balan system to bring peace. Hopefully I can do that without putting planets to the sword. I prefer negotiations over destruction. By now, you must have heard of my victory against the superior rebel forces arrayed against me at the Battle of Arteccia. You will also have heard of the peaceful return of the Glorious Golden Eel System to its allegiances to the Emperor. I would encourage you to follow the Glorious Golden Eel System in a peaceful and tranquil return to the serene lordship of your Emperor."

Kris halted. She was starting to ramble. She'd made her point.

"Admiral Longknife sends." She turned back to Jack. "So now it is out of the bag. Let's hope that does the trick."

"And now we wait," Jack said. "Are you hungry?"

"Yes. Lunch would save us from gnawing at our livers, as the ancients put it."

So, Kris and Jack shared a meal. As they talked the situation over, it became clear that she was overdue for a talk with Admiral Tong.

"I need some advice," Kris said. "You know more about the Iteeche Empire than anyone I know. Did you follow my message to the Planetary Overlord by any chance?"

"Yes, My Most Eminent Admiral. My communications watch did provide me with a copy of that rather interesting message. I know of similar bids for reconciliation, but none have been made in at least a thousand years."

Kris raised her eyebrows at that. "Do you think anyone on that planet will know what to do with an offer that comes from such ancient times?"

"That is always the risk when you attempt to step outside the norm. However, you have presented them with a very reasonable and honorable proposal that can stand on its own four feet. I agree with you that any leadership team that is so invested in this system might prefer turning their coats to seeing all their hard work turned over to a leadership that no doubt will care less about the future of this system. We will just have to wait and see."

"If they do offer to change allegiance back to their Emperor," Kris asked, "what can we expect of them? They've got an army of over a million men. What do I do with them?"

"After you accept their newly sworn loyalty they are yours to command."

"They will accept my commands?" Kris repeated, incredulously.

"Yes. If you give them orders, they will obey them instantly."

"You mean if I landed four hundred thousand men and took off four hundred thousand of these former rebels, they will follow my orders to invade the next planet and not take the opportunity to stab me in the back?"

The Iteeche admiral on the screen paused for a moment. When he continued, Kris could hear the teacher that he'd been before he was sent off to die in battle.

"I've been studying your art of war through your history. One situation I found interesting was one fought by your legendary Julius Caesar. He was also fighting a civil war just like we have here. He fought a campaign in Spain against another rebel."

"Spain was called Hispania in those days," Nelly provided.

"Thank you," the Iteeche admiral said. "He fought for a month or so, outnumbered, still he managed to maneuver his enemy into one bad position after another. Each time, he allowed them to walk away from a battle that would have meant many dead soldiers. I think he finally got them in a position where his army was between the rebels and water. Faced with this situation, the leaders of the rebel legions fled, leaving the men to fend for themselves. Do you know what your war commander did?"

"I imagine you are about to tell me," Kris said.

Admiral Tong met Kris's response with a laugh that, like all Iteeche humor, sounding like he was coughing up a hairball. "Yes, I will. He sent his recruiters among the soldiers of the abandoned army. Men and officers, they came over to him, more than doubling the force under his command. They followed him to the ends of the Earth obeying his orders and fighting his battles. You can expect the same from these soldiers."

"I have a hard time understanding this Iteeche Way," Kris said.

"But this is how you must wage your battle against the rebels."

Kris was still not persuaded. "When I captured ships, I had to remove the admirals and ship captains. Will I have to purge these troops of their higher ranks, and if I do, where do I get my new officers?"

"Just like in your Caesar's day, the political leaders will likely have to be reassigned to other duties, assuming they do not flee. However, the officers from the generals down to the most lowly recruits will, once they give you their oath of allegiance, fight by your side and follow your orders to the death."

Kris shook her head. Everything about this situation was crazy. Could she really trust that the Iteeche would behave just as Admiral Tong believed? It would certainly simplify her choices if they did so.

"Kris, there is a call coming through from Sam. He sounds very agitated."

"Thank you, Nelly, and thank you, Admiral Tong. Once again, you have given me more knowledge about this Empire I serve and the Iteeche Way. No doubt, I will get back to you again."

"From the sound of it, you will enjoy our next call much more than the call you will be taking in a moment."

"No doubt, Admiral, no doubt."

A very angry Iteeche came on the main screen a moment after Kris ended the call.

"What do you mean offering the rebels *my* planet!"

So much for the Iteeche long history of beating around the bush and avoiding confrontation.

"Sam," Kris said, "It is so good to see you."

"Yes, yes, it is good to see you," he rattled off, "but what about *my* planet?"

"I have not done anything about your future Planetary Overlordship," Kris said smoothly. Butter would have melted in her mouth.

"Do not think me a fool. My communication watch on this Battleship of State intercepted your message to those rebel traitors. You are offering to let them continue to rule this planet. This planet that was offered to me and my clan."

"Your Overlordship, I think there is some minor confusion on this matter. You will surely be the Overlord of a planet before this war cruise is finished. You will lord over the first planet that I capture. That still may be this system, but I have chosen a different approach and am negotiating for this system even as I prepare to capture it. If they lay down their arms and return their allegiance to their proper Emperor, yes, I will allow them to continue to manage this system. Someone may be appointed Supreme Planetary Overseer. Still, is it not better to have planets peacefully and serenely returned to their Emperor rather than fought over and returned to the Emperor a burned-out husk of what they were?"

"You have created new Planetary Overlords before," Sam spat. "You allowed for the peaceful return of a system like the Glorious

Golden Eel to the Emperor after handing it over to new lords for exploitation. Do you do that only for the major clans. Why isn't this *my* planet?"

"May I point out that the leadership of the Eel system fled before me as my ships arrived. I found shipyards with nearly complete battlecruisers melted down into huge masses of goo. It is to my advantage to have this planetary Overlord surrender his nearly complete battlecruisers to the Combined Fleet. If that means leaving his lordlings in their positions, I will do that. We have other planets to conquer. Don't worry. I'm sure there is a planet for you to rule."

Kris's hope that her small attempt at soothing the upset small clan lordling would resolve his concern. It did not. She ended stuck on the line for the next half hour as the two of them rehashed the same points over and over before Kris finally managed to end the call.

24

Exasperated with the politician and the phone call, Kris turned to Jack. "And to think, Father wanted me to be an assistant to my Member of Parliament brother. I would have had to do that all day, every day, for all sorts of fools and jerks."

"At least Sam wasn't shooting at you," Jack said, offering the only benefit he could find for the half hour wasted.

"I'd rather be in a battle than talk to him again," Kris countered.

The fleet continued to accelerate toward Balan 4. Just before they flipped over to begin deceleration, a message arrived.

"I am the Planetary Overlord for the Balan system," an Iteeche announced by way of preamble. There was no one else visible on the main screen. "I recognize that you have overwhelming force and that my planetary defenses are quite outnumbered. I also understand that you are asking me to surrender to you and swear my allegiance to the Emperor who now sits on the throne."

The Iteeche paused to glance off the screen at someone.

"It is also my understanding that if I surrender my planet and all forces in this system to you, that you will allow us to continue our present policies and plans to improve the resources of this system without outside efforts by other Clan lords and lordlings. Do I understand your offer correctly, and can I trust that you will do as you say?"

Again, the Iteeche looked at someone off camera. This time he shook his head, curtly, which for an Iteeche began at the hips and twisted his entire body.

"May I offer an additional proposal to your suggestion that you might appoint a Supreme Planetary Overseer? You command the Imperial Combined Fleet and want our system to add ships to your force in much the same way the rebellion has used us to build ships for them. Would you consider appointing one of your senior admirals to oversee our system and assure that we remain loyal to the Emperor and provide you with new ships and naval supplies?"

The screen went blank and Kris found herself staring at Jack. "Did what I think just happened actually happen?"

Jack gave her an expressive shrug. With only one set of shoulders, he had to work hard at it to beat an Iteeche shrug. "May I suggest another call to Admiral Tong?"

"Yes. Nelly, get me Admiral Tong and hold any calls from Sam until I finish with my admiral historian."

"Will do Kris," Nelly said just as the requested admiral appeared on screen.

"I take it that you heard that offer the same time I did," Kris said.

"Actually, my Most Eminent Admiral, I was, how do you Humans put it, indisposed at the moment."

"Can you look at it now?" Kris said, wondering if the look on the admiral's face was what an Iteeche looked like when embarrassed.

She watched as the admiral viewed the offer on another screen. When it finished, the Iteeche ran the top finger of his upper right hand along the rim of his beak.

"That is very interesting, My Most Eminent Admiral. Does he understand fully what you intended to offer him?"

"It appears so," Kris admitted. "He repeated much of it back to me. I'll need to talk with him to make sure we see eye-to-eye with each other. I have one question for you."

"Only one?" actually was accompanied by a bit of a raised

eyebrow. Could the Iteeche be using more facial muscles now that they had Humans around who used theirs so extensively? *Interesting.*

"Well, one to start with," Kris said. "About him wanting an admiral to function as whatever it is that we intend to leave behind to see that we get ships, supplies, and not a new rebellion. Why would he expressly ask for a Navy admiral?"

"Am I correct in saying that what you want is an officer who would mainly involve himself with military matters? He would see that supplies are forwarded to the Combined Fleet and not the rebels. That any battlecruisers built are commissioned into your fleet and not the rebels and keep his nose out of running the system."

Kris nodded.

"I think he understands that as well," the Iteeche admiral said. "However, I don't think he's worrying about your needs. He's asking for an admiral because of his needs to keep their own programs progressing as they want them to."

"And why I would need an admiral to do that?" Kris asked.

"If you appoint any Clan Lord or lordling, they would inevitably turn matters in the direction that most favors their clan. It is inevitable. You heard from Sam. To him, the system is a treasure trove that his clan views as nothing more to plunder and despoil."

"You must have listened in on our rather lengthy conversation," Kris said.

"I had someone of my staff do the listening. He provided me with points that I suspect tell me all I needed to know."

"If only your staff could have cut my own conversation with Sam so short."

"Yes. No doubt. However, we Navy personnel, be we officers or sailors, have no clan. We have no hopes of advancement through clan honors. A junior son may be put over us as a fleet commander. If we win victories, he will bask in the glory and advance his standing in his clan. We, however, who serve below him will get only our Navy pay. Our advancement is based on merit. We don't always succeed, but we try to promote the best man to officer and CPO."

"So Balan's Planetary Overlord is willing to have an admiral looking over his shoulder as Supreme Planetary Overseer," Kris said. "He expects that an admiral will concern himself with the war fighting ability of what they produce and will leave the running of the planet and its improvements to the civilians."

"Yes, My Most Eminent Admiral, that is what he is expecting."

"How often does this happen?"

"That is hard to say. Usually, major clans are swapping planets around. Both the rebels and loyalists may come from the same clan, just different branches. However, here you have minor clans that want to get in on the fun and profit of running planets. Would they recognize the advantages of this prosperous planetary system continuing to develop itself and making itself wealthier and more productive? Would they instead want to bleed off resources and wealth to benefit their clan chiefs back on the Capital?"

The Iteeche admiral ended his series of questions with a shrug involving all four arms.

"Yeah. And here I thought that bringing in the minor clans was a fun thing to do," Kris muttered.

"I have heard you Humans say, 'no good deed goes unpunished.' "

Kris snorted. "You are learning too much about us," she said glowering, though her lips were too upturned to make it believable.

"Well, the wind blows good to some and bad to others. There is often no way to know until you reach a safe port or crash upon the rocks."

"And I seem to live in a very windy age," Kris said.

"Yes, you do, My Most Eminent Admiral. Now, how may I serve you?"

"Do you have an admiral that you would recommend for the job of Supreme Planetary Overseer?"

"You like that title?"

"When we Humans offer someone a big job with little benefits and no extra pay, we try to give it a big title."

Admiral Tong made the strange, strangled sound that passed for an Iteeche laugh.

"Sometimes you Humans seem almost Iteeche. So like us and so alien, all at the same time," he said as he gasping for breath after laughing. "Yes, I do have an admiral I can recommend to you. He was a good student of mine in the War Academy."

Again, Admiral Tong fell into lecture mode. "He was also among those of us sent off to immolate ourselves in battles we could not win. Like myself, he chose survival over suicide by combat. He was one of the first to join Admiral Coth when he called that you were looking for good officers and didn't consider one defeat a permanent mark on a man's record. He is loyal to the Empire, the Navy, and you, likely in that order, or he may be like me and unable to tell the difference between the three. He is a good man to have at your back."

"Could you please have him brought over to my flag so I can meet this man of such sterling repute?"

"That I shall do. When?"

"In two hours."

"I keep forgetting how quickly you Humans move. Yes, he will be there. Now, before you go, there is one thing about this message that you may not have understood the full import of."

"What is that?" Kris asked. A red light was flashing on the lower right-hand corner of her screen.

"He has offered to surrender all forces in his system. You asked for the battlecruisers under construction. He has countered by offering you all the warships tied up to the piers in his system. He's asked for an admiral and offered a thousand battlecruisers in return."

"I missed that. Are you sure?"

"No," The admiral admitted. "However, the words appear to say that."

"We'll have to approach Balan 4 carefully. If those battlecruisers don't get out of here, I'm afraid that I will need to look a gift horse in the mouth. I take it that the skippers on those ships would be just as loyal to me as the Army personnel."

"Yes. If they swear allegiance, they are yours."

"You've given me much to think over, Admiral. Now, I really must go, I have an annoying light flashing on my board. No doubt Sam wishes to bend my ear for an hour this time."

"I will have Admiral Linn report to you in two hours. I must confess. I am glad that you are the politician and not I."

"Admiral, I ran off and joined the Navy to avoid a life of politics. My father is an elected Planetary Overlord. Trust me, it is even worse when you must persuade more than half of a planet's population that they want you to be their Overlord."

Now Kris got to see eyebrows come down over the admiral's two middle eyes, not much, but a bit more than a twitch. "Someday you must tell me of this horror story."

"No doubt, if you sail with me long enough, you shall hear me drone on about it."

Kris was right, it was Sam waiting impatiently to bend her ear. And he did not want to stop just because he had said all there was to say. He refused to accept that the Planetary Overseer should be anyone but a Clan Lord. It was amazing the vituperation the loyalist Clan lord suddenly had for the rebels.

"They will stab you in the back. They will throw anyone you leave behind into irons and send them off to the rebel Clan Lords to be tortured and murdered. How can you trust those who have turned their coats once and now offer to turn them again?"

"I assure you, Most Eminent Chooser, I will be leaving nearly half a million troops behind to back up this Supreme Planetary Overseer. We Humans are not babes in the woods where intrigue is concerned."

"Yes, I don't doubt that you are. I just wonder if you are intriguing against me."

"I assure you, you will have a planet soon enough."

"Please be sure that you do. Remember, these Battleships of State are full to the brim with other Clan Lords who expect planets. You sailed with three sets of Lords eager to step in and rule three planets. There are many lordlings that are expecting fiefs to rule. They will not be happy if you do not capture three planets for us. We are Iteeche and we do know how to intrigue."

"I don't doubt that you do, Sam. However, remember that I offered to capture only two, maybe three planets. Now, if the transfer of allegiances goes quickly and smoothly, I fully expect that we will have supplies and troops for three more planets. I do, however, require time to attend to the present situation in the Balan system."

Despite Kris's suggestion that he let her tend to acquiring a system, he still kept her for an hour as he yammered on with his demands, and Kris did her best to sooth his injured ego and restore his dreams of vast riches for himself and those who would serve under him.

When she accepted the ships from the minor clans, she had no idea just how petty the politicking was at that lower level in the Clans' pecking order.

Finally, she was able to escape without gnawing her leg off.

After a quick supper with Jack and Megan where they got stuck listening to her vent her frustration at wasting so much of her day being a politician, Kris checked the situation.

Her Flag Bridge was getting feed from every sensor known to man. Everything was going smoothly. Indeed, beyond smooth. All one thousand of the battlecruisers tied up on the three Balan stations had gone cold steel. Their reactors were completely secured.

That required another call to Admiral Tong.

"Have you seen the report of the battlecruisers closing down their reactors?"

"Yes. I think you now have proof that they have no intention of going anywhere."

"Admiral, what does it take to start a ship from cold steel?"

The Iteeche gave a quarter shrug. Only one shoulder went up. "Plasma must be brought from the station reactor to fire up one reactor. Then that ship fires up another and so it goes down the line of piers. It is a slow process and not one we like doing."

The Iteeche admiral paused for a moment, apparently lost in recollection of how this process worked. "We have to use a flexible hose with the required superconducting magnets to keep the plasma from breaking loose and wreaking havoc on the station while it's being transferred from the station reactor to the nearest ship. It's a long, dangerous, and carefully done process. I don't think they could fire up all three hundred or so ships at each space station in less than two days More likely three or four. It all depends on how many meters of hose they have on each station. Oh, and whether or not it needs refurbishing if it's gotten aged or hasn't been tested in fifty years or more."

"Ugh," Kris said. "He's risking that potential problem."

"That is a major message, my Most Eminent Admiral. It also answers one matter that was tickling my interest."

"Oh?"

"The battlecruisers are tied up one to a pier. That will allow us to dock one of our battlecruisers directly across from the ship with cold steel. That will take a lot less hosing and it will likely need less twisting and turning. Yes. Someone organized his ships so that he could make you this offer."

Kris chuckled. "If I'm going to be played, I prefer that it be done this way. So, you think this Planetary Overlord was hoping I would spot what he was doing for the system and its infrastructure and make him the offer he's fishing for."

"Pretty much."

"Thanks, Admiral Tong. Now I must prepare to meet with your Admiral Linn."

"I hope you like him. Most in the fleet do."

"Not all?"

"He lost a battle and ran," Admiral Tong said simply.

"So, he has the approval of those who have fought a battle but not of those who are still virgins to this business, huh?"

"Precisely."

"It's been good talking with you. I'm looking forward to our next conversation."

"No doubt."

Kris broke the comm link and took the short stroll to her day cabin, just off the bridge. The fleet was still at Condition Baker, so Kris's quarters were a bit cramped, but she found it comfortable.

She had only had time to check the fleet's status and that the situation on the planet ahead was stable before she heard a knock at her door.

"Enter," she said.

25

Admiral of the 4th Order of Iron Linn was a tall, thin Iteeche who moved gracefully on his four legs while keeping his arms moving slowly at his side. His central eyes focused on Kris while the other two took in the room around her.

Kris had the distinct feeling that Admiral Linn would be a tough opponent in a ground fight. With warriors like him, no wonder the Iteeche War had lasted so long.

He presented himself before her desk and gave her a snappy Iteeche salute with both hands shading his two central eyes.

Kris returned it. "Nelly, produce a stool for the admiral. Take a seat. Admiral Linn, you come with high praise."

If the Iteeche was surprised to see a stool rising from the floor beside him, he didn't show it. He settled himself on it and answered. "I fear that my old teacher is under the misperception that I was a better student than I was. I got lucky on a few exercises and seem to have made a name for myself."

Kris chuckled. "We had a great general named Napoleon. He said that he would rather have a general who was lucky than one who was good. I find that the harder I work, the luckier I get, don't you?"

"I see that you have discovered the secret. A good swimmer makes sure ninety percent of the effort is below the water."

"I think we're singing from the same page of the hymnal. Now, if we pile one more cliché atop this pyramid, it is going to bury us alive."

The Iteeche admiral chortled and laughed. It was a small one, but a hairball nevertheless. "Admiral Tong told me that you had an impossible job to do and that all I'd get for it was a big title. He didn't tell me anything else. What do you have in mind for me?"

So Kris quickly brought him up to date with the situation in the system they were invading. She let him know her desired outcome. "I need battlecruisers for the Emperor and naval stores and supplies for my ships. I do not want the planet's present management's initiatives at improvement and expanded infrastructure delayed at all."

In conclusion, Kris said, "I know that there are bound to be conflicts between my goals for the Navy and my goals to improve this system. I don't doubt that some of the locals will see this as an opportunity to cut back on warship production and supplies to the Navy and the Army we leave behind here and jack up their local efforts. You'll need to be watchful for that."

"No doubt. If I wasn't Navy, I might feel the same way. Do you have a report of what munitions and equipment have been provided over the last six months?"

"No. However, as soon as I appoint you, I expect you will request and require that it be provided to you. I'll include it in the negotiations I expect to have. No doubt, we will have to reduce our verbal proposals into articles that you can use to hit someone over the head with. I doubt you could use them as a basis for legal action."

"Yes. It is hard to find a court that has purview over matters such as these. I suspect that is what wars are for."

"Sadly. I hope that the Empire can strengthen the rule of law so that more of these irritations can resolved short of war."

"So, the stories about you are right. You are a bit of an optimist and a romantic."

"Better to dream dreams of what can be than live with no vision for the future of your kids."

"Again, your kids. A romantic idea."

"Many of the officers and staff at Main Navy as well as the Imperial Guard now have better housing. They are living with companions and many of them are choosing to share their seed together and choose a child of their flesh," Kris pointed out.

"Yes, I have heard of that. It's very interesting. A sailor on a battlecruiser is not likely to have a companion to share his quarters." The Admiral paused, then all four of his eyes grew wide. "You have your companion on this ship. Have you had your children here as well?"

"Several times. They came out on this very ship with us when we came from Human space. I was prepared to fight the rebels with my children behind me when they jumped us."

"Yes. I really like the tune they use for your song about that battle that wasn't. You can almost hear the pitter-patter of running rebel feet as they flee from your fleet of target drones."

"Yes. We did pull a good one off there. What the Iteeche Navy is lacking is a feminine side. You have no women on the ships. We do. Occasionally, that means we have pregnant women and children on our ships. So far, it has not kept me from winning my battles."

"No, it certainly has not.

"Now," Kris asked. "What do you want for ground support? I'm willing to march off four hundred thousand troops and take on that many soldiers from Balan."

"I talked with my friend, General Compeel. He is the one I would request to command my ground forces. He proposes that we mix one of your brigades with two Iteeche. That would leave most divisions with two local brigades, including one Human brigade. Same thing, one in three division HQ and support units, along with their artillery brigade, would swap with one in our Order of Battle Corps. Army staff will be split down the middle: local and us."

"Do you think that will keep you safe if there is an uprising?"

"That, and a major presence of military intelligence. You can't make a rebellion if you can't speak the word. Also, we may not have the tiny listening devices you have, but we have some pretty good ones, now that we've learned how much of an advantage they bring.

These hicks haven't had the intrigues and back-stabbing we have in the capital. We should be able to run them ragged."

"Don't underestimate your, ah, well, in this case, your sudden ally."

"Oh, I assure you I won't. However, in my study of you Humans I came across a word you sometimes use. Paranoid."

"Ah, yes. A good word. I've often thought that my own paranoia has kept me alive more times than I can count."

"It is strange for you to admit such feelings. I understood the word to mean people are 'out to get you' when they aren't, and that that is a bad thing. As an Iteeche, it is just considered good Clan business."

Kris started to open her mouth. She started to say something funny, then she thought better. She hadn't been raised in a mating pond like an Iteeche. She hadn't spent the first several years of her life in constant fear of being eaten by something bigger. Of course that was imprinted on every Iteeche's psyche. What for Humans was an aberration was for the Iteeche just the normal attitude toward life.

Kris listened while Admiral Linn further outlined his plans. Apparently, he and his friendly general had gotten quite down in the weeds. After a half hour, Kris was reasonably sure the Iteeche understood her intent and was prepared to carry it out.

"I will keep my eye on the local Planetary Overlord, but I will not keep him under my thumb. I will not start throwing my weight around unless they mess with ship production and supplies to you. That, and if intelligence begins to hear chatter of a rebellion."

"You understand my intentions clearly," Kris said, "I'd like you to develop a comfortable relationship with the Planetary Overload so problems can be handled over a shared dinner."

"I will do my best to do that, Most Eminent Admiral."

With that, the meeting ended.

26

That left time for another call to Admiral Tong before supper.

"I was expecting your call, My Most Eminent Admiral," Tong said for greetings.

"So I could tell you that you sent me a great manager for the Overseer job?"

"Well, I *was* expecting to hear how the job interview went."

"It went very well," Kris said. "He sounds like a good choice. He understands where I want a tight hand and where I want him to hold the reins loose. I think he'll do us both proud. I discovered that he was already discussing with an Army general how to distribute the Balan troops among our loyal soldiers on the troopships, and the same for the troops we leave behind."

"Yes. He gave me a quick rundown on what they thought. I agree it's a good business. No doubt, some senior personnel in both the Army and Navy will hitch a ride on one of the local Battleships of State. Two of them have kept their reactors hot. No doubt, someone wants to make a gracious exit."

"Oh, I missed that. I was concentrating on the battlecruisers. Thanks for pointing out that there are options for as many as want to run to do just that. Now, what about the fleet. How do we manage a thousand new rebel ships?"

Admiral Tong didn't even hesitate. "It just so happens that their thousand are organized into thirty-two flotillas, each with four squadrons. If we pulled one squadron out of each of their flotillas, we'd have thirty-two squadrons to distribute among our flotillas. If we took two squadrons out of each flotilla, half of the ships that stayed here would be Balan, half would be ours."

Kris nodded agreement. "And the sixty-four squadrons would be swallowed among our two hundred and sixteen flotillas. However, the fleet here would only be fifty-fifty."

"Yes," Admiral Tong said. "So, may I suggest we take one more squadron out of sixteen of Balan's flotillas. That would leave half the flotillas here with three loyal squadrons and half with two. Exactly how we staff one or two task force headquarters will depend on who runs for the battleships. Same for the ship captains. I may shuffle some COs and XOs around until I'm comfortable that I can trust them not to try to stab us in the back."

"I like your attitude. Even with eighty former rebel squadrons in my fleet, they will still be a small part of those flotillas and the rest of my fleet would be all loyalists."

"Very much so, My Most Eminent Admiral," Tong said.

"With that settled, I can now get an early supper. Thank you."

"We should dock during the third watch tomorrow morning. I will call you as soon as we know how many of the local Battleships of State want permission to leave for the far jump."

"Thank you," and Kris cut the circuit.

"Nelly, can you get Jack? Damn, I almost said Jack and the kids. I miss those cuties."

"I miss them, too," Nelly said. "Ruth asks such interesting questions and the view she takes on things is always a surprise. I find talking with her so refreshing."

"You need to share some of those moments with me," Kris said.

"I keep them in a special storage. I guess you would say close to my heart. Johnnie is a scamp. More often, Hippo is trying to keep him in line. Fortunately, we removed the off button on Hippo and Johnnie can't turn him off. Ruth wouldn't think of deactivating Daisy. She wants to talk to her all the time. Daisy is getting to be quite the chatterbox on the family net."

"No surprise there," Kris said, smiling fondly. She remembered herself at Ruth's age, when she could laugh and ask any question she wanted of their nanny. That was the year before little Eddie was kidnapped.

"Oh dearest, I so hope we can keep your laugh, your smile, your questions," Kris muttered to herself.

"Here is Jack," Nelly said.

"Hi, hon. Has your day been survivable?" he asked on net.

"The question is will the decisions I make today be survivable a month from now."

"You hungry?"

"Terribly, Jack. Can I meet you at the wardroom?"

"Admiral's or ship's?" Jack answered back.

"I need to feel the background chatter of my fellow soldiers," Kris said. "We can talk about the classified stuff over a nice pillow, or maybe turn the shower into a hot tub."

"I vote for hot tub."

After a nice supper, Kris and Jack had just gotten comfortable in the newly created hot tub in their quarters when Nelly announced she had a call coming in from Admiral Tong.

"Audio only, Nelly. Yes, admiral. You've caught me in the bath."

"I hope you are not alone in it," the admiral shot back.

"She isn't," Jack contributed, and got a splash for his reward.

"I promised that I'd immediately get back to you if any of the Battleships of State took flight."

"Yes," Kris said.

"Both of the ships that had fusion up are underway for the farthest jump. Six battlecruisers detached from the station and took up position on their flanks."

"I thought all the battlecruisers were cold steel," Kris said.

"We were both right. All the battlecruisers are cold steel.

However, just before they sailed, we got some very strange readings off the battlecruisers and battleships. They first transferred plasma to the battlecruisers who shared the piers with the battleships. Then another pier got plasma from one of them. It is not like the signature for this action is in our standard book for analyzing signal intelligence. Sorry, My Most Eminent Admiral."

"These things happen. I've tried a few moves that aren't in the book. Tell me, Admiral, how many passengers can an Iteeche Battleship of State carry?"

That got Kris a shrug. "I don't know, my Most Eminent Admiral. It all depends on how big they are. I think these ships are of a middling size. They likely were designed to carry a thousand in luxury. If desperate, they could probably take on four or five thousand before the air got seriously bad. Mind you, with five thousand crammed aboard, comfort would not be on the passenger list."

"I don't imagine so. And the battlecruisers?" Kris asked.

"Again, we use a crew of a thousand. They could likely carry twice as many. Some would sleep on the racks. The other half could sleep in the high gee stations."

"So, basically, you're telling me that we don't know."

"Correct, My Most Eminent Admiral."

"Tong, you're going to have to cut back to just admiral or we'll lose a year out of our lives."

"It is not easy to change a habit of a lifetime. However, Admiral Coth warned me this might happen. Very well, Admiral. Have you considered calling the Planetary Overlord?"

Kris blew out a troubled breath. "I really didn't want to get out of this tub and get dressed in uniform again, but I guess I have to."

"I would offer to call," Admiral Tong said, "but I doubt I'd have the necessary pull."

"Still, thanks for the offer."

She and Jack got out, dried each other off, and threw on a fresh set of khakis. Both then returned to the flag bridge.

"Nelly, get me the Planetary Overlord on the horn."

"I advised him immediately that you would want to talk to him. He is awaiting your call. He asked me why you were calling."

"Did you tell him?"

"No, Kris."

"You should have asked me. I might have told you to. Now we'll have to wait for him to find out what happens if he doesn't know."

The screen came on, showing a very serious Iteeche face.

"Yes, Your Most High Admiral. How may I help you?"

"Two Battleships of State and six battlecruisers have detached from the station and are running for the most distant jump out of the system. Would you care to explain?"

"I can offer no explanation. I did not know about it until your computer asked me to stand by for this call. I polled my subordinates and discovered that several of them were no longer at their post and that my own personal Battleship of State was no longer at the pier."

"I had thought that we had an agreement that people didn't have to run or disrupt the system's economic operations and development."

"Some of them remember your reduction of the reigning Clan Lords of Zargoth."

"Yes, but there was no fighting in the streets there. At Arteccia and the Glorious Golden Eel, matters went much smoother. I hoped they could be that smooth here on Balan."

"You have not heard that Arteccia has been retaken by the rebels?"

"I heard," Kris admitted. "That is the reason for this war cruise."

"Then you do not know how the reconquest went down on Arteccia?"

Kris frowned, and let a long sigh out. "No, but I suspect I'm about to find out. What happened when the rebels retook Arteccia?"

"Every clan lord and lordling was marched naked to the center of their city and relieved of their heads."

Why was Kris not surprised? Hadn't she been told that there was a nice Iteeche way to solve these civil wars that didn't involve a lot of Iteeche getting killed? Well, clan lords and lordlings getting killed. No one cared if the average Iteeche died. However, all that was something to talk to Admiral Tong about. Right now, she had a very skittish Planetary Overlord and a lot of people wondering if they should have grabbed the last boat out.

"Sir, you have my pledge both as a Longknife and as a Human admiral. We do not commit war crimes. If you surrender to me, you are my responsibility to protect. I will protect you from any Iteeche, civilian, clan, Navy, or Army. Under no circumstances would I abandon you. Anyone who comes for your head, comes over my dead body."

The Iteeche was blinking his eyes, and when you have four eyes, that's a lot of blinking. "You make me believe that that is true," he admitted. "Why would you do that?"

"For the opposite reason that the rebels murdered those lordlings on Arteccia. I want to bring peace. They want to prolong war. By jacking up the bloodshed on both sides, they reduce the fight from a war into a slaughterhouse."

Kris shook her head. "Sir, I most definitely want to resolve this occupation without bloodshed. I need to show other planets that they can surrender to me and not be put to the sword. I hope you are equally resolved to settling this matter the same way. Still, do not doubt that I will use whatever force I have to achieve the Emperor's success. However, if I can, I will achieve it with the least bloodshed."

The Iteeche studied Kris from his side of the screen. "I find that I do believe you. I have no desire for bloodshed. We can arrive at a mutually acceptable resolution of our situation. I will surrender the entire Army and Navy presence in this system."

"I will leave you with the same thousand ships, maybe more, to guard you. I hope that you will continue your investment in your own defense. Every battlecruiser built here will remain here for your defense. I may swap some of my ground combats with yours, but you will be as strong when we leave as when we arrived."

"That means more to me than you can possibly believe," the Planetary Overlord said.

"Knowing what you know, and I now know, I can believe it. Now, could you get me a list of those who have fled? I will need to pull replacements from my Battleships of State. If Army or Navy personnel are among those who fled, I will need to begin searching my ranks for those to promote, and that usually means two or three promotions to fill all the resulting empty slots."

"I see your problem. I will have a report to you in the next hour. It may be incomplete, but it will give you something to start with."

"Thank you. We will dock tomorrow morning on your space stations."

27

At 0900 hours the next morning, Kris's battlecruiser fleet matched orbits with the three space stations. There was no question, all her ships could not dock. Kris would have to shoehorn as many in as possible, then swing the rest at anchor behind the stations in divisions of four.

Kris saw to it that Admirals Kitano, Tong, and Linn's flagships were docked close to hers. She had also fielded an "ultimatum" from all three of the future Planetary Overlords that their Battleships of State must be docked as well.

All agreed that zero gee was not compatible with their good digestion. Kris had intended to dock all nine Battleships of State. They were all of a different size and they were not made of Smart Metal. There was no way to anchor them to each other. Still, ultimatums did not go down well with her digestion.

About a tenth of the minor lordlings positions had come open with the flight of the two Balan Battleships of State. It took a while for volunteers to be found to fill them.

"This wasn't what we signed on for," was the most frequent complaint. "We were supported to serve together. Control our own planets."

Kris kept her temper, if only just. They'd had their jobs drawn out of a lottery barrel. Nobody knew who they would be working with. Of course, working with another junior clan lordling was one thing. Working with people from the major clans, who had been rebels-in-arms just hours before, could be considered something else.

The Planetary Overlord, whom Kris named Larry, was waiting for Kris as soon as the *Princess Royal* sealed locks with the station. Kris greeted Larry with full honors and laid it on with gold plate and jewels as the *P. Royal* went from Condition Able to full Imperial Able Plus.

The Planetary Overlord's eyes, all four of them, didn't quite bug out of his head as he joined her on the quarterdeck with Admirals Tong and Linn as well as General Compeel.

Trailing the Planetary Overlord up the gangplank were his acting Navy and Army chiefs of staff. The Iteeche who held those jobs yesterday were beating feet for the exit today. He also had his senior advisors from several Clans as well as what Kris took for a number of lawyers.

That was fine by her. She had a small gaggle of JAG officers standing by. They'd drawn up the Surrender and Future Management Agreement according to her wishes. It was likely now that her lawyers and his lawyers were about to adjourn to work out any nits.

Hopefully, they wouldn't have too many matters to refer to their seniors.

While Jack led the lawyers off to meet with their Human compatriots, Kris invited Larry to join her in her quarters for refreshments. Once again, Nelly had done Kris's quarters up fantastic as well as palatial. Then her cooks did her proud, serving up several delicacies fresh from her water tanks.

Clearly, the Planetary Overlord had not expected such treatment, nor had he even considered it possible from a Navy officer.

"You are full of surprises," Larry said.

"If we are to bring this war to a conclusion," Kris pointed out, "we need to pull a few surprises out of our hats."

Kris turned the conversation over to Admiral Tong and the other

Iteeche even after Jack rejoined her. She listened as the two sides swapped questions and answers with them flowing in both directions. She was quite surprised at how well-informed Admiral Linn was on the industrial side of the Iteeche Empire. He probed deep into not only the status of Balan's military and naval capabilities, but also the industrial base that supported it.

It turned out that Balan could make 160 battlecruisers a month, a full five flotillas. Further exploration showed that the adverse impact on the rest of the economy would be minor.

"We'd have to cut back on producing any intersystem freighters, but we've got plenty of them and we can work the old ones a year or two past their date with the ship breakers," the Minister of Industry offered.

The new Navy Chief of Staff agreed.

Kris turned to Admiral Tong. "If we were to peel five flotillas off of each wing, that would add eight hundred ships to Balan's defense. In two months, they'd have a full two thousand. We were expecting to have to provide protection for the system from minor raiders." She left the rest of the question unsaid.

"I wouldn't mind that. In two months, they'd be up to two thousand. In four months, they'd be reaching for twenty-four hundred. Might I ask, if we're still campaigning at that time, that Balan second to us two flotillas each month after that?"

The Planetary Overlord nodded. "You'll help us for the next four months, then we'll still be adding four flotillas each month to our defenses, but we send two to assist you in your campaigns. That seems more than fair."

Kris invited the Balan delegation to lunch with her. It was what one would expect in an Imperial Palace, but hardly the fare aboard a warship. The lawyers were served the same food, but for them, it was a working lunch.

After the meal, the Balan delegation gave Kris a thorough briefing on what was going on in the system. None of it came as a surprise. However, the extent of it went well beyond what she had monitored from space.

Larry, himself, presented his assessment of the political climate on the planet below. Most of the most fervent rebels among the military had fled, as had many of the middle management types that had pushed for the civil war with an eye toward their own promotion. Most of the lower clan lordlings had remained neutral in the debate, likely because they saw little in it that benefited them, and a lot that could cost them their neck. Most of the senior clan lords had stayed, choosing to believe Kris's offer of protection. Not all, but most.

Kris had several hundred positions to fill, more than she had originally known. She made a call to the Planetary Overlords in waiting and asked them to distribute the vacancy notices among their subordinates.

They did so, with ill humor.

Suppertime came, and Kris again put on a spread fit for an Emperor. She included Admiral Kitano and several of the Iteeche admirals that were being considered for commanding the Balan fleet as well as generals that would be given commands in Balan's Army.

The conversation around the tables was usually light, but often divided into a discussion of specific issues that would face those who commanded at Balan. It never grew heated but stayed to just the facts. Indeed, the only thing that inspired grumbling among her guests was that if they ate like this every day, their clothes would soon not fit.

Kris let the dinner conversation go long. It appeared to be quite productive. She visited each table and each visit turned into a report on what they'd settled over dinner. Before dismissing her dinner party, Kris brought the lawyers in. A count showed that not one of them had been killed and there were no visible cuts or bruises.

They had reached agreement on all the important things, and even most of the minor ones. Admiral Linn's title of Supreme Planetary Overseer had proved hard for them to swallow. A final appeal was made to Kris and Larry. He accepted Admiral Linn's title with a quick wave of his right hands.

"A rose by any other name would smell so sweet," Kris said, wondering how it would translate into Iteeche.

"If the Overseer and the Overlord can see eyes-to-eyes, there will be no problems," Larry said. Kris had made sure during the meal to have Lynn sitting at Larry's right elbow and she was at his left.

They had gotten along fine and ended up exchanging jokes about a place they had spent time on in their early careers. It was a cold, icy rock that they all hated, but was a good bonding experience for those that were no longer there.

Kris signed the treaty of surrender first, followed by the Overlord and the Overseer. Several of Balan's high ranking civilians and military personnel signed as well. Then it was back to Kris's side for the signatures of the military personnel she was leaving in charge.

She wished that she had more civilian representatives handy to add their signatures to the fancy parchment Nelly had produced. However, she still didn't have word of who would do what from the overlords-in-waiting.

Kris was starting to wonder if her biggest problems would be from loyalist civilians than her new allies from the rebellion.

Then Nelly cleared her nonexistent throat. "Admiral Longknife, we have a problem on Balan."

The conversations around the rooms came to a roaring halt. Everyone turned to Kris as she stood up. She wanted to be seen by everyone here.

This is how I solve problems.

"Nelly, what's the problem?"

"A water main has blown up at a junction of two large aqueducts. Several million Iteeche will be without water in a few minutes. Loss of power and communications will follow shortly thereafter, assuming Balan uses the same construction codes as Zargoth. Water will likely flood communications, power, and sewage very quickly. Maybe even close down the rolling roads."

Kris muttered a few words she didn't use when the kids were around.

"Nelly, get Commander Longknife. Alert the Marine crime scene investigating team. General Compeel, can you provide a company of troops with more on standby?"

Kris turned to Larry. "Can you arrange for our people to work with yours? I know jurisdiction is often a touchy problem at crime scenes. I think you want to get to the bottom of this as quickly as I do."

"Yes. Definitely. Tom is my Minister of Planetary Security. Would you please accompany this Commander Longknife and see that nothing stands in the way of our finding this saboteur."

"Of course, Sir. Where do I go?"

"Wait for her on the quarterdeck," Kris said. "You can't miss her red hair."

In a blink the Iteeche was gone leaving Kris with a serious question. Who could have done this and why? It certainly could be a rebel that didn't make it when the ships were leaving.

However . . .

NELLY, HAVE ANY PEOPLE FROM THE BATTLESHIPS OF STATE GONE ASHORE? MORE IMPORTANTLY, HAVE ANY OF THEM TAKEN THE SPACE ELEVATOR DOWN?

KRIS, SEVERAL HAVE GONE ASHORE. A FEW WENT BELOW TO ACQUIRE FOOD AND DELICACIES FOR THE SENIOR CLAN LORDS' DINNERS. WE COULD NOT FOLLOW THEM ONCE THEY LEFT THE SPACE ELEVATOR.

SO, WE HAVE A POTENTIAL PROBLEM, PLENTY OF SUSPECTS, AND NO REAL WAY TO PROVE ANY OF THIS. NELLY, REVIEW WHAT YOU KNOW ABOUT THOSE THAT WENT BELOW. ARE ANY OF THEM TRAINED IN EXPLOSIVES?

There was only a slight pause before Nelly answered. KRIS, THERE IS LITTLE MORE THAN THEIR NAMES ON THE PASSENGER LISTS. SOME SHOW MILITARY RANKS, BUT WITHOUT ME, YOU COULD NOT BUILD A BOMB AND KNOW WHERE TO PLACE IT FOR MAXIMUM IMPACT.

THANK YOU, NELLY, FOR TELLING ME ONE OF THE MANY THINGS I DON'T KNOW.

Further thought was interrupted. "Kris, you have a call coming in from Commander Longknife."

"Longknife One here. How's it going Meg?"

28

Lieutenant Commander Megan Longknife, *aide de camp* to Grand Admiral Kris Longknife, was used to being rousted out of bed or hauled away from a meal. It came with the job. If she'd wanted regular hours, she could have stayed on distant Santa Maria. Certainly, she could have avoided volunteering for a second tour as Kris's dog robber.

Yet, here she was, still chewing her last bite of supper, being helped into a full set of space armor.

"I'm not making the same mistake I made at Zargoth," she muttered to herself and the young Marine helping her get into her play clothes. On Zargoth, she'd made the mistake of dropping down the beanstalk in just a blue shipsuit.

Bad planning.

When she and the Marine were satisfied, and Gunny had looked her over, she holstered her sidearm and headed for the quarterdeck on the double.

That place was filling up fast. An Iteeche in what may or may not have been a uniform, but who looked most officious, strode from Kris's day quarters. A Marine squad with a cart full of gear arrived from the left as she entered from the right. Behind the Marines that

Meg took for the forensic team, came another squad of MPs. These had been trained to work with the local police and coordinate all the different efforts going on. At least all those that didn't require a Longknife to stick her nose in.

Quietly behind them followed a small squad, two Marines with long rifles, and two more with scopes strapped to the top of their packs. So, Kris was sending Meg down with not one, but two sniper teams. Either this was going to be a hot job, or the admiral wasn't taking any chances on sending too little.

Across the pier, a Marine company was forming ranks only paces from the brow of the *Defiant*.

Kris was definitely going heavy. In front of them, a long line of eight-wheeled infantry fighting vehicles waited to transport them quickly to the space elevator's ferry station.

Megan turned to the Iteeche and introduced herself. He responded with a name a foot long. She followed Kris's practice of naming him Tom for short and letting Lily remember to use the full name when she spoke to him. He was the Minister of Planetary Security.

Meg was coming up in the world. She now had a higher class of juvenile delinquents to babysit. Of course, it could be that he was along to babysit her. No doubt, they'd have a fun time before this was over.

LILY, I THINK WE NEED A FLATBED STATION CART. ONE WITH A HANDRAIL IN FRONT FOR TOM AND I TO HOLD ON TO.

A moment later, such an electric cart rose from the deck right next to the brow and motored silently down the gangplank. It not only had the requested handrails, but also wide steps on the back to make it easy for an Iteeche to mount.

Tom studied the sudden addition with a jaundiced eye. All four of them. "They told me that you Humans enjoyed playing with the magic metal. I see that I am dealing with one of the best."

"Yes, sir. I am honored to have one of Nelly's children at my neck.

She is one of the sentient computers. Please call her Lily if you chose to address her."

The Iteeche cleared his throat. "I can't believe I'm saying this. How do you do, Ms. Lily?"

"I am fine, Sir, thank you," Lily replied with equal formality. "I am looking forward to finding the culprit who has put your people at risk."

The Iteeche raised four eyebrows. Only for a few millimeters, but still, he eyed Megan with puzzlement.

"Lily will likely do a lot to apprehend the criminal," Megan said. "Nelly's kids are very smart and often underestimated. Few folks get a chance to do it twice."

Meg looked around, everything seemed in order and ready to go.

"An Iteeche company is approaching this pier on A deck," Lily said. "They also have been reinforced with a platoon of MPs and two sniper teams."

"Very good," Megan said, "Please get me a line to Kris."

A holograph of Kris and several Humans and Iteeche with her formed in the air before Megan and Tom.

"Longknife One here. How's it going Meg."

"We are ready to depart the *Princess Royal*, Your Highness. Do you have any last instructions for me or Tom?"

"Nope. Find the bastard who did this. Bring him before me in chains if he's one of ours. Let Tom have him if he's a local. And, of course, make it quick."

"Do you have someone checking to see if anyone remembers one of our Iteeche going dirtside, or should I start beating that tree as well?"

"Don't worry. We'll handle everything topside. You take care of what's dirtside."

"Aye, aye, Admiral. Longknife Two out." And the holograph vanished.

"Ready to go, sir."

"After you, Miss."

Megan rendered honors and led the bemused Iteeche civilian

down the brow to their waiting cart. The Marines, in full battle rattle, followed her across the gangplank and quickly mounted up. More electric powered infantry fighting trucks waited for them there.

Megan took the lead, heading the entire formation for the elevators up to the main deck of the station.

As expected, a reinforced company of Iteeche Marines waited for them on A deck. They were also using eight-wheeled infantry fighting trucks. As Meg and Tom exited the elevator up from the pier, they motored silently toward the ferry station.

Megan fell in behind the Iteeche with her three special squads rolling around her. Behind them came the Royal US Marine Corps company.

Pity the poor SOB who took a pot shot at this crew.

As they entered the station, they went straight to the loading dock. The last scheduled ferry had been held for them.

Tom looked around at all the heavy metal parked around them. "Would you mind if I said that I felt a bit exposed in that nice station truck that you provided for me? Don't you feel the same?"

"I sure do, Sir," Megan said. "We'll be riding with the MPs as soon as we depart the ferry. I didn't think it would be a good idea to start off by locking you up in a metal box where you couldn't see what was going on around you."

"I appreciate that concern," he said. "But when we get down?"

"Lilly will add this Smart Metal, magic metal if you prefer, to several of the gun trucks. She can also turn the Smart Metal transparent. That should give us the option of watching what's going by if we want to."

"You think of everything," Tom said.

"Only because I've been here, Sir. A local blew up the rolling roads in one major city on Zargoth. It caused a series of cascading crises, much like I think this incident will. I'll get a lousy fitness rating if I can't do it better this time than I did last time."

"Did you catch the culprit?"

"Actually, we didn't. We were too busy fixing the problems to do much of a police sweep. Our sniper team did take out a shooter who took a pot shot at me. Maybe that was the guy. Or it could have been the guy who tried to do it to another town. Security was tight and that guy got shot dead before he managed to cause any trouble."

"I'm beginning to believe that I might like you, Longknife. Are you also related to the Hammer of Iteeche Longknife?"

"I have the honor, or pain in the butt, depending on the day, of being his great-great-granddaughter. The Grand Admiral and I are cousins from different generations and from quite different limbs of the family tree. I come from a lost colony a quarter of the way across the galaxy. Her folks stayed home."

"Halfway across the galaxy. I didn't think you Humans had colonies that far afield."

"We haven't. Our exploration ship took a wrong turn four hundred years ago, added twists to it, and became totally lost. We were surviving, just barely, when Ray Longknife took off for a meeting. His ship was sabotaged and stumbled across us when we were in a heap of trouble."

"Don't you Longknifes do that a lot? Walk into trouble, I mean."

Megan chuckled. "Jesus, Mary, and Joseph, has the Longknife legend spread this far?"

"I don't know what the Longknife legend is, but if you ask any Iteeche older than ten years they will tell you that Longknifes mean trouble. Either them causing it, or them in it."

"No wonder the boss lady can't get any respect," Megan sighed.

They got a drink in the VIP lounge. Every ferry seemed to have one. Megan had to settle for tea provided by a Gunny who thought ahead.

A half hour later, Meg's rump battalion moved off the ferry smartly, only to find several rigs that had to qualify as limos and police cruisers blocking their way.

"I believe my boss laid on a welcoming party," Tom said.

Megan opened the aft hatch of their gun truck and soon found herself talking to the governor of the district, the mayor of the capital, the baron for public security, and the baron for public services.

Unlike the minor lordlings she'd dealt with on Zargoth, these folks all sounded quite motivated to get this problem solved.

The police escort led the battalion to where the break was. Megan and Tom joined the four local officials in a very large limo, and discussed their problem along the way.

There wasn't much to discuss.

"The explosion occurred just after suppertime," the governor said.

"A quarter of the capital is now without water," the mayor added.

"We have lost communication access in that quarter. Power is going down slowly around the break. Sewage went when we lost water."

"Do you have any idea who did this?" Meg asked.

The other four Iteeche looked at Tom for permission to respond to the two eyes.

"Since our Planetary Overlord is about to surrender to her cousin, I strongly recommend that you answer any of her questions."

"Yes, sir. Ah, how may we address you, woman warrior?" the governor asked.

"I am Commander Longknife," Megan said. "Longknife 2 is my radio call sign. Any further questions?"

"No, Commander Longknife," the governor said, then lightly pointed with his lower left arm at the police official.

"We are going from apartment to apartment, asking if anyone saw anyone plant a bomb. However, that could have been done below ground, and we doubt anyone saw it."

"Has anyone been working below ground today?" Meg asked.

"No, Commander Longknife," the services baron said. "We had no one working on any of the sub-surface services."

"So, did anyone see anyone go below?" Meg asked, then demanded, "Are you going at this investigation slowly, or did you just fail to think of that?"

The four Iteeche began staring at each other.

"Answer her," Tom ordered.

Finally, the Baron of Police said, "The officers in the area did a standard search and interrogation for someone who had planted a bomb. I was told not to do anything to disturb the scene of the explosion."

How the Don't Disturb turned into a Don't Look Under the Street was something that Meg would leave to reflect upon another time.

She settled on asking for now, "How long until we get to the scene of the explosion?"

"Six point three minutes," the governor replied.

"Lily, get me the leaders of my squads and companies."

"Aye, aye, ma'am," came from Megan's neck.

Tom sat still while the other four Iteeche eyed the source of the words coming out of the air and looked uncomfortable. The Baron of Public Services' fingers made strange signs that he strove to conceal.

I guess they have magic against the evil eye, too.

"Team, I want to stop a block away from the site of the explosion. Forensics, I want you to check any service hole covers for explosive residue. Lieutenant, I want you and your best evidence tech to take a look at the site of the explosion. Determine if there is any chance of finding any evidence."

"Aye, aye, Commander."

"Company skippers, check your date of rank and the highest ranking person is in charge of our perimeter. Please deploy the Marines to assure that we are not disturbed. Snipers, pair up, Human and Iteeche, and find two good vantage points. If you see anyone getting ready to shoot at this force, take them down."

"Aye, aye, ma'am."

"MPs, again, check to see who is senior. I want you to liaise with the local police and coordinate a second search that includes asking if anyone saw anything that looked suspicious: a stranger carrying a large package, a vehicle stopped next to a service access hole. Anything out of the ordinary."

"Aye, aye, ma'am."

"Any questions? Any suggestions?" Meg paused. There was no response. "Okay, crew, the Grand Admiral wants this solved and solved quickly. I want to know where those explosives came from if it is at all possible."

"Aye, aye," came across the net.

"Okay, we're ready to get this show on the road," Megan told those who shared the limo with her.

The five Iteeche exchanged glances.

Finally, Tom said, "That was quick."

"Pardon?" Meg answered

"You did not negotiate with anyone. You did not refer to historical precedent. No one suggested that you consider a different precedent or that a clan might not want you to do that."

Megan wondered if she was discovering another speed bump between the Human and Iteeche mindset.

"I am Commander Longknife. I outrank everyone in my task unit. I also report immediately to Grand Admiral Longknife, Imperial Admiral in command of the Emperor's Combined Fleet. I gave the orders. I asked for suggestions to improve them. I expect mine will be executed quickly. Baron of Security, will we have a problem working with your officers?"

"No," he said.

"Baron of Services, will you have people on scene that my people can work with?"

"I was told not to disturb the scene of the explosion. However, I do have workers standing by to begin solving this problem. However, I must tell you that water gushing out of aqueducts this size is not the gentle thing you splash on your face. This water hits you like a brick wall."

"I understand the strength of water in large doses and at high speeds," Megan said. "As soon as we have recovered any explosive residue that we can find, I will be eager for your work details to begin fixing what they can. You may find us very helpful."

The Iteeche didn't look very persuaded.

"Lily, get me Longknife 1."

"Yes, Megan, what can I do for you?" a small holograph of Kris said almost immediately. The Planetary Overlord was at her elbow and in the holograph.

The four Iteeche who had no experience of this sat bolt upright. If an Iteeche could smile, Tom was doing his best not to.

"I need a hydraulics engineer and a work group to assist some Iteeche in controlling the broken aqueducts. I'll also need Smart Metal, ah, magic metal, to patch the pipes and maybe spin together a couple of pumps to drain the underground."

"I'll have them on the next ferry. Everything going okay?"

"Nothing to report yet, Admiral. We're still a few minutes out from the scene of the explosion."

"Good idea calling for the hydraulics engineer. Call me if you need something or have something."

"Will do. Longknife 2 out," and she cut the line.

"Now you see," Tom said softly, "our lowly Navy officer can call down the world on your head."

The rest of the ride to the sabotage site was very quiet.

29

Lieutenant Commander Megan Longknife stood with her hands on her hips, observing the mess someone had made of this street. At least the street wasn't one of the rolling roads.

Thank God for small favors, but holy mother of God, what a mess.

The explosion had ripped up the street. It had fallen back into the hole, then flooded. Muddy water flowed down a low hill to collect in a shallow depression. That depression was rapidly filling up while flooding the bottom two floors of several apartment buildings. The unnamed lake, Lake 1, was about to overflow its banks. Excess water would soon be flooding into another, lower depression. The buildings at the bottom of that hill had businesses on their bottom floors. They might also have parking garages under them.

Megan needed to stop the flow of water, and fast.

"Lily, dispatch flitter quad choppers to check out the tunnels under this street as soon as someone gets a service hole cover off."

"I'm waiting, Commander." Lily wasn't usually that formal, but they were on stage in front of very class-conscious Iteeche.

"A cover is off. I've dispatched four flitters to it. I'll put flitters down every cover as it opens."

"Good, Lily. Anything on the explosive used?"

The Iteeche officials standing at her elbows perked up at that.

"We have taken samples of what looks like explosive residue, Commander. However, we have to test it to be sure. We are dealing with an area where harsh chemicals might well be present in daily use," Lily answered.

"Sorry, Lily. I'm anxious," Megan admitted.

"You apologize to your computer?" Tom asked. The Iteeche around him seemed just as interested in the answer.

"My computer is sentient. None of us like to be micromanaged."

"Micromanaged?" Tom's mouth struggled to get around the word. Apparently, there was no Iteeche translation.

Now I'm the alien.

"A good officer informs a subordinate of the ends desired, then delegates the authority to achieve those ends. Micromanaging is when a bad officer won't quit looking over the subordinates' shoulder and keeps telling them how to do their job."

"Oh," Tom said. The answer dropped like a lead balloon.

"Commander, you might want to join the forensic team," Lily observed, helpfully. "They expect to soon have several samples of explosives through their field-testing devices."

Megan felt like a mommy duck leading her ducklings toward where Marines huddled over the ramp of a gun truck. There were several differences. These ducklings towered over her. Also, ducklings would have formed a line, single file. The Iteeche jostled each other, unable to agree on a pecking order. Tom followed with the governor and mayor, one on each shoulder. Meanwhile, the two barons couldn't decide who was senior, and finally ended up walking side by side.

"What do you have for me, Lieutenant?" Megan asked as she joined her forensic team a hundred meters back from the big hole in the ground. The sound of roaring water provided their background. It also smelled of mud with a hint of residual explosives.

The first lieutenant leading the forensic team looked to be a mustang. Most lieutenants barely needed to shave. This woman had the maturity to not even blink when a commander descended on her with a pack of well-dressed, and therefore high-ranking Iteeche. Definitely, she'd earned her sergeant's stripes before putting on officer's bars.

"All of our sample wipes showed evidence of strong chemicals," she told them. "We're about to get a full report of what are on the service covers. We also took some from the roof of the access passageways for the water pipes. They are likely to have fewer random chemicals."

A thin printout began to stream from a port on the machine that looked a lot like a whole batch of tiny microwave ovens. The printout stopped, was cut, and another printout began immediately. When a half dozen hung from the slot, the LT broke the last one off, then divided them all up.

"The chemicals at the top are listed in black," she explained. "They rarely go into explosives. The next list of chemicals is in yellow. They can be used in explosives, but they also have other uses. The bottom of the list is in red. If you find those suckers, somebody made a bomb."

At the bottom of all six lists showed five or six chemical compounds in glaring red.

"I think we have a winner," the LT said.

"And it is . . . ?" Megan asked.

The LT scowled, "C-14. One of the most common explosives known to man. Apparently to Iteeche as well."

Megan turned to Tom. "In Human space, we require every manufacturer of explosives to include tags in the explosives. That way, if one is used illegally, we can trace it to the manufacturer and to which plant on what planet. Likely even the production batch. Do the Iteeche Empire have the same requirement?" Megan asked but even as she presented the question, she knew the answer would be no.

Tom shook his head. "How can you put something in an explosive that isn't destroyed in the explosion?"

Megan knew that Tom was asking a rhetorical question, but she answered it anyway. "We're looking for explosive residue. There's always some of the chemicals that don't get exploded and miss out on the main event. That's what we've just tested. If this was made from Human manufactured explosives, we'd find a few taggants that had also missed out on the fun."

"Oh," was Tom's response. The rest of the Iteeche just stared blankly.

"Lieutenant, are there any taggants in this explosive residue?" Megan asked.

"No, Commander. I already ran one sample through, checking just for tags."

"Well," Megan said, with a sigh, "at least we know no one used Human C-14. So, where does that leave us?" she asked the mustang.

The LT shook her head. "Not a whole lot to go on. C-14 is your explosive of choice for a quite a few things, from military to construction to mining. It could have come from anywhere."

"How much would be needed to cause this much damage?"

"I hate to say this again, but hard to tell. Commander, we haven't gotten a look at the area around the explosion."

"Okay," Megan said, trying not to let exasperation into her voice. "More than a thimbleful, less than a truck load?"

"Oh, yes commander. Something at least the size of an average briefcase. I doubt if it was larger than a suitcase or backpack. A duffle bag would likely be too much."

"Mm," Megan muttered. That was helpful, and it did define the problem a bit better. She turned to Tom.

"Could you arrange for the local Iteeche security forces to re-question the locals? Did any of them see someone, likely well-dressed, looking out of place and carrying something between the size of a briefcase and a backpack?"

From the look on Tom's face, neither briefcase nor backpack translated well.

"Lily, give us an in-scale picture of a briefcase and backpack."

A holograph immediately appeared with an Iteeche holding a briefcase. On his back was a backpack.

"We don't have anything like that," Tom said. "Can you make it an over-the-shoulder satchel?"

A moment later, two Iteeche glowed, one with a small of the shoulder satchel, the other with a large, say ten kilo, haversack. That got the Iteeche's attention. The Baron of Security signaled for several uniformed people. They came running.

They and the baron talked in hushed tones, then the senior police officers took off running, no doubt to tell every beat cop to question people again. No radios here, the message could be hand carried down the chain of authority.

That was the Iteeche way.

Megan made a note of other Iteeche ways she was seeing today. The baron did not ask Lily to show the police officers what the satchels looked like in terms of size. She'd read somewhere that knowledge was power, and some societies required that it be husbanded out to the members of lesser status.

She suspected she was encountering such a society. She was not surprised, though it could complicate her job.

The Marine LT was still at Megan's elbow. "Ma'am, it's none of my business, but why is water still gushing out of this hole in the ground?"

"It hasn't been turned off?" Meg asked.

"Nope."

Megan sidled over to the Baron for Public Services. She'd gone through Tom to get the police moving on canvasing the locals. She'd suspect that it would go over better if an Iteeche gave the order. That had worked smoothly.

Asking a mere question of the baron of the water works didn't seem like it would put any noses out of joint.

"Has the water been turned off?" she asked the baron. Sugar wouldn't melt in her mouth.

He glanced around at his superiors. If Megan wasn't mistaken, this was what an Iteeche looked like who had been caught out.

"Yes, of course the water is now off," the Iteeche stammered.

"Are you sure, because my lieutenant tells me that there's still plenty of water gushing out of that hole in the ground."

"I ordered it be turned off. I was told it had been turned off," came out way too fast.

"Tom, could you arrange for me to talk to the supervisor of the workers who maintain this section of line?"

"Why would you want to do that?" he asked Megan. "It is beneath you. Why would you want to get your hands dirty? Besides, they are of the lowest class. If you talk to them, they'll start acting above their station."

Megan knew that she would need Jacques to unpack everything in that statement.

"Tom, I serve Grand Admiral Longknife who commands the Imperial Combined Fleet. She sent me to do a job, and I have no intention of reporting to her that I did not move heaven and earth to both find out who did this and get the people in this part of town water, electricity, and communications. Now, will you please point me in the direction of the men who do the actual work of keeping water flowing?"

Tom turned to the others.

WHAT'S HAPPENING, LILY?

THERE IS A GENERAL CONSENSUS THAT YOU HUMANS HAVE NO SENSE OF PROPRIETY, AREN'T BEHAVING LIKE A PROPER ITEECHE, AND HAVE NO CLASS. I GET THE GENERAL FEELING THAT THEY THINK YOU'RE A HICK FROM THE LOWEST CLASS LAST CHOSEN.

CAN'T PLEASE EVERYONE.

"Tom," Megan said.

"Yes."

"Your boss, the Planetary Overlord, is trying to negotiate a surrender with my boss, Grand Admiral Longknife, that will leave you and your associates here still running this planet. Do I understand that correctly?"

"I thought it was already signed."

"You thought wrong. Now, if this no-account hick from the lowest class, last chosen, makes a call to the admiral, your boss and all of you will be sent packing and we will install a leadership cadre more responsive to our questions and interests."

"You can't do that," the District Governor spat.

"Tom, you've seen me talk directly to the Grand Admiral with your boss standing at her elbow."

A half dozen Iteeche seemed locked in indecision. They'd clearly decided that Megan was a minor flunky they could ignore. Meg gave them five seconds to change their opinion, but they held on tightly to it.

"Longknife 1, this is Longknife 2. We seem to have a problem down here."

"Longknife 1 here. What seems to be the problem?"

A holograph of Kris and the Planetary Overlord appeared between Megan and the six officious Iteeche.

"First question. Has the surrender treaty been finalized yet?"

"No. I'm waiting for the results of your investigation. Do I have a rebellion on my hands or something else?"

"Longknife 2 here. Sorry, I can't answer that question. However, I've run into a different problem. It seems that high ranking Iteeche don't sully their hands talking to low-born workers. I'm being told that the water's been turned off, but the water's still flowing. I need to talk to the guys who do the job."

"For all the dark fates and their sharp fingers, Tom, do what this woman says. If I am still Overlord of this Planet tomorrow, I'll sack the lot of you and replace you with pond scum. Understood?"

"To hear is to obey," Tom sputtered.

"Longknife 2 out."

"Longknife 1 out."

Megan turned to the six. "Who do I talk to?"

Her question was punctuated by the boom of one huge explosion.

30

"What was that?" wasn't helpful, but it came from all six Iteeche.

"LT, do you have drones up?"

"Yes, ma'am," the mustang sounded off. A Gunny Sergeant held a thin battle board where both of them could see it. Megan joined them to make it a trio.

A building down the second hill where Lake 2 was filling, had blown up. It was toppling over, into the building next to it. Both were fully involved in flames. It looked like flaming wreckage was sparking fires in four other buildings.

"More sabotage?" Tom spat. "We must see that the perpetrator makes a Full and Most Sincere Apology to the Emperor."

Having stood at attention through one such mass apology in the Imperial Presence, Megan was not interested in doing it a second time. It had involved poisonous snakes and ax wielders taking heads off only after the most excruciating pain was about to end.

"May I strongly suggest that you get some fire fighters down there to keep it from spreading, assuming you have any water pressure to use?" Megan snapped.

The six very senior Iteeche just stared at each other. Clearly,

Megan had asked them a question that was way below their pay grade. Apparently, as in the capital, firefighting was something provided by each clan for their own buildings.

Shaking her head, Megan turned back to the reason she was here. "Who maintains the water pipes here?"

All the other Iteeche turned to the Baron for Public Services. He looked for all the world like a deer caught in the headlights of a hundred-thousand-ton starship.

One of the Marines trotted up to Megan.

"Ma'am, my sergeant isn't sure, but he thinks he's found a water manager. Our translation app isn't the best, but he told me to tell you."

"Thanks, Corporal," Megan said, and followed him back toward a group where a few Marines were talking to three Iteeche in work clothes while a dozen more Iteeche in worse work clothes waited nearby.

Megan joined the corporal jogging back to his sergeant. She noticed that the high ranking Iteeche chose to stay put. That was fine with her.

She made sure to block the view of these supervisors from the head high muckety-mucks with herself and the corporal's body.

"Can you tell me why the water has not been turned off?" she asked without preamble.

The three Iteeche kind of cringed inward and if a seven-foot tall Iteeche could manage it, make themselves small.

"We were asked to turn off the water at the next valve up for both the water aqueducts," one of them said. "However, in both cases, that valve has been frozen in place for years and we're afraid that if we break it loose, the entire valve could shatter in our hands and we'd have another flood. This time, one we caused."

Megan had learned that lower class Iteeche lived from hand-to-mouth. If they lost their job, they, and anyone dependent on them, starved to death.

"Can you turn it off at the next valve up stream?" Megan asked, doing her best to sound reasonable.

"His Lordship of the Water System said that we would be taking water away from too many buildings. It was better to just let the water flow."

"He didn't suggest you risk breaking the frozen valve?" Megan asked.

"Oh, no. If he gave orders that destroyed official property, he could be charged with treason."

Megan knew that humans did some stupid stuff. Still, the Iteeche had to have us beat hands down.

Smoke was drifting their way. It was acrid and caused both Humans and Iteeche to cough.

"LT, Longknife 2 here. This smoke stinks. Does this tell you anything about the fire?"

"Yes, ma'am. It's chemical in nature. If I may venture a wild ass guess, I think someone stored flammable chemicals too close to a transformer. The water shorted it out and we've got ourselves a fire that floats on water."

"I was afraid you'd say that. Keep me informed. Has the engineering task group showed up, yet?"

"Not in sight, ma'am."

"Thanks."

Before Megan could ask, Lily replied, "They are down the beanstalk and should be here in ten minutes.

"Do you know anywhere we can get some foaming fire suppressant, Lily?"

"Are you giving me permission to do a full search on what serves as the Balan information net?"

"Log the request," Megan said, "then do it." She glanced back at the six top managers. Clearly they were no smarter than they'd been a few minutes ago.

"Longknife 2 to Longknife 1."

"Yes, Meg."

"We had another explosion here. Our best call on it is that water shorted out a building's power and that exploded some chemicals stored way too close to something explosive. At least, that's what we got from examining the smoke. What we do know is that we have a fire that floats on water. If we don't put it out, we could have everything the water touches go up in flames, and God only knows what else these buildings have in their basements."

"What are you after this time, Meg?" Kris asked.

"Enough foaming agent to cover a couple of blocks of flooded streets. You know how the fire departments run in the Empire. I can't get anyone to respond to these fires. More than likely, if I did, I'd get water pumpers that have no water to pump."

"Can't get there from here, huh?"

"Exactly, ma'am."

"Admiral Tong, General Compeel, do either of you have access to foam firefighting equipment?" Kris asked.

The holographs in front of Megan shook their heads.

"If we have a fire, we open the space to vacuum. That kills it," Tong said.

"We blow things up," the general said. "We don't put out the fires."

That was logical.

"Sorry, Meg, but this hot potato stays in your lap."

"Longknife 2 out."

"Longknife 1 out."

Megan was getting a sick feeling in the pit of her stomach that there was no way to get anywhere from here. She'd seen how General Bruce used Smart Metal™ to smother apartment fires when the embassy was under rocket attack. That wasn't going to happen here.

First, she didn't have nearly enough Smart Metal™ to smother something this big. Worse, there was no way she could be sure the buildings had been evacuated. If she locked these burning apartment buildings under a dome of Smart Metal™ she ran the serious risk of killing a whole lot of Iteeche.

Megan needed a new firefighting plan, but first, she needed to turn off the water. She turned her back on the lowly supervisors and quickly strode back to their lordships. She stopped well short of them.

"I am about to use my authority to order the pipe supervisors to turn off the water well up the way from here. It seems that the next valves up from these breaks are all broken."

The Baron for Services actually cringed. "I had their replacement in my budget for the last ten years, but the money was never there," he whined to the governor and mayor.

"We will talk about this later," the Lord of Planetary Security bit out, eyeing the baron as he might a bug.

"But if she closes down those aqueducts, a quarter of the capital will be without water. I will miss a mandatory goal for the year. I could be sacked."

Oh, now I know where this is coming from.

"It's not my fault. It's the budget for maintenance. It's always cut."

"Be silent," the security lord snapped, then turned to Megan. "You have the authority to do whatever you think is best. Do it. You need not refer any matter to us."

Well, that covered his ass ... and left mine out in the wind.

"Thank you, Your Lordship. Now, if you will excuse me," Megan said, turned on the s of her feet and shouted, "Turn off the flow of water! Now!"

Two naked runners were dispatched to carry the message to Iteeche, who apparently, had been standing by for an order.

"Lily, have you found any foaming agent?"

"No, Megan. Either I have the wrong word for it, or they don't have any."

"That would be hard to believe," Megan muttered, not really finding it all that hard to believe. "Lily, can you get me some pumpers that can suck the water that is already out in a lake and then throw a fine mist or spray to cool down the fire?"

"I do have a design for two firefighting machines. I can combine what you need from both of them into one fire engine."

"Good. Skipper," she called.

The commander of the Royal US Marine company trotted toward her.

Megan didn't wait for him to arrive. "Captain, if you have anyone in your company who knows anything about firefighting or ever wanted to fight fires, now is their time."

"I have a corporal whose father was a fireman. Is that close enough?"

"It will have to do," Megan said. "Lily, turn as many of the Iteeche armored gun trucks into fire engines and get them moving. Arrange for a single control station to work everything."

"Doing it," Lily said, and several Iteeche found themselves standing on the outside of the gun trucks as they transformed into something . . . red.

The rig now had only four wheels. Out the back was a boom with a hose, ready to plop its end down into a pond and draw water. The other end had another boom. At the end of that boom was a nozzle that would swivel as the fireman aimed it.

The first of these rigs began to roll toward the fire. A Marine raced to meet it and hopped aboard as it went by him. He slung his rifle and settled into a seat surrounded by knobs, buttons, sensor readouts, and a whole lot of stuff Megan could only guess at.

The Marine shouted a cowboy cry, as if he was breaking a bronco. Behind him, the water pipe sought Lake 1, and began to suck water. Ahead of him, the forward boom aimed toward the fire below. A fine mist issued from it and began to fall on the fire.

It hissed as it fell onto the flames and steam rose from the burning chemicals.

Maybe we can cool down some of these chemicals.

The mist turned into a thin sprinkle. The amount of steam coming off the fire slowed. In a moment, the Marine took it back to a mist.

"We need more of these if we're going to do anything about that fire," the Marine shouted to no one in particular.

Three more Iteeche gun trucks turned into similar engines. Three Marines climbed aboard them and, following the lead and with advice from the first Marine firefighter, they began to lay more mist on the flames.

Steam rose from the flames in a boiling mist. A pungent odor left anyone who had to breathe it choking.

"Lily, give me an overhead view and pass it along to your mom."

A holograph again appeared in the air in front of Megan. It showed panicked refugees fleeing every building in the immediate area. Many were struggling to breathe as they ran.

Not a few fell and were trampled underfoot.

The situation was bad and only getting worse. The one bright spot, water was no longer gushing from the bomb crater in the street.

A column of engineers rolled up. A major dismounted. "How can I help you, Commander?" he asked.

"If you know anyone who knows how to fight a fire by cooling mist, or has a better idea on how to put out a floating fire without foam, I'd appreciate the help."

The major spoke to his commlink and a squad worth of Marine engineers dismounted and examined the situation. More of Lily's unique fire engines transformed, and one by one, these engineers drove them down the hill. A few started draining Lake 2 to fight its own fire. Others continued draining Lake 1.

Engineers set to work draining the explosive site, sending more water gushing down into Lake 1.

Megan surveyed what she'd gotten done in the last ten minutes and liked it. Smoke and steam still rose from Lake 2. It spread out in a huge polluting cloud, making life miserable for everyone downwind.

"My Lords," Megan said, addressing all six Iteeche. "Do you think it would be a good idea to have people under that smoke evacuate their homes and businesses? Those fumes cannot be good for your people to breathe."

They looked at each other as if they had never heard anything so preposterous. "It is their fate to live where they live. Maybe their luck has run out, but they will live or die as is their destiny."

In all Megan's life, she had never heard anything so preposterous.

No. No, she did remember something like that mindset. The survivors of the Earth survey ship, the Santa Maria, had expressed similar thoughts about the deaths of their colleagues and friends.

"Their number just came up."

"Their luck ran out."

These hard-working survivors, struggling to make a niche for themselves in a world that offered so little had lived on the edge of death every day. They had to develop a fatalistic attitude because they had so little control over whether they lived or died.

So, why did these clan lordlings take the same attitude toward their own kind? Was it because this fire was burning on the land of a clan that wasn't represented among the six?

A sickening thought stomped into Megan's consciousness. It was an unusual, but not unheard of, practice by the Iteeche in a war to gas an entire planet and then take it over for the victorious clans to repopulate with their people. Where these people fleeing from the apartments around her from a clan that was on the outs with someone in power? If these people died, would another clan higher in the pecking order step in? Would they choose more younglings from their mating ponds and fill up the niche left by the vanished population?

Megan knew she didn't have enough information to drop this bomb on Kris. Still, she'd have to keep her thumb on the pulse of developments. If a few more actions authenticated her gut instinct, Kris would definitely want to hear about this.

Pulling herself out of such thoughts, Megan joined the engineering major examining the hole in the ground. The LT joined them.

"Here's the take I have from the tiny flitters I've got up the pipes since they are starting to drain," the LT said.

The three of them studied the video take coming in.

"That's the end of the damage," the major said. "I can seal that with Smart Metal. I'm going to have the devil's own time repairing the break, though. See, all around the hole the bomb made, the ground has washed away. I need gravel and dirt to fill in the hole and pack it down hard before I put in new pipes."

"No way to bridge it?" Megan asked. She knew it was a dumb

question, but since she wasn't the engineer present, she figured dumb questions were her forte.

The engineer frowned into the muddy water of the hole, apparently giving serious consideration to Megan's dumb question. "I could suspend a pipe across the space using a suspension bridge arrangement. However, I'd need a solid foundation for the towers, and right now I can't see how I could support four towers. Maybe eight towers, considering our mad bomber hit us at the intersection of two aqueducts. I have no idea what the soil is like below this soup, or how far I'd have to drive piles to reach something solid. Throw in the question of where I'd get pile drivers, and you'd be setting an impossible mission for me."

Megan called the three Iteeche supervisors over to them and posed the next question to them. "Where do we get a hundred cubic meters of gravel to fill in this hole?"

The three stared at each other and said not a word.

Megan chose to walk over to the Iteeche lordlings rather than shout a question at them or call them over to her. Tact didn't cost her that much time.

"Wise Choosers," she said, hoping that qualified as "Gentlemen." "How can we get gravel and gravel-moving equipment here?"

Their eyes looked about as blank as the supervisors. Clearly, her question was above one set of pay grades and below the other.

Megan was getting seriously pissed with this Imperial hierarchical society that not only seemed to limit who knew what, but also who knew what anyone else knew.

Oh, and no one had a commlink, so you couldn't just get on the net and talk to them. Teen Meg had hated being at the end of a commlink when her mom was nagging her about this or that. Now that she knew what it was like to live without that commlink, she was becoming more and more grateful.

She strode quickly back to the Iteeche supervisors. None of them had any idea how construction was handled. What they maintained was there when they got the job.

"I don't remember seeing any construction down here in the capital. They sing songs about all the work being done on Planet 3 and the asteroids, but I've never seen any dirt being moved or any buildings going up," one supervisor admitted. The others nodded agreement.

Megan walked away from all three groups to find herself a place where she might talk to Kris in private.

"Longknife 2 here to Longknife 1."

"What's up?"

"Not a lot. Can I talk to you in private?"

"Give me a second." As Kris walked, she said, "I've got some very antsy high-level people up here that can't wait for us to sign this surrender so they can get things going."

"That's why I'm calling. Admiral, is there any chance we can toss them back and go conquer another planet?"

"That bad?"

Megan filled Kris in on what she'd discovered. She ended with, "I'd need to look at their books, but from where I'm standing, maintenance has been shorted for years. Nothing has been built in the capital in anybody's memory. No one knows if there is any gravel available to fill in the crater we have here. None of the maintenance people know where we can locate big construction equipment to fill in that hole. These Iteeche don't know much more than what their pay grade requires them to know. Nothing above it. Not even what's below it. I don't know how many layers of management I've got between the mayor and his barons and the guys actually doing the work so I can't find out how to get there from here."

"I'll have our imagery hunt you up a sand or gravel pit," Kris said, going immediately into problem-solving mode.

That was fine for Megan. She didn't want to cry on any shoulder that was nearby. Now then, a certain redhead back at the capital had a great shoulder to cry on.

"You show me where the gravel is, and I'll have Lily knock us together the dump trucks we need as well as other construction equipment. I may need more Smart Metal, ma'am."

"I'll have Admiral Tong send you an engineering battalion from the invasion force as well as a battalion of Marines in Smart Metal gun trucks you can mess around with."

"Thank you, ma'am. We are starting to make progress. We've turned off the water upstream on the two water lines. As soon as we can identify how far back we have to go from the explosion to build a cofferdam, we'll do that and get the water back on."

"Very good, Commander. Keep up the good work."

For about the next five minutes, Megan did her best to keep Kris happy and keep up the good work.

Unfortunately, a building on the opposite side of Lake 2 became involved in the fire despite their best efforts to cool the flames. More gun trucks were switched over to pumpers with remotely controlled nozzles. Sometimes the water played over the building in a stream as hard as concrete, pouring water through a window or other break that left the fire open to assault. Other times, they sprinkled or misted what they could to cool the buildings next over to try to limit the spread.

The major in charge of the engineers fighting the fires reported they hoped to bring all the fires under control in half an hour, an hour at worst.

The more they drained the lake to fight the fires, the less surface the fire had to float on. Or maybe it was burning away all its fuel. Still, they were making progress.

Kris sent Megan a gravel pit twenty klicks away, but usable. "Although there may be someone there in a hurry to demand payment. I suggest you ask the mayor to accompany the first team you send there. Arrangements may be needed for payment before you can extract any gravel."

"You're kidding me," Megan answered.

"Meg, if the Navy wanted gravel from a pit on Wardhaven, we'd have to pay for it. Most definitely, we'd have to pay for it if my Grampa Alex owned it. Avarice seems to be a trans-species norm."

"Aye, aye, ma'am. I'll talk to the mayor."

"Longknife 1 out."

Megan began the walk back to where they'd set up an HQ. A gun truck had been sacrificed to create a pavilion with comfortable stools for the Iteeche lords and uncomfortable chairs for the humans.

Megan did not want anyone hanging around headquarters. She needed work done.

She was not yet to the shady entrance when there was a sudden reduction in the amount of noise around her. She glanced around. Most of the gun trucks had cables leading off them to power the hand tools the invading troops were using.

Longer cables powered the tools Balan's workers were using. Suddenly, they were looking at their tools. Nothing worked.

"Megan, the local power net has gone down in this area."

"Thank you, Lily. For how far?"

"We have drones out searching. It is hard to tell. Most traffic at intersections is directed by Iteeche traffic police. However, people are streaming out of buildings. Those without windows can hardly see in the dark."

"Keep me appraised."

A few moments later, Megan was about to enter her HQ when a flash of light occurred, immediately followed by the sounds of an explosion. A pressure wave a second later knocked Meg down and almost blew her ear drums out.

Megan didn't need to be told. Her problems had just gotten a lot bigger.

31

"Get me imagery, Lily," Megan demanded.

A second later, a heliograph of an aerial photograph of the area appeared in front of Megan. Smoke billowed from a skyscraper a half dozen blocks away. She turned in that direction as dark black smoke began to rise in the air.

Something really nasty just blew.

"Longknife 1 to Longknife 2. What's going on down there?"

"We've got a fire in the area that lost its power about five or ten minutes ago. I've cut off the water to that area so I can seal the breach. Pardon me, Admiral, but I'm going to need a whole lot more Smart Metal that I can turn into firefighting equipment. Can Admirals Tong and Kitano rustle up some Iteeche who might have firefighting skills? This situation is rapidly getting out of hand."

"Do you know what just exploded?"

"No, ma'am, but I'm getting suspicious that the Iteeche Empire not only doesn't have any building codes to speak of, but also any hazardous material laws. I'm pretty sure the first fire was caused by improper storage of hazmat. I'm willing to bet my tiny pension that this next one is also stowage of something that needed electrical power without a backup power supply. Why don't you ask the Planetary Overlord while I speak to the governor and the mayor?"

"It's a deal. The admirals are launching a call for volunteers. We're holding the next ferry for our gear. We'll get a small invasion fleet flowing in your direction."

"Thank you, Admiral."

"And Commander Longknife, I'm making you On-Scene Commander. You pulled my sorry ass from under a pile of rocks. There is nobody better qualified for this. Understood?"

"Yes, ma'am," Megan said. She didn't add on a reminder to Kris that the Santa Maria side of the family wasn't part of the Longknife legend. Her people did not pull elephants out of hats like the Wardhaven side of the family did.

With a shrug, Megan set about her business. After hanging around Kris, maybe enough of the legend had rubbed off on her that she could pull a cow out of a hat.

An Iteeche colonel rolled in at the head of a brigade. He headed straight for the headquarters, or maybe Meg. She was still standing in the shade of the awning above the headquarters' door.

"Commander Longknife, I was told to report to you for assignment," the colonel said. He held his voice steady, giving nothing away concerning his attitude to his orders.

Megan doubted the Iteeche colonel was very happy reporting to a Human commander for his orders. Still, she'd saluted him first, and let him return a much sloppier honor.

"Thank you, Colonel, we're desperate for any help we can get. All of our troubles stem from too much water in the wrong place and not enough in the right place. If you would, please, join the Human major of engineers who has been working on closing off the water. He needs magic metal to close the pipes as close to the break as possible. Then we'll need to address why the power went down. If you have any spare men and magic metal left, we'd appreciate it if you could start fighting the fire over there. That will involve drawing water from outside the area where we turned it off."

"You seem to have quite a few problems, Commander," the colonel said.

"And more keep coming." Megan glanced off to where the billowing black smoke was still rising high in the sky.

She added, "A couple of minutes ago, we didn't have that particular problem."

"Should I hold some reserves to address the next problem?" the colonel asked.

"I'd love it if you could, but I would strongly suggest that you put everything you have on the line. I'm told a major force is flowing our way on the next two ferries."

"A very good idea," the colonel said. He saluted and returned to his convoy. Megan had to hurry to respond to his honor, he was so quick to take his leave.

With all her resources committed to at least one of her many problems, Megan took a moment before she returned to the Iteeche lordlings of the capital.

"Lily, could you get me that mustang who was checking for forensic evidence?"

"Yes, Commander," came a moment later.

"Lieutenant, we seem to have two buildings that spontaneously combusted. You mentioned that chemicals were involved in the first one. Have you examined the smoke from the second?"

"Yes, Commander, we ran several drones through it to get air samples of what was burning. We lost one drone that we took in too low, but the ones we got back show evidence of a powder that needed to be refrigerated. I'm guessing that it was already too warm before it lost cooling."

"So that's what happened," Megan said.

"That's what started things happening, ma'am. There's a lot of crap in that smoke. I won't bore you with the long list I've got. Suffice it to say, the explosion started a fire that spread quickly to several other things that should not have been stowed anywhere close to each other. Ma'am, I'm looking at so many stupid mistakes I don't know where to start. On any Human planet, we'd have laws against letting these things be in the same building."

"No hazmat rules?" Megan asked.

"From where I'm standing, I see no evidence of either building codes or hazmat control, Commander."

"Thanks for your opinion. Now I've got to go beard the lion in my HQ."

"I'd kick their asses halfway back to the Imperial Capital if I could, Commander."

"Yes, Lieutenant, I'd enjoy doing it if it was only a private that did the stupid. I've got to talk to the governor of the capital region and the mayor of this town."

"Better thee than me," the Marine officer said.

"Thanks for those words of encouragement."

Choosing between a frown and a scowl, Megan chose the frown. Her face frozen Navy hard, she turned to enter her HQ. As she entered, her guards snapped to attention. Marines at their terminals stayed in their seats but sat up a bit straighter.

The Iteeche lordlings didn't even stop their conversation to take notice of her. Megan sighed; her bad day was about to get worse.

32

Lieutenant Commander Megan Longknife, *aide de camp* to Grand Admiral, Her Royal Highness Kris Longknife, strode up and down the aisle of her command center, ignoring the Iteeche lordlings as they ignored her.

A check of the screens showed no major changes. The two fires around Lake 2 were still spreading. Now, more apartment buildings were involved. Someone had organized slides. As Iteeche from the higher stories found themselves trapped, the slide gave them a way out. It was frightening to go into. Even as Megan watched, more Smart Metal™ was added to them so that the top was enclosed fully for safety.

The number of Iteeche appearing at the bottom increased after that.

"Commander," the sergeant working the station said, "there are Iteeche soldiers searching the buildings, hunting for kids, elderly, and anyone trapped. We've created fire retardant coats and boots, breathers, helmets, and face masks. They're as protected as any firefighter in Human space."

"Very good. No Humans in the buildings?"

"The major fighting those fires strongly suggested that the folks in those buildings would prefer to see four legs rather than two."

"Probably a good call."

The next station was centered on the new fire. "Commander, the colonel turned his engineering battalion over to the folks working at the explosion," a staff sergeant reported. "He took his two leg infantry battalions over to fight this fire. We detached two sergeants over to him. They're turning any Smart Metal he has into what he needs. He appreciates the help."

"Maybe the Iteeche will finally decide they need more people who can turn magic metal from a block of nothing into a fire hose and pumper," Megan muttered.

She'd dodged her next meeting for as long as she could. She turned to where the five lordlings huddled together ignoring everything going on around them as beneath their dignity.

Careful to keep her feelings of helplessness and rage under control, Megan strode quickly for the exit. Outside, she glanced around and then told Lily.

"Get Kris."

"Longknife 1 here. What's up Longknife 2?"

"Are you in a private place where we can have a talk that could involve me screaming nasty things about the procedures and policies of the Iteeche clans, ma'am?"

"Wait one," Kris said.

"Pardon me, a call of nature cannot be ignored," Kris told others.

Less than a minute later, Kris said, "How bad is it?"

"Unbelievable."

33

"As a quick executive summary," Megan said, beginning her report to Kris, "the Iteeche lords have no idea what a hazardous material is and none of them know of any Imperial policy for the caring, handling, or storage of the stuff. It's a clan prerogative to stow anything anywhere and no one likely knows what is in any of these buildings."

"Good Lord," Kris said. "Don't they have any idea of the risk they are taking?"

"The answer I got was if an Iteeche dies, it was just their fate. That seems to be the answer to all their unsafe conditions. 'Oh, the building fell down. It was just their fate to die today'."

"I wonder if they take the same attitude toward their palaces," Kris muttered.

"You do recall the palace that blew sky high when a bomb you had aimed at it hit their magazine?"

"Yeah, I was wondering what a magazine full of explosives was doing in a palace. I guess I know now. They dump stuff anyplace they can find the vacant space."

"Kris, they can't be this stupid," Megan did her best not to scream at her boss and cousin.

"As we have said all along, they have a population problem. If a mass of Iteeche die, that gives those in power more opportunity for patronage. 'Oh, we had a thousand people die. Good, now I can give my loyal followers a chance to be Choosers,' or something like that."

"They're crazy," Megan cried.

"They are *alien*," Kris said, softly correcting her *aide de camp*. They are alien and they have had at least five thousand years to perfect a social structure that bind all of them to their alien ways."

"Yes, Admiral," Megan said, calming herself.

"The first time I heard someone say there is a right way, a wrong way, and the Navy way, I thought it was stupid. I've been Navy long enough to accept that there are just rules that govern the way a large body of people operates. Now we know of the Iteeche way," Kris said with a shrug. "You don't change five thousand years of social norms in an afternoon."

Kris paused, then went on. "Enough of this. What do you need to concentrate on next?"

"Ending the flow of water, then getting the water pressure up where we need it to fight fires. The latest explosion needs water. As soon as we can put a cap on the aqueduct, we can turn the water back on."

"Then that, I would say, are your orders."

"Aye, aye, Admiral."

"Longknife 1 off."

"Longknife 2 off."

Lieutenant Commander Megan Longknife squared her shoulders and turned her back on her own HQ with its pack of unhelpful Iteeche clan lordlings. She marched for the big hole in the ground made by the first explosion.

Megan's first stop was with the forensics team.

"Lieutenant, do you have anything new for me?"

The LT looked up from where she was overseeing the processing of more explosive test strips. A staff sergeant was eyeing one of those samples through a microscope.

"We may have found chunks of the bomb embedded in the surrounding buildings. It's hard to tell because there are a lot of chunks of concrete, steel rebar and road along with the few tiny bits of metal we found."

"Any better chance you can tell me where that bomb came from?" Megan asked.

"Maybe. We've run a batch of explosive samples up the beanstalk for the *P. Royal*'s mass spectrometer to analyze. It's the best one within several hundred light years, so it may be able to detect a surprise or two, but it's too soon to have an answer."

"Keep at it. We need to know if this job was home grown or if it can be led to someone that just arrived."

"Yes, Commander, all of us figured that one out. We'll have something for you as soon as we can, but not now."

"So, buzz off and quit joggling your elbow, Longknife, huh?"

"I couldn't have put it better myself," the LT said, while holding back a grin.

"Thanks. Let me know when you're sure. It will go straight from my ears to the admiral's."

"I figured as much. No review of my work, just turn it into an action item. No pressure here."

"Of course not. You're working for a Longknife," Megan said, not even trying to hide her grin.

"I'll be very careful to get it right the first time."

"I'll see you when you're ready," Megan said and marched off to micromanage another part of this mess.

At the hole, water was down to a dribble. However, Megan didn't need some expert in measurements to know that the hole was a whole lot bigger than it had been when she first saw it.

It would take a lot of gravel to fill in all that water-logged space.

Until then, there was no way to repair the shattered aqueduct, aside from capping the pipe.

An Iteeche colonel of engineers was the senior officer present, and Megan reported to him. He showed no interest when she presented herself as a lieutenant commander. That attitude took a radical change when she finished with Longknife, then added, "I'm the *aide de camp* to the Grand Admiral."

"What can I do for you?" was much less arrogant than the first look she got.

"How is the work going at capping the shattered pipes? We need to get water back up to fight the fires." Megan ran a glance around the limited horizon. In addition to the three fires she expected to see, two more had sprouted.

Apparently, they had sparked off without a boom to gain everyone's attention.

"If we aren't careful, we're going to burn out this end of town," Megan said.

"Yes," the Iteeche colonel agreed. "Your Human engineers are handling the job of capping the aqueducts. They have the best magic metal spinners."

"Thank you, Colonel. Do you mind if I talk to them?"

"No, feel free to. I am using most of my men to fight the fires. Your major loaned me two spinners to help us convert gun trucks to fire engines and lots of hose."

"Lily, could I see an aerial view of this area?"

A holograph appeared in the air in front of Megan and the Iteeche colonel. He looked surprised by the sudden image in the air before him, but he made no superstitious sign against unknown evil.

"I have been told some of you Humans can do that."

"Yes, sir. Lily, zoom in close on the outskirts, where the outer white blends into black."

In a moment, it was clear that the black blur was Iteeche fleeing on foot from the area that was without power and water. The mob looked dangerous as it hastened away. That was a situation where children got lost and people got trampled.

"Colonel, if I helped you convert some of your gun trucks into buses, you could you help those people get away."

"I would hate to be without my gun trucks if we come under attack."

"Yes, Colonel, but it seems much more likely that hundreds or thousands of Iteeche may die if that mob panics and stampedes. We have had no evidence of hostilities from the locals."

The Iteeche officer pointed all four of his eyes at the big hole in the ground.

"If you wish," Megan said, "I can call the Grand Admiral and get you an order to spin out the buses to pull people away."

Left unsaid was that the order would cover his ass.

"I believe that I can give that order, Longknife."

"I can begin spinning out the buses," Megan said.

"You?"

"Yes."

All four eyebrows went up, "Please do."

In a moment, most of the gun trucks began to morph into buses. Those made from gun trucks with anti-matter reactors became double-decker buses with two articulated cars trailing behind the powered bus. Other buses were also double-deckers, but with only one car attached to the first. These operated on batteries that were quickly charged from the bigger buses.

"We can provide the driver of each bus with a screen that shows him the safest way to get around the damaged area so he can begin to pick up passengers. One bus to a street."

"How will the driver know where to go?"

"Colonel, if you don't mind, my computer Lily will coordinate this rescue."

"A computer can do this?"

"My computer will do this in her spare time," Megan said.

"I have heard of such things, but never expected to see such a mythical marvel."

"I am not a myth," Lily said from Megan's neck. "I will have no problem helping your drivers be where the need is greatest."

"Thank you, I think."

"You are welcome, I think," Lily said, with a laughing lilt to her voice. "Now, if you could have your drivers organize their gun trucks into a single file line with at least a hundred meters between each one, we can begin."

"Thank you, Colonel, I'll leave Lily to work with you."

"How?"

"Lily, you want to set aside a net channel for you and the colonel so he can talk to you?"

"Can you dial your commlink to channel 1313?" Lily asked.

A radio tech quickly appeared at his colonel's elbow, unloaded his pack radios, and adjusted the net status. He handed his headphones to the colonel who, of course, blew in the mic, then said, "Testing, one two."

"I read you fine," came from his headphones.

Megan started walking for the hole even as the colonel dispatched runners to carry his orders to the mounted troops to reorganize their rigs. She shook her head. He had a radio; yet he sent runners to carry his orders to his subordinates.

Then she rethought herself. That radio looked mighty heavy. Maybe they didn't want to have too many of those lugged around the battlefield. Or maybe it was the Iteeche Way to transmit information and orders by word of mouth. The saints only know what kind of job these poor runners could get if they lost this work.

She found the Human major of engineers at the edge of the big hole in the ground. He had his head in his battle board.

"How's it going?" Megan asked.

The poor man jumped. "Sorry, ma'am, I was just so intent on what's going on down there I didn't notice you."

"Major, I suspect we could have driven a motorized brigade past you and you wouldn't have noticed it."

"Likely," he said, his eyes going back to the visual on his board.

Megan eyed what held the major's attention so strongly. It meant nothing to her.

He, however, began to mutter an explanation to her.

"We've scanned the shattered aqueduct," he said. "We think we know where it is sound, although the amount of shock going up the pipe has me more worried than I want to be."

"Yes?" Megan said.

"I know you want this pipe working again, at least as far as this. You've got that fire."

"I have three fires out in that direction," Megan pointed out.

The major glanced up, then slowly turned around, eyeing all the smoke billowing in the distance from burning buildings.

"Good lord. Where'd all these fires come from?"

"Apparently," Megan said, "The Iteeche Empire has no rules controlling the storage and use of hazardous material."

"You're kidding me," the major sighed, not sounding at all like one who doubted what he'd just been told.

"Nope. I just discovered this little lack on the part of the Empire. No one can tell the clans what to store or where to store it. Worse, what to store next to it."

The major just shook his head. "I guess I should be glad that we're here to help."

"Unless the reason we're here is why we have this mess."

"Yeah. Okay, moving right along. We've been drilling holes in the concrete walls of the aqueduct to give our cofferdam anchors to the wall. We're putting in three rows a half meter apart. The cofferdam will be convex, with the front end strong, but flexible, so that it can be compressed by the pressure of the water. The back couple of centimeters will be stronger, but brittle, more to hold the pressure coming back on it."

"When will you be ready for us to turn the water back on?" Megan said, asking the critical question.

"Give me five more minutes to finish drilling the holes," the major said. "I'm ready to strip metal off of several of those Iteeche engineering vehicles and convert it to a steel alloy."

"What kind of alloy do you want?" Lily asked from Megan's neck.

"Actually, I want two alloys. The forward part of the plug needs to be strong, but compressible. That's the reason for the convex form.

Let the water expend most of its force on the nose of the steel bulge without breaking the plug loose. The back also needs to be convex, but harder. It can even be brittle. I want it to hold on tight when the water forces the front back on it."

"I've got just what you want," Lily said. "High tensile steel with a bit of manganese, a dash of nickel, and just a drop of molybdenum. Do you want any aluminum in the mix to lighten it?"

"I need strong and unmoving," the major said. "Weight is not a problem."

"Then I'll keep it heavy," Lily said. The nearest engineering vehicle was a track-laying tank with a massive mortar for a weapon and a bulldozer blade at the ready. As Megan watched, the entire fifty-ton monster began to melt. Its Human driver hurriedly scampered out of the rig as it began to shrink around her.

The driver of the next rig didn't wait. He piled out of his vehicle before it began to melt out from under him.

The Smart Metal™ dissolved into a puddle of roiling liquid that changed color as the atoms shifted from one molecule to another. Soon, a small snake began to wiggle its way from the pool toward the large hole in the ground. It was thin, but long and getting longer, as it stretched from the first engineering vehicle to the shattered end of the gaping water pipe. From there, it slid down into the hole, but once inside, crawled along the top of the huge shattered aqueduct.

The line thickened up, going from a few millimeters to a centimeter, then three, six, nine, twelve, and finally fifteen centimeters in diameter. It seemed to pulse as Smart Metal™ coursed through it toward the hole. The second rig threw off tendrils that quickly thickened up until it joined into the conduit coming off the first line.

Even as the last holes were drilled into the walls of the reinforced steel and concrete aqueduct, the first row was filling, forming a perfect half-sphere plug, bulging toward the flow of water. It waited there to break that torrent's own force and power when it came to rage against the waiting steel.

Megan knew that Lily was almost maxed out. The feeling that the entity who shared her brain was gone often happened when her computer was almost at maximum utilization.

That was verified when Lily said, in a most computer-like voice, "The plug is in place."

"Let's get started on the next hole we have to stopper," the major said.

Megan turned toward the gaping aqueduct behind her. She heard drilling machines trundling their way out of the blocked tunnel. They'd likely need a bridge to cross from there to the new hole. At least water was not flowing anymore from that raged maw.

As Megan took her first step toward the new challenge, the building in front of her blew out with a massive explosion.

34

Megan was right; Lily was almost maxed out. She was busy directing buses to where they were needed, finishing up the work on the plug, and melting down more rigs for Smart Metal™ she could use for the next plug. It took her a fraction of a second to realize the flash of light meant an explosion.

Megan was in space armor. Her experience on Zargoth had taught her the lesson to never go dirtside unprepared. That saved her life.

Her facemask was open. Lily immediately closed it from all sides. She just barely managed to get it in place before a steel splinter nearly slammed into Megan's eye. As it was, Meg found herself staring at a very sharp and long splinter from a metal bolt, only a few millimeters short of her eyeball.

It took her a while to notice that threat to her mortality. The flash from the explosive dazzled her eyes, blinding her. The destructive blast from the explosion picked her up and hurled her against the building behind her.

When Megan got her senses back, she found herself embedded in the building's outer wall, a meter off the deck.

She needed help from others to pry herself out of the bricks and help her to the deck. Her suit's armor had super-hardened under the pressure of the blast. The impact on the wall was spread all over her body; the armor kept her shoulders, hips, and back from bending as they sustained percussive hits.

She found herself laid out on a stretcher as her vision slowly came back. When it did, she was staring at the jagged edge of the metal splinter. Fortunately, it was encased in transparent Smart Metal. Megan grabbed hold of the rear of the splinter and slowly pulled it from her faceplate. The metal shard looked scary as all hell.

A moment later, the faceplate reabsorbed the hole and was good as new.

A medic was trying to figure out if Megan was just as good as new. "How many fingers am I holding up?" he asked.

"Just the right number, corpsman," Megan said, climbing off the stretcher and shoving the woman aside. "Now in exactly ten seconds, the Grand Admiral will want a report from me about what's holding us up. Get out of my way."

"I need an MP," both of them shouted.

"She doesn't," Megan snapped. "I do. Who's the senior MP in charge?"

"I am," a voice came on net. "Captain Wilson, ma'am."

"Have you got a cordon around this latest explosion?"

"Yes, ma'am. I also have overhead video take. There's an Iteeche beating feet. We are tracking him."

A moment later, Lily announced, "Call coming in."

"Longknife 1 here. How are you, Megan?"

"Surprisingly well, everything considered, Admiral. This new armor is quite effective."

"Two explosions in one day. That doesn't sound like a coincidence."

"It isn't, ma'am. We've got a suspect under observation and are moving to cut him off."

"So, I'm interrupting you."

"As much as I hate to say it, yes, ma'am."

"Get back to me as soon as you have time, then, Commander."

"Aye, aye, ma'am."

"Longknife 1 off."

Megan hated to cut her cousin off, but she did have very pressing matters.

She turned back to the search. "Captain Wilson, get that running Iteeche. I want to talk to him. Then the Grand Admiral will want to interrogate what's left of him when I'm done."

"Understood."

"Lily, give me the video off of that drone."

A holograph appeared in front of Megan. She had to close one eye before it settled down. Maybe the corpsman had a point.

A red circle showed a single Iteeche moving quickly up one street, then cutting diagonally across a street, walking up a narrow alley, then hopping into one of those three-wheeled cars the Iteeche used.

It took off, speeding down the street before doing a two-wheeled turn onto another street.

Meanwhile, the drone came in for a perfect dive bomb attack. When the drone rose back up into the air, a splat on the top of the little rig wasn't bird droppings, but a tracker.

That three-wheeler would not vanish from this search.

Meanwhile, the high drone showed a small fleet of gun trucks racing to cut them off. About half were Human; the others were larger to accommodate Iteeche.

Whoever was in charge of this chase wanted to make sure it was no chase at all.

A dozen rigs got ahead of the target tricycle. They spread out to close down the three roads on either side of target. To the rear, gun trucks were speeding up the three roads on either side of the target's track.

Megan noticed how there were no small alleyways for the trike to dodge around in the part of town the chase now entered. At precisely the right moment, gun trucks slammed around two corners, and four gun trucks charged at the oncoming target, blocking all lanes.

The driver of the trike slammed on the brakes and did a hard U-turn, only to be confronted by more gun trucks charging from the rear. He went hard on the brakes again. Slowed, he hopped the curb and bounced over the grassy verge surrounding a luxury high-rise.

The Human rigs in the chase hit the curb and bounced right over it. The engines complained as wheels spun, throwing clods of grass behind them, as they raced after the much smaller rig.

The driver slammed the tricycle to a halt, meters from the side door of the high rise. Together, he and his passenger dashed for the building, confident of escaping inside and vanishing.

However, every option they could choose had an anticipated response.

Four Iteeche and four Humans deployed from the door only moments before the two fleeing Iteeche reached it. The Humans hit the Iteeche with sleepy darts. Other Iteeche grabbed the two and forced beak spreaders into their mouths. No way were they going to use a poison tooth to escape interrogation.

The Iteeche hog-tied these fellows, tossed them on two trollies, and rolled them toward the two idling Human gun trucks that quickly lengthened to add room for two restrained passengers.

The overhead zoomed in to let Megan, and likely Kris, get a good view as cables slipped out from the two truck beds to attach to the manacles holding the prisoners tight. A moment later, each disappeared behind a spreading cover over their rig. No doubt, that quickly became armored.

The two gun trucks with prisoners moved off slowly, allowing the other rigs involved in the chase to join up with them. That provided a very tight security cordon around the prisoners.

Two drones dropped low to give a very good look at the eight blocks around the column. If someone tried to break these two free, they'd have a fight on their hands.

It looked like no one was trying. The luck of those two Iteeche had run out.

Megan looked around. She spotted two Marines that looked nearly identical, grabbed for the closest one, and had to reach farther up to get a grip on his shoulder.

"Marine, you are about to become my seeing eye dog as well as my cane," Megan said.

"Sergeant, the commander wants me to be her walking stick," the Marine called.

"From the way she's wobbling, she needs two," the sergeant replied.

"She needs to be on a stretcher and evacuated," the corpsman shouted. "She's got a concussion that would fell an elephant."

"Corporal," the sergeant called, "take the other side of Commander Longknife and see that she doesn't fall down."

"You mean land too hard when she falls down," the corpsmen got in.

"Marine, you can tell a Longknife anything you want to, but it won't make a bit of difference," retorted Megan.

"Yes, Sergeant."

"Now you go take care of people who will listen to you."

"Yes, Sergeant."

Megan found herself with her arms on two strong shoulders that stayed with her as she stumbled toward up the street. She wanted to meet this bomber close, but not too close.

35

M egan watched with one eye closed as two rigs, gun trucks in front but police vans in their back half, rolled down the street. They did quick three-point turns to back up to her. The Human MPs opened the rear hatches. Iteeche MPs yanked the two restrained Iteeche from the back and dumped them at Megan's feet.

The MPs made no effort to ease their landing.

"Which one of you blew up that building? Blew up those aqueducts?" she demanded.

They said nothing. With their beaks wide open, it might have been hard for them to answer, but they didn't even gurgle.

"Lily, tell the forensic LT that I need her here with her explosives residue kit."

"She's on her way," Lily answered immediately.

The two Iteeche exchanged looks of sheer terror. The word must be getting around that if you talked to a Human that had a second voice coming from around their neck, you were in way over your head.

Two Marines arrived, four until Megan remembered to close one eye.

"Tell me which one of those has the most explosive residue on them. One drove the getaway car, the other blew the bomb that's giving me a hell of a headache."

The Marine sergeant swabbed them down, each getting a dozen pads.

Each wipe turned from white to pink. Some darker, some more pale.

The LT stood at Megan's side, frowning.

"Do you find something interesting here?"

"Yes, ma'am. The swabs turn pink when they find hints of explosive residue. If one of these guys was in a getaway car with the bomb maker, one should be lighter, the other darker."

"But?" Megan asked.

"Both look to be about as pink as the other. I'm going to withhold judgement until we get the field trials back. Maybe even until we run the lab tests back on the *Princess Royal*. This is way past intriguing."

"Provost Marshal," Megan said, turning to the senior Iteeche MP now present. "Can you tell me which clans these two are from?"

"No, Commander," the colonel replied. "They have no ID. Their clothes are of a common weave you can buy in any bazaar. The same for their boots. I'd love to know of their clan, Ma'am, but I have, excuse me, *we* Iteeche of the Empire, have no way to know who they are or where they come from."

Megan wanted to rile at him for not having a fingerprint database, but she wasn't sure Iteeche had distinctive fingerprints.

"Lily, do we have a doc who can take blood for DNA sequencing?"

"Commander, all the doctors are busy with the dying and badly wounded."

"What?"

"Ma'am, you got off easy," her computer told her.

Megan turned back to see the wreckage around the explosion. Then she jacked up her face plate to telescopic magnification.

The place was heartbreaking.

It was not so much what the explosion had hurled at them,

though Megan had almost been blinded by one flying shard. It was where the explosion had hurled *them*.

An Iteeche engineer had been thrown against one of their vehicles. He was bent over it, his legs at the wrong angle, his back wrong, too. His screams were cut off as quick-acting pain relief took effect.

One Iteeche Marine looked like he'd been hurled down the street, then rolled over and over again as his bleeding body traded energy, using his own flesh to slow him down.

In Lake 1, several bodies floated, some in one piece, others not. Iteeche and humans splashed through the shallows, trying to get the fire away from the injured as well as the dead. They were unable to tell the two apart yet.

Across the gaping hole, a half-dozen Marines slowly and carefully removed the body of a Marine. Her slight hips and shapely legs had been stopped by the wall below the window. The glass had not slowed down her upper body. Instead, her back was shoved through the window, and bent the wrong way.

Her armor had failed.

What the Marines were slowly picking out of the wreckage was little more than a rag enclosed in shattered armor. Even from where she stood, Megan could see tears streaming down a hardened old Gunny's cheeks.

Tears spilled down her own.

That said nothing of the lumps under this or that pile of wreckage that did not move.

The first explosion had done great damage to the city's life blood. The second had slaughtered those responding, those striving to help the people of the city get their homes, lives, and livelihood back.

In fury, Megan turned back to the two cringing in the street in front of her.

"Provost Marshall, could you please cut those clothes off of those criminals? Lieutenant, bag and tag their gear, then swab them down thoroughly. I don't want any chance that we won't have all the evidence to see that these two make their date with the snakes."

"Convict them?" came from behind Megan. She turned to see the five Iteeche lordlings strolling up behind her.

"They clearly are guilty," the Governor of the Capital District snapped. "Shoot them."

"Belay that order," Megan barked. "If either of those murderers dies before Admiral Kris Longknife can interrogate them, I swear I will have the five of you shot."

The five clan lordlings were clearly shocked to be treated that way. Before they could open their beaks, however, the Provost Marshall shut them down.

"This crime was committed against the officers and men of the Combined Fleet. Our Commanding Admiral has taken jurisdiction over this case. The Human Commander is correct. Our admiral will pass judgement when she has extracted as much information about this attack as she wishes."

Under the Provost Marshall's hard stare, the five civilians gave ground.

Another sergeant and a corporal arrived from the forensic unit. The Iteeche MPs began to shear the two prisoners of their clothes with little care and less concern. They both ended up with some long scratches across their skin.

No one offered them any medical care.

Megan found herself surveying where they stood. Her two prisoners lay in clear sight of way too many windows from the surrounding streets. It was a sniper's free fire zone.

"Lily, convert one of the gun trucks into a covering for us and our prisoners."

One of the gun truck/police vans began to melt and reform into a temporary hut.

"I don't mind getting out of the sun," the Provost Marshall said, "but why bring this foul bait into your nice air conditioning?"

"I don't care if their fingers and toes melt," Megan growled. "What I won't have is somebody from one of the surrounding buildings putting a bullet through their brains."

"Oh. Right. Good thought."

The LT and her sergeant finished swabbing down about every centimeter of the suspects' exposed skin.

"Commander, I'm going to run half of these test strips up the beanstalk and have them tested in the lab."

"Is there anything you're ready to share with me yet?" Megan asked.

"Questions, ma'am. Provost," the mustang officer said, acknowledging the senior Iteeche present. "We have two explosions. I think they were different, but I don't have proof of that yet. They could have been built in different locations, but I don't know that yet. We have two potential culprits, both of whom show much more evidence of explosive residue than one of them should. Could we have hit the jackpot and snared both bombers? I think that is too much to expect, but I'm not going to assume or reject any data until I have a full set of test results."

"Understood. Now, Lieutenant, you tend to your knitting, and I'll tend to mine."

"Happily, ma'am," and the LT strode off with a jaunty air.

"Lily, get me the Human engineering officer in charge."

The voice that came on net was not the same voice she'd been working with. "Lieutenant Colonel San Simon."

"Commander Longknife here. Are you fully involved in plugging the last water pipe?"

"Pretty much, ma'am."

"Do you have any spare assets?"

"May I ask what for?"

"I need a jail. I have two prisoners I don't want them going anywhere or getting killed. Can you modify a local Iteeche structure into a secure building?"

"Do you have Smart Metal we can work with?"

"Yes. Can you burrow my jail into a brick building without bringing it down?"

"There's another company about due. I'll see if we can give you a construction platoon."

A few minutes later, an eager first lieutenant and a less confident gunny sergeant reported to Megan. She explained what she wanted, and gave them Smart Metal™ to be used in reinforcing the Iteeche construction.

After ten minutes of surveying the inside and outside of the building, a diamond saw made short work of the first floor's exterior wall. A modified bulldozer moved the wall back as Smart Metal™ kept the entire front of the building from collapsing. The Smart Metal™ jail slid easily into the largest room of the building. The removed outer wall trundled back in place, and, for all anyone would care to see, there was nothing to indicate there were detainees inside.

Well, there was *something*. Down the street from the building modified for a jail, there was a thin balloon of metal.

If somebody wanted something to shoot at, they now had a target. Megan combed a company of Human combat Marines out of the security work they had been scattered to. They took up posts on the tallest buildings around. Micrometer wavelength radar was established at high points, ready to spot any incoming fire and backtrack to its point of origin.

Megan finally took the time to take some pain meds. Lily made her a more comfortable chair, then made sure she didn't fall asleep.

With half the pipes carrying water, some of the fires were brought under control. As night fell, the engineers worked under lamps, trying to figure out a way to bridge the gap from the blocked pipe to the empty one across from it.

Meanwhile, reports came in concerning looting in the empty buildings. The Governor and the mayor ordered Iteeche police and soldiers to move into the blackened streets. Apparently the Rules of Engagement were liberal; every few minutes, shots rang out.

Megan had never seen an Iteeche jail. Apparently, the concept was strange to the Provost Marshall. A drunk tank for sailors to sleep it off, yes. A brig for minor infractions, yes.

Strike an officer, and there was no need for incarceration. Spacing was the usual punishment. It was filmed, both what took place inside and outside the air lock. The civil lords over the fleet thought that solved any problem.

Megan wondered what Admiral Tong thought of that.

About midnight, the corpsmen allowed her to get some sleep.

Shortly after dawn, Kris ordered Megan to report to the *Princess Royal*. The work dirtside was done. The water flowed through all the pipes through a marvelously engineered repair. Communications and power were back online.

The only question left was who did it and why.

Two Longknifes wanted to know the answers to those questions very, very much.

36

Megan boarded an enlarged gun truck with her prisoners in the back, chained and separated by a wall. A full brigade accompanied the prisoners, two battalions of Iteeche and one of Humans.

There was no doubt in her mind that Kris would personally see these prisoners.

Apparently, however, Meg dozed off just after the drive began. She must have slept through the entire beanstalk ride up, because the next thing Megan knew, her vehicle was pulling to a stop at the brow of the *Princess Royal*.

Rubbing sleep from her eyes, and trying to ignore a pounding headache, she dismounted. Two squads of Human Marines from the *P. Royal* removed her prisoners and hurried them up the gangplank and into a brig just off the quarterdeck next to Admiral Longknife's day quarters.

Also waiting for Megan on the quarterdeck was the LT from the forensic team.

"You ready for this?" Megan asked her.

"I have the facts. Someone else will have to interpret them," the mustang LT said crisply. Apparently she got more sleep than Megan, or, being a former Gunny, knew how to sleep wherever and whenever.

Likely with her eyes open.

Kris was waiting for them at a conference table in her day quarters. Interestingly, only Admiral Tong represented the Iteeche. Jack sat at Kris's other elbow. This was to be a small, likely decisive, meeting.

"Tell me exactly what facts you have," Admiral Longknife demanded.

Megan turned to the LT. "This is your bailiwick."

"Admiral, we've examined two explosions. The one that destroyed the water pipes used sophisticated military plastic explosives. The second explosion used a common civilian compound, something like T-ammonal, a mixture of trinitrotoluene, or TNT if you prefer, ammonium nitrate, aluminum powder, and a bit of charcoal. It is less effective, but the objective was to blow a building apart, create blast, and launch destructive flying debris, which we all experienced," the Marine lieutenant said ruefully.

"Based on our spectral analysis, I can say that the second package of explosives was manufactured here on Balan. The first explosion, however, came from elsewhere. Like hundreds of light years from here."

"How can you know that?" Admiral Tong asked.

"Sir, we are all made of stardust," the Marine officer said.

When the Iteeche admiral merely stared at her, she continued.

"That is not just poetry, but also a fact. After the big bang, the first generation of stars were huge monsters that burned through their fuel fast, from hydrogen to helium, then larger elements up to iron before they went supernova and blasted their elements through space to seed the next generation of stars. Those of us who live in the same interstellar neighborhood are made of the same star dust from either one of those supernovas or a later one."

"I see," said the Iteeche admiral, though he sure didn't sound like he did.

"Each star burns the same, only differently. Each star's dust has a fingerprint. The main elements are the same. However, the ratio of different isotopes in the mix vary. When you take the mix of stable isotopes of the most common elements like carbon, oxygen, nitrogen, and iron and compare them, you find extremely slight, but measurable differences in their isotopic ratios. All the stars in the same cluster have this fingerprint, or marker, if you will."

The woman officer eyed the Iteeche admiral. He nodded and she continued.

"Based on our analysis of the explosives and the metal parts of the bomb that we found, the C-14 bomb is from someplace else. The other bomb is from here. With a bit of work, we could likely locate the sources for the minerals."

The Marine officer glanced down at her battle board, then swiped one page.

"We also have done a full spectrograph of their clothes. No surprise here, the fellow covered in residue from the C-14 bomb wore fibers and metal from the same other part of the galaxy. The other Iteeche, the one who handled the local bomb, wore clothes from Balan's neck of the galaxy. I imagine if we were to take tissue and bone samples, we'd find the same parallel, Admirals."

The lieutenant finished her report with a final, "I await your orders."

The room fell silent. Megan eyed Kris. She could almost hear the wheels spinning in her cousin's head. Meg leaned back, eager to see how the Great Longknife Legend worked its magic again.

37

Grand Admiral Kris Longknife, Commanding Admiral of the Combined Fleet and all ships presently in the process of capturing the Balan system, frowned. She knew of the stardust story. She had just never expected it to have bearing on a crime she wanted solved.

Kris took a long few minutes to think all this through. The case wasn't nearly as airtight as she would have preferred. Even if she did prove the explosives and clothing placed the bomber on the Imperial Capital planet, she had only the bomb residue to connect them, and no connection to any clan waiting expectantly on the Battleships of State. Still, any connection, no matter how tenuous, might be used to pry a door open that was currently slammed shut.

Finally, Kris said, "I think we need to know whether or not this C-14 was manufactured in the Imperial Capital system."

Admiral Tong twisted his body around to face her, then raised two of his four eyebrows.

Kris went on. "If it came from anywhere else in Iteeche space, it tells us nothing, but if it comes from the capital? Well, we have several Battleships of State tied up next to my flag that just came from there."

"I see. And for that you need a sample of something from the capital to compare your other samples against. Though, even if you find that the C-14 is from that area of space, will we really have established that it is from the capital?"

"No," Kris admitted. "But we shall have certain evidence that a reasonable person might find interesting. Possibly creating a connection."

The Iteeche grunted, then raised his commlink to his lips. "Leal, please bring me your new stool immediately. I'm over on the *Princess Royal* at the moment."

"Sir?" was loud enough to make it through the Iteeche's commlink.

"No whining, Leal. With luck, I'll give most of it back to you."

"Yes, sir," sounded very dejected.

Ten minutes later, Kris knew why. Captain Leal showed up with a sailor pushing a stool ahead of him. The stool looked much like the stools Kris had been creating for the Iteeche from Smart Metal, only this stool had the smell of leather and wood about it, something that metal objects missed.

What immediately caught Kris's eye was that this particular stood rolled on wheels and had a central spindle up from the six wheels that allowed the stool to swivel. Whoever sat on this stool could spin it around and roll it about.

"My flag captain had this made while we were orbiting the capital. He had to order it special from a couple of craftsmen at the bazaar, didn't you, Leal?"

"Yes, sir. They promised me that they used the finest local products. Iron, copper, and tin from their own mines back in the mountains. Leather from freshly-caught seals, and freshly-grown fiber for the padding. Is that important?"

"Yes," the Iteeche admiral said.

At the Human Marine lieutenant's request, the Iteeche Sailor set the stool upside down on the table between Megan and the lieutenant.

Kris and everyone with her at the table eyed the contraption. "Very good," she said.

"Thank you, Most Eminent Admiral," the Iteeche captain stuttered out. "I have often thought that I could be more productive if I could take some of the weight off my feet."

"We'll make sure this is not destroyed," Kris said. "Right, Megan?"

"I hope so. Lily, to what extent is this station chair over-engineered? Keep in mind the Iteeche weigh more than us."

"So, you're teaching your gramma to suck eggs, huh?" Lily quipped.

Megan looked surprised at that retort. Kris chuckled softly. Nelly was often that cheeky.

There was a knock at the inboard door.

"Enter," Kris called.

A Human Marine sergeant came in at a trot, carrying a metal toolbox. He set it down on the deck and eyed the upside-down stool.

"What do you want, Lieutenant?"

"We want to take some samples from the metal on this stool, but we don't want to destroy its utility."

"Understood. How large a sample will you need?"

"Two- or three-square centimeters of metal, leather, and fiber if you can get it. No need for them to be square, though."

"Right, ma'am," the sergeant said, eyeing the stool. "Whoever did the leather left extra hanging. I can snip a strip for that. The leather is held by bronze nails. I can pull one and replace it with a Smart Metal one that looks just like it."

"Good," Kris said."

Now the sergeant carefully studied the steel supports for the wooden stool. After a moment, he concentrated on a large central strake that stretched along the bottom of the stool.

"The central strake that runs from front to back needs to be the strongest. These two lateral strakes at the end bear the least load. Let's see how much metal I can get doing a thin scallop cut. I'll keep the area around the screws untouched, okay?"

The sample quickly went into an evidence box intended for hot items.

He repeated this three more times. At the end of his work, he had four strips locked away.

"If you'll excuse me," the LT said, "I'll oversee this going through the *P. Royal*'s mass spectrometer. I doubt if any ship of the fleet has one as overpriced as hers."

"Be glad I demanded it," Kris said. "Admiral, would your captain care to accompany my lieutenant?"

"I've read about how you Humans are mad about maintaining a chain of custody," Admiral Tong replied.

"Studying up on us Humans?"

"I'm hooked on police procedurals at the moment. Your story telling techniques are so much more visual and have a strange power. Much more powerful than our singing," the admiral admitted. "I'm borrowing from your ship's entertainment library. It is catching on among my junior officers. I had one ensign do a Bogart on me yesterday. We Iteeche will need to find something we can trade. Your media is addictive."

"No all of it is true," Kris was quick to point out.

"You may have to add a voice-over to that effect. It was nice to see that some of your cops are just as forceful as any Iteeche public service officer is."

"Yes," Kris groaned inwardly. "We must do some voice-overs."

One door closed behind the two officers and the opposite door behind the sailor as he left to return his captain's stool to his ship. Kris said, "Megan, do you want to bring your prisoners in for a talk?"

"One at a time, ma'am?"

"Yes."

"Are we going to interrogate them?" Admiral Tong asked eagerly. "Which of you will be the good cop? Which the bad cop?"

"Likely neither," Kris said, dryly.

Megan stepped out and soon returned with a naked Iteeche. His skin showed splotches of blue, pink, and purple from the application of explosive residue compounds that had not been completely wiped away.

The Iteeche prisoner looked terrified.

Megan looked puzzled as to what to do with her prisoner.

NELLY? STOCKS OR A GIBBIT?

I'M NOT SURE STOCKS WOULD SERVE WELL. ITEECHE HAVE AWFULLY THICK NECKS.

YEAH. GET US AN X CROSS TO MANACLE HIS ARMS.

A solid, 30 cm square wooden beam rose, rough-hewn, from the deck. It even showed wicked splinters. At its top, it sprouted two cross beams of similar strength in the shape of a double Y. Kris would have expected something like that at the bottom, but Nelly skipped it.

Megan and the two hefty Marines that dragged the Iteeche in got one of the prisoner's left arms manacled to the top crossbar, then the other left arm to the lower cross bar. They quickly repeated the process with his right arms.

Kris did her best to suppress a smile. Was she the only one that saw how Nelly slipped in some extra chains so the prisoner's hands could reach up and over?

On the deck, the two manacles on his left legs were hooked by a loop of metal and secured to the deck.

Oh, Smart Metal™ is so nice to have around.

In a moment, the Iteeche's right side was also locked down. He hung there, his head down, waiting for what would come next.

From the look on his face, he expected it to be brutal, quick, and final.

38

"So," Kris said, beginning her interrogation. She stayed seated, made no threatening moves toward the fellow, and kept her voice low. "You blew up the capital's water supply just as it was surrendering to me."

He said nothing, which wasn't hard to explain. He had a wickedly hard metal dental dam blocking his mouth open.

"Megan, has his mouth been searched?"

Her *aide de camp* gave Kris an affirmative nod. "We removed two hollow teeth that had poison in them."

"Somebody really wanted you dead," Kris said to her prisoner. "Meg, I don't know if you or Lily were the one that came up with the idea of the metal dental dam." *Or where you got it from.* "I really don't want to know. It has saved his life, but let's let the poor guy close his mouth."

"Yes, ma'am," Megan said. In a moment, the metal dental dam flowed down his chin like saliva and vanished into the deck.

The Iteeche bomber worked his beak, maybe to get feeling back to his face. Maybe to search for another way out. He finally huffed a sigh and glared at Kris and the Iteeche admiral.

"You might as well admit it," Kris went on. "We found all sorts of residue on you indicating that you handled the C-14 plastic explosives. Didn't you even think of using gloves?"

The Iteeche gave Kris a puzzled frown.

"How can you tell I handled the explosives?"

Admiral Tong issued a coughing Iteeche laugh.

"Next time you attack someone, don't go near the Humans. Admiral Longknife, am I correct in saying that some of the streaks on his skin are from that explosive residue compound you use?"

"Yes. It paints a very pretty picture." Kris said, then changed the subject to sheer terror.

"Have you ever been to a ceremony where an Iteeche make a Most Sincere and Very Complete Apology to the Emperor?" Kris asked, diffidently.

The terror in the prisoner's eyes expanded. Jerkily he shook his head. Since his neck didn't move that much, it had to start at his hips. His effort ran afoul of his chains and lurched to a stop.

"He would have seen several such Very Complete Apologies carried over the media. We broadcast them for all to see."

"To encourage the others," Kris said, bitterly. "Well, have you seen such apologies in the media?"

"They are shown before sing-alongs for a month afterwards," the Iteeche admiral told Kris. "You've seen them, right?"

Now the prisoner struggled to raise his head up and down.

"You see, clansman," Kris said. "You are a clansman, right?"

The prisoner stood stock still.

Yep. You work for the clan. I wonder how high up.

"Well, whatever you are, I find apologies lacking in the proper science."

"How would you Humans apply your science to our apologies?" Admiral Tong said, playing straight man to Kris's horror.

"The snake bite is so random. From the way the Iteeche dies so fast, clearly, the snake is injecting too much venom."

"Well, it's a snake bite," Tong said.

"Yes," Kris went on, so reasonable, "but if we milked the snake of its poison beforehand, we could inject just the right amount of snake venom into the Iteeche. He'd take more time to die and suffer more agony. You Iteeche really need to update this way you execute people. Be scientific."

The Iteeche admiral stroked the few small hairs on his chin. "I see. You have a point."

"Would I have to go all the way to the Emperor to get this changed?" Kris asked, just sounding curious about something as if it didn't mean a horrible death or an even more horrible death to her listener.

"Well, My Most Eminent Human Admiral," Tong said, sounding extremely helpful, "as Admiral Commanding the Imperial Combined Fleet with a mandate direct from the Emperor's hand, you could probably implement it in matters concerning the Combined Fleet immediately. That way, those afraid of changing a single thing in the Empire might see how it worked for you and be more willing to accept the change."

"Good," Kris said. "Now, I take it that someone who blew up the water supply on a planet I'm in the process of capturing would indeed be in my jurisdiction. I could experiment on him," Kris said, eyeing the prisoner eagerly.

He was weeping where he stood and had lost control of his bodily functions. The blowers in the room kicked into high, wafting air from vents behind Kris and removing it through vents behind the prisoner.

It was a lot nicer with him down wind.

"Yes," Admiral Tong said, leaning forward. "I definitely think both the fleet and the people of Balan would be very happy to watch this one die slowly."

The man tried to fall to his knees. He likely didn't notice when Nelly lengthened the chains on his arms so he could.

"Please," he pleaded. "I haven't seen anyone die worse than a Very Formal Apology. Please. You can't do that to me."

"Tell us what we want to know," Kris said, again diffidently, "and we'll see what we can do about that."

The Iteeche shook his head. "No. No. I can't tell you anything. They'll kill me."

The Iteeche backed up until his rump bumped against the timber. He struggled to his feet. "I can't tell you anything."

"So, you're afraid that if we don't kill you, that they will kill you?" Kris asked.

The Iteeche prisoner nodded.

"What if I promised you that you can live out your life to a happy old age? Maybe even become a Chooser."

The prisoner eyed Kris as if she was crazy.

"Admiral Tong, I've heard songs about being the first lander on a new colony. If you don't do something stupid and let the planet kill you, you can become a major landowner. A businessman. A leader of a local branch of a clan even if you were born or your papers say you are outside of the clans."

"That's what the songs say," Admiral Tong said. "It's hard work and the fates are at your elbow every night. Still, they may choose you for wealth or they may choose you for death. It's your risk. It seems to me that it's a lot less risk than a needle with snake venom in it or taking your chance on the streets of Balan."

The prisoner had clammed up. He had nothing more to say.

"Okay, I can understand your feelings," Kris said, as if no one in the room had a care in the world. "However, you have to understand, this colonizing offer won't be on the table forever. I intend to make the same offer to the guy caught with you. If he tells me which clans you two are from and names a few names for me to talk to next, he gets the offer and it's off the table for you."

The prisoner slumped against his chains.

"Megan, you and the Marines set him up in a temporary brig in my night quarters. Lily can do that for you. I don't want to hear a peep from him."

"We'll make it soundproof," Megan assured Kris.

"Oh, and you might want to hang around him. He might change his mind. You can never tell."

"No, you can't," Megan agreed.

39

Kris didn't pay much attention while they walked the next prisoner in. She had Nelly projecting the image from her night quarters onto Kris's eye so she could see how that went down.

Her bed had become a cell even before the guard detail and prisoner entered the room. They tossed him in the tiny cell and slammed the door shut.

About that time, the new prisoner was hauled in and secured to the X.

In the other room, the prisoner was complaining that his cell was too small. Megan turned it into a long, thin arrangement that looked like a dog run and the Iteeche began to pace up and down its length.

Kris left him to stew and turned to the new prisoner. He was shackled like the previous one. He was already crying and making puddles of brown and yellow at his feet.

The blowers were going as fast as they could. Kris would just have to put up with it.

Again, Kris told the prisoner that the local excruciating way of executing prisoners could be improved upon if the Humans just applied science to it.

The prisoner's beak dropped open and just kept dropping.

Kris shared the idea with Admiral Tong as if it was a new concept. She waved her hands as if she hadn't a care in the world, and coming up with new ways to viciously kill people was her favorite pastime.

Most humans would be groveling on the deck, begging to do whatever they could for Kris if only they didn't die like that. The Iteeche did no such thing. Apparently, this prisoner, like the last, just assumed they were dead and the only matter on the table was how they'd die.

Once again, Kris had to drag the prisoner around to offering her a quid pro quo.

"Of course, we might be able put you on a first ship to a new colony. Rework your papers so no one there knows who you are. You might prefer this pioneer life to some other options. I might be persuaded to give you a chance for a long life if you give me the name of your clan and who put you up to this."

He was already shaking his head before Kris got the words out of her mouth.

"There's no place in the galaxy I could go that they would not follow me. No place that they would not kill me slower than you would kill me. No. No way."

"Okay, but I should tell you that the offer is on the table. The woman who brought you up here is next door, encouraging your friend to give us what we want. Whoever speaks first gets the colonizing deal. Whoever holds out the longest, gets the needle."

Kris turned away from her prisoner. "Sergeant, take the man back out. Stay close. He might want to tell you something. Oh, and give him some room to walk in. Pacing might help him think better."

A few minutes later, the brig off the quarterdeck showed a long, narrow cell that was perfect for pacing. Just for chuckles and grins, Kris had Nelly time the two. They were both pacing their cells at about six klicks an hour.

Kris ordered meatloaf sandwiches brought up as well as a live fish lunch for Admiral Tong. After reviewing the matter, she ordered the same meals for the prisoners.

"At best, they deserve a raw yam," the Iteeche admiral said. "More likely, we'd just let them go hungry."

"Yes," Kris said, "I know. However, remember, I'm trying to show them that we want a different outcome to our mutual problem. By treating them differently, they might get the point."

"You Humans are absolutely crazy," Admiral Tong snapped.

"No, sir. We are alien, something I must often remind myself when I'm talking with even my best Iteeche friends and associates."

"It is so strange to view oneself as the alien," the Iteeche admiral said, thoughtfully.

"But it gives us a new perspective, doesn't it?"

"Kris, the food is ready," Nelly reported. "I could have it appear in the cells and at Megan's side."

"Yes," Kris said, suspecting where this conversation was going.

"However, I think delivering the meal by a cart pushed by a wardroom steward would have a greater impact."

Kris smiled. Her computer was getting very good at measuring how the impact of certain actions on Humans and Iteeche affected them.

"Very good idea, Nelly. Make it so. Oh, and deliver a sandwich to the sergeant guarding the other miscreant. I expect Megan will want sit down for lunch. Match his action to hers. Understood?"

"Oh, perfectly, Admiral. We will play them like they were penny whistles."

"Nelly, I doubt if anyone has been able to buy anything for a penny in centuries. Now, get along with this bit of judicial theatre."

The Iteeche admiral raised all four of his eyebrows. "Am I detecting a bit of caring for our prisoners in you, My Most Eminent Admiral?"

"Yes, Admiral Tong, you are. These aren't the real criminals. Yes, they followed orders and got their hands dirty with the explosives that threatened to leave millions homeless, and killed our troopers. However, they were merely the pawns maneuvered into position in someone's game of chess. Do you have a board game like chess?"

"Your translator is working fine. Yes, we have a game that matches wits in a bloodless game of medieval warfare."

Kris nodded. "I don't want the pawns. I want the bishop or paladin. If I can squeeze them for names and proof of how high this went, I will ship them off to try their luck at the bottom of a new colony. I want the king. The queen. Those are the individuals I'd request be given the long, slow, and excruciatingly painful apology to the Emperor."

Admiral Tong took a long while to meditate on Kris's ideas and objectives.

"I would have called them traitors and executed them immediately," he said, slowly. When next he spoke it was slow and thoughtful, as if each word was a newly discovered land.

"I begin to see what you have been talking about. Our clan lords play their games for power and a larger following. They send puppets out to do the bloody work for them, usually killing pawns from the other side. Never do they sweat. Never do they bleed."

He turned to eye Kris, focusing all four of his on her own two eyes as if he looked into her soul.

"I begin to understand why you brought the coup to a halt before too many soldiers died. If you had not been there, it would have been a bloody brawl with entire blocks of houses demolished and many soldiers and women and children caught under the rubble.

"Instead, when the guns fell silent, apartments still stood. Few of the lower ranks on either side were dead. Instead, two Clan palaces were smoking wrecks and two Clan chieftains lay dead among the scattered debris."

"They refused to end the firefight," Kris said. "Their soldiers were checked. I would call them all checkmated. It was time to quit and they refused."

"They refused," the Iteeche admiral answered, still thinking on each word, "because so few of their fighters had been killed. You and I know that you had them trapped with only killing zones to their front and flanks. Still, it is the Iteeche Way that the Clan Chief orders the troops forward, and they die trying. Occasionally, the fight goes a surprising way. It costs the Clan Lord nothing to throw the dice again."

"Yes," Kris agreed. "So, I raised the price on that last, worthless roll of the dice. I made it deadly for the Clan Chief. How do the powers that be feel about my change to the Iteeche Way?"

"Umm," the admiral grunted. "It is hard to tell where the feelings for the one 'adjustment' you made to the Iteeche Way ends and the next one begins. Housing for junior sailors, Guardsmen, and Marines so they can share their lives with a chosen woman. The need has always been there, but no one has dared strive for it. The Clan Chieftains have their harems. They dole out time with the girls in them as a reward for services rendered. Now, you change all that for your sailors and Marines. I have no idea where that is going or where it will end. You have men and women, pair mated, crewing your ships."

Kris glanced at Jack.

He nodded. "Yes, Admiral. Do you have a woman that you would like to share your cabin with?"

"We already have a thousand males on each of our warships. How could we support another thousand that make no contribution to us fighting the ship?"

Kris cleared her throat but said nothing.

"Yes, yes. I know a woman commands here, but . . ." the Iteeche admiral ran out of words.

"You cannot see an Iteeche woman in a laser team, standing an engineering watch, helping feed the crew?" Kris let her words just hang there.

The admiral with too many eyes began to sputter his thoughts, but a chief steward's mate interrupted by wheeling in a cart with their lunches laid out in a beautiful symmetry.

He laid the lunches before Kris as if it were a banquet, not a sandwich with pasta salad.

"Have you served the prisoners?" Kris asked.

"I serve you first, Admiral," the chief said with the kind of gentle reproof chiefs have had for officers over the last thousand years. So, Kris received the gentle correction that was reserved for those seniors in rank only and who either don't know their proper place, or more like her being a Longknife, refused to stay in.

"Thank you, Chief. Once we are served, please serve the officer keeping a prisoner company in a cell in my night quarters. Then do the same for the sergeant and his prisoner in the cell just off the quarterdeck."

"Aye, aye, ma'am."

"Nelly, get me the two Humans overseeing our prisoners."

"I have them."

"Yes, Admiral," and "Yes, ma'am," came in rapid fire.

"I want you to dine with our prisoners. Nelly will be raising tables and chairs, or stools, for all four of you facing each other through the bars. I want you to make this a friendly repast between comfortable associates, if not friends. Sergeant, beer may appear at your table. Unless you have a serious problem with alcohol, I'd like you to drink it. I'll be looking for something like alcohol for your prisoner. This goes for you two, Megan. Befriend our bombers."

"Yes, Admiral," Megan snapped.

"Ma'am," was pained from the sergeant.

"Sergeant, yes these guys pulled the trigger, but I want the guy who gave them the bomb. I want the guy who gave the order to put the bomb in place. Do you understand?"

"Yes, ma'am. This guy is a little fish. We want the big fish."

"Precisely. If you must, get them drunk. Try not to actually get drunk yourselves. I want them to spill names."

"Understood," Megan said. "Aye, aye, ma'am," came from the sergeant. Kris rang off.

She immediately turned back to Admiral Tong. "The reference to little fish and big fish is an ancient Human phrase. Do little fish sometimes get used for bait to catch bigger fish in the Empire?"

"Long enough that I understood your words exactly. Thank you for checking to see if your phrase was offensive. I will try to make the same effort if I think some of our traditional aphorisms might be misunderstood."

"Thank you. Now, Nelly, show me what's going on with our prisoners."

40

K ris watched as a holograph appeared on the table in front of her and her guests.

First the chief went to Megan. Either Nelly or Lily pulled a table out of the floor and a seat for the young commander. The chief set Megan's table just as carefully as he had set Kris's, then he turned to eye the situation on the other side of the bars.

Before he had to ask, Megan's table stretched out, giving plenty of room for two to eat. The prisoner had stopped pacing and eyed her meal like any man who hadn't eaten in twelve hours or more, though the dead and cooked meal must have been off-putting.

When the table expanded and the chief laid out a meal fit for an Iteeche, the prisoner actually showed dismay and backed up a bit. Likely, having the meal laid out under his nose but on the other side of the bars must have looked like a vicious torture.

The table set, the bars rose just high enough to admit the table's edge, then opened further to allow the meal to pass into the cell.

A stool rose from the deck to give him a seat at the table. In order to accommodate him, the table had to raise a good half yard higher. Megan's side of the table soon rose just as far. Her chair converted to a tall bar chair.

The Iteeche looked on, his beak slack, his mouth hanging open.

Megan sat, then invited the Iteeche to share the meal with her. It took him a bit to step forward. Megan had to have his meal pulled back to her side of the table so she might taste the contents and assure the prisoner there was no poison. She also tasted the whiskey. Considering the horrible taste of the rotgut that the Iteeche favored, Megan deserved a medal for not making a face as she tasted it.

Satisfied he wasn't about to be poisoned and make a Complete and Formal Apology to the Emperor, the Iteeche finally sat down. He filled a mug with whiskey, sat down, and took a sip.

"This is very good. The best," he told Megan, as he took a deeper pull on the mug.

"We serve it when we entertain," Megan said. "I don't think the Admiral carries anything less than the best."

"You actually work for the impressive Human admiral?"

"Yes. I have that honor. I am her aide. Think assistant for minor things."

"Like chasing down bombers and doing miraculously fast repairs?"

"I do whatever she tells me to do," Megan admitted.

On that note, both Megan and the Iteeche criminal began to eat. As he did so, he kept wagging his head back and forth.

"You are feeding me live lollarm. The chum is sliced so finely as are the yellow seaweed bulbs, and you have warmed the saltwater to just the right temperature. You are treating me to a meal fit for a Clan Lord."

"It's the same meal that Admiral Tong, the deputy commander of the Combined Fleets, is eating with Admiral Kris Longknife," Megan explained.

"Why are you treating me like this?"

"Why should we have the cook make two Iteeche meals? The Clan Lords who came up from Balan are eating this."

The Iteeche paused, spoon halfway to his mouth. "I didn't expect to be fed. If I was, I doubted that it would be better than a half-rotten yam."

"We don't have any half-rotten yams in our fleet," Megan told him.

"I thought that was what the Navy fed sailors? They have a choice between red or yellow yams, boiled or baked."

"We're trying to improve the food in the ship's messes," Megan said.

The prisoner began to talk about his favorite places to eat in the Imperial Capital. Megan let him talk, encouraging him with a remark or small question. The interrogation proceeded apace with him doing all the talking. Megan provided some careful direction, discussing the décor of some of the eateries she'd enjoyed on Wardhaven as well as some that Kris's flagship had been turned into for Imperial visits where she wanted to impress visiting dignitaries with the palatial nature of her battlecruiser.

That resulted in a quick tour down to the places to eat on the Battleship of State he'd come in on. It didn't last long as he realized he was talking too much about something close to home.

He also didn't notice just how slow his beaker of whiskey emptied. A few moments after he poured another mug and returned the pitcher to the table, it had refilled to almost the same level. He drank quite a few cups.

"Nelly, is any of this conversation helping you locate where he lived in the Imperial Capital?"

"Sadly, the answer is yes and no, Kris."

"You're not being helpful," Kris sang back at Nelly.

"Each clan has its palace and district. Some palaces for the smaller clans aren't much bigger than a small apartment building. The block may be their district. However, all of them have annexes, places farther from the Imperial Palace where many of the minor clan officials live and work. Iteeche who are clan affiliated, but just one step up from servant, guard, or soldier. Apparently, this guy is one of those very junior types. What he's describing to Megan has helped me locate him to a fifty hectare area, but it is way out and a jumble of different clans. There are even Iteeche living there with no clan affiliation at all. Think slum, Kris, with Iteeche packed in like sardines."

"Okay, pass that along to Megan. How's the sergeant doing? Any better?"

"He has the guy drinking and talking as openly as Megan. I think the two of them are getting along even better. However, we have a major problem with locating anyone on Balan. No maps. Apparently, a map is a top secret document. People know where they live and how to get around their neighborhood, but they don't know where anything is."

"You're kidding me," Kris said, exasperation creeping into her voice.

"Sorry. We are working on remedying that. I've got drones out mapping the capital city and going up and down the streets, looking for the names on the doors or windows. We're not having a lot of luck. A lot of apartments have no name out front and many of the eateries are located in basements with no sign out front except maybe a picture of one or two of their specialties. Many are very similar."

"This is ridiculous," Kris burst out. "How do they deliver the mail?"

"Kris, the lower levels don't send messages and the high clan lords send a runner."

Kris turned to Admiral Tong. She hoped her face didn't look as if she was pleading.

"I am sorry, My Most Eminent Admiral, but your computer, ah Nelly," he hastened to correct himself, "has the right of it. Our ships are so much the same that it is an accepted fact that we will sail with two or three missing and two or three aboard that got confused."

Kris wanted to face-plant on the table, but kept to the decorum as befitted a flag officer.

"Nelly, can you run some of those places by our guests from Balan? See if they know any of these locations the prisoner has named."

"I am already doing that. Unfortunately, I am having no better luck. The Lords know their way around their district. They know where the Planetary Overlord's Palace is as well as their equal or superiors. They take their meals either in their palaces or in places that befit their rank. The chasm between the upper crust of this society and the lowest commoner is vast with no real way to span it."

Kris closed her eyes and counted to twenty, then started over and counted to thirty. "How can anyone run a planet like this?" she finally demanded.

"Kris, this is feudalism pure and simple. Actually, it's not all that different from ancient Earth during several times in its early history. A peasant, serf, or slave had no idea where they were or what was going on. Their local lord was only slightly better informed and knew little beyond his lord's realm. You had to be a duke or count or something to pay any attention to the king."

"How did we get out of that?"

"Literacy and bureaucracy," Nelly provided. "If you can't read, you can't read a road sign. The bureaucracy was mainly to see that the king got his taxes. It put an end to tax collectors and soldiers riding into town, taking anything that wasn't nailed down, and eating up most of it before it got to the king."

"Thank you for the lesson in government, Nelly. I do have a degree in the subject."

"But you're having problems applying it to something that is borderline anarchy."

"You got that right, Nelly. Now, how do we crack these two?"

"I am amazed," Admiral Tong said, "that you have them talking as much as you have. If I had turned them over to one of my interrogators, we would have a lot of blood on the floor, but very little said through their bloody mouth."

Kris stared at the overhead. Her family had some experience in getting information, even willing help from some of their enemy's troops.

"Admiral," she said, still thinking, "what level are your ship programmers?"

"Mid-level. You might think of them as warrant officers."

"And you need more of them, don't you?"

"Yes."

"If you had two new ones added to the fleet, is there anything that you could do to make their past life disappear? Make sure that they could go ashore for a beer and not be mugged and dragged off to die slowly?"

"There are ways to change an Iteeche's appearance," the admiral agreed.

"Do you have a problem with me offering these two jobs as programmers on two of your ships?"

"They are traitors and deserving of the honor of making a Most Sincere and Very Complete Apology to the Emperor."

"Wouldn't the Emperor be served if someone higher up in the clan made that apology?"

"I might think so, but I was always taught to see that a traitor made his apology as soon as possible."

"Has what you've seen this morning shown that there might be an advantage to slowing down the rush to judgement?"

It took a long moment for the admiral to answer. When he did, it was a curt "Yes." Then he added more thoughtfully. "Yes. I think you have once again shown the weakness of the Iteeche Way." After a pause, he added, "Or the way that it supports the continued power of the clans."

Kris nodded, but remained silent. She did not want to interrupt a man fighting such a bitter battle with himself and what he had been taught all his life.

When the Iteeche admiral leaned forward and said, "Make the job offer to these fools. They may just be drunk enough to agree to it and start talking."

Kris had Nelly pass the word along to Lily for Megan to deliver. A text message went out to the sergeant. Kris watched as his commlink beeped. He read part of the message, then looked at his prisoner.

"I'm being told to make you a better offer than being sent to a start-up planet. The other guy is getting this offer too. You might want to decide this quick. The first one who takes it gets a warrant officer's job in the Navy, programming the magic metal." He went on reading the offer to his luncheon partner.

Meanwhile, Megan was doing the same. When she finished, she was met with an incredulous stare.

"The Navy would train me to program magic metal and use me to move it around in your ships?"

"Yes, we move walls around to make loading go faster. We expand the ship to give sailors more room to live in."

The Iteeche looked at Megan sideways, using three of his four eyes. "You wouldn't dare trust me to program this magic. What would keep me from just programming the hull over the bridge to vanish and let vacuum onto the bridge?"

"You wouldn't have the code to program that part of the ship. The hull, engineering, and some of the space around the lasers is under a much longer and more complex password. All the computing power on an Iteeche battlecruiser couldn't hack that password in ten thousand years. But it wouldn't matter, the code is changed every day or two. As I said, you could move walls. In your department only."

Here, Lily widened his cell.

"You could make tables."

Lily now turned the table into gold, the legs loaded with fancy curlicues. Sparkling diamonds, rubies, and emeralds filled the center of the swirls.

"You could work on coming up with a better stool," Megan finished, and her own chair converted into a recliner and let her get comfortable.

"You might be asked to work with the Marines to produce tanks and fighting vehicles from a standard pattern."

Here, Lily really outdid herself. A gun truck, complete with eight wheels grew out of the deck.

"You expect me to believe you made an infantry vehicle in this space?"

"Actually, yes. It's armored. A shot would have no impact on it."

A 12-millimeter automatic appeared on the table in front of Megan. She picked it up and shot it at the truck. The soft lead bullet turned into a splat on the front of the rig.

"Here, you take a shot," Megan said, and passed the weapon through the bars to her prisoner.

He took it gingerly. He pulled out the magazine, checked its load, then, with magazine still in one hand, the gun in the other, he said, "Why give me a gun? Why give me a chance to kill you?"

"Because I doubt that you *could* kill me," Megan told him. "Why give up your own life for mine when you can have a long life in my Admiral's new Navy?"

The Iteeche slowly reloaded the magazine and pushed it home with a click.

"You may shoot from where you sit, or you can stand. Don't move any closer to me or the weapon will explode in your hand."

"So, you've given me a bomb. Kind of sounds familiar."

"Actually, I have given you a standard weapon," Megan said. "It's just that Lily, the computer around my neck, has more computing power than several Iteeche flotillas worth of battlecruisers. If you take a hostile act against me, she will likely know it before you can even finish the thought. You may shoot at the gun truck, like I offered. Anything else will not go well for you."

The Iteeche stood. He took three steps back from the table.

Unknown to him, Lily stood ready to immediately convert his cell from bars to a solid bullet-proof wall the instant that he began to swing his weapon toward Megan. The bullet would splat on the cell wall, and that would be the end of their negotiations.

"I should tell you," Megan said, as if she didn't much care, "that your associate is trying to sweeten the offer. He wants to be commissioned an ensign." Megan knew nothing of such bargaining. Still, knowing what she knew of buying anything in an Iteeche bazaar, haggling seemed in every Iteeche DNA.

The Iteeche raised the automatic and fired at the gun truck, aiming for the same spot where Megan's slug hit. He missed it by less than five millimeters. It also deformed until it was almost flat.

The armor showed no effect.

"I will take the offer. Now, can I bargain for ensign's rank?"

"Let me check in with my admiral," Megan said.

She left her prisoner to stew in his own juices and stepped into Kris's day quarters. Across from her, the sergeant was coming through the opposite door from the quarterdeck.

"Come, sit down. Would you like some tea?" Kris said.

41

Kris was in no rush to finish the plea bargains. At least, no hurry to finish within the next five minutes.

She waited until her two prison negotiators were seated at the table and had poured themselves a cup of chamomile tea before she said, "I've been following your negotiations. You have both managed to arrive at the same point at the same time. Admiral Tong, you will be the one hiding these men in your fleet. Are you willing to pull this off?"

"I hate to give comfort to traitors," the admiral answered, as if almost in physical pain.

"Admiral, may I ask you a question?" Kris said.

"Of course, My Most Eminent Admiral," he answered quickly.

"You command a fleet that has battlecruisers with crews that were in rebellion against their Emperor until only a month or so ago. We are looking to add a thousand ships from Balan who have not quite finished their surrender. Now, I admit that these two planted bombs that killed my people and caused me great inconvenience. However, some of the ships under Admiral Coth's present command are in ships that destroyed our own ships in the Battle of the Arteccia

System. How is this different? How is it wrong if it gets me the names of the clans that have violated my trust?"

"When you talk of it in that way, I agree with you. You are once again, Admiral, pointing out the strange logic of the Iteeche Way. However, you Humans have a saying, 'A fish cannot discover water.' Until you Humans came, I had no idea what I was swimming in."

"Thank you, Admiral. You have a standing invitation to Wardhaven. I wonder what water we are swimming in that you could tell me about."

The admiral laughed at Kris's offer.

"I may take you up on that. Now, about our situation. I can give these men new papers and put them into an apprenticeship. We should be able to keep them out of harm's way in the fleet with not too much trouble."

Kris measured her options, then turned to Megan and the sergeant. "I'm not willing to offer too much until I find out what they have to offer me. We have promised them a warrant officer's rank. Tell them that what they tell us will decide if they enter the Navy as a warrant officer, chief warrant officer, or ensign."

Megan looked at the sergeant. "I think we have our marching orders. See you back here in a few, Sergeant."

They put down their still-steaming tea and headed back to work.

Megan found her prisoner staring at the automatic in his hands. The barrel had spooled itself up into an interesting roll of metal.

"I wondered why you did not retrieve your gun," the Iteeche said, and handed it back to Megan through the bars. She took it, rolled the barrel out straight, and set it on her table next to her drink.

"You do that as if it is nothing. As if you do it every day."

"We program Smart Metal to what we need," Megan said, with a shrug, "whatever we need it to be. That's the job we are offering you."

"But at what rank?" the bomber shot back.

"Admiral Longknife has told me to make you this offer. We will help you disappear into the Navy. You will be protected from the wrath of the clans by the Navy's security net. We will bring you into the Navy as a warrant officer and train you as a Smart Metal programmer. Depending on the quality of the information you give us, you may be brought into the Navy as a chief warrant or as an ensign. It all depends on who you can name for us."

For a long moment, the Iteeche wore the closest thing Kris had ever seen to a frown on one of his four eyes. Finally, with a sigh, he began to talk. He was from a minor sept of a medium-sized clan. The guy he'd been caught with was from a different minor sept of that clan. A senior clan lord had provided him with the C-14 and instructions on how to blow the water lines to cause the most trouble. He'd later been ordered the night before by the same lord to work with the other fellow to build and position the second bomb.

"How did you get through our security perimeter to plant the second bomb?" Megan asked, saving Kris from having Nelly tell Lily to have Megan do it.

"Not all of the tunnels under the city were flooded. There were things some people liked to do and not be noticed. Between the storm sewer and certain other private tunnels, we got the bomb in place without having to go up to the surface."

"Then why was the other guy running just blocks from the explosion?"

Now the Iteeche did scowl. "That is a question you must ask him. He was supposed to have met me several more blocks out, then he called me to meet him way too close to the bombing. I should have just left him like a fish gasping for water on land as the tide goes out."

Kris had Nelly search for information on the clans this prisoner had implicated.

"The other prisoner has named the same clans," she told Kris.

"Good, now, why did this other nutcase go back in?"

"The sergeant already asked him."

"Show me."

The holograph again showed the sergeant and the prisoner seated. Now they were across the table, and the bomber was refilling his whiskey glass. From the low level of whiskey in the jug he had likely drunk it dry at least twice. Maybe more.

"I'm sorry, but I don't get it," the sergeant said. "You said you had a timer on the explosives. If I'd set a bomb, I'd have been halfway to the next star when it went off. Why were you only a few blocks away, on street level, and not a whole lot of blocks away running up the sewer drains?"

The Iteeche took a long pull on his glass, just about emptying it. Then he let out a deep sigh. "My boss's boss told me that they weren't sure the timer would go off on time, so they rigged a backup. If I pushed a button, I could blow up the building, but I'd need to be above ground to do it."

The guy finished his drink, then refilled it again. "The time came and went, and nothing happened. I used the tunnels to get back inside your security cordon, then slipped up to the surface and ducked out to get a good line of sight to the building."

He took another drink.

"It blew just as I was about to push the button. It just *blew*! Late, but it blew. With all the smoke, dirt, and dust spewing out of the access to the tunnels, I panicked and ran. I figured that if I was caught, I could bite my tooth and die with glory for the cause."

Another long drink.

"But you jammed that metal cage in my mouth and I couldn't close my *teeth*!" he shouted. "So, you caught us both, and I've lost my chance to be a clan lordling and I have to start all over again in the Navy. The *Navy* of all places. Only the leftovers from Choosing are in the Navy."

"I think you may find that not to be the case," the Marine sergeant said.

The Iteeche snorted. "So, when do I get started in the Navy?" He made it a four-letter word.

"First, you might want to sleep off all the whiskey you've drunk. Second, we'll just have to wait to see how the intelligence you've given us develops."

"Oh," the Iteeche said, and reached for his bottle. He watched, eyes growing wide, as it drained before him.

"Don't you think you've had enough?" the sergeant said.

"I don't know if I'll ever have enough," the Iteeche said, then rolled out of his chair and sprawled across the deck on his back.

"Nelly, give me a view of the sergeant's prisoner's cell."

He, also, was sprawled on his back, snoring.

"Nelly, we don't want him to choke to death on his own vomit. I might need to use him again. Roll him over on his stomach and get his bunk under him. Let his head half-hang off the side."

"You care this much about this . . . traitor?" Admiral Tong snapped.

"I may need him to tell us more. So, yes, I will keep him alive, and I strongly suspect that when he's in your command, you do the same. The next time I need to break a prisoner and get him talking, I may have him or his associate over there talk to them. If people can trust you, they'll talk. If the word gets around that people vanish, they don't talk."

"But you intend to make them disappear into my fleet?"

"Yes, but I don't have to tell anyone that. I could tell the clan lords we're likely to be talking to tomorrow that I'm shipping them off to do time at a Human prison."

"Oh."

"Yep. Keep your options open."

"And your opposition confused," the Iteeche admiral added.

"You got it. Now. What Iteeche clan chiefs do we talk to first and how do I swoop in and take a whole lot of Iteeche into detention without causing me any more trouble?" Kris mused.

42

Kris expanded her small number of confidants seated around her table. At the moment, that was exactly one. She added a stool at her conference table for Larry, Balan's Planetary Overlord.

"I have some confessions I'd like to share with you," Kris said, and let him view holographs of the two Iteeche bombers spilling their guts.

When the show ended, the Overlord was livid. "I will arrest that one's supervisor immediately. We can have both of them immediately offer a Most Sincere and Very Complete Apology to the Emperor at the same time. I'd arrest the other supervisor, but he is on a Battleship of State and, I assume, under your jurisdiction. Still, we can have all four of their apologies on the media before sunset."

"I would prefer not to," Kris said.

"You want the apologies sooner?" the Planetary Overlord asked.

"Actually, I have made arrangements for these two bombers to disappear as soon as we resolve this matter."

"You cannot let treason prosper!" said the Planetary Overlord, interrupting Kris.

"I assure you, this treason will not prosper," Kris cut right back in. "However, I want the real traitors, not the poor fools they set up to take the fall."

"Fall?"

"Pardon me, poor translation. I want an apology from the members of the clans higher up the food chain. These are small fish. There are bigger fish above these two. Then there is the biggest fish that ordered all this. That is the apology I want filmed and broadcast to the winds."

The Planetary Overlord eyed Kris as if she had two heads.

Admiral Tong broke in with an explanation. "Do you cut the finger, then the hands, then the arms off of an octopus?" he asked the other Iteeche.

FINGERS, HANDS? Kris asked Nelly.

OUR TRANSLATIONS ARE FAILING IN BOTH DIRECTIONS. HUMAN WORDS DO NOT FIT HANDS AND FINGERS. SIMILARLY, OCTOPUS DOESN'T QUITE FIT THE CREATURE. OKAY?

THANKS, NELLY.

Meanwhile, the admiral was still talking.

"I have seen a picture of how the Humans think of fish hunting. A small fish swims along placidly. Behind it is a big fish, ready to swallow it down. A bigger fish follows it, mouth open. Behind all of them is the biggest fish, ready to snap them up. My Most Eminent Admiral considers these bombers just small fish, following orders."

Larry eyed the Iteeche admiral askance. He still was not getting the picture.

"She wants to reel in the big fish behind those that gave them the orders. Once she gets that fish talking, she can drop a hook into the water to snag the bigger fish who is the only one who can tell us who the biggest fish is. That is the fish our Human Commander of the Imperial Combined Fleets wants to see make that apology. Oh, and she has an idea for making that apology most painful and very long."

"How?"

So, the Iteeche admiral told the Planetary Overlord of Kris's idea for skipping the snake-biting part of the ritual and using a syringe to measure out exactly how much venom was needed for a long, excruciating death.

"Do not mistake the canny way our admiral hunts. I would never want to be the one she pursues."

"Hmm," Larry said, thinking long and hard on what he'd just been told. Then he turned to Kris.

"So, how would you Humans go about reeling in the fish you are after?"

"I would cast a broad net, take them all into custody, then interrogate them one at a time. I'd let my commander, here," Kris said, giving Megan a well-deserved wave of approval, "talk to them one at a time. As we get each one's confession, we find out who ordered the bombings. Then we talk to them. We do this as often as we have to until we get to the top."

"You would go after a clan lord?"

"Who is most guilty of the crime, the one who sets the timer, or the one that ordered the entire operation? Who will profit most from the bombings, the little fish, or the biggest fish at the top?"

The two Iteeche exchanged glances, then began to talk quickly to each other. Nelly wisely did not translate their conversation. At least, not out loud.

"KRIS, IT IS JUST DAWNING ON THE PLANETARY OVERLORD HOW OFTEN THEY HAVE PROMPTLY EXECUTED THE LITTLE FISH AND NEVER EVEN THOUGHT OF PURSUING THE CLAN LORD BEHIND IT ALL. I THINK LARRY IS SHAKEN BY THE REALIZATION OF HOW THE ITEECHE WAY SHIELDED THE REAL CRIMINAL.

SO, NELLY, IT LOOKS LIKE ANOTHER FISH IS DISCOVERING WATER.

DISCOVERING WATER AND THE FISHBOWL THEY SWIM IN. I SUSPECT THERE WILL BE SOME SERIOUS EFFORTS TO BREAK THE GLASS.

I FEEL LIKE THE SNAKE IN THE GARDEN OF EDEN HANDING OUT FREE APPLES LEFT AND RIGHT.

KRIS, ISN'T THIS WHAT YOU WANTED? TO BREAK THE

GLASS? TO HAVE THE ITEECHE FREE THEMSELVES OF THE CONSTRAINTS THEIR SYSTEM HAS CONFINED THEM TO?

YES, NELLY, BUT IF YOU SHATTER THE FISHBOWL, WHAT HAPPENS TO THE FISH? THEY END UP FLOUNDERING AROUND ON THE FLOOR, GASPING FOR BREATH.

YES, KRIS, BUT WHAT IF THE FISHBOWL IS BROKEN OVER THE OCEAN? WHAT IF THEIR EYES ARE OPENED AND THEY DISCOVER THE ENTIRE SEA TO SWIM IN?

AREN'T YOU BEING A BIT OF AN OPTIMIST, NELLY?

I WORK FOR A LONGKNIFE. IT'S EASY TO BE AN OPTIMIST WHEN YOU EXPECT MIRACLES.

THANK YOU, NELLY, FOR THAT VOTE OF CONFIDENCE.

YOU'RE WELCOME. THEY ARE FINISHING UP.

The voice in Kris's head fell silent.

"What would a Human who hunted the biggest fish do now?" the Planetary Overlord asked.

"I would dispatch my police officers and soldiers to make the arrests, but I'd wait until two hours after midnight, when everyone is asleep. Then I would swoop down, capture them, haul them off to solitary cells so they couldn't concoct a story to confuse me. Then I'd start working my way up the food chain. I don't know if Admiral Tong has told you, but I'd offer lesser penalties if they talk, an excruciating death if they didn't."

"How do you keep them from taking the honorable way out?"

Kris smiled. A moment later, a dental dam appeared on the table. "I make sure we jam this into their mouths before they know what's happening," she said, tossing the device over to him.

The Planetary Overlord looked at the object. Admiral Tong then held it up and slipped it between his beaks and into his mouth. He had to pull it out before he could say, "No one will bite a tooth with this jammed in their mouth."

"Very good," Larry said.

Over the next hour, they worked out the logistics of an operation. This would be an all Iteeche drill, with Iteeche arresting Iteeche.

As the day wore on, several more battalions of Marines would go down the beanstalk to reinforce troops around the bombed area. People were coming back and traffic was horrible. There were also needs for security to assure that no one got into the wrong apartment.

That would keep the Iteeche Marines busy for the daylight hours.

Platoons of Iteeche Marine MPs would also be mixed in with the line beasts. They would lead the assault on the clan headquarters along with the police of the Planetary Overlord.

However, no one would get any orders before midnight. Indeed, Nelly intended to guide the lead arresting vehicles while more followed, unaware of where they were going. Not one Iteeche would know what they were doing until the trap was closed. Then and only then would the raiders open their order and discover that they were to arrest every Iteeche on the top three floors of a luxury high rise.

This sept wasn't large enough to have a palace, so they had to settle for the upper floors of a very nice high rise. To save money, most of their minions were housed in less pricy quarters several blocks away. They included the supervisor who had passed along the orders to the bomber. He'd skipped over two layers of minor supervisors to go direct to the bomber.

Kris guessed that was meant to reduce the chances of a leak. Now it improved the chances of getting the top Iteeche.

The raid on the Battleship of State that housed the sept of the first bomber would be more complex. Clearly, everyone in that sept had to be snapped up.

However, there was the matter of the minor clan chief. Was he involved in this project? If he was, how many of his people were? A major potential problem was that this sept was riding in the lead Battleship of State.

This ship housed a third of the Iteeche who would rule the first planet.

That raised a very serious question. Had the frustrated Planetary Overlord-to-be been a part of this scheme? Should they snatch Sam at the same time as the others? How do you hold a Planetary Overlord while you decide he's a mass murder?

That was a very thorny problem. It likely came with plenty of poison dripping from every spine and barb.

43

Kris held this secret in a very small circle of confidants. However, there was no way for her to keep the guessing game in the rumor mill from churning out crazy ideas.

Some, of course, were very close to the truth.

The word that the two bombers had been captured and failed to suicide got out.

Jack suggested that they had enough mangled and unrecognizable Iteeche bodies on hand that a pair of unrecognizable corpses could be "identified" as the bombers

So, they produced two badly burned bodies and created the first media circus ever to occur in the Iteeche Empire. They even left the mouths hanging open so the camera could see where they'd each crushed a suicide tooth.

Unfortunately, someone around the initial arrest reported they were alive.

Larry had several people, from middle clan rank to clanless, report all sorts of places where the bodies had been found. Some insisted there had been no explosion, others insisted there had.

Who was it who said that the truth needed a bodyguard of lies? Kris provided this truth with an army of lies.

Meanwhile, Admiral Tong and his undercover agents kept the Battleships of State under close observation. Several of the cooks from the battleships went ashore to buy fresh fish and vegetation with their own bearers. Those from the Battleship of State they were interested in quickly were replaced by undercover agents and slipped into the kitchens aboard. From there, they spread out, taking food to different dining rooms. That quickly gave them a map of who was billeted where. That map was quickly passed ashore to the select group planning the invasion of that Battleship of State.

The rumor mill continued to churn. With the cooks and helpers aboard, Kris and Admiral Tong heard plenty of new stories. The flood of guesses was like a tsunami, slamming through the ship and washing away the truth.

Several minor officials from quite a few septs did their best to slip off the ship. Many of them attached themselves to a line of carriers following one of the replacement cooks ashore to get more delicacies.

No sooner did they slip away from the line and head for the space elevator than MPs in plain clothes picked them up and hauled them off to a solitary cell on the *Princess Royal*.

It took little pressure to get them talking. They were terrified to start with and only wanted to assure their Iteeche interrogator that they had nothing to do with the bombings. They'd only heard about it after the fact.

Unfortunately, most of their stories were hearsay, and all from different storytellers. However, a few central themes began to take shape.

Most of them agreed that the identified clan was involved, "but not me," was quick on the lips of those who shared the same sept with the bombers or just the middling clan relationship. That tightened the noose around that clan lord.

There were reports of the clan chief dining with the future Planetary Overlord, but those were mostly fifth- or sixth-hand. At least they were until a clerk in the office of the Clan Chief tried to run. It didn't take long for him to verify that supper with the Planetary Overlord had been on the Clan Chief's schedule the day they docked.

"Really, I have no idea what they talked about," he insisted. "No one tells me anything about what goes on in clan meetings. I know nothing."

Megan sat in on this interrogation, her back against the wall, listening and not interfering. The questioning had been returned to the interrogators. Kris didn't want any Iteeche to fell supplanted.

However, it seemed that the several of the official inquisitors hated how easily they were getting people to talk. A few had continued the standard Iteeche torture that was included with any talk with the police. After a few minor parts of the story fell from the beaks of black and blue Iteeche, Megan began to sit in on the interrogations.

Megan notified Kris when the Iteeche MPs were finished with this slight fellow. She stepped away from the wall and circled the clerk where he stood, his feet chained to the floor in an otherwise bare room.

"Tell me," she said, tossing on the table in front of the Iteeche what passed for a delicious candy bar. "When was this dinner meeting scheduled?"

"A couple of hours before we docked," the Iteeche clerk immediately stammered out, his eyes focused on the sweet.

"How many hours before?"

"I don't remember for sure. Three or four hours."

Kris scowled at the holograph of the interrogation. This minor bureaucrat could not know when the Planetary Overlord of Balan chose to offer to surrender, so he would not understand how important the timing was.

As Kris turned back to the holograph, her key staff for this operation was watching with her.

"Who asked for the meeting?" Megan asked.

The Iteeche looked up from eyeing the food on the floor and named a clan lord from yet another minor sept in a different clan.

Kris's scowl grew deeper. Yet another clan to add to the raid. However, that clan lord could easily be the cutout between the pissed off future Planetary Overlord and the clan that did his bidding.

This was getting very interesting.

The questioning continued, with Kris trying to wean the MPs of their rough manhandling of the Iteeche in their charge. They grumbled, but got less heavy-handed as the day wore on. Despite the lighter hand, the minor clan lordlings in their custody continued to sing like birds.

Their talkative questioning added little to what Kris knew, but added layers of detail to the picture. This only whetted her appetite for a talk with the clan lords that had their fingers in this pie.

Kris and her key staff planned the takedown assault. Then they looked at it from a different perspective, then looked at it again. At that point, Jack was detailed to be the Red Team and figure out how he would screw up the lightning assault on the Battleship of State.

Time flew swiftly.

Kris and Jack slipped away for a few hours' nap. It quickly slipped into stress relief, and they napped happily in each other's arms. Kris sometimes wondered when she and Jack would become an old married couple. So far, they'd avoided that fate.

She definitely wanted to continue in this wonderful state as long as she could.

At midnight they were awoken to dress for the night's mission. Kris intended to be on the team that took down Sam, the troublemaking future Planetary Overlord. The two of them needed to have a nice, long talk.

44

Grand Admiral Kris Longknife, admiral commanding the Imperial Combined Fleet crossed the brow of the Battleship of State *Ever Victorious Sunrise*. The two guards were asleep on their feet as she and her strike force arrived. The thermos of drugged tea, brought up by one of the inserted "mess stewards," likely accounted for that.

Kris would have to remember how vulnerable a ship was once its mess crew had been suborned.

Her team moved swiftly and silently through the sleeping passageways of the palatial Battleship of State. The cooks that would prepare breakfast for the crew would not rise for another hour. However, the cooks that her troops had slipped aboard this extravagant barge were up.

They guided the different squads of the strike team to their target. They'd kept the clans that Kris was interested in under close observation. Now, except for an occasional sailor or insomniac, the squads moved quickly and unobserved into their assigned places.

Each squad had a pair of Human US Marines on point and rear, with M-4s loaded with sleepy darts. Innocent Iteeche who stumbled into the strike squads were put to sleep and left in storage closets.

So it was that two hours after midnight, Kris's strike team stood outside the door of the suite of rooms reserved for the highest clan lord on board. This trip, it held a particularly disagreeable lord from a middling clan who had won the lottery to be Planetary Overlord for the first planet Kris captured.

Time and time again, Sam the Iteeche had insisted that the Balan system's decision to surrender did not make it any different from one captured after a long battle. He wanted to govern the planet for fun and profit. He dreamed of spoils that would enrich his clan for hundreds of years to come.

Kris, however, wanted the existing Planetary Overlord left in charge to continue the improvements in infrastructure that he was investing in.

There were three different people with three different demands, and only one planet to share among them. Someone was in for disappointment.

That someone was likely sleeping comfortably on the other side of that door.

The Human Marine engineer stepped back from running a scan on the doorsill. He didn't look happy. Kris slipped up to the front to eavesdrop on the discussion. Jack followed hot on her footsteps.

She refused to glance back his way. No doubt he was wearing one of his worried looks. He'd just have to worry.

"They've got three different locks on this door and five sets of hinges on the other side," the combat engineer said. "It's going to take a lot of explosives to open this can of worms."

While the Iteeche in nominal command of this team considered this problem, Kris stepped into it.

"Have you considered taking a laser to the wall and just cutting the locks out?"

The two of them turned to her. The Human raised an inquisitive eyebrow. The Iteeche let all four of his eyes grow wide.

"In the last few years," Kris said, "I've broken into a lot of places I wasn't wanted and out of a few places I was. Do you have the equipment?"

In a moment, the Marine had pulled a small hand laser from the tool kit at her waist. She drilled a shallow test hole, then slowly worked it deeper. On the fourth try, she broke through the metal wall near the door.

That established, she deftly cut around all three of the locks, peeled back some of the metal, then packed a very small amount of explosives around each bolt. A layer of bulletproof cloth closed up the wall, ready to trap the shock of the explosion inside and add to the force on the locks.

NELLY, ARE ALL THE TEAMS IN PLACE?

WE HAVE TWO TEAMS THAT ARE FACING THE SAME SERIES OF LOCKS. I PASSED ALONG THE SPECS ON HOW THIS COMBAT ENGINEER PEELED BACK THE WALL. THEY SHOULD BE READY IN A MINUTE. MAYBE LESS.

STANDBY TO COORDINATE ALL THE EXPLOSIONS, NELLY.

STANDING BY. ALL THE DOORS ARE RIGGED. I AM READY.

GIVE THEM A COUNT OF THREE THEN BLOW ALL THE DOORS.

"We go on three. One," Nelly whispered softly. Her voice came from every commlink in the passageway.

"Two."

On "Three," a low "whomp" came from the door.

A Human Marine swung a door knocker to smash the door open, then quickly got out of the way as a small parade of Iteeche stormed into the conversation room of the suite. Occupying a good third of the room was a deep pool of water.

Both pool and room were empty, as was the dining area of the suite. Groups of three or four Iteeche MP's moved purposefully around the pool and gathered at the doors into what was likely the bedrooms.

The Human combat engineer was called to check those doors with his sensors. Only one was locked, and it was a lock easily defeated. An extra two Iteeche were assigned to that one.

Kris crept up behind them. She very much wanted to discuss

matters with this obnoxious and greedy Iteeche who was causing too much trouble for Kris's tastes.

Once again, Nelly whispered a three count from every commlink in the room.

On three, doors were silently opened and Iteeche, all seven to eight feet of them, tiptoed their three to four hundred-pound bodies into the room. The second Iteeche from the lead held a dental dam readily at hand.

The first any of the sleepers knew that their world had changed was when that gag was jammed into their mouth, keeping them from doing anything that would cause Kris to miss talking to them.

There was a lot of screaming and squawking as the lights came on.

The screaming came from the three female Iteeche that were sharing the potential Planetary Overlord's bed. The squawking came from the one guy in the bed who now could not close his mouth or speak clearly.

The female Iteeche were all hurried out of the room. There were a lot of splashes as they were joined in the pool by a lot of bedmates.

Kris, however, was only interested in the male Iteeche. An Iteeche Marine corporal had jammed the dental dam between the guy's beak even as he still slept. It being made of Smart Metal, Nelly programmed it to expand.

In the blink of an eye, Sam, the hopeful Planetary Overlord, had his beak spread wide open. The teeth inside his mouth were also held wide apart. No way was he crunching his teeth together and crushing a poison tooth.

That might explain why he was squawking so much. That, or the way the Marines had trussed him up like a calf ready for branding.

Then he caught sight of Kris standing well back from the struggle of strong Iteeche.

He let out a primal scream as he tried to lurch out of the bed and struggled with the big Iteeche MPs to get to Kris. She scowled; he was not making a case for him being merely misunderstood. There was no sign of contrition that might earn him mercy.

Kris turned and led the Iteeche out of the room. The demanding future Planetary Overlord followed, strung up on a pole carried by four strong Iteeche Marines.

The pool was now full of unclothed women Iteeche. They whispered nervously among themselves. None showing any signs of grief as their recent bed mates were perp-walked past them and out the door. Kris would have really liked to pause and ask those women what they thought of their life and of their clan lordlings, however, she had little time.

The long line at the gangplank was moving slowly. Some of the prisoners moved like sleepwalkers. Others were still struggling with their guards. Every few minutes, one of the lordlings would get so out of hand that he'd be hogtied and rolled aside. When a pole arrived, he was slung under it. Thus, many clan lords left the Battleship of State struggling and screaming.

The Iteeche Way apparently didn't allow for sedating prisoners.

As Kris waited her turn to go ashore, she watched the scene unfolding before her eyes. She had personal searing memories, of being relieved of her command and perp-walked off her own ship. She'd wrapped herself in dignity, since that was all she had left, and led her guards as if they were her honor guard.

The charges were trumped up and political, but vindication was a long way off at that moment. As she studied the Iteeche around her, struggling with their guards and being forced into less and less dignified positions, she couldn't help but wonder. *Was this a sign of their guilt?*

Kris would have to be careful about that thought. She had no idea if the Iteeche law required a prisoner to be considered innocent until proven guilty. It didn't matter. As a Human and emissary to the Iteeche Empire, Kris had to uphold her own standards. The case against these Iteeche would have to be made beyond a reasonable doubt to her before she would do anything to these Iteeche.

She had to, if for no other reason than the agony the Iteeche Empire would lay on these lordlings if they considered them guilty. A

Most Sincere and Very Complete Apology to the Emperor was a horrible way to die.

Kris's turn in line finally came. She crossed the gangplank; the Iteeche require no honors. A station cart was waiting for her. No sooner did she settle into it than it set off for the *Princess Royal*.

From the outside, Kris's battlecruiser looked at Condition Able, Imperial Plush. However, looks were deceiving. The space normally reserved for the forward lounge was occupied by four stories of prison cells. Each new deck held eight cell blocks that could be entered only by one hatch.

Every cell was fully equipped for the comfort of its occupant, but there was only one prisoner to a cell. Each cell was soundproof to prevent any contact with the Iteeche on either side. However, they were not intended to be solitary or to make the occupant feel isolated.

Instead of blank gray walls, each cell showed a surround view of favored Iteeche locations. They could sing along from inside a huge stadium. Several beach scenes were available, as well as meadows, mountains, and other pleasant locations. The cell could be cycled through all these options to help its occupant find the one he wanted. There was even a bride auction with hundreds of lovely, nude and nubile Iteeche lovelies on the block to see just how high a bride price they could bring to their clan before they disappeared into a great lord's harem.

Kris found that one disgusting, but it was popular among the junior lordlings.

Leaving Nelly to keep an eye on the prisoners, especially the yelling and bellowing of the clan lords and the frustrated Planetary Overlord, Kris turned her focus elsewhere. She was most interested in two interrogations.

She kept a close eye on the supervisor who had been named by the first prisoner. A pair of Iteeche intelligence officers from Tong's command applied the usual Iteeche techniques to breaking him. Sitting with her back against the wall, finding it easy to make herself look small among all these towering Iteeche, Megan observed the proceedings.

That fellow's clan chief was also being interrogated. However, the two Iteeche in the room were being quite nice to him, treating him with deference. They even got him a flask of whiskey. It being metal, there was no way for him to notice that it kept refilling itself every time he set it back on the table in front of him.

Kris asked Nelly to let her know if anything interesting developed there, then returned to the supervisor. Bruises and open cuts now showed on his face, and his hands and feet were chained to a very uncomfortable stool. It was clear, this heavy-handed approach to breaking the Iteeche was going nowhere fast.

A dental tech arrived and pulled a tooth without anesthesia. That set the prisoner to howling.

The two interrogators retreated to a corner to discuss what to do next. One was in favor of hot needles under his fingernails. The other preferred pulling more teeth. "He'll remember us for however long his miserable life is every time he bites into a nice soft yam."

The subject of the conversation whimpered where he sat.

Megan rose and joined the conversation. "Could I talk with him for a bit? You guys have been working hard and could likely use a break. Why don't you take thirty and get yourself a snack and cup of tea in the mess? I heard the cooks laid on quite a spread for you guards and interrogators."

The Iteeche eyed the prisoner, then looked at the five-foot six Human. "You sure you can handle him?"

Megan patted her service automatic. "If he causes me any serious trouble, I'll just put him to sleep."

"Oh, right, you Humans are so soft in the heart that you do that. You are way too easy on crap like this. We'll have to fill out all sorts of paperwork to get anything fun released to us," one complained.

"You can fill the paperwork out while you're on break. Maybe get a second cup of tea while you do it."

That seemed to please them. They left the cell exchanging cheerful words and expectations.

Megan waited until the cell quieted, then strolled over to stand in front of the shackled Iteeche.

"Now you are mine."

45

Lieutenant Commander Megan Longknife circled the restrained Iteeche prisoner. He looked about as threatening as a pan of her nana's pastries before they went into the oven. Still, he was the central pin that could bring a huge conspiracy crashing down.

She needed to break this pin and start this scheme tumbling to its destruction, and with it the likely destruction of several clans.

Megan shook her head in disgust, and the four eyes of the Iteeche grew wider. If his chains allowed it, he would have cringed farther away from the Human.

Actually, her disgust was for the disloyalty of the clans to their presumed all powerful Emperor. Even though just shy of half the Empire was in rebellion, the other half's only concern was to jockey for positions that would bring them more power and wealth.

So far, at least one major clan had crashed and burned badly for their attempt.

You would have thought that would have been a sufficient warning to the other so-called "loyal" clans and septs. Apparently, it hadn't.

Maybe the Iteeche clan lords were just too dumb to learn. That, or too locked in their millennia-long games of power.

Megan turned to this poor minion of the clan system. Her voice alternately dripped honey and poison. The prisoner spun between relaxation and panic. It was a mixture guaranteed to make him open to anything that might allow him to survive this mess his clan lordlings had gotten him into.

Megan cheerfully explained how the Humans intended to refine the traditional Iteeche apology. "We've already gotten a snake and milked it," she whispered eagerly in the Iteeche's tiny ears.

Lily provided a full video of the milking process.

"We figure we can get four or five apologies from that one bite," she added, pride in the economics of horror.

The Iteeche's face froze in terror.

"This is how we think it would go. You know, compared with the wasteful, old-fashioned way of apologizing."

Two videos began to play out. One was from the last Formal apology to the Emperor where a hundred officials had been executed at the same time. The camera view zoomed in from above to focus on just one. The snake bit and the condemned clan lord began to scream and wither in pain as his muscles knotted up and began to crack his bones.

Beside that poor damned soul, a second video had opened up. Four big Iteeche each held an arm of someone that looked very much like the prisoner. A Human jabbed a needle the prisoner's arm and stepped back. The guards held on for only a few seconds more, then quickly released the prisoner as the Iteeche let out a blood curdling scream and collapsed onto the deck in agony.

For the next few minutes, the prisoner sat, eyes riveted on the two deaths. One ended in five or six minutes with an axe severing his head. Then it vanished.

The death throes of the other went on and on. While the spasms were less brutal, bones still shattered, only slower. The dying Iteeche's howls of pain and screams of agony were unending.

At one point, the Iteeche standing by forced a breathing mask on the dying Iteeche.

"Why?" the prisoner pleaded.

"Your lungs are all knotted up and you're not getting enough oxygen. We can't have you dying too quickly."

"You rancid pond scum! You monster from the darkest deep! You . . ." the prisoner ran out of air. When he gasped in two deep breaths, he let out a primal scream. He tried to look away.

Lily locked his head in a Smart Metal™ brace and forced him to watch.

He shut his eyes tight, refusing to see.

Small grippers latched on to his eyelids and pried them open, forcing him to see the final death throes of the condemned prisoner. They were accompanied by screams that were only interrupted by gasps for breath.

MEGAN, I HAVE TOLD THE ITEECHE INTERROGATORS TO TAKE THEIR TIME.

THANK YOU, LILY.

"Why hasn't the axe men cut off his head?" the prisoner gasped.

"Why end his suffering?" Megan answered. "The agony of death will continue long after the body seems to have collapsed. That's why we're giving him oxygen. He'll suffer for hours before he finally loses full consciousness."

"Why would you do that to me? I don't matter. I'm not a Clan Chief or lord."

"Yes, I know," Megan said. "However, you know who gave you orders to blow up the aqueducts. He's the one we want to have a nice long talk with. He's the one that would face the needle and the long death. You, could very easily live a long and successful life."

"How?"

"Ships are always leaving for the new colonies. We can change your name so that the clans would never find you. We can add you to the first wave of immigrants and drop you in the first wave. Half of those die. We could also ship you to a young colony that has survived the worst of the start. You decide whether it will be you who makes the Most Sincere and Very Complete Apology to the Emperor using the needle injection, go to a raw colony, or to one that is in the early stages of progress. Which choice will you make?"

A few minutes later, the supervisor stumbled off, his arms in the firm grip of two MPs. He was headed for a holding cell. In a few days, he'd ship out to a colony ten years into its development. He'd likely survive there. Maybe even prosper.

Megan passed the clan lordling's name along to Kris and collapsed into her chair. Lily turned it into a comfortable recliner with a very pleasant back massager. Megan was grateful for the care. It had been hard enough to watch executions the old-fashioned way. This new way was horrible beyond comparison. No doubt it would be easier on the watchers than it was to those dying. However, Megan's ears still rang with the screams; she feared that she had added another potential nightmare to her nights.

Fifteen minutes later, a young lordling was hauled through the cell door. He was a soft fellow. Still, even after being strapped to the stool and with his arms in restraint, he sounded too ambitious and confident as he coldly promised vicious reprisal on the two guards in place of answers to their questions.

He was quite shocked when his failure to answer the question got him slugged in the gut. That brought on a new wave of threats that ended with him punched hard in the throat.

The protrusion that might pass for a jaw on an Iteeche was too small to really get a fist into.

In Megan's opinion, the guy hung on the edge of a confession. He'd look like he was about to break, then pull back. After the fifth repeat of that, Megan again sent the interrogators off, this time to a long lunch.

They left, talking among themselves about how good the snacks had been and how good lunch might be.

Megan let the hatch to the cell close and the room fall silent. She stalked around the prisoner several times, as if she was picking the most painful point at which to begin her questioning.

Finally, she began with almost a cliché. "We can do this the easy way, or we can do it the hard way. Which would you like?"

"What can a weak Human do to hurt an Iteeche?" the lordling sneered at Megan. Big mistake.

Lily didn't need a command. The chair sent electrical shocks through the prisoner. Everywhere his body touched the stool, he got shocked. His legs, his bottom, even his arms. They were secured to what appeared to be ruggedly hewn beams of wood. Now, they too, sparked.

In his restraints, the Iteeche lordling's body danced and spasmed for a few seconds. Then, just as suddenly as it began, it was gone, leaving the prisoner slumped in his restraints, gasping for breath.

"Do you still wonder what a 'weak Human' can do to you?"

"H-how c-could you do that?" he stammered.

"With magic," Megan said, diffidently.

"Magic metal, not wood," the Iteeche spat, as he rubbed his shoulders against the so-called wood.

"Now, as I said, easy way or hard way. Which will it be?"

The Iteeche focused all four eyes on Megan. "What's the easy way?"

"You give us something and we give you something. If you answer our questions correctly, we change your name. Your total identity. The clans will never find you."

Megan took a long breath before continuing. "We will find you a billet on a colony ship, headed out for the rim of the Empire. You can lose yourself among colonists scheduled to be the first to land on a new planet. There, you can take your chances with the bugs, worms, and other things that kill colonists who don't starve to death because their crops fail."

Megan paused to let that option sink in. "Alternately, we could put you on a ship headed for a colony that has survived the worst of the beginning. Give you a better chance of surviving and still make a place for yourself."

"I'd be a dirt-grubbing farmer," the prisoner spat, again.

"Do you have any special skills. Are you a doctor? An engineer? A mechanic?"

"Of course not, those all require getting your hands dirty."

The arrogance of the young fool seemed to have no bounds.

"Okay, I'm going to let you in on a secret. Here's what happens if you don't tell us everything we want to know." So, Megan told the lordling how he would die if he didn't give up the names. She avoided showing him the video.

Iteeche were normally a pale cream color. By the time she finished her description, the prisoner would make a ghost look well-tanned.

With a deep gulp, he began to spill his guts. "If I tell you who ordered me to arrange the explosion on the planet, are you sure I won't die that way?"

"I assure you in the name of Grand Admiral Kris Longknife that you will not have to make an apology to the Emperor."

The prisoner took several deep breaths, then asked, "What will happen to me?"

"Well," Megan said, keeping her voice matter-of-fact. "Depending on how helpful you are, you could go on one of those two colonial ships. If you insist on not going, we'll turn you loose. You can make your way in a much-reduced clan. I'm sure your talking to us won't have a negative impact on your advancement," Megan said, knowing very well that he'd be dead before midnight.

"Could I be made a clan lord on one of the colonial planets?" he stuttered.

"I understand that the clans don't set themselves up on colonial planets for thirty or forty years," Megan said, reminding the lordling of what he knew already. "They wait until the early colonists have created the infrastructure that makes the planet a civilized place to be. I guess we could try to slip you in then, but what clan role could we put you on?"

The prisoner realized the hopelessness of his situation. If he kept his present name, there were way too many senior clan lords who knew about his role in the operation. He could guess his role in the downfall of the clan.

He'd be a dead man.

Clan roles were tightly held. There was no way to slip his name into a minor lordship billet. Everyone from that clan on the planet would know he wasn't one of them.

The Iteeche closed all four of his eyes and took a deep breath. Then he began to talk. Ten minutes later, the guards walked him out to a holding cell, next to the supervisor he'd ordered to get a bomb made and planted.

They were both headed for successful startup colonies, though each would get a different one. There they would make their way in life like every other early colonist.

By getting their hands dirty.

Megan herself felt dirty. She wanted to wash all of this off and send it down the drain to be consumed in the reactors.

Instead, she reported to Kris. The admiral knew she was coming, and she knew what she'd report. Still, she made time to have tea with Megan, seated on the couch across from her.

"How bad was it?" the admiral asked.

"Kris, I say this as your cousin. If you can avoid playing that video Lily and Nelly concocted, you'll be a lot happier with this day."

"I understand. I turned the sound down a few seconds into it. I still have nightmares about that execution of a hundred rebel clan lords."

"This kind of execution will just go on and on. It feels like forever."

"Take the rest of the day off, Meg. I'd like to have you with me at dinner tonight. I'll be entertaining three clan lords and a guy who will never be a Planetary Overlord."

Megan rationed herself a huge Irish sigh before saying, "I'll be there, Admiral. I've got to get a shower and enough food in me to calm my stomach. It's in a knot."

"Understood, Meg. Job well done. Now, go relax. If you need time to debrief this horror, you have my permission to go to the head of the line and talk to any of the ship's therapists immediately."

"I may take you up on that, ma'am."

Megan finished her cup of tea and headed for her quarters. They weren't as palatial as Kris's, but with the ship expanded, she had plenty of room to put in a massage tub and fill it full of hot water before she turned on the jets.

She blanked her mind, relaxed, and took a trip to the beautiful hills of Santa Maria, then laughed softly as her mind's eye insisted on starting with the mountain that had been cut off perfectly at about the middle of its former height.

No one had figured out where the rest of the mountain went when it vanished. Megan's great-grandma had been one of the flighty teenagers to pull that stunt ... and live.

She might be a Longknife on one limb of her family tree, but she had some real crazy Irish on several of the other branches. It truly took the luck of the Irish to get her this far.

"Jesus, Mary, and Joseph, protect me tonight. I'll be dining with snakes on the table, and poisonous ones they'll be."

46

Grand Admiral Kris Longknife was entertaining as befit her rank and that of her putative guests. Her day quarters were as grand and imperial as Nelly could make them. Ancient statues vied with holographs of forests and waterfalls on one side of the room, a beach sunset stood frozen on the other.

Offset near the center of it all was a round table set for seven Iteeche and only four Humans.

The three lords of middling clans circulated among her and her other guests. Each had been allowed to walk down the passageway and enter Kris's day quarters unescorted by guards for the last hundred yards.

That was intended to restore some of their lost dignity from spending the day in a solitary cell. After all, this was a dinner in their honor.

The fact that the passageway they trod was lined with weapons detectors and explosive sniffers wasn't mentioned to them. Still, Nelly reported when each of them had proven unarmed and safe.

If they hadn't been, Nelly would have slammed the door in their face. They would have found the passageway converted to a very small bomb-proof cell.

Now, however, they exchanged small talk, waiting for the supposed Planetary Overlord they would work for when they landed.

Sam entered with a flourish and began to work the room as if this were the usual clan social where the juniors would fawn over the seniors and wait for any nugget of wisdom that dropped from the lips of their betters. The three lords from middling clans quick made a beeline for his august presence. However, several other Iteeche, all in uniform, were just as quick. The circle around him as he held court was large. The elephant in the room was ignored.

No one spoke of the day. No one spoke of the cells. Of course, since none of them had been interrogated, there was little to say about their day. However, being experts in saying nothing, they proved to be quite successful in doing just that.

Marines in full dress uniforms, with weapons well out of sight, entered, carrying trays of hors d'oeuvres.

For the Iteeche, there were lovely ceramic bowls divided into four quarters. Each portion held a different tasty treat for the Iteeche to spear and enjoy live. Different bowls held different tidbits; each Iteeche chose their own bowl.

The pecking order was quickly established. Sam, the future Planetary Overlord had first call. The three middling clan lords managed to avoid any conflict. Only after they had chosen were the nibbles offered to the admirals and general.

For the Humans, the small finger food was tiny crab puffs and slivers of fish or meat on miniature crackers. Cubes of different cheeses also lay scattered artistically around the plate, mixed in with slices of fruit or vegetables. They were all the same so there was no dispute about who chose first.

The ship's chefs had outdone themselves again.

Kris let the conversation center on every little thing except what everyone wanted to talk about: the explosion.

General Compeel shared with the clan lords the success of the huge operation that moved four hundred thousand soldiers down the beanstalk to join the garrison of Balan. Meanwhile, the same number of troops from Balan went up the beanstalk. Not a ferry had a vacant seat going either way.

Admiral Tong passed along to all of them that the fleet was ready to sail. The thousand local ships had shaken down well with the five wings of the Second Battlecruiser Fleet. The two thousand ships to be left behind to guard Balan were organized and had drilled operating as an independent task force.

"We're ready to sail any time you give the order," Admiral Tong told Kris.

"Good, because I want to give that order very soon. We have planets to conquer."

"You think we can leave soon?" the expectant Planetary Overlord asked. "So, you have solved the puzzle of the explosions?"

"Yes," Kris said, then, after a pause, added, "We captured both of the bombers while they were attempting their getaway."

"You did?" said the big fellow. "We heard all sorts of things. That you had them. That you didn't have them. That they'd suicided before saying anything."

"Oh, I would not allow anyone to suicide on me," Kris said. "We have a new device that forces the mouth open so poison can't be obtained. After we remove the tooth, we have no trouble with the prisoner avoiding their fate."

As one, the four clan lords' tongues went to the void in their mouths where a poison tooth had been removed earlier in the day.

"Have they made a Most Sincere and Very Complete Apology to the Emperor?" the future planetary overlord asked.

"We Humans have recently refined the technique for making such an Apology." Kris led them to the table as she told them about the idea of "milking" the poison from the snake and injecting it in a smaller dosage.

"We even have a pretty good idea about how it will go. If you'll take your seats."

The table was round. Kris sat, and offered the hopeful Planetary Overlord the stool at her right hand. He sat.

Admiral Tong slipped into the next stool, then waved the clan lord who they knew had blown up the aqueduct to join him.

Admiral Linn, the future Supreme Planetary Overseer for Balan took the next seat, while ushering the clan lord who attacked the first responders to join him. General Compeel took the next stool and waved the clan lord who had only carried the messages for the future Overlord to sit beside him.

Megan, Admiral Kitano, and Jack rounded out the table.

While the four Iteeche civilians had been checked thoroughly for weapons, every one of the uniformed personnel at the table had their sidearm handy.

"My computer, Nelly, has made up a hologram of what such an execution might look like compared to a normal one. Nelly?"

Two half-sized Iteeche were projected in the middle of the table. It was so real that Kris could see sweat running down the prisoners' naked bodies and the tremble of their narrow chins. Also obvious were the dark bruises and cuts on their bodies. Nelly had modeled them after what she'd seen at the apology a hundred Clan Lords had recently made to the Emperor.

Disembodied hands held both of them in place.

A red-clad snake wrangler opened the lid on a glass jar. The snake struck as a Human injected the other Iteeche.

Both Iteeche screamed and fell to their knees. For a moment, nothing seemed to happen, and the two doomed Iteeche just knelt there, whimpering. Then their bodies began to knot up and tear itself apart.

One body tore itself apart quickly. The other was much slower. However, the agony on either face as they screamed their lungs dry at the torture was no different.

Kris could not look away. She was like a bird, mesmerized by a snake. The slow death was so horrible to look at that she had to struggle to hold herself back. When the last death throes were over, she needed to be ready to strike like a snake at these four Iteeche Clan Lords. She would have only a moment to extract a confession from them before that golden opportunity was gone.

So, Kris studied the Iteeche lords as they watched in horror. From the looks on their faces, she had a pretty good suspicion that they were seeing their own deaths. Since death to traitors was the eternal mantra of the Empire, none of them saw any way out of this scenario.

The last spasm, last jerk, last uncontrolled gurgle ended.

For a moment, there was silence.

Then the holographs on the table were replaced by the initial bomber. His confession was cut down to just the basics.

"That has nothing to do with me," his clan lord snapped. "I knew nothing of this."

Kris paused the parade of figures across the table. "Be careful what you say, gentlemen. The last one lying to me is the one who dies that death."

"What do you mean?" the clan lord who only carried the water asked.

"He told the truth. We are providing him with a new identity and shipping him off to a colony world on the rim. He may die there, or he may live and prosper."

"You are saving him from making a Most Sincere and Very Complete Apology to the Emperor?" the not-so-future Planetary Overlord demanded.

"Yes, I am," Kris said. "I think the one who ordered him to blow up my planet is the one who needs to make such an apology."

The named supervisor now spoke from the center of the table. When he finished, no one said a word.

"Shall I show the next one? We have interviewed him."

"Have you also offered him a free ride to the colonies so he can grub in the dirt?" his clan lord said, snidely.

"Yes, I have," Kris answered

"Are you such a fool that you trust a traitor's word?"

"When several other people verify portions of the story," Kris said, "yes, I begin to trust the word of a traitor. Now, I'm about to play the next confession. Once I start it, only one option will remain on the table for some of you."

Four gulps were audible from around the table.

"I had nothing to do with those bombs," the water carrier half-shouted as he jumped into the conversation. "I was just asked to invite that clan lord to a meal with our future Planetary Overlord."

"Shut up!" the never-to-be-Overlord screamed.

Megan stood and waved that junior clan lord toward the door to Kris's day quarters. It opened before they got there. Four Iteeche Marines were waiting for him. It was a most hangdog Iteeche clan lord that walked into their custody.

"I'd heard from several sources that you invited this junior clan lord to your table," Kris told the never-to-be Planetary Overlord.

"So, what of it? We have plans to make for when you finally capture us a planet," he replied, wrapped in invulnerable dignity.

He had no idea how moth eaten that garment was.

"Or when you get a chance to take over this one," Kris said, then turned to the clan lord who actually ordered the bombing of the water aqueducts. "Shall I start the holograph of the junior lordling's confession?"

The Iteeche leaned forward, rested four elbows on the table, then put his four palms over his four eyes. Without looking at Kris, he began speaking.

"I didn't want to do it. Why should I do it? What good could it bring to me and my clan? Still, he threatened to see that I held my job for little more than a moon. If I didn't help him get this planet, I and my entire clan would be out of our jobs and starving on the streets before you even jumped out of the system you conquered and gave to him."

"No trust, huh?" Kris muttered to the grasping Planetary Overlord.

"Why should I trust you?" Sam shouted. "You promised this first conquest to me and my clan. You promised! Then you played this crazy game of semantics like some blind Imperial philosopher. You peeled your words until they had no more meaning than a flower stripped of its petals. What was there to trust?"

"My word," Kris growled. "Megan bring in the guards."

"You will not!" the Clan Lord snapped. "I am the master of a clan. You have no standing over me. I demand to speak to the council of clans. Let them hear my words and it will be you making that horrible new way of apologizing to the Emperor. You Humans never know when to leave well enough alone."

"Very well," Kris said. "I had planned to bring you back to the Imperial Court for you to make your apology personally to the Emperor before all the clan chiefs. You will accompany me through my battles from a solitary cell on my flag."

"I will not! I knew what you were up to. We Iteeche are not fools! Not one of those Battleships of State will sail unless I am aboard mine. Not one."

Kris raised her eyebrows. "That will be interesting to see. Especially after I tell them what my next target planet is. Guards, remove these three Iteeche from my sight. I've had enough of them."

The rest of them shared a much more comfortable dinner after the four Iteeche were removed.

Next morning, Kris gave the order for the invasion fleet to sail before the battlecruisers pulled up anchor. Each of the nine Battleships of State detached from the space station right on schedule and followed the troop transports as they headed for the least-used jump point out of the Balan system.

47

The battlecruisers were in the lead as the fleet headed into the first jump. Three jumps later, two of them the advanced type, they jumped into the target system.

Longnae was one of the three richest systems left to the rebellion. It had two occupied industrial planets, two more worthless ones being mined, and a richly exploited asteroid field.

If they were going to try to stop her sweep through their gut, this was a likely place for them to defend.

Kris was not disappointed.

Longnae 3 and 4 were both circled by space stations. From them came the hum of a battle fleet ready for combat. The weird noise from their reactors made it nearly impossible for the *Princess Royal*'s signal analysis team to separate them out.

"Ten thousand? Twenty thousand? More?" Kris asked.

For a long five minutes, the head of Sensors Division polled his three leading chiefs. They added in a pair of sensor operators first class to the assessment.

Shaking his head, the Sensor Division Officer headed for Kris.

"First off, Admiral, the enemy ships are packed onto that station like cans of sardines. The piers are dangerously close together."

"That doesn't sound so good," Kris said.

"Yes, ma'am. However, there is something else. We think part of our problem is caused by a new reactor. Lots of them."

"A new reactor type? What can you tell me about it?"

Sensors let out a sigh. "As I said, they are crammed in so close together that we can't separate one from another. They all just kind of form a line of static with every spike too close together for us to make anything out of it. We also think there may be some heterodyning between the different engines. One signal may be modifying another, so that what we see from the same reactor once may be different from the next one, depending on how close or how powerful the reactors around it are."

"I repeat, Commander, is what we are facing closer to ten or twenty thousand?"

Sensors shook his head slowly. "Admiral, you're asking me for little more than a guess at this range. I think we might be able to pull the noise apart as we get closer."

The look on Kris's face must have hastened the commander to add, "Closer to twenty thousand than ten thousand. It could be over twenty."

Kris frowned. "What makes you say that?"

"We're assuming that these are battlecruisers with three reactors. What if there are more ships with fewer reactors aboard?"

"Do you think the Iteeche have managed to spin out a new class of ship?"

"I'm not saying anything, because I don't know anything. However, the reactors seem to be a bit strange, strange enough to modify the standard music we get off of the usual reactors both we and they use. There is something not right here. I'm not sure we can assume that what worked last fight will work for this attack."

Kris nodded, finally accepting that one of her usual miracle workers had come up empty handed.

She asked Jack to report to her day quarters and converted the conference table into a large map board. If she wanted 3-D, Nelly could add that later.

Jack found her pondering the map of the Longnae system.

"You look worried," Jack said, as he rested his hands on the table beside hers.

"I am."

"How so?" her husband asked. He rested a hand on her shoulder and rubbed it for a second. A moment later, he was standing behind her, working on both sides of her backbone, from shoulders to the small of her back.

Kris breathed in slowly, enjoying the warmth of Jack's touch on her back. She let the stress in her flow out through his fingers and her breath. Still, she only allowed herself a very brief minute.

"While we were playing patty cake with the clan lords, the rebels came up with a surprise."

"What kind of surprise?"

"Nelly, give me a replica of what a sensor board should look like when it's scanning a thousand battlecruisers."

A moment later, the table opened a window. It showed three bars: one tan, one white, one gray. Across them ran reports, traced out in green, red, and black. The squiggles told their story in a moving series of peaks and troughs. Strangely, the peaks and valleys of one strip were usually mimicked by those above and below it. There was some variance, but not much.

"That's what the space station above Longnae 4 should look like. Here's what it does. Nelly?"

The table opened a window with the sensor take that had everyone puzzled. In place of regularly repeating sine waves that were closely mirrored by the tracings of the signals above and below, it showed something totally different.

These traces were a jagged series of ups and down, with data in none of the three bars reflecting in any of the others. Indeed, occasionally the green trace would shoot off the chart. Other times it crashed to the lowest data point.

It was the same for the other two bars. They showed short jagged movements that edged up or down overall. Interspersed with that pattern were sharp spikes also going up or down.

"Nelly, can you spot any sort of a pattern in this jumble?"

"Kris, I and all my children within the fleet have been searching for a pattern since this first came in. So far, the major excursions have not been repeated in any kind of a pattern. Every time we spot a pattern in the low grass, it lasts for only a few seconds, then it takes off like a wild thing again. Sorry, Kris, but they either have a jammer with capabilities way beyond anything we could mimic, or they've done something that naturally produces the most random noise I've ever heard."

"So, let's assume that the Iteeche computers have not suddenly gotten better than ours," Jack said. "What does that leave us?"

"A new reactor for a new class of ships," Kris whispered.

"Nelly," Jack said, "could you filter out what would be the normal sensor take from a fleet of battlecruisers?"

"I will try," Nelly said. "I may have to search a bit to find the right place to slip in the canceling data."

For several long minutes, the different squiggles shimmied and shook as Nelly tried to find a place where injecting the normal battlecruiser reactor readout could fit into the present readout and make everything fall into a useful pattern.

Finally, the screen went back to its previous uninformative mess.

"Kris, there *must* be several other input sources for the data. I've tried several million ways to fit the battlecruiser noise into these patterns and I've gotten nowhere. Every attempted match left patterns that are still way too random."

"Thank you, Nelly."

"What do we do now?" Jack asked. "Turn around and go find another planet?"

"That might be the smartest thing to do," Kris mused slowly. "However, we have a major rebel fleet here. We left Balan with two thousand battlecruisers for its defense. It seems to me that with our six thousand warships, we ought to be able to take on this unknown fleet. After all, I've never had a larger force under my command."

"That is true," Jack said. "However, I don't remember you ever sticking your head in a lion's mouth without checking how loose its dentures were."

"I know," Kris said slowly. "Yes, I know. So, let's stick our head in this noose very carefully. Nelly, set a fleet speed for Longnae 4 at one gee for the battlecruiser fleet. When the attack transports finish coming through, let the soldiers have it easy. If we have them head in at .4 gees, we should have plenty of room to maneuver."

"And if we get a surprise?" Jack asked.

Kris studied the system. "We've got a couple of gas giants between us and Longnae 4. They're a bit off our course, but they'd give us a place to swing around and reverse course. Maybe refuel as well. There's a rocky planet fairly close to 4 that we can also swing around."

"That assumes they haven't read your own book on defense," Jack pointed out. "They could be using it to swing around and put themselves on a parallel course for a running gun battle as you approach their planet."

Kris made a face at Jack. "I had hoped that you hadn't noticed that." She shook her head. "I'd much rather be defending this system than attacking it."

"I'm glad you hear yourself admitting that," Jack said.

Kris nodded. "They're in a good position to mount a defense. They've got an unknown number of ships, with some way of masking their reactors that confuses us. Yeah, what's not to like."

48

The approach to Longnae 4 was slow . . . and it remained uninformative. The noise coming off the five space stations orbiting Longnae 4 and the other three space stations orbiting Longnae 3 continued to run together. Sensors could not take a count of reactors, so the force ahead remained unknowable.

The sensor division head was often seen walking the passageways shaking his head and mumbling to himself. That might have been something to worry about. However, Nelly remained just as befuddled.

"It is as if they had plastered reactors all over the surface of the stations," Nelly said. "Assuming they have, and this isn't some new jamming, how could they dock that many ships that close without having some of them smashing into the piers as they docked?"

Nelly seemed to shake her non-existent head. "Even if they did risk packing their ships in that tight, there would inevitably be some pier strikes. There would have to be spaces in the noise where a ship crashed as it tried to catch the hook. Kris, this is driving me crazy."

"Is this the first time you haven't been able to solve a problem?" the admiral asked.

"It's the biggest one I have failed to hack," Nelly admitted, "and the one that bothers me the most."

Kris pulled her focus from the puzzling planets ahead to eye her own fleet. She had it formed up in the normal fashion, five wings in a cross shape. The cross could be spread out to prevent the enemy from engulfing it or concentrated to bring more fire to bear on a smaller area.

Kris preferred that flexibility in battle.

She had a bit more than 1,200 battlecruisers per wing. However, 200 of them were green as grass. They'd only had the brief time since they departed Balan to shake down, learn Kris's drills, and operate with a fleet this large.

There were 640 experienced combat battlecruisers that had had come with Kris to the Imperial Capital. All the rest of her 6,000 had only a few weeks of drill under her command. Kris would have to be careful both with what she ordered and the way she ordered it. Confusion could easily slip into the ranks of battlecruisers if half understood her order one way, and half another way.

The more Kris reflected on her situation, the less she liked it.

However, she was an experienced enough battle commander to know that the other side of her battle board had their own problems. To date, she had been beating the rebels like a drum. Those ships up ahead were most likely just as green as her own crews. Maybe more so.

She surveyed the system. It was devoid of any sign that ships were moving about. That included merchant ships as well as warships. She remembered a saying from back when Navies were wet and powered by sail that went something like the Royal Navy drank their grog while the French kept to port. While it compared two alcoholic drinks, it was also meant to point out that Navies are meant to be used, not kept swinging around the anchor.

Her fleet, though its time was short, was doing what warships did. Drill, drill, and drill some more. Could the same be said for that unknown mass of ships ahead, tied up to the space station's piers? As happened so often when she went into battle, she would have to wait for the end of a horrible day to know the answer to that.

The answer began to come clear when the space stations above Longnae 3 sortied a battle fleet. Warships by the thousands detached from the stations and set a course for the worthless rock that was Longnae 5 at 1.7 gees. That was double the normal gravity for an Iteeche.

The enemy's intention to swing around the fifth planet and settle on a parallel course for Longnae 4 where they could take Kris's fleet under fire became obvious.

"Kris," Nelly said, "Most of the battlecruisers have detached from the bases around Longnae 3."

"Yes," Kris said, waiting for the next shoe to drop.

"I am still having problems making sense of the hash coming off the stations. The noise is all over the place and too close and confused for me to separate it into a coherent signal."

"I'm sure we'll find out soon enough," Kris said.

Kris was sitting down to lunch with Jack and Megan when Nelly cleared her throat.

"Yes, Nelly?" Kris said.

"The noise from Longnae 3 is now detaching from the stations there and accelerating at 2.1 gees for Longnae 5."

"Do you have a coherent signal?" Jack asked while Kris waited for Nelly to get to the point.

"The signal is coalescing into an intelligent blend of signals."

"Spit it out, Nelly," Kris finally ordered, exasperated by the wait.

"We are facing a fleet of small- to medium-sized ships, all with one reactor of traditional Iteeche design such as we saw in the Iteeche War ninety years ago. They appear to be armed with a few large lasers. The weapon systems are different, but the same in some ways."

"What do you mean, Nelly?" Kris asked.

"Even though the lasers are 20-inch and 22-inch guns, they all have two capacitors. Smaller, but two."

"Does that mean what I think it means?" Jack asked.

"If you think it means they can fire a large laser for only a few seconds, then reload one laser at a time to get off a second shot, yes. Depending on what electrical power they're drawing from the reactor, they should be able to reload the two small capacitors faster than they could reload one big one."

"Any idea what the range is on these lasers?" Kris asked. "Our Fast Attack Boats were armed with 18-inch pulse lasers. They packed a wallop but only at a short range."

"It's hard to tell," Nelly answered. "Some appear to be armed with cast-off lasers from ships that were upgraded to 24-inchers. Others, I'm not so sure. I also have to wonder where the reactors came from. They match the signatures we took off Death Balls during the war. Biremes and Tri-remes had two or three reactor pods around the sphere. Quadri-remes and Penta-remes added four or five pods, then double or tripled the reactors and were laser mounted. Toward the end of the war, the Death Balls had gotten huge. That gave them a lot of firepower, but also left them a large target."

"Tell me something I don't know, Nelly," Kris grumbled.

"Somebody hit the archive library of reactor designs and came up with all the different reactors they had on those different ships: smallest, small, medium, big, bigger, biggest, large, largest."

"I get your point," Kris snapped.

"They must have mass produced a lot of those old reactor designs, then build ships around them for any guns they had on hand. It was all those different reactor designs, complicated by the new power system that gives them five or six times the power of regular ships that made it impossible for me to match all their different signals to what we had in our archives."

"How many are there?" Jack asked.

"I'm still having problems sorting them out," Nelly said.

"Still?" Kris growled.

"Somehow, they've got the signals still squashed up together. I spotted a few as they began to launch, but as more got into space, the clutter went back to hash. I don't know how they can get so much noise out of this mess, but the signal is far enough away that they all blend into one big mash up."

Kris must have looked ready to tear into her computer, because Jack jumped in before Kris could say something she'd regret.

"Okay, Kris, we know they've made a major industrial effort to slap together ships from spare parts, old designs, and whatever they could pull together. Nelly, are these ships Smart Metal?"

"I don't hear any hum from that frequency, Jack. I think they threw whatever they had at this project."

"Ouch," Jack said.

"Ouch," Kris repeated. After taking five deep breaths, she focused on the battle board. "So, we've got an unknown lot of small attack craft. Likely fast as well. We can't get a solid count because they've got themselves clumped so close that all their reactor noise merges together."

"Sooner or later," Jack said, "Someone's bound to screw up and ram someone else."

"We can only hope so," Kris muttered. "We can only hope."

49

Hope is not a solid strategy or a battle plan. However, as Kris continued toward Longnae, that was all she had. No enemy skipper made any mistake. Not one of them took it in his head to ram the ship nearest him.

However, the time came for the fleet around Longnae 4 to sortie if they intended to join the fleet coming from Longnae 3. That finally answered Kris's question.

Ten thousand more battlecruisers were not what Kris wanted to face. Still, she expected her fleet to be able to fight outnumbered three-to-one and win. Fifteen- to sixteen-thousand rebel battlecruisers would amount to less than three-to-one odds.

However, it was the smaller ships that Kris wanted to observe. They were close enough to get a solid visual on them. The first pictures cleared up a lot of questions . . . and left Kris with more.

In order to get enough range for the smaller ships to circle Longnae 5 and turn back to engage Kris's fleet, all those small ships with their different reactors were lashed to a central fuel tank. The reactors on the six to eight ships connected to that auxiliary tank of reaction mass were so close as to make sensors go bonkers.

To make matters worse, it seemed like every collection of small ships was different. Any effort to extract data from one clump fell apart when Nelly tried to match it against any noise coming from another close to it.

The signals from the different configurations simply merged into one huge scream of static.

Kris had to take her hat off to this bunch. They not only had thrown together a huge scratch force that was very likely going to make a hash of Kris's fleet's fire control computers, but by mixing and matching, they'd confused the best and suckered Kris right into their trap.

Which missed the point entirely. Kris was exactly where she wanted to be.

So, she called a council of war on net with Admirals Tong and Kitano.

Quickly, Kris brought them up to date on the latest intel. "So, we face 16,000 battlecruisers when the two forces merge. As for the new ships, let's call them cruisers, it looks like there are at least twenty thousand strong. Maybe twenty-five. Nelly's still prying each cluster apart and counting noses."

"The Magnificent Nelly is having trouble?" Jack asked.

"Each cluster has to be individually looked at," Nelly said. "Worse, some of the reactors are heterodyning on each other so that two or three appear to be one. I believe that my estimate based on signal noise will likely be off by as much as ten percent, plus or minus."

"That bad?" Admiral Kitano remarked.

"Pretty much," Kris's computer answered. "Until we have a solid visual on all of them, we're going to be in the dark."

Admiral Tong cleared his throat. "Pardon me for asking, but could the different cruisers that are clustered around that reaction fuel tank possibly be hiding more ships that have their reactors closed down?"

"I wish you hadn't mentioned that," Kris answered. "Yes, you're right. I have a hard time believing that even a system as large as this one could knock together this swarm of attack craft. However, there could be one more surprise in store for us."

"If I was in their shoes," Admiral Kitano said, slowly, "I'd pick a highly productive system and concentrate my forces there. They know you go for the wealthy systems. It's kind of hard to maintain surprise when you're picking your targets from a short list of the rebellion's most productive planets."

Kris couldn't disagree with that. Could it be that she'd finally bit off more than she could chew? She had certainly taken bites out of the rebels. Could she have gone hunting a fox and ended up facing a bear?

Shaking her head, Kris chose to bull through this. "Their level of training has to be low. The quality of their equipment also is questionable considering its likely obsolescence as well as hasty construction. Remember folks, the view from the other side is likely just as scary as the view was from this side."

Kris found a feral grin spreading across her face. Not only was the view from the other side likely very troubled, but she could make their situation even scarier.

"Admirals Tong and Kitano, let's steer a course closer to Longnae 5. Why not start this fight sooner and see how they take to that?"

"It will also give us more room to maneuver as we close Longnae 4," Admiral Tong said.

"Yep. Let's see how he reacts to us serving up a change to his battle plan."

She issued the order, and 6,000 battlecruisers edged over ten degrees but kept their deceleration at one gee.

Kris waited to see how her opposite would react to her not only not running but steering her ships closer.

50

Zom'sum'Ka'sum'Quin, of the Quin'sum'Domm clan, Imperial Admiral of the Second order of Steel, stared at his battle board as if it might show him the thoughts of his old teacher Commander Tong. For a Last Chosen with no clan, that man was one fine teacher at the academy.

He was also his opponent for this developing battle. True, the Human Kris Longknife was somewhere in the pile of stinking seaweed and dead fish left high and dry by a storm. Still, the word was that Tong had been raised up by the loyalists to command this fleet of the combined fleets.

It was he that Zom must defeat. With a third to a half of the Combined Fleet wreckage in the Longnae System, it would be an easy matter to sail his fleet to the Imperial Capital and put an end to that poseur the senior clans had raised up to sit as their puppet on the throne.

His enemy was following a standard five-wing formation: van, main body, and a rear guard with an upper and lower wing protecting the flanks of the main body. That allowed them to concentrate their firepower where they wanted without allowing him to flank and engulf them. That might have worked if he had 10,000 ships to face their 6,000.

Zom, however, had his own plans. His 16,000 battlecruisers were divided into nine wings. Two extra wings extended the line fore and aft of the usual three wings. The other two extra wings were above and below the high and low wings.

Four of Tong's wings would be rolled up by a force double that number.

If that wasn't enough of a problem, 25,000 unarmored cruisers with lasers big enough to burn the hide off of a battlecruiser would be mingled in with the battlecruisers, filling in the intervals between wings, charging through those holes in the line to close with the enemy, pouring on more gees than any Iteeche warship had ever taken.

Tong would find himself engulfed both by stinging bees as well as battlecruisers easily his equal in speed and maneuverability. With Zom's fleets outfitted with new high gee couches, this would be a very different battle from any ever fought in the Empire.

This victory would lead the way for a new Empire. The ocean was about to suffer a sea change. The water that had grown cold, the fish who had grown sluggish, were about to be upset and overthrown by an upwelling of warm water, full of young and eager fish, ready to feed on those that were fat and slow.

The old Empire would be preserved. These fools who dragged the Humans into the Empire's private affairs could rot in the dark depths.

Zom's ruminations were interrupted as his number one staff officer cleared his throat. "Sir, it appears that the Imperial admiral has made an adjustment to his course."

"What is old Tong up to, Number One?" Zom asked.

"He is now on a course to pass closer to Longnae 5, Sir. The battle will be joined sooner and last longer."

"That is not something that I expected of Tong. He always struck me as a bit of an old ninny, always following the War College's standard solution," Zom said, eyeing the change in course. For a bunch of green skippers, those six thousand battlecruisers did the course change quite smartly. Still, he would expect nothing less from ship drivers drilled by his old teacher.

"Sir, is it possible that he may be under the influence of the Human Kris Longknife more than you expect?" his Number One asked, most tactfully.

"Tong was never under anyone's influence. Would a battlecruiser captain who allowed himself to be swayed easily have turned away from a lost battle and come back alive?"

"No, sir."

"Of course not," Zom answered both his Number One and himself. He gazed long and hard at his battle board, studying the developing battle from every angle. He had a good eyeball for the way battles developed on the board. He'd won many a simulation with just a glance at the board.

Now, his instincts said it was time to sail for battle.

"Number One, order the fleet to up acceleration to 2.5 gees. Set a course for Longnae 5 that will have us joining up with the Longnae 3 fleet sooner. We can then form up before we swing around that small gas bag."

"To hear is to obey, Admiral," the junior officer said, and stepped back to give the execute order for the plans already distributed to the fleet.

Admiral Zom took a deep breath as his body grew heavier on his high gee couch. He had seen this battle many times in his mind's eyes. Now he would make it a fact in space.

51

Admiral Kris Longknife studied the vectors as the two rebel fleets upped their acceleration, then she went to supper. By the time she dropped by her flag bridge to make a final check before hitting the rack, the rebel commander's intent was clear.

Nelly reported she had found it quite a struggle to get a head count.

"Each cluster around a huge fuel tank had to be analyzed individually. Each cluster was a different collection of types of ships," she told Kris.

"There were six different reactor types, five of which dated back to the Iteeche War almost a hundred years ago. Their designs have been updated a bit. The sixth reactor is the one presently used by most Iteeche freighters built in the last ten years."

Six different reactor signatures showed up in windows flowing down the right side of her board.

"Still, the noise coming off of those six reactors should not have delayed me as much as it has. However, there was a different mix of six or more reactors coming off many of the clusters," Nelly reported.

On the board, each of the six reactor signatures however, had been broken down to five to twelve slightly different signatures.

"I doubt if they did this intentionally," Nelly said.

Kris studied the various reactors' electronic signatures. Some were wildly different. Some were hardly noticeable. Taken as a whole, however, they created a racket that made them hard to get a handle on.

"So, "Kris said, "could this be a function of the production methods? Are we looking at the product of a whole lot of different fabrication plants?"

"Kris, these may be handmade in factories. They could be the product of machinery and Iteeche labor rather than a standardized and automated fabrication plant. Even among these half-dozen there are too many variations for anything fabricated by standardized production functions. When they turn on all these dissimilar reactors at the same time, I get a hash of a signals like the ones that have been making it so hard for me to count noses around these tanks."

"Have you got an estimate, yet?" Kris asked.

"I know that you are facing sixteen thousand battlecruisers. Traveling with them are somewhere between twenty to twenty-five thousand single reactor cruisers with lasers ranging from 16-inches to 22-inches. All appear to be using smaller capacitors and more of them."

"So, we're facing something like a garage sale of reactors, motors, and weapons. Any idea which are newly built and which were pulled out of long storage or a museum?"

"Impossible to guess, Kris. The question I do find intriguing is this: did the Longnae system manage to knock all these cruisers together? You know that the fleet in front of us has to be a concentration of battlecruisers from several systems. Did they also send along their hand-me-down flotsam and jetsam?"

"Would it matter, Nelly?"

"It would mean there are likely several more thinly defended planets ready for the picking," Jack put in.

"Nelly?" Kris asked again.

"Jack has a good point," Kris's computer said.

"There's also the matter of the fleet you're facing," Jack continued.

"It's thrown together," Kris pointed out. "Where did they get their ranging sensors and fire control computers, assuming they have any?" Lasers were worthless without the complete system to aim them.

Jack shook his head, his eyes still on the battle board and the developing fleet action. "Kris, you know as well as I do that quantity has a quality all its own. If they get enough laser fire criss-crossing space, we're bound to run into some of it."

Kris didn't like Jack's point, but, still, he had one. "Nelly, could we turn this fleet around and get out of here?"

"It would be a tight run, but we could swing around Longnae 6 and head back for the jump."

"And our transports?"

Nelly took a bit longer to answer that one. "It would require some very smart ship handling. Any collisions at the jump point could leave a lot of wreckage drifting there. More ships would pile into them and the entire fleet could become backed up for some time."

Kris spent a long moment examining her options. They boiled down to one, really. Charge her way through. Fight them, even if they were using her own defensive battle plan against her.

"Jack, I've always wondered how I'd do fighting my own plan. He's hoisting me on my own petard. He's got his fleet out here and intends to spend as much time on a parallel course as he can. That is exactly what I would do if I was him."

"So," Jack said, "what would you do if you were you on the offensive?"

Kris let her eyes wander the battle board, measuring distance and accelerations for two different forces.

"Nelly," she said, still thinking, "we're close to the point of flipping ship. How much sooner would we pass Longnae 5 if I set our deceleration at half a gee?"

The battle board blinked, and new vectors replaced the ones that had been there for most of a day. It showed Kris's 2nd Battlecruiser Fleet arriving ahead of the rebel's main force and a bit more ahead of the smaller one.

Kris's battlecruiser force would sweep by the enemy ships while they were slowing before their swing around Longnae 5. She'd have time for several broadsides at them as the two forces raced by each other. The shooting done, Kris would head direct for Longnae 4 and the rebels would be faced with a long rear chase.

"That looks good," Jack said, "but it leaves our transports hanging out there in our rear."

"Yeah, that was a bad idea, wasn't it?" Kris admitted. It was a bad idea to let the enemy get between her and her vulnerable transports. She again studied vectors and accelerations.

"We could have them change course for Longnae 7," she muttered, finally.

"Keep our transports well out of reach of his guns," Jack observed.

"Yeah. We could always send them on a grand tour of the star system until we've taken Longnae 4 and can take off after whatever ships they have chasing them," Kris answered.

"That might do it, Admiral," Jack admitted.

"Nelly, pass along our latest intel to Admirals Tong and Kitano. Tell them I want to talk to them at 0830 tomorrow morning. If anyone has any idea how we catch these bastards in their own trap, I'd be glad to hear about it."

"Aye, aye, Admiral," Nelly said. "The message is sent. They will be waiting for you to call them right after breakfast."

"Now, Nelly, inform Admiral Tong that I wish to steer five degrees closer to Longnae 5 and cut deceleration to .5 gee."

Aye, aye, Admiral," Nelly again replied. "The order has been received. Admiral Tong has issued preparatory orders to the fleet."

"Tell him to execute."

"Aye, aye, Admiral. It is done."

Kris felt herself get lighter as her weight dropped by half. She did not feel a five-degree change in course.

Over the next several minutes, Kris peeled a flotilla out of each of her wings, a total of 160 battlecruisers and got them and her transport fleet on a course that would take them well out of the way of the coming fight.

"Very good, Nelly. Now, Jack, I'm tired and I'd like to have my mind emptied of my worries for a few hours. Do you have any suggestions?"

"I may have a few, Admiral," Jack said.

His long legs got him to the hatch that entered their day quarters faster than Kris's tired legs could. He opened the door and ushered her into their quarters, not at all like a general, but definitely like a lover.

52

Admiral Zom, Commanding the First Combined Fleets of the True Loyalists was awoken from a sound sleep by his Number One Staff Officer.

"The Human Kris Longknife," he almost spat the word, "has sent her ships in all sorts of wild directions as if they were mindless pollywogs dodging hungry fingerlings."

Zom dressed and carefully covered the distance to his flag bridge in less than five minutes. Walking at two and a half times his usual weight was a pain. However, he liked to sleep in his own bed. Many of his crew were already sleeping at their battle stations in their high gee couches.

On the way, he wondered what had caused his Number One to assume the Longknife Human was commanding the fleet opposite them.

He eyed his battle board for a moment as he slipped onto his high gee couch, then frowned. "Are these projected vectors correct? How long have her ships been on these insane courses?"

"We first spotted something strange about half an hour ago," Number One said, sounding very stressed. "We waited for a quarter of an hour for the tracks to firm up, then I went to wake you. In the meantime, we checked with several other flagships and they all are showing the same course adjustments. I ordered every ship to check their search sensors and they have. What you see is what she is actually doing," the staff officer said, stuttering a bit as he finished.

Admiral Zom ordered his battle board to extrapolate where the Human's fleet deceleration would place it in thirteen, twenty-six, and thirty-nine hours. When those new vectors were overlaid with his present course and acceleration, the results were enough to make an admiral wish to be a fingerling again.

Zom growled at the display. "We must slow down to round Longnae 5. Meanwhile, she will whiz by us in a flash. Our fire control systems will hardly be able to target a ship with that much energy on it. They would find us as easy to hit as ducks floating on a pond."

Admiral Zom made a face at his board. "Worse, when she finishes shooting us up, she will be between us and Longnae 4."

"We will also be between her battle fleet and her invasion transports, Most Eminent Admiral."

"Show me the transports," Zom demanded.

The scale of the battle board zoomed out to show much more of the system. Then the board went blank for the better part of a minute while its computer calculated the information on the course the transports had been following for the last half day.

When the screen came back, Admiral Zom barely managed to suppress a groan. The transports had changed course at the same time the battlefleet had reduced its deceleration. They were now headed for Longnae 7. That would open up a large number of options. The troop ships could return back to Jump Point 5. They could take off for Jump Point 3. They could aim for Longnae 6 and let it sling them around and direct them toward the industries of Longnae 4.

Not one of those choices need be taken until they were on approach to Longnae 7. In the meantime, any ship that he sent after them would be conducting a long, stern chase.

There would be nothing to keep the battle fleet of that tadpole keeping the throne warm from ordering its own Marines to occupy

Longnae 4. Then that Human's battlecruisers could take off to intercept his ships for a second time. Would that battle go any better than the potential only one a day away?

"Battle board, assume my fleet increases its acceleration to three gees."

The board went blank again as the computer did the necessary calculations. The flag bridge was cool and drenched in shadows as he and his staff waited in silence for the results of his question.

The board came to life. Again, it showed where the two battle fleets would be in thirteen, twenty-six, and thirty-nine hours. Admiral Zom saw that his fleet would still be rounding Longnae 5 after his enemy's fleet had sped by. There would be no battle. That was not the way of his old Tong. No. The Human was showing her yellow belly.

However, he could accelerate to catch up with the fleet commanded by that Human. In all likelihood, the enemy would have the advantage of firing salvo after salvo at his stern. Her ships would be targeting his vulnerable rocket motors and fusion reactors that, if hit, could destroy the ship quicker than any other laser strike.

He could not let his enemy get ahead of him.

"Battle board, recalculate assuming a 3.5 gee acceleration and deceleration by our fleet."

"At what point do you intend to flip ship and begin deceleration?" the computer asked.

"Six hours from now," Admiral Zom snapped, picking a time off the top of his head. He had to accelerate as much as possible before he began the deceleration. He needed to pick up minutes to get his fleet there faster.

Once again, the board went blank. Once again, the Iteeche standing around the board were silent as the seconds ticked by. At their stations around the flag bridge, watch standers did their duty but it was easy to tell that they behaved as if they were walking on eggs. No one wanted to disturb the admiral while he was making life and death decisions.

The board did not come back in a minute, or in two minutes. It was closer to five minutes later before the screen came to life. What it showed explained the delay.

The intent had been to use Longnae 5 to swing the force around back toward the planet they were set on defending. The results on the board showed a fleet sling shooting around the small gas giant. However, lots of ships failed to complete the course reversal and headed off in all kinds of different directions.

The battlecruisers swooped low, then shot into a high elliptical orbit. Rocket engines quickly brought them around to a course headed for Longnae 4. The gunboats, however, were not so lucky.

Depending on the size of the reactor and the mass of the ship it powered, that class failed to make any kind of an orbit, but rather did a slingshot off the planet, and headed for points unknown. Some managed to swing around, but it was slow and took up a good chunk of space.

They would never rejoin the battlecruisers.

Other ships never managed to turn the corner and just kept going. Admiral Zom measured their situation with a sailor's eye and shook his head. The best these ships could hope for was to make for Jump Point 5 and use it to jump into an empty system.

With luck, they might be close enough to a gas giant so they could refuel and aim themselves back at the jump. Zom scowled. Jump 5 was never used; he had no idea what lay in that next system.

"Number One, orders to the fleet. Prepare to go to 3.5 gees in ten minutes."

"To hear is to make it so," the staff officer said, and moved off to the comm section.

"Battle board, what deceleration would I have to use in order to have my entire fleet successfully swing around Longnae 5? Assume I accelerate at 3.5 gees for the next six hours?"

The board went blank.

Admiral Zom relaxed into his high gee couch and eyed the bridge. They were professionals, going about their duties.

"You, Boson," the admiral snapped.

The Boson's mate immediately snapped to attention. "Yes, My Admiral."

"What kind of midrats is the galley handing out tonight?"

"I do not know, Sir. None of us have taken a break to drop down to the galley."

"Well, you or somebody see that the galley sends up midrats for everyone on my bridge. I would prefer brown bread with white berry preserves, but I'll settle for rotten fish just now. Oh, tea and coffee as well. Tonight, we will likely need both."

"To hear is to have it done," the bosun answered, and left the bridge at a brisk walk. The young and strong handled higher gees so well.

The board still hadn't come back with an answer, so he took the moment to get up and roam the bridge. He peeked over shoulders and watched the actual information coming in.

His fleet was at a hard 3.5 gees. All these thousands of ships were holding to their assigned location. Despite so many of the ships having been cobbled together in haste, not one of them had suffered a breakdown or fallen out. The battle was developing so well. Now, if that Longknife woman would just play her part.

Stored at the rear of the bridge were the new and improved high gee stations for the rest of the bridge crew. They had come aboard in the last month, manufactured by a steel foundry on Breda 4. Someone deserved to rot in the deepest depths of the dark abyss for not thinking of such things when the Human programmers were still working on the battlecruisers.

Then, of course, everyone agreed that warriors went into battle standing tall. The idea of sitting or reclining at a battle station was an abominable thought. Everyone remembered how the Humans had zoomed about in the Human War, but no one expected to be facing them again.

All the battlecruisers ran through their trials at never more than 1.5 gee.

However, no sooner had the rebellion decided to send its Human programmers and engineers packing than the Longknife woman showed up. First thing she did was start zooming Iteeche battlecruisers around at two and three gees. The Human ships even did four or five gees.

"All hands, prepare for three point five gees in ten minutes," blared from the ship's communications system. "All hands, prepare for three point five gees in ten minutes."

Admiral Zom could almost feel the thud of four thousand Iteeche feet hitting the deck as sailors and officers were roused from their sleep and pounded off to their battle stations to slip into their high gee stations.

A Marine guard marched over to the admiral's station and began pumping it full of water. The admiral returned to it and stepped into it. It had padded holders for all four of his legs. This version allowed him to flex his knees as the station reclined to its full forty degrees from the vertical. This version had additional padding under his hips, back, and shoulders. There were even supports for his arms. Although he could not move them, he could adjust the armrests before locking them in place.

It was quite an improvement from the high gee station he'd used just three months ago. Feeling ensnared by some monster, Admiral Zom eyed his battle board from within the station, then reclined at a mere five degrees.

At that moment, the battle board lit up and filled with information. In the version before him, his entire fleet managed to swing wide around Longnae 5 and come to a parallel course with the enemy fleet. However, the numbers beside the ships were appalling.

If he accelerated at 3.5 gees for the next six hours, he'd have to decelerate at 3.7 gees for most of the rest of the way to Longnae 5. Short of that planet, he'd have to take the fleet up to 4.0 gees, and hit 4.5 gees as his fleet rounded the planet.

Even then, he'd have to accept a quite wide orbit coming out from Longnae 5. Likely that would put his ships way too close to the enemy fleet.

However, that might not be such a bad idea. The shorter the

range between his fleet and the enemy, the more likely his lasers were to inflict damage.

Admiral Zom frowned at the results. All this assumed that his ships and crews were still combat ready after pulling those hard gees. How many of his ships would have fallen out of formation, shooting off into space at any point in the swing around their pivot planet?

The clan chiefs had assured Admiral Zom that the new gunboats could handle anything the battlecruisers could. However, Zom had walked the tight passageways of a battlecruiser at Condition Zed, ready for combat.

At Condition Zed, the large comfortable battlecruiser vanished. Its hull thickened up, as did all its strength members. It became a very tight nut to crack. The gunboats were designed to fit around every reactor their planet could manufacture. The yards had thrown them together using any parts at hand. Were they rugged enough?

This was the first test of such emergency construction. It was a hasty merging of traditional steel, well-tested reactors, and lasers of all sizes and manufacturing. Eighty years ago, the Iteeche would have been so proud of a fleet like this.

Eighty years ago, a fleet like this could have swept the Humans before it.

Now, however, the Humans had these abyss-spawned battlecruisers. Ships that they could program so easily and so quickly. Yet, the Iteeche Empire and its rebels had failed miserably in stealing their control and programming arts. It seemed as if the Iteeche computers could not relate to the magic metal.

"Number One, attend me," Admiral Zom said softly.

His Number One staff officer moved cautiously to his side. He could still move about because he had yet to ensconce himself in a high gee couch. "Yes, Most Eminent Admiral."

"Listen to me as I list my options and tell me if I missed one."

"Yes, Most Eminent Admiral."

"We can ignore Longnae 5 and shoot close aboard the Human-led fleet for one pass, then head for Jump 3 and leave this system. We can then seek another planet to defend and prepare to meet the enemy fleet there."

"Yes, Most Eminent Admiral. What do you think the ruling council would think of that?"

"They might very well have my head. At best, I would be relieved of my command."

"Most likely."

Admiral Zom noticed the lack of "Most Eminent Admiral," from his Number One staff officer. *Might some of his admirals chose to mutiny and fight this battle?* If the fleet crumbled into a half-dozen admirals all giving different orders, it would be massacred. *No, he had to keep command.*

"Secondly, I can follow a safe course around Longnae 5, pivot the entire fleet there, but be way behind this Human Longknife woman. When we joined battle, we would be decelerating with our engines and reactors vulnerable to their fire."

"I would hate to fight that battle," Number One said carefully.

"Yes, I agree. Third, I can ride hell for deep abyss, lose a part of my fleet as we pivot on Longnae 5, swing close to the foolish supporters of the tadpole on the throne, and maybe get in some good hits as they pass us. We could match course with the enemy fleet and steer close or bear off, depending on how the gun battle goes."

"Yes, Most Eminent Admiral."

Zom kept his face perfectly bland. However, that last remark told him what course of action his Number One would back.

"Do you see any other option?" the admiral asked.

Number One did not fire back a rote acceptance of his admiral's ideas, but instead leaned over the battle board and studied it for a long minute. Finally, he said, "We risk losing an unknown portion of our fleet as we wheel tight around Longnae 5. We will not know how many we lose until we have done it. The builders insist that the new ships are as strong as our battlecruisers."

"If I had a livre for every time a builder did not deliver on his promises, I could buy myself a mountain retreat," the admiral growled.

"Yes, Most Eminent Admiral. Still, I must throw my support behind your third option. Go for broke and let the abyss swallow those who cannot follow you."

"Very good, Number One. Let us get into our new high gee stations. I think we will be spending a lot of time in them."

"Oh yes," the staff officer chuckled, and began to adjust his station.

At the end of the ten minute warning period, the fleet accelerated to 4.0 gees.

53

"Kris, the rebel fleet has just gone to 3.5 gees acceleration."

Being roused from a pleasant sleep, Kris was a bit groggy. "Repeat that," she ordered as she blinked her way out of what was likely to be her best sleep for the rest of this battle.

"The admiral commanding the rebel fleet has increased his acceleration, from 3.0 gees to 3.5."

"What's that in Iteeche gravities?" Kris asked as she sat up in bed.

Jack was already up, and rummaging through their clothes locker. "Do you want khaki or ship's knits?" he asked.

"In Iteeche gees, the rebel commander has gone from 3.5 gees to 4.0," Nelly answered Kris's question.

"Shipsuits," Kris said, answering Jack's question. "I don't know when we'll have to go into the high gee stations." It was usually better to be unclothed before you slipped into the tight confines of one of those things. Simple blue shipsuits were easier to slip out of.

Jack tossed her a soft jumpsuit as well as two booties for her feet.

"That must be a real pain to put on three gees for an Iteeche. I wonder if they've got high gee stations to soften their weight?"

"Likely they've got something better than they had before you got called back to play patty cake with the clans in the Imperial Capital," Jack shot back, not even trying to keep bitterness out of his voice.

Kris scowled. She'd known when she was called back from the front line of the civil war that the rebels would use this time to regroup and come up with new surprises for her. She'd already seen several classes of new, smaller warships. Now she was about to learn about what was inside them.

With her own ships decelerating at only half a gee, Kris had to be careful as she paced off the distance between her night quarters and her flag bridge.

Nelly had Kris's battle board already up to date with the enemy's acceleration. She had course estimates assuming they stayed at this acceleration for two, four, six, and eight hours.

It took only a glance to tell Kris that the eight-hour duration would scatter the hostile fleet all over this system's outer rim.

"Eliminate the eight-hour estimate," Kris said, and that cleared up some of the clutter.

"What speed did you base these courses on, coming out of Longnae 5?" Jack asked.

"I assumed 3.5 gees deceleration," Nelly answered.

Kris shook her head. "All of these courses have the rebel fleet going wide of the mark as they go around their pivot planet. They should be flipping ship and starting to decelerate, not the other way around. Only the course where they stay at three gee for two hours gives them any chance of ending up within attack range of us."

"Yes, Kris," Nelly answered.

"That sounds like a waste of time, going to three gees for just two hours," Jack said, confirming Kris's thoughts.

With a sigh, Kris stuck her neck out. "Nelly, assume that this admiral wants to get in range of our fleet sometime after he does his U-turn. How many gees will he have to pull going around Longnae 5 to get in such a position?"

The board flickered and new courses appeared. With gees

appended to each course at different times, it was very messy. "Nelly, show me just the course he'd have to take after six hours at 3.5 of his gees."

The clutter disappeared. One course now enclosed Longnae 5, looped high around it, then settled down on a course that ran parallel to Kris's at extreme range. The two fleets were about even, so they would be exchanging salvo for salvo, trying to melt the heaviest armor.

The enemy fleet was at 3.5 gees as it approached the planet. It increased to 4.5 gees when it was five hours out, then five gees for the swing around the planet. It had to stay at five gees for four hours after that in order to slow down enough to match course with Kris's fleet as well as to avoid crashing through her formation.

"Do you think he might be willing to crash our line?" Jack asked.

"I haven't taken the Iteeche for suicidal," Kris said.

The two of them eyed each other. There was a lot about the Iteeche that they didn't understand. They'd had to pry mouths open to keep assassins from swallowing poison. Was that there to help them avoid torture during interrogation or to assure that their bosses didn't have to answer embarrassing questions? Or maybe a bit of both?

"Nelly, is Admiral Tong awake?"

"Yes, ma'am. His Number One staff officer woke him about the time I woke you."

"Amber as well?"

"Do you really think that if you're awake, everyone else isn't as well?" Nelly said, giving Kris some attitude.

"Please ask both of them to join our discussion."

A moment later, the main screen filled with an Iteeche and a Human, both in soft shipsuits.

"What may I do for you, My Most Eminent Admiral?" Admiral Tong said.

"Hi, Kris. No rest for the wicked," Admiral Amber Kitano tossed at Kris, along with a broad grin. "When do we start the shoot?"

"That all depends on when and if our illustrious enemy gets in range. Admirals Tong and Kitano, are your boards the same as mine?"

Nelly projected Kris's battle board on another edge of the screen. Both admirals glanced down at their own boards.

"One-for-one match," Amber said.

"I concur, My Most Eminent Admiral."

"Admiral Tong," Kris said, "We're likely to be short on time and long on problems today. Could you allow yourself to call me Kris? Amber does."

It took Admiral Tong a long moment to process Kris's request. When he answered, it was with a question of his own. "You want me to adopt your informal Human ways of address. Yes?"

"To me, Admiral Tong, you are both a professional associate and a personal friend. We have a hard job ahead of us. My friends call me Kris. Can you accept me as a friend? Admittedly, I will always be admiral in public, but in private, we can let our hair down and move the conversation along quickly."

The Iteeche admiral nodded slowly. "Yes, I can accept your offer to be informal as you Humans are. Thank you for this honor... Kris."

"Good. Now, Tong," suddenly Kris stopped. "You don't have any other name, do you?"

"No, I am Tong."

"Good. Tong, does your intelligence have any reports on the rebels getting better high gee stations?"

"We have a lot of reports, Kris. The few times we managed to get schematics of the upgraded high gee stations and made a test model, they failed miserably when used above three gees. It is my opinion that they don't have anything that will help them take more than what they are taking right now."

"It sure looks like they intend to take a try at it," Kris said.

"Yes," Tong said. "I think we are about to see someone try. His best option would be to head for Jump Point 5 or 3 and get out of here. However, since he likely has a nominal superiority of three to one or so, he has to attack or be ready to make a formal apology to someone."

"Yeah," Jack said dryly. "Who does an Iteeche apologize to if he's in rebellion against the Emperor?"

"I'm sure his clan chiefs will come up with someone," Tong answered back, just as dryly.

Kris, however, was eyeing her board. "I have a feeling some of those cruisers are going to skid right out of orbit and come careening our way. Nelly, what happens if a ship can't hold more than three gees as it goes into the turn?"

"It depends, Kris. If they hold four or five gees for part of the turn, they could come out anywhere along our path. If they slow too soon, they end up way behind us and will be wandering off to nowhere."

"After we win, we'll have to send some ships off to rescue the crew before their air runs out." Kris said.

"You're assuming we win," Jack said.

"I always assume we win. If I ever face defeat, I prefer it to come as a surprise," Kris muttered as she studied her board. "There's not much we can do for the next dozen hours. I suggest we go back to bed and get some rest. Then we can come out swinging later. I'm sure nothing will happen the way our opposite number thinks it will, or anywhere close to what I want."

With a chuckle, the two admirals cut the call and the flag bridge again became the quiet domain of shadows. Watch standers sat at their stations, tending the data that streamed into the bridge. Some monitored the loyal fleet. Others watched the rebel fleet. For now, no one had anything to say. There were no changes in their readouts to remark upon.

"Has anyone ordered up midrats?" Kris asked no one in particular.

Heads turned in her direction, but no one said anything. Finally, the captain commanding the watch came out of the gloom. "No ma'am. The hostiles have been too rambunctious for us to take time out for coffee."

"God willing, you've got a long and boring watch ahead of you. Call down to the galley and tell them you deserve fresh bread and plenty of whatever goes on it."

"Thank you, ma'am. I will, though I doubt anything less will show up."

"No doubt. Now, if you will excuse me, I need my beauty rest."

The captain raised his eyebrows, more to Jack than Kris. Clearly, Kris would have to be more reserved. She didn't want people to think her vanity was fishing to be stroked.

Admirals couldn't afford vanity or strokes.

54

Admiral Zom watched the tracks extend slowly on his battle board. It was like watching paint dry, only worse.

That Human admiral Kris Longknife held her forces at a deceleration of hardly more than two thirds of a gee.

"Battle board, what is the enemy task force deceleration in Human gees?"

It took a moment, but the answer came back, "Half of a Human gee."

Zom slowly shook his head against his high gee station. The Human was flaunting her strength and her position. Decelerating at little more than two thirds of an Iteeche gee, she was letting her fleet build up energy as it fell deeper into the system. At some point, she would have to go to higher gees. Maybe much higher gees, to make orbit around Longnae 4.

How punishing would those deceleration gees be to his ships and crew?

Even after little more than an hour at three gees the woven mats of the high gee station were being crushed by the weight of his body. They had been told that these mats would absorb the pressure of 4.0 gees. They had been told that when they were crushed in one spot, they would still support the other parts of the Iteeche body.

Zom would like to have whoever designed this mat on a couch on his bridge. He'd cut off his tentacles and feed them to him an inch at a time. The matting had collapsed under his hips and shoulders. He was rubbing himself raw on fragments of matting. The rest of his body was doing pretty much the same. Even his knees were feeling the weight and the cuts of raw matting.

Zom activated the water tank and water began to fill the space below the mat on his couch. As it filled, the admiral still had to tolerate the fiber of the matting, but at least he didn't feel his body rubbing against the hard steel of the high gee station.

A nasty voice niggled at the back of the admiral's mind. The fiber mats were supposed to have lasted longer. Would the waterbeds also fail?

Zom eyed the board. His fleet took on velocity as it accelerated to the flip point, then it would start shedding energy. Still, all of this happened at such a slow pace on his battle board. Having had enough of watching paint dry, Zom closed his four eyes and did his best to drift off to sleep.

When he weighed over three times what he should have, it was no easy job to slow his labored breathing, calm his heart, and drift off to sleep.

Somehow, Zom'sum'Ka'sum'Quin of the Quin'sum'Domm Clan did.

55

The next morning Admiral Kris Longknife, commanding admiral of the Imperial Iteeche Combined Fleet, and presently in command of the 2nd Battlecruiser Fleet stopped by her flag bridge as soon as she had showered and dressed. No surprise, nothing had changed.

Once again, Kris and thousands of ships and crews that might live or might die in the coming clash, were in the unrelenting grasp of physics. The gravity well around Longnae 5 dictated every move her ships and her opposing fleet could make.

For Kris, it was slowing down her deceleration so that she zipped by the planet faster than she would have preferred. Every minute she kept her fleet at less than one gee deceleration, the longer she'd have to have her ships blast at two or even three gees to catch the gravity well of the target, Longnae 4.

However, her move was forcing her opposite number to burn a lot of reaction mass, getting to Longnae 5 faster so he could twist his course around that planet's gravity well and send his ships hurtling toward Kris's ships.

The rebel admiral would get a chance to exchange laser fire with

Kris's fleet as the two zoomed by each other. Still, Kris's would have enough velocity on her ships to quickly leave the rebels behind.

No doubt, the Iteeche admiral would then pour on as much acceleration as his ships could bear. His aim would be to catch up with her and fight her for the rest of the run into Longnae 4.

The approach to the resource-rich industrialized planet would be a wild and bloody business.

"Nelly, are we getting anything new off of our enemy?" Kris asked.

"Many of their reactors are in distress," her computer reported. "Up to this moment, no ship has suffered an engineering casualty and had to fall out of formation. However, I expect that to change quickly when he increases his deceleration to four or even five gees."

"So, he's burning his candle at both ends," Kris said.

"And he's got a stick of dynamite in the middle of his candle. Sooner or later, things are going to go boom."

Kris frowned at the board. She had 6,000 battlecruisers in her force. The rebels had 16,000. Kris was comfortable with odds of less than three-to-one. However, the 25,000 single reactor cruisers were a question mark to her. They carried just a few lasers, but there were a lot of them.

Just how well these strange new additions to the enemy fleet would do in battle was a huge question in Kris's mind.

With a shake of her head, she went to breakfast with Jack.

In the wardroom, Kris found herself looking around as if something was missing.

"You miss the kids mobbing us for breakfast?" Jack asked.

Kris sighed. "I think you're right. Their noise. Their enthusiasm. Their questions. They can be annoying when they come at you like puppies, but still, I love it, and yes, I'm missing them. Regardless, I'm glad they are back at the embassy, safe with their grandparents and far away from all these threats."

Neither she nor Jack could add anything more to that thought, so they got their breakfast and settled down at an open table to eat. There wasn't a lot to say, so the meal went quickly and in silence.

Megan joined them halfway through, but she was good about spotting when Kris needed silence and said nothing.

Done, Kris bussed her own table. She was a grand admiral, but she preferred to hold to the simple things of life as long as she could. There was no reason to ask some steward's mate to wait on her. Soon enough, she'd be demanding much more of everyone. Demanding their sweat and tears if not their life's blood.

Kris returned to her battle board. There wasn't a lot she could do at the moment. Even her in-basket was empty. Everyone was preparing for battle; no one had time to generate reports.

The important reports were on the screen now. The status of every one of the six thousand ships was visible on the main screen. A question to Nelly could call up any ship.

"Nelly, give me a look at the ten battlecruisers with the worst performing reactors and motors."

Ten ships names cascaded down a new window. Bar graphs showed their reactors all in the green. They were closer to the yellow zone than the average for the fleet which Nelly also projected in a bar graph.

"Very good. Keep an eye on the fleet and let me know as soon as a ship touches upon the yellow."

"What do you intend to do with ships that are at risk of engineering casualties?" Jack asked.

"If I can, I'll likely detach them to look after the damaged ships," Kris said. "If I am too hard pressed, I'll have to keep them in the line and hope for the best."

Jack nodded. Kris had made those hard calls before. She was willing to make them again.

"Kris, the rebel fleet has their first reactor problem."

"Show me," Kris said.

Nelly quickly zoomed the system map down until it just showed the rebel battle array.

Kris had the standard five wings formed into a cross with each wing 1,200 strong. The advanced guard held the seven flotillas of 224

Human battlecruisers. The Human warships were the ace up Kris's sleeve.

Earth's massive R&D base had come up with a surprise. Quantum computers worked by slowing light down for a tiny fraction of a second while the calculations were done. Someone back on that crowded planet had developed slow crystal. It slowed the light of a laser down and let it scatter all along the hull of a Human battlecruiser, where it radiated most of the damaging energy back out into space.

Only someone with Nelly's sentience could watch this happen, and she described it to Kris as water cascading over a fall. "If you look closely, you can even see a bit of a rainbow."

The crystal armor could be overwhelmed with enough hits, but the Human warships were usually able to withdraw from the heat of battle for a bit. There they'd cool down, mend ship, and then return to the fight. Kris could count on one hand the number of crystal-clad ships she'd lost.

Now Kris studied the enemy battle array. It might have intimidated anyone less confident than a Longknife.

Her opposing admiral had changed the basic array. He'd added a scouting wing ahead of his advanced guard. Another wing trailed the rear guard. Both the upper and lower wing had a top and bottom wing above or below them.

Each wing had 55 flotillas of over 1,700 ships. The five traditional wings would fix Kris's fleet in place while the four more widely spread wings engulfed her from the top, bottom, and sides.

But that wasn't her worst challenge.

Forward and aft of the top and bottom wings were the hordes of massed new ships. Kris had no idea what their fighting quality was, but 6,000 ships, each with three-to-one lasers, even in a mob formation, had to prove the maxim that numbers produce a quality all their own.

Maybe her battlecruisers could take one of them out with each salvo. It would still take 15 broadsides to eliminate them all . . . more than likely, twenty. That would tie up her fleet for five to ten minutes.

What would the rest of the rebel fleet be doing while she concentrated on these annoyances?

In the end, the question came down to whether or not her ships were good enough to kill seven or eight enemy ships for every one of them.

For the closest she could get to that question in the present, Kris asked, "Nelly, is Admiral Tong awake?"

"Yes, Kris."

Without further request, the Iteeche Admiral appeared on Kris's screen. "Did you rest well?" he asked her.

"Very well," Kris answered. Iteeche officers always said they rested well before battle, whether they did or not.

"How are our green sailors shaking down?" she asked him.

"Amazingly well. The ones that sailed with us from the capital are almost old salts. The new crews and ships from Balan are coming along. Like every admiral in our Empire's long history, I would prefer more time to train, but with the changes you and your Nelly have made to our ships, their lasers and their fire control systems, we should fight with the fury of ten because our hearts are pure." The admiral coughed softly, then added softly, "And our ships are better."

"Let us hope so," Kris said.

"I have drills going on every waking moment," the Iteeche admiral said. "Our ships are trimmed to Condition Baker so that a quarter of each battle station can get something to eat from the mess deck or wardroom. The high gee stations are already parked at their battle stations, and one quarter of them are sleeping in their high gee stations. It will only take us five minutes to go from Baker or Charlie to fighting Condition Zed."

Each of those conditions reduced the size of the ship as more Smart Metal™ flowed from habitability to armor. Corridors narrowed and staterooms shrank at Condition Baker. At Charlie, one could hardly move around the ship and most quarters were packed up and stowed away. At Condition Zed, you could hardly move from your battle station, but the ship was small, hard, and target-ready to snap out at any ship that dared cross its path.

Kris was half a day away from ordering Condition Zed.

Satisfied that all that could be done was being done, Kris stood. She took a final glance at her battle board. The ships on it continued to hurtle toward their coming fight. Only reactor failures could save the rebel ships from their rendezvous with Kris's battlecruisers.

She turned her back on the questions and went to lunch.

The officers had only a single wardroom at Condition Baker for junior and senior officers. Kris could have kept her flag mess but didn't. She listened to the hard edge on voices. Laugher was a bit brittle, but everyone seemed eager. No one was sitting in a corner morosely staring at their food.

Kris walked her own tray through the steam tables, then found a seat in the middle of the wardroom. She was available if anyone felt the urgent need to bend her ear, but the junior and senior officers left her to herself and her table mates.

Jack and Megan joined her. They ate in silence, each of them more interested in the conversations going on around them than any they might need to share at the moment.

After what would likely be their last hot meal eaten before battle, Kris returned to her flag bridge. Nothing had changed on the board.

Someone, however, had brought up the high gee stations for her, Jack, and Megan. As Kris stripped out of her shipsuit and slid down into the high gee stations that looked for all the world like an Easter egg with its bright blue paint job, trouble began.

On her board, a rebel ship suddenly blossomed into a bright star, then vanished away to nothing.

Somewhere among the new construction, one of the single reactors had been pushed too far . . . a failure occurred and promulgated at the speed of light.

It might have been in the magnetohydrodynamic electrical generation system, or the superconducting magnetic containment field for the plasma reactor. Whatever it was, the failure occurred in less time than it took to bat an eye.

Where once had been a ship with its crew of eager rebels, now only a cooling ball of gas spread through space.

With grim determination, Kris let her high gee egg tighten its mesh close around her. Then she filled the sides of the egg with hydraulic fluids to absorb four gees easily. Maybe five, if Kris had to order it.

The egg elevated so Kris could still see the battle board and share it with Jack and Megan as they studied it for surprises. If some awaited her, they were well hidden at the moment.

Another small ship sparked into a star as its reactor ate it.

Kris would not want to be the admiral facing her. He had some horrible decisions to make.

56

Admiral Zom blinked as a third one of his gunboats blew up in less than a minute. He'd expected problems, but nothing this bad. Over the next minute, two more ships self-destructed.

As he weighed his response to this developing disaster, a full two minutes went by without any ship destroying itself. He allowed himself a breath of relief.

Just then, a ship cut its deceleration. That sent it careening through the forward upper wing. It survived a glancing blow to another one reactor ship before slamming into a second. Both gunboats blew themselves to pieces.

That defined the two extremes of the problem facing Admiral Zom. If he did nothing, he risked destroying his ships as engineering casualties blew ships to atoms. Alternately, he could authorize captains to reduce deceleration before their reactors failed. That, however, ran the risk of a ship colliding with another as it shot through the rest of the fleet that was still decelerating.

His third option, ordering the entire fleet to reduce deceleration, was out of the question. The reduced deceleration would send the fleet whipping around Longnae 5 and hurl it off on a course that would totally miss the enemy fleet.

There would be no battle.

Admiral Zom placed a call to the skipper of the *Defender of the Domm Clan's Honor No. 273*.

"How are your reactors handling the pressure?" he asked.

"Let me check with Engineering, Most Eminent Admiral."

A moment later, the captain of his flagship was back. "Our reactors are fine. They are still in the green. We should have no problem maintaining a 4.0 gee deceleration and even going to 4.5 gees as we round Longnae 5. Engineering says we could even do 5.0 gees."

"Yes, Captain. Good. Let me know immediately if that changes."

"To hear is to make it so," the skipper answered as Zom cut the call.

If his hands did not weigh so much, the Iteeche admiral would have pounded the arm rest. Of course, the Human-designed battlecruisers could manage 4.5 gees for the Humans, even if it was a killing 5.0 gees for an Iteeche.

No, the 16,000 battlecruisers of his fleet were not the problem. Now, it was the hastily designed and built Iteeche gunboats with single reactors that were failing as they struggled to decelerate at 3.5 Iteeche gees.

Who had set the specs for those ships? Hadn't anyone told them of how the Humans slammed themselves around in space at absurd speeds?

Of course, the Human-commanded fleet was decelerating at a lethargic half of a Human gee. It was that Longknife woman's decision to race by distant Longnae 5 that had forced him to risk his fleet at this absurd high gee deceleration.

Had she known the new construction was not so well tested? That its engineering crews and hastily built reactors might fail under the pressure?

There was no way to tell if she'd just gotten lucky or had known what she was getting him into. Either way, he damned her to the deepest abyss of the dark deep for doing this to him.

As he dithered, four more ships sparked themselves into tiny stars, then disappeared into the cold void of space.

There remained only two choices for him. He could authorize every skipper on one of those death traps to reduce deceleration if their reactor or supporting engineering activities began to show signs of failure. Alternately, he could order them to take courage, like cavalry men of old, committed to a charge against the guns, to carry through to saber the gunners at the end of their charge. At least, those that survived until the end of the charge.

Admiral Zom had often thrilled to the songs of those old battles. As a youngling, he'd reveled in the courage of warriors who sought immortality in songs in the mouth of the cannon. He had often wondered if he would have the bravery to do something as glorious as they had. To risk all to be remembered in song.

Now, he found himself facing just such a charge. Only it was not him hurtling himself and his beast at the guns. No. He was safe on a battlecruiser. It was others he was ordering to charge the guns on faltering mounts. It was others whose equipment would immolate themselves before they could come to grips with the enemy. *Would his role in this magnificent charge even be remembered?*

He wondered if he should order the ships' companies to sing one of those proud ballads. If he did, would they? *Were his sailors as courageous as those riders of old? Would they respond with bitterness as he ordered them to sing even as he ordered them to die?*

Admiral Zom shook his head, as much as he could at 3.5 gees. How could he even be thinking thoughts like these? Of course, his men were as bold and courageous as those Iteeche of old. What had gotten into his head?

It was those damn Humans. Somehow, some of their poisoned thinking must have seeped into his head. He had heard how the Human Kris Longknife always seemed overly concerned with saving lives.

She would take a planet with hardly a death among the clan lords and never a fight on the planet. She even bragged about how the planets she captured were in such pristine condition after she took them. Dishonored clan lords were even shipped back to their clans for reassignment.

More of those Humans and their cursed dishonor!

Admiral Zom ground his beak together and sat tight in his high gee station. On his battle board, ships would sparkle for a moment, then vanish into the emptiness of space.

Admiral Zom remembered a message that one Human admiral had sent as he took his men into battle, a battle he did not live to see the end of.

"Comm, send to the fleet. 'Your clans expect every one of you to do your duty to the greatest destiny of our people. Let us fight so that they will sing songs about us for a thousand years'."

With a sigh, the rebel admiral gazed at his battle board. All of his problems came from that Longknife woman's decision to cut her deceleration and zoom by his fleet. Tong would never have done this; this had to come from the twisted mind of the Human Longknife. The War College would flunk any student who risked such high gees so close to the planet that was the invasion target.

Of course, he was risking such high gees to get into the fight with the despised Human. *What would War College teachers say about him in the years to come? That he had met the Human insanity with insanity of his own?*

What they said would depend on him winning.

Zom settled back into his high gee station. The fibers of the compression mat had been worn down until they no longer bothered him. The layer of water under him did a much better job of supporting him against the pressure of three gees.

The merchant who sold him on adding a cushion of water to the high gee couches said that the idea had been found in the romance stories of the Humans. They used it for their obscenely incessant mating that led to no procreation.

Only the Humans would do such a thing.

At least, for the moment, it allowed his fleet to hurtle toward the enemy ships at high gees. That would be a joke. The defeat of the Human-led fleet came to be because of an obscene Human tool.

57

"Kris, the enemy admiral has just sent a message to his fleet," Nelly reported.

"What does he have to say?" Kris asked. Despite her fleets' half-gee deceleration, Kris was snuggled naked in her high gee egg. It would be a while before she began ordering her fleet around at high gees. Still, she and her entire fleet had moved to high gee stations in preparations for the coming fight.

"Your opposite number has just exhorted his fleet that, 'Your clans expect,' or maybe that's demand, 'every one of you to do your duty to the greatest destiny of our people.' That could mean race. 'Let us fight so that they will sing songs about us for a thousand years.' What do you think of that, Kris? Unless there are some Iteeche exhortations like those that I don't know of, Zom has borrowed from Admiral Nelson before the Battle of Trafalgar and Prime Minister Churchill before the Battle of Britain. Who would have thought we had an anglophile across the battlefield from us?"

"I'm not surprised," Kris answered. "I've been devoting as much of my spare time as I could to the history of the Iteeche Empire. No doubt, you have translated every book you could get your hands on, Nelly."

"Yes, Kris."

"In many ways, we are cross-pollinating each other."

"Some might say poisoning," Jack put in.

"No doubt," Kris agreed.

"Still," Jack went on, "It is strange to hear someone who very likely considers everything from us Humans as poison allowing the thoughts of Humans to seep unexamined into his own exhortation to his fleet."

Kris didn't have a quick comeback for Jack. It left her very thoughtful. Soon, in the heat of battle, she'd need to get inside the head of her opposite number. She'd need to figure out his next move before he even did. Would this reflection from her husband help her?"

"Thank you, Jack. I think you have something I need to mull over."

"You think the enemy admiral may have read too much of your file?"

"He's trying to fight his battle the way I would, so yes, he's read a very big file on my fighting methods. But it's not me he's studied, not if he's quoting Nelson before Trafalgar or Churchill during the pivotal war of the bloody twentieth century. He's done his best to get inside my head. That may give me a special hook into his head."

Another light sparked among the 25,000 single reactor warships of the enemy fleet. The four divisions of them were organized rank-on-rank, with some ships struggling to hold their place in formation. Even if the reactor wasn't blowing up, they were not providing a steady stream of plasma.

Ships jockeyed constantly to hold their place in the line. Long lines were their basic formation. They looked like a phalanx of old, men standing shoulder-to-shoulder and back-to-back. It had been the first organized battle array, and the most primitive. The phalanx could stand strong on defense, but it had a nearly impossible time maneuvering in battle.

It could charge forward, or fall back, often in a rout, but it could not face right or left if it was taken on the flank and moving over even moderately rough space would break it up.

Kris had to wonder how much tactical mobility her enemy admiral expected from this mob of newly designed, constructed, and crewed warships. She had her own problems. His must be much worse.

Could those small ships charge down on her in swarms that complicated her firing computer solutions? If she ignored them, could they slip in among her ships and cause havoc and destruction? Did she risk overestimating them and tie up her fleet's guns, or underestimate them and risking the loose of her battle?

"Jack, when the battle is joined, I'm going to have to make a split-second decision on what the fighting value is of those new warships. If you think I need to revisit my initial estimate, please tell me."

Jack nodded. "Understood. They look to be slippery little bastards. If they appear to be worth more or less than you're valuing them, I'll let you know."

"Thanks. This looks to be one fast and slippery battle. Help me not get fixated on one of these threats and miss another."

Meanwhile, several ships had struggled out of formation. Most had dodged their way out of the mass of new warships. However, one had slashed a sister ship in two before exploding. A second ship had nipped the stern of a ship still under full deceleration and had ruptured its reactor. Both the ships had vanished in one huge gas cloud.

"Nelly, do you have any estimate of how many of these new warships will be left when we engage the enemy?"

"I cannot but guess, Kris. I still expect the hostile fleet to have to go to four or even five gees as it rounds Longnae 5. Any estimate developed based on casualties at 3.5 gees deceleration will be worthless at that brutal deceleration."

"Right, Nelly. Thanks for the advice."

"I can have an estimate after one minute into the highest gees, Kris."

"I expect that engineering casualties are only going to get worse as engines and reactors heat up."

"That is true."

"Keep paying close attention to our reactor readouts and let me know if anything changes, either with our engines or theirs."

"Will, do," Nelly said.

Kris eyed the battle board. Her main interest was the angle on the bow when she engaged the enemy.

The fleet would likely be broadside to broadside, not that the battlecruisers fought that way. Like ancient submarines, their weapons were in their bows and sterns. Still, if they were on a parallel course, she'd have on fight on her hands.

If the enemy swung around and came at her on her forward quarter, she'd be shooting up their stern if they began decelerating immediately. That would give her some good shots at their vulnerable sterns with their reactors.

Kris blinked her eyes closed for a moment, then groaned.

She'd misjudged the battle. Badly.

"Nelly, show me what the situation will look like if they manage to swing around Longnae 5 the way we think they will."

The enemy force swung wide and began immediately to accelerate toward Longnae 4. Kris's fleet, having put off serious deceleration, whipped past them with time enough for a few salvoes, then continued to fall faster toward their target.

Meanwhile, the enemy fleet put on acceleration, aiming to catch up.

Kris, for her part, would have to order her fleet to begin deceleration sooner, using two or three gees, or later, applying three, four, or maybe even 4.5 gees. All that time, the enemy fleet would be juggling their acceleration and deceleration, trying for an advantageous position.

The most important question for Kris was: would her enemy give up his chance to make orbit around Longnae 4? Kris had to make orbit.

If the rebel commander decided that he didn't, then he'd have the advantage on Kris for the rest of the battle. At any particular point, he could command his ships to juggle their gees to achieve a preferred range or angle on the bow.

Kris reflected on that for a long five minutes. She finally concluded that she might have to split her forces again, having a small detachment aim for the planet while her larger force parried the rebel's actions. She had a small enough force as it was. To pare it down even further sounded like folly.

Still, she'd seen it done before.

Oh, right, and she'd also picked off the smaller force.

Then again, she'd gotten between that force and their target. Was there any way the rebels could get between her and the planet?

She didn't think so. Still, she'd have to keep her eyes open. Every move she made gave the enemy a vote and a move of their own.

For the next two hours, she and Jack tried different ways to strike at her fleet and foil those strikes. It was enough to make her brain spin.

In the end, time came for supper. The *Princess Royal* was still at Condition Baker, so the three of them dismounted their high gee eggs, pulled back on their shipsuits and went to the wardroom for another warm meal.

The wardroom was quieter now. The loudest noise was the crash of trays and crockery when two ensigns collided on their way to return the dirty dishes.

Most of those eating had the cold determination of those who knew what was coming and were ready for it. The *Princess Royal*'s crew had been through this all before. Several times before. They knew to trust their shipmates and trust their training.

Still, a few of them threw Kris furtive looks, as if they wondered how she might pull this one off. They'd been with her when she'd used this very same tactic to beat her enemy like a drum.

How would she do against her own game plan?

Kris returned to her egg and got comfortable. A glance at the board showed her enemy was entering his approach to Longnae 5. When would he slam on the brakes and hike up the deceleration? Sooner and he might be able to keep it at four gees. Later and he'd have to jack it up to five gees.

Still, the longer he kept his ships pushing their reactors, the more likely they were to overheat and fail with catastrophic results.

Even in the few moments that she watched, waiting to see what he'd do next, four ships sparked into tiny stars. Just as quickly, they vanished from view.

Kris would not want to be in his shoes.

58

Admiral Zom could only stare at his battle board as ship after ship exploded. Others broke ranks, cut their deceleration, and threaded their way through the crammed ships in formation with them until they fell out the bottom.

That worked fine for the two huge forward masses of gunboats. The two rear groups were more complicated. Most managed to steer out the unengaged side of the array and avoid the battlecruiser wings and gunboat phalanxes.

Every once in a while, an overheated reactor would fail or burp and send a ship careening through the formation until not one, but two ships ended up blowing themselves into expanding clouds of superheated gas.

All of this took place without an order from him. Admiral Zom had not been able to bring himself to give the order to the fleet captains to use their discretion to withdraw from the formation if their reactors were close to failure. No Iteeche commanding officer had ever given such a lame order and he could not bring himself to be the first.

Still, what admiral in the last 5,000 years had been sent into battle with ships that blew up one after another long before they came in range of the enemy guns? The entire situation left a bitter taste in his mouth. He could only guess what the captains and crews of the pieces of floating crap called gunboats must feel like as they watched their reactors go slowly into the red and measured their honor against their life.

Do they struggle longer to bring this worthless piece of junk into the fight? Did they give up and quit while they had enough fuel to aim themselves at a planet where they could be refueled before their engines failed and hurled them out into the empty void of space?

"Number One, can we determine if one of those worthless classes of knocked-together gunboats is suffering more engineering casualties than the rest? Is any single type of reactor failing at a higher rate?"

"I do not know, Most Eminent Admiral," his senior staff officer answered.

"Well, find out. If one class is clearly a botched job, it is better that we order it out of the line. As it is now, every captain and Sailor in every ship is wondering if they could be next. Let's cut down on our catastrophic failures if we can."

"To hear is to make it so," the officer said and began talking into his communication unit. How long it would take him to get a reply was anybody's guess.

For eons, Iteeche sent runners across the battlefield to take a commander's orders to his subordinates. "To hear was to make it so," was not just a reply to an order. It was how the order was delivered.

Now, matters moved too quickly. In battles of yore, commanders issued orders and they were obeyed. No battle commander in ancient times asked his juniors for anything but to die for their lord.

Now, he needed information from his subordinates. Now, he needed to know which class or classes of ships under his command were blowing up. He needed to know this and get them out of the line before they sapped the morale, if not the courage, of his other ships.

Even weighing over three times his normal weight, Admiral Zom ground his beak together, frustrated that he had been given such defective ships. Of course, it would have helped if they'd done their acceptance trials at something greater than two gees and that for only two hours. Time had been of the essence and construction was rushed.

No one knew how much time the fracas at the Imperial Capital would delay the Human Longknife's next campaign. No one could guess how much time they had to put together a fleet that could stop her. Still, the rebellion had set out to build four major fleets and station them around some of the most productive planets.

It meant leaving a lot of planets unprotected. They'd known when they pulled most of the fleet back from the Balan system that they would lose them. What they hadn't expected was for the entire fleet of battlecruisers left there to surrender when his Longknife Human showed up.

Reports were still scarce, but she seemed to have captured the entire system without firing a single shot.

How could any commander, much less a Human, manage that?

Zom knew he was dithering. There was not a lot to take his attention away from his battle board as more ships ballooned into bright stars that faded in a blink.

"Do you have any information?" Zom demanded of his Number One.

"They are consulting their subordinate admirals and asking them to ask the question of their subordinates, My Most Eminent Admiral."

"Tell them to hurry up. I don't know how many ships the crews can watch blow themselves to dust and atoms before their bowels run thin and they give into fear."

"Surely, no captain would do such a thing, Most . . ."

Zom cut his subordinate off. "They *are* doing that, Number One. Get me what I need. Is every class of ships blowing up, or is it limited to just one or two classes?"

Once again, the Iteeche admiral forced himself to study his battle board. Here and there, ships exploded. Here and there, ships slipped out of line, cut their deceleration, and began to race ahead of the fleet.

Now, a long thin line of ships reached out in front of his fleet on the unengaged side. Zom wondered how many of those ships flew an admiral's flag. He would have to ask among them and have the senior admiral take command.

Maybe that admiral could get them to a safe harbor. Maybe he could lead them in pursuit of the troop ships. Maybe he should make a complete and sincere apology when the battle was done. Still, he and his subordinates could be of some use in the coming defense of the Langnae system.

"I have gotten some initial reports," Number One ventured carefully.

"Tell me what I want to know."

"Two classes seem to be suffering the largest numbers of failures," he said.

The new construction fell into six classes, depending on what reactor had been put into them, and what armament had been plugged into the reactor. The three larger reactors powered large gunboats. All three were armed with cast-off 20- or 22-inch lasers, all concentrated in a forward battery.

There were also three classes of frigates that had smaller reactors. Their armament was hastily slapped together short-ranged lasers of 18- to 20-inches copied from the Human pulse laser. Frigates would have to get in close to do any damage, but still, if there were enough ships swarming the battlecruiser fleet and if there was enough gunk in space from destroyed ships and noise makers, there was a chance that some might get through to mow the enemy down.

That was what the true loyalists were counting on. They would over-match the followers of the false emperor and that Longknife Human. They would die no matter how many of the admiral's own ships went down to dusty death.

"Which two classes?" Admiral Zom demanded.

"Most of the failed reactors seem to be powering the medium and the light frigates, Most Eminent Admiral," Number One stuttered out.

"The smaller two classes of frigates, but not the heavy frigates or the larger gunboats? That sounds preposterous."

"Yes, Most Eminent Admiral," the staff officer sputtered.

"Keep me informed if that changes any."

"Yes, Most Eminent Admiral."

Admiral Zom suppressed a sigh. The newly designed and constructed ships accounted for 25,000 of the 41,000 ships in his fleet. They were over 60 percent of his attacking warships.

He had 5,000 of each of the three types of frigates. Gunboats accounted for another 10,000 warships.

If he sent 10,000 of the frigates zooming off into the outer solar system, he would lose some 25 percent of his force.

Could he afford to face the Longknife Human's fleet of 6,000 battle-cruisers with 31,000 ships? She had won against better odds that that.

Of course, she'd been the one defending, using just this battle plan. How well would she do attacking against her own tactics?

Would the courage and moral of his own crews and captains fail if he let them continue this charge while destiny's demons rode hell for leather at their stirrups? Should he ask them to, or keep silent and just expect them to wait for their own reactor to go critical?

Whatever he was going to do about that problem, it was time to decide before he jacked up his deceleration.

"Number One, send to fleet. Go to four gees deceleration on my execute order."

Two minutes later, all the acknowledgements were in from his subordinate commanders.

"Execute."

He had weighed over three times his normal weight for the last eighteen hours. Now his weight nudged up to four times normal.

The water supported him as he sank deeper into his couch. Still, the weight on his chest grew and each breath became an effort.

On his battle board, the fleet began its swing around Longnae 5. They would dip down, down into the very top of the atmosphere. Down until their hulls burned as the friction slowed them down a bit more so that they would not go rocketing off into deep space but rather whirl around and head back sunward.

Back into a battle they had to win.

59

"Nelly," Grand Admiral Kris Longknife asked her computer, "do you know anything about the ships that are blowing up? Do they have the same reactor type or something?"

"Yes, Kris. I should have told you sooner, but you seemed intent on your problem and didn't ask me if for the information, so I didn't jiggle your elbow."

"No problem, Nelly. What have you got?"

"We've had no problem identifying the battlecruisers. They are all the latest classes with either twenty 24-inch lasers or smaller ships up-gunned with sixteen new 24-inch guns. No surprise there," Nelly said.

"My problem was the jumble of noise coming off of what I could only describe as an unreadable hole in space. When ships started blowing up, the rebel commander ordered his ships to detach from their auxiliary fuel tanks. I finally got a good look at his fleet. He has some twenty-five thousand ships built with six different reactor designs. Six to eight ships were clustered around a reaction fuel tank that fed mass to the different ships tied up to the tank. That way, they could get range out of ships that couldn't carry nearly enough fuel."

"And they were too close for you to get a discrete reading off of the individual reactors," Kris said.

"Right," Nelly answered. "Once they blossomed out into individual ships, I could identify six reactors from a design we fingerprinted during the Iteeche War. They have large reactors ten times the size of the smallest reactor, with four different sizes in between."

"Which ones are given to self-immolation?" Jack asked.

"No surprise," Nelly said. "It is the two smallest reactor types that are going critical under the heat and pressure. The third largest reactor is taking the strain okay. None of the three largest reactors have suffered a failure yet."

"How many of those reactors do they have in their fleet?" Jack asked.

"Ten thousand ships, minus the ones that have blown up. It accounts for twenty-five percent of his total force."

Kris scowled. "So, he's reluctant to order them out of the line. He needs them for when he finally attacks me."

"He's allowed ships that are showing a serious risk of a reactor failure to fall out and slow their deceleration," Nelly told them. "But he can't see his way through to letting them all fall out of the charge."

"Crazy Iteeche," Jack said.

Kris felt goose flesh. "Just crazy Iteeche?" she asked.

When Jack was slow on the uptake, Kris answered her own question.

"What of the Coast Guard Auxiliary, manning the runabouts only safe for in-orbital trips, some with entire families crewing them? They took the pressure off of Fast Attack Squadron 8 at a horrible price when six battleships threatened to blast Wardhaven back to the stone age. What of the reservists or volunteers or civilian ship drivers that showed up to punch a hole with their flesh and blood so our twelve mosquito boats could get close enough to smash the battleships with our shipwrecking pulse torpedoes?"

Jack nodded solemnly. "Hard to forget them."

"Yeah, hard to forget them," Kris agreed. They'd held center stage in too many of her nightmares.

"But we're not threatening to blast any planet back into the stone age," Jack pointed out.

"No, but aren't we, from their perspective, threatening their entire way of life?" Kris asked. "I think they're wrong. I think they need to walk forward with their eyes looking at the distant horizon, not looking back over their shoulder. Still, they're out here to risk their lives for their perspective."

"And we for ours," Jack said, nodding.

Kris had to agree with Jack. If the rebels won, their policy towards Humans would range from isolating their Empire to engaging in war. Again!

Kris wasn't just fighting for the poor kid on the throne. If she didn't manage to win this war for him, Humanity could face a dismal future.

Nelly reported on Kris's own fleet. The ship maintainers had taken the time at half a gee to do everything possible to assure the fighting quality of her ships. Weapons and engineering were as close to 100 percent as any operational fleet ever can be.

Her 6,000 battlecruisers were ready for the coming fight.

Or were they?

Kris expanded the enemy array on her board, then expanded her own, putting them across from each other. There was one thing she could do to get her ships ready. Right now, at half a gee, was the best time to do something.

"Admiral Tong, I would like to modify our array."

"What do you have in mind?" he asked.

She quickly explained. Five minutes later, orders had gone out to the fleet and flotillas began to reorganize themselves. It went on for a bit longer than either Kris or Tong liked, but they were green ship drivers operating in close quarters for the first time in most of their careers.

While this bit of ship movement occurred slowly, but smoothly, Kris's battlecruiser fleet continued to fall toward Longnae 4. At this velocity it would take some serious juggling of deceleration when the time came, but that time was not now.

The enemy fleet was now on its final approach to Longnae 5. The admiral had increased their deceleration to nearly four gees. That was still 4.5 gees for an Iteeche. The rebel admiral chose to increase deceleration early so he'd require five gees for less time. Still, the fleet would have to manage that killer deceleration for at least an hour, maybe more, as they rounded Longnae 5.

It would be brutal work, and reactors would overheat at that close encounter with a gas giant and its upper atmosphere.

Kris relaxed into her egg and let her eyes slowly roam over the lines and vectors on the battle board. *What would he do? What would she do in response?*

The dance with death was coming. Kris would have to be sure about her every step. She and her fleet could not afford a misstep.

Her mind wandered as the course vectors grew longer. As rebel ships fell out of their battle line, cut their deceleration, and zoomed ahead of the rest of the fleet. As overtaxed reactors gave up the battle and blew ships into vapor and junk in cold, deadly space.

Kris eyed the developments and forced herself to get out of her head. To stay in her gut. To wait for the sound of the bell that would release her into the fight.

Soon, it would be just her standing against an Iteeche admiral with thousands of ships moving to their orders.

For now, Kris measured each breath and waited.

60

Admiral Zom had never heard of anyone who cracked their beak. Still, he wondered if there was any way to mend a one. It was bad enough how long he had been grinding his beak together for the last few hours. Now his jaw clamped together a beak that weighed almost five times normal.

But it was about to get worse. "Number One, take the fleet to five gees on my execute."

The preliminary order went out to the fleet.

Admiral Zom could almost hear the groans of the sailors and officers of his ships. He could almost hear the groans of reactors and auxiliary equipment as they prepared to take on the greater burden of yet more weight.

He could also hear the silent sound of fingers hovering over switches.

Switches that if thrown at just the right moment might save a ship from obliteration. Of course, if courage failed and an Engineering Officer threw the switch too soon, it would also save their lives, while sending them off on a tangent that would take them out of the battle.

Admiral Zom could only wonder at the courage of those captains on ships with potentially defective reactors who held to this suicidal mission. How they must tremble, hoping that their ship would not be one of those cursed with whatever it was that blew ships into hot gas and scraps of wreckage.

A glance at the board showed fewer than a hundred ships whose captains had taken them out of the line.

Around his flag, the ships' skippers held the fleet to its course and deceleration. *Where did the Empire get such men?*

"Decelerate at five gees. Execute," Admiral Zom ordered.

Immediately, the dead weight of his body went from four and a half of normal to a full five times. The pressure on his chest was brutal as his lungs struggled to suck in air and expel it back out.

The admiral could only view his battle board from his high gee couch if it was angled no more than forty degrees from the vertical. He felt the weight of his insides begin to slip toward his hips. His stomach was pressured from above until it begged to expel his last meal.

Zom eyed his board. There really was nothing he could do at the moment. The fleet would struggle around Longnae 5 at five gees. Those that made it would be there on the other side to join him in fighting the Longknife Human and the misguided sailors following the boy pretender.

Closing his eyes, Zom used his thumb to push the button that laid his high gee station out flat. His body's weight now pushed down on the waterbed. The water leveled out in the mattress. Breathing was still a struggle, but his insides no longer felt like stones pressing against his heart, lungs, stomach, and guts.

A loud pop startled Admiral Zom. Without thinking, he glanced around for the sound. He should not have done that.

Even as he heard a sound of water gushing out, then sloshing around the deck, he felt the scream of agony from his neck.

While he struggled to find a less painful way to rest his neck, he demanded, "What happened?"

"The water cushion in a Marine guard's high gee station failed, Most Eminent Admiral."

Zom made an effort not to grind his beak together. It did no good to make himself a casualty.

"Number One. Send to the fleet. 'All hands who are not needed specifically for duty are to recline their high gee stations parallel with the floor. Report to me how many water mattresses have failed.' Get me the tally as soon as you can."

Around him on the bridge, gears ground painfully as all his staff and support personnel reclined their beds.

Even as they did it, the painful situation on the high gee station with no water played out. The Marine was now level, and on his back. He groaned with each breath he took as his body ground against itself and the hard mattress. His breath struggled as he gasped for air in small pants that grew smaller and smaller still.

Admiral Zom could feel the weight, like a slab of stone, on his own chest. Still, the water below him softened each breath. The downward pressure flattened his diaphragm as he let out a breath. He was barely able to gasp in another shallow breath and hold it, trying to drain every atom of oxygen from the captured air before he had to give up and let the weight drive it from his lungs.

Each breath was a struggle. Each movement risked pain.

With his own struggle for breath and that of those around him, it took him a while to notice that the Marine no longer rasped air before he panted in a small gasp.

The Marine was dead. Dead because someone delivered a water cushion that was not up to specs and had a defective point. Maybe a bubble in the plastic that weakened a single spot in the water cushion that made all of it defective and worthless.

If he survived his encounter with this Human Kris Longknife, Admiral Zom promised himself that he would have a serious and most painful apology from all those clan men of importance that provided this faulty equipment.

The admiral would laugh in their faces as they writhed in pain. He would kick them in their beaks, their guts, their most sensitive flesh, as they paid the highest price for what they had done to his men.

It would be a minor price for them to pay for the loss of so very many brave and courageous men.

Even under the weight, Zom grimaced. He would have to win this battle before he could do anything to those cheap clan lordlings.

Longknife Human, you will have to die so that I can see that they die, too. Too many have already died. Their sacrifice cries out for victory.

Admiral Zom could no longer see his battle board. However, even flat on his back, he could not avoid the agony of watching his fleet's bitter decimation. The lights that sparked on his board reflected off the overhead. He could not fail but count them as the number rose higher and higher.

Still, bitter as it was, he did not release the frigates from their course. From their duty. If they would not flinch, he would not either.

Admiral Zom closed his eyes. It did him no good to observe the slow attrition of his fleet. At the end of this hour, he would decide what acceleration they need, coming out of the swing around the gas giant, to send them hurtling after the puppet's fleet.

His ships would get one shot at the Human's fleet as they zoomed past them, still carrying too much energy on their ships.

After that one shoot, he would accelerate his ships after them. At some point, that fleet would have to begin decelerating if they wanted to make orbit around Langnae 4. That would be when the real fight would begin with them both decelerating on parallel courses.

That is when ships would vanish with each broadside. Each salvo. That is when he would decide the fate of the Empire for the next 1,000 years.

Admiral Zom checked the timer on the main screen. The alarm would go off in exactly half an hour. That was when he'd need to make his next decision. For now, he lay back, closed his eyes, and struggled to keep his heart from pounding out of his chest, and keep his lungs moving to provide oxygen to his blood.

For the moment, survival was all that he could do.

So, he set his beak and concentrated on surviving.

61

Grand Admiral Kris Longknife watched the rebel fleet as a major chunk of it completed its swing around the gas giant and began the climb out of its gravity well. It was show time.

She had only minutes before her ships shot into range of that massive collection of ships. The fire fight would be brief as she left them behind in less than a minute. However, even now, they began to put on acceleration that would catch them up with her later.

Kris studied her board, looking for the best way to arrange this blazingly short encounter to her benefit. No doubt, the rebel commander would prefer for her to allow his broad arms to hug her close, bringing every one of their guns to bear.

That was the last thing Kris intended to do.

"Send to fleet. On my mark, take all ships to Condition Zed. Begin hull rotations, decrease deceleration to .49 gees. Two minutes later, decrease to .48. Stand by for a close encounter of the shooting kind.'"

Kris chuckled at her own joke. Maybe it would loosen up taut nerves. Maybe it would be wasted on minds focused on picking out a target and tracking it until the firing solution was accurate to the thirteenth decimal place.

Around her, the *Princess Royal* hummed as it prepared to shrink down into the smallest possible target. Water coursed through her hull, filling a honeycomb of chambers that would cool the hull from any laser hit. Her battlecruiser wore a coat of crystal that could absorb most laser hits and spread it around the hull and radiate it back into space.

For the Humans, this armor was a Godsend. For the Iteeche, the armor was technology that the Humans refused to release beyond the rim of their populated space.

Iteeche battlecruisers, both loyal and rebel, would burn as the lasers cut through their hulls. The spinning surface of the battlecruisers would move the laser-burned armor away from the spot hit and to someplace where it could cool. That assumed that too much energy was not applied to too small an area.

Kris gave the execute order and her fleet shrunk from comfortable to a nearly solid block of Smart Metal™. The crew were all in their high gee stations at their battle station. There was little reason to move around inside the ships so every possible scrap of metal from passageways and quarters went to the hull for armor, or the honeycomb behind it to cool it when a laser hit.

Slowly, her fleet edged ahead of the rebels. They'd gone into the swing around the gas giant at five Iteeche gees, about 4.35 gees for Kris's Humans. They'd come out of the swing accelerating at 4.0 gees. As expected, the rebel-advanced vanguard led the way. None of the battlecruisers had failed, though Kris had to wonder how the crew had taken to all the extra gees. She knew their high gee stations were a lot less effective than the ones she provided to the loyalist ships.

The massive blocks of over 6,000 recently built little ships had quite a few holes in their formation. At a continued heavy gee acceleration, the skippers had little extra they could pull from their reactors to keep pace.

Kris eyed that and wondered if there was some advantage for that among the holes for her and her fleet.

"Send to Admiral Tong. Vanguard, main body, and rear guard, should take the battlecruisers of the rebel's advanced guard under fire. Top and bottom wings, concentrate your fire on the new construction with one of the three most powerful reactors. They should vanish like moths drawn to a fire."

Kris could not hear the sound of fire control sensors switching on and aiming themselves at the onrushing hostiles. She couldn't hear it, but she sure felt it. If not through her teeth, then through her soul.

Just ten seconds later, Nelly said, "All ships have acknowledged your order, Admiral."

Another small window appeared on the main screen. Apparently Tong had every warship monitoring her channel, and gave them orders to respond directly to her.

Considering all the squadrons, flotillas, and wings between her and the last ship, it wasn't a bad idea to have them take their orders from her and send their acknowledgements directly back to her. It was a kick to think she personally commanded 6,000 ships. It was also a kick in the gut.

Her command was huge, yet it would turn on a word from her. How scary could life get?

"Admiral Tong, please have the Iteeche battlecruisers fire on rebel battlecruisers by divisions," Kris ordered. "Please have each ship in the upper and lower wings fire their forward battery at a single ship. Have a second target selected for the rear battery. I'd like to see how many of these newly constructed ships we can destroy in the short time we're in range."

Four battlecruisers targeting one rebel ship at a time ought to be lethal.

"Admiral Kitano, please have the Human battlecruisers fire by pairs. The improved fire control and computer systems on the Human ships should give them the lethality of four Iteeche ships," Kris commanded.

"Aye, aye, Admiral," the Iteeche responded.

Her fleet was barreling down on that tiny, unmarked spec of space where they'd come in maximum range of the rebels: 270,000 kilometers.

"Fleet, on my execute order, go to 1.5 gee deceleration and begin

Evasion Plan 3." Kris paused to watch as the numbers on her screen quickly rolled up to 6,000 warships responding.

"Execute," she ordered. "You have weapons release. Good shooting."

And may any available God have mercy on a lot of souls in this small patch in the vastness of space.

Kris felt herself take on weight then lose some of it. Her head slammed into the restraints as the ship dodged left and dropped out from under her.

It was just another wonderful day that she wasn't stuck in an office.

The lights dimmed as the massive capacitors began to draw power into them even as they emptied. It was likely the twelve 24-inch lasers in the forward battery could fire for an extra second based on what electricity they soaked up between the time the ship's lasers started firing and ran dry.

Kris had established a standard doctrine that she would rather have the next shoot start a second sooner than empty the power.

The ship dodged twice while its batteries reached out at the speed of light to slash into a ship that *Princess Royal* and the *Intrepid* shared for a target. Kris snuck a peek at the gunnery board for the *P. Royal*; Guns was aiming the twelve lasers at four spots on the hide of a distant battlecruiser. With luck, he might get burn-through on one or two.

Kris could be that confident of her ship's shooting not just because she had tightened the laser in their cradles. Nelly and her kids also lent a hand to Human squadrons to refine their firing solutions and get them to the guns faster. The Human squadrons were the deadliest ships in the fleet.

Kris eyed her board. It was not showing her what was happening on the other side of this shoot. She scowled but kept her mouth shut.

When there was something to tell her, she would be told. Until then, other people had jobs to be done even as she waited.

62

Admiral Zom was still recovering from the five gees. Only a few hours ago he'd thought 3.5 gees was unbearable. After hours in excess of 4.5 gees, 3.5 seemed so relaxing.

Still, his neck hurt, and he was breathing rapidly as he refreshed the oxygen in his blood.

However, he had a problem barreling down on him with the certainty of death. Even as he accelerated toward Longnae 4, the swing around Longnae 5 had them skidding off a direct course.

At the top of that skid waited that Human Kris Longknife and her battle fleet. His board estimated that they would be in range for hardly enough time to fire, reload and fire again, and that only if they did the reload faster than they usually did in drills.

Ordering the fleet from Condition Charley to Condition Zed, Admiral Zom prepared for the fight.

"Prepare to engage the enemy fleet. This shoot will be short and pass quickly. We should be in range for less than a minute. Still, I expect every ship to meet the enemy with two volleys from each battery. We will commence Dodging Plan C on my mark. We will get the outer skin of all battlecruisers rotating at twelve revolutions per minute. Ships will fire by squadrons. Wing and flotilla commanders will allocate targets to each squadron. All ships will fire as soon as their squadron commanders establish that your target is in range."

The nature of physics had given the Longknife Human a heaven-sent gift. The Humans called it "Crossing the T." She would be able to bring all her ships to bear on just the ships of his two vanguard wings and the array of gunboats and frigates on either side of those wings.

Still, the forward battlecruisers would be getting good shots at her fleet. Too bad he couldn't identify just which ships were Human. He'd concentrate on them. Killing the Longknife abomination would end any hopes the false emperor's clans had of winning this war. Maybe with her gone, they'd call it quits.

They were coming up on maximum range for the 24-inch lasers. The beams would be weak, and lasers were notorious for not hitting anything that far out. Still, those battlecruisers would be in range for forty seconds. He had to try to do some damage.

Certainly, that Longknife Human would be doing her best to do hurt his ships.

He was only moments away from coming in range.

"Execute Dodging Program 3. Fire when target is in range."

The order given, Admiral Zom waited for word.

His flagship slowed by a fraction of a gee, then dipped down. A few moments later, it dipped down again, before going right and up. Zom banged his head against the restraints of the high gee station, but he still elevated his head and bent his legs so he could get a good look at his battle board.

Now, it could begin to tell him something.

While getting information from ships, flotillas, and wings was slow, the admiral did have one ace up his sleeve. One of his clan's younger chiefs had bought a gizmo off of a Human. It could be aimed at an area and would count the number of reactors in that chunk of space. Each of his nine wings had two ships, one at each corner of their rear. Each of those battlecruisers had a device aimed at the rest of the warships, tracking the reactors in the wing.

He might not know if a ship suffered the loss of one reactor, but if all three reactors on a ship suddenly ceased to report, he had a pretty good idea that ship was not going to report any more.

While the center force had 1,920 ships, the other eight wings had a tally of 1,760. Each ship had three reactors. Verbal reports coming in told him several battlecruisers had a reactor down for repairs. Still, the total per wing was still at the maximum number. Apparently, a lame reactor still counted as available to have its nose counted.

The Longknife Human's wings swept into range of Zom's advanced vanguard. Both fleets opened fire.

In an instant, the Iteeche admiral recognized his mistake.

He had ordered his ships to fire by squadron. Flagships of each squadron led seven other ships in-line. Only now did Zom realize what that meant. For a fraction of a second, the entire squadron was not in range. During that fraction of a second, the flag was in range of the enemy fleet.

So that was why the Longknife Human had juggled her ships around, going from five columns of seven or eight flotillas to seven columns of five or six.

The flotilla at the head of each of the enemy columns swept into range. Each one led with a squadron in-line abreast followed by three more. In the blink of an eye, 56 battlecruisers were in range of the 24 flotilla leaders. Another 56 of the Human's ships would sweep in range at the same time 24 of his ships.

In other words, the misguided fools following the child opened fire at his first 48 ships while they held their fire, waiting for the rest of their squadron to pull in range.

Twenty of them vanished while they held their fire upon his order. That messed with the rest of their squadrons mates, as they waited for the order to open fire, an order that never came.

Twenty-eight of his flotillas opened fire at 28 Imperial ships, but Zom's other ships fired erratically.

It didn't matter. The Human side was dancing around, making itself an impossible target even as they flipped end-over-end to bring their rear battery to bear.

Meanwhile, the enemy's second flotillas came in range, rendering less damage that the first round of firing. Only ten ships in his first flotillas burned.

Then the Human's lead ships finished their flips and their lasers slammed into his lead ships again. Twelve more of his ships dropped off the board.

Thus it went, as one flotilla after another came in range. Eight, ten, then twelve of his ships vanished from the count.

Then it got worse. The top, middle, and bottom wings of the Human ships pulled in range. Every moment another row of 6 flotillas would come in range, but during that same moment, so would another 6 loyalist flotillas. Now, there were 12 flotillas in range in less than the blink of an eye.

In that blink of an eye, lights began to sparkle amongst the horde of newly-constructed single reactor ships. A hundred ships blinked out of existence, leaving the admiral gasping for breath.

He watched as the other fleet went through its flip, something they did so smoothly, and his crews did so poorly. A moment later, more of his newly built gunboats and frigates began to spark and bubble away into nothing.

Instead of being the surprise on which he would base his victory, the charge of these single reactor gunboats was turning into mass suicide.

Worse, a glance around the horde of gunboats showed that the enemy was picking and choosing. Ships vanished here and there. The gutting knife of death passed over this one to choose that one. Which of his ships was she picking?

"Number One, find out which of the gunboats are being selected for destruction."

"What?"

"Look at my battle board. She is picking and choosing which of the new construction to destroy."

"How could she?"

"I don't know. Maybe she has made a pact with the devils of the deep to control death. Tell me the names of some of the gunboats that have been blown to bits."

It had taken him too many seconds to discover that question to ask. It wouldn't matter when he got an answer. The enemy fleet was firing again. It had taken them only twenty seconds from the time the forward battery finished firing before her fleet was blasting his ships again.

Just about every ship of the enemy fleet was firing right at the twenty second mark. *How was that even possible?*

The deadly ships that had led the slaughter with their hard shooting were firing again. One after another, the four squadrons of each of the Longknife Human's seven flotillas cut loose. Over 100 ships vanished over the next six seconds. Then, smart as could be, they flipped ship and fired their aft battery. Another 67 Iteeche ships vanished.

It was clear to Admiral Zom now. He was firing by squadron. Most of the ships facing him were firing by division. However, those seven leading flotillas were shooting by pairs. It totaled some 220 ships, give or take a few. They fired four salvos; he lost over 300 ships.

All three wings of the enemy fleet had fired on his two vanguard wings. Over 3,000 of the Longknife Human's ships had destroyed over a thousand of his. He had yet to hear reports of those damaged.

It became clear after the first salvos hit that the gunboats in both the top and bottom array were the targets. Now it was beyond a doubt that the enemy picked the larger gunboats and skipped the frigates.

In the less than a minute that the two forces were in range of each other, nearly 5,000 gunboats in the forward arrays had been blasted to wreckage.

The butcher's bill was yet to be tallied precisely but it was clear even now that 1,300 of his battlecruisers had vanished and close to half of his gunboats were now twisted wreckage spinning in space!

Admiral Zom wanted to rage. He wanted to kick the bulkhead and maybe roar at some cringing sailors. How could the ships under that Longknife Human's command have done this to him in less than a minute?

What had she done to her ships that he had not done to his?

Consumed by fury, Admiral Zom forced himself to study what visuals he had on the other fleet and his own.

It was immediately clear that her ships had dodged and bobbed much faster than his ships had. That would clearly make them harder to hit. Still, from the video of the brief battle there were few sparks of her ships blowing up.

"Computer, count the number of enemy ships that blew up."

It took two minutes for the computer to come back with a curt, "Seventeen."

"Seventeen!" Zom bellowed. "How could we have only gotten seventeen of her ships? Computer, recount. Any spark, any flash, any evidence of a ship exploding. Count it."

The computer was calculating for three minutes, but when it finished, "seventeen," was still its answer.

Admiral Zom slumped back in his high gee couch. It was true that the enemy fleet had escaped out of range before most of his fleet could come up. Still, how could he have traded 1,300 of his battle-cruisers and 5,000 of his gunboats for just 17 enemy ships?

Going into this battle, he had thought he outnumbered the Longknife Human by almost seven-to-one. Admittedly, the small, short- ranged, gunboats had accounted for a third of his force. Take them away and the odds dropped to a bit better than four-to-one.

Admiral Zom watched as the enemy fleet zoomed away from him. It had hardly begun to decelerate towards Longnae 4. His fleet had decelerated hard to make it around the gas giant. Now he had to accelerate hard to catch up with the Longknife Human. Sooner or later she would have to begin decelerating and then he would have her.

It was only a matter of time before they were again in laser range.

Of course, his ships would have to be firing more than they had been this pass.

"Number One, what is wrong with our deep damned ships today?"

63

Kris ordered her fleet back to Condition Baker, and allowed chiefs to dismiss one in four watch standers to get a hot meal and a warm shower before returning to their battle station to doze or drill, depending on the iron whim of his or her chief.

The most pressing needs taken care of, Kris climbed out of her egg, donned her shipsuit and stood beside her battle board, her shoulders hunched as she leaned on it. She thought better standing up and staring down at the universe.

"Nelly, get me Admiral Tong," Kris ordered.

A moment later, a very happy Iteeche filled much of her forward screen.

"Admiral Tong, that was a very good shoot. Give the crews a Very Well Done."

"It will be my pleasure," the admiral agreed, and waved at someone off screen, likely a comm officer, to get the message disseminated to the fleet quickly.

"Now, what's the butcher's bill?" Kris asked.

"I was hoping you'd tell me. I'm sure your Nelly kept a better tally than my ship's computer could."

Kris could almost feel Nelly preening at her neck. For a computer, the gal was getting awful vain. However, she did stay quiet. Apparently, Nelly wanted Kris to give her the order.

After a brief pause, Kris allowed herself a tiny shake of her head and said, "Okay Nelly, what are the total casualties for both sides?"

"Twelve hundred and ninety-seven hostile battlecruisers lost containment and exploded or suffered major, but not catastrophic, damage and have dropped out of the battle formation. Many are adrift in space."

"What about those non-Smart Metal ships with only a single reactor?" Tong asked.

"Seven thousand, five hundred came in range during the shoot. They turned out to have no ice armor. We'd kind of expected that based on their mass and density, but it was nice to find out we were right. If we hit them, we destroyed them. However, they weren't very good at jinking. I don't know why that wasn't a major design requirement. We hit six thousand nine hundred and twelve, Admirals," Nelly reported.

"Our gunners thought the small rebel ships were quite energetic, dancing around all over the place," Admiral Tong said. "We thought we missed more than we hit. I guess we must have hit more than exploded."

"What about the battlecruisers?" Kris asked.

"The same thing," Admiral Tong said. "Lots of dancing around. I don't think they were revolving their hull armor nearly as fast as we were. That might have cost them ships."

"I hope they don't do better next time we meet," Jack drawled, dryly.

"Yes, let's hope. What were our casualties?" Kris asked, and changed the topic. She could have had the ships she lost listed on her board, but she waited for Nelly to pass the word.

"Seventeen of our battlecruisers were destroyed. Twelve from among the thousand ships we acquired at Balan," Nelly added softly. More proof that training was essential to surviving in battle.

Nelly went on, "Another sixty-four were damaged, but not enough to have to pull out of the line. Two Human battlecruisers were hit, but their crystal armor worked."

Kris shook her head. "I wonder if our opposite number has this loss count."

"I'd hate to be in his shoes if he does," Jack said.

"I'd hate to be part of his flag bridge crew," Admiral Tong said. "If he's a clan lordling, this may be the first time in his life that he's facing adversity."

Kris could easily agree with the Iteeche admiral. Adversity was a hard tool for annealing character, but she had yet to find anything that worked nearly so well. Into each life some rain must fall, or it's a pretty dry life.

She turned her mind from the preliminary battle she'd just fought to the critical one that lay in the future. Her main concern was where to meet that battle.

"Let's see, Nelly. If we stay at 1.5 gees and they set out to overtake us, where do we meet?"

"Your enemy is now accelerating at 3.5 Iteeche gees. That would give him more energy on the boat when they come up on us. He'd whiz by and then have to decelerate. Let's assume his nav computer is half decent and he cuts his acceleration, or keeps it up and flips ship to decelerate into our meeting engagement. You're about twelve hours out from that fight. Oh, and Kris, you'll have to decelerate at three gees for the last twelve hours in order to make orbit on Longnae 4."

"If he matches course with us," Kris mused, "he'll be back doing 3.5 gees again."

"Yes. His ships and crews have to be tired of that by now."

Kris let her mind wander, following vectors and thrust projections. Always, the maximum range of the 24-inch lasers was a circle around each potential position of her ships. Of his ships.

Finished with the thinking, Kris had Nelly run some projections on a few of her possible options. Satisfied, Kris said, "Nelly get me Admiral Tong."

"Yes, Admiral," the Iteeche said.

"I want to take the fleet up to 1.75 Human gees. Will that be a problem for your Iteeche crewmen?"

"That will be just a smidge over two gees Iteeche," Nelly put in, helpfully.

"If they can't lift double their weight for a bit," Admiral Tong snapped, "they don't belong in my Navy."

"What do you intend to do for the next dozen hours or so?" Kris asked.

"Once the crew gets some food and a dip in the tub, I'll let them sleep in their high gee carts at their battle station. I already have the ship engineers mending and fixing. They can take care of their own needs after they take care of the ship's needs. I intend to be back up to a hundred percent on every ship before we get into another fight."

"Good," Kris said, and closed down the call. She turned to Jack.

"You hungry?"

"I could eat the horse you rode in on," he said.

"I don't think the supply situation is quite that bad. At least not yet. But don't make any suggestions to the officer mess's president. He doesn't need any more ideas about how to find stray meat for the stew."

"No. Not at all," he answered her.

At the hatch into the passageway, Kris glanced back at her board. Nothing much had changed. She allowed herself to go enjoy lunch.

Maybe, after that, she and Jack could enjoy a tub soak.

She rotated her shoulders, trying to get some of the tension out. Jack rested a gentle hand between her shoulder blade and did his best on the walk to the wardroom to unkink a few muscles.

64

Admiral Zom was tired of laying on his high gee couch. He was tired of staring up at the overhead whenever he wasn't risking his neck to angle it up so he could see his battle board. The tube intended to help him evacuate fluids when nature called itched.

If he hated this, what must his sailors feel toward this enforced torture? First, his fleet accelerated at hard gees. Then it decelerated. Now it accelerated again at the same hard gee. He knew why he'd done it. How many of the sailors did?

Still, sailors really didn't matter. They performed their duty to the clan that fed them. That was enough.

Speaking of feeding, his stomach growled. Zom could not remember the last time he had eaten. He reached down to rummage in the pocket sewn into the side of his high gee cot and found a wrapped candied yam. He unwrapped it and slowly began to eat it.

At high gee, you had to chew your food until it was little more than spit in your mouth, otherwise your stomach could not digest it.

He also had to bring his cot up to forty degrees from the vertical to make sure that he didn't choke on his food. There were so many things to fighting a battle the new Human way.

He'd done so much, yet still they slaughtered his ships like smelt swimming upriver in shoals. What could he have done differently?

"Number One, do we have any video of the enemy battlefleet during the last fight?"

"Most Eminent Admiral, they were barely into the 270,000 kilometer range of our lasers."

"Certainly, someone took video of what the enemy was doing," Zom snapped.

"I will canvas the fleet, Most Eminent Admiral," Number One answered, and began talking into his comm unit.

Half an hour later, Admiral Zom was watching a brief video on the main screen of his flag bridge. It had been magnified and slowed down, but it was clear that the enemy ships were dancing around like spring bugs doing their best to evade hungry fingerlings.

"They never stayed on one course more than three seconds," Admiral Zom mused softly. "Every two or three seconds they're up, down, left, right, faster, slower. Yet each ship did a different dance. Whether they were turning toward our ships to fire or returning to their base course, they never quit bouncing."

No wonder so few of his ships had made hits.

His staff officer stayed quiet. Zom wondered what he was thinking ... or if he ever thought at all.

"Our ships did their own dodging, but apparently not so well. I wonder what our dodging efforts looked like?"

"I don't know, My Admiral," Number One staff officer said.

"Then have a few flotillas go back to Dodging Program 3 and let's get some video to compare."

"Yes, My Admiral."

That Number One staff officer was now addressing him merely as "My Admiral," told Zom a lot. Someone didn't approve of all this hunting around for the source of their catastrophic losses. "It was just their time to die. Their fate. Their destiny."

That kind of thinking had gotten him into this mess. That and the few survivors of the previous defeats who had managed to escape destruction or capture to carry back reports on how this Longknife Human fought.

They had changed their tactics and equipment. A week ago, it had seemed enough.

It had not been nearly good enough.

Every survivor brought back stories of how the Human and allied Iteeche ships danced around, making it nearly impossible to hit them. Spies from the capital reported on new high gee couches. They shared how the Humans and Iteeche fought while reclining on them, allowing their bodies to survive the brutal pressure of two, three, or even four times their weight.

The newest high gee stations were the best copy they could make of what the spies described.

Zom ground his beak together. The spies said the enemy used the magic metal to make the high gee "eggs" and that the warriors went into them bare. Both claims were hard to believe. Dozens of programmers had tried to create the cushioning needed for a such a station and all had failed. They were either too brittle and fell apart, or too strong and inflexible. Those were no better than laying down on the deck.

The Human programmers had offered every builder a high gee station for their ships. Every planet had rejected those offers. Warriors went into battle standing on their own four feet.

Now, the Human programmers were gone and Zom was left fighting a Human-led fleet that he could not match with these thrown together couches whose water cushions blew out under the pressure of high accelerations.

"My Admiral," Number One staff officer said, somewhere between respectful and obsequious. "We have the video of four of our flotillas operating for three minutes under Dodging Program 3."

"Put it on the main screen. Put the enemy ships above it."

The two videos appeared, the enemy below, his own ships above. The two told him nothing. His own ships were clearly dodging faster than the Human-led fleet.

"Computer, change the timing on the videos. Make one Iteeche second equal to five Human seconds."

His ships slowed down. The enemy ships sped up. This view showed an enemy fleet that moved as if its feet were in a bucket of kelp syrup. His fleet now was much more lively; the ships changed course every two or three seconds with much harder turns.

His ships were sluggish, each course change taking effect slowly. The hostiles slammed their ships into the change of directions.

At times, his ships doubled back on themselves. For example, one ship went down and right, then up and left, only to end up in the same space. If it was trying to evade a laser, it had done a good job of charging right back into it.

"Do you see the problem?" he asked Number One.

"Yes, My Most Eminent Admiral," the staff officer said. With the proof right there in front of him, even this mindless sand flea could see it.

"What do we do?" Number One now wanted to know. "They obliterated half our vanguards. What changes can we make in the next half day that will make things go any differently?"

"Are you suggesting I turn and run from an opponent I outnumber four-to-one?"

"She has defeated forces that outnumbered her four-to-one and sailed away with more ships than when she started the fight. A lot more ships."

Suddenly, Number One staff officer was sounding like someone who had seen a ghost and became a true believer in ancestor worship.

"I think we can do much better than we did this last fight," Admiral Zom said. "Battle board, show our course and vectors to intercept the enemy fleet, assuming we stay at 3.5 gee acceleration as long as we can and then flip and match course and deceleration with the enemy."

"There are too many variables," the computer responded.

So, Admiral Zom went through an iterative process, inserting his assumptions for when the Longknife Human would jack up her deceleration.

He was halfway through this effort when Number One said, "The enemy fleet has increased its deceleration from 1.5 to 1.75 gees."

"So, she doesn't want to have to weigh four times her normal self. After today, I can't blame her."

"Computer, I wish to generate a random number list. Two lists, each using digits from one to seven."

A long list of random numbers began to cascade down the screen in front of him.

"Now, assume that the first and last three numbers mean a course change of 40, 30, and 15 degrees right or left of course. Use the second list in the same way for up and down."

"That can be done," The computer agreed.

"Good. Then go through the list eliminating any numbers that cancel each other out. For example, a down, left followed by an up, right. That would put the ship back in the exact same space it left."

"Yes. I can eliminate all of those."

"Now, prepare a program that will control the helm of each battle-cruiser. Let each ship start the random numbers at a different random place on the list. Also, have them skip ahead fifty after using a hundred pairs. That should keep it random."

"It shall be done," the computer replied.

That should give that Longknife Human something to worry about.

Number One staff officer cleared his throat, then cautiously said, "My Most Eminent Admiral, may I point out that their ships seem to dodge much harder than ours do?"

"Yes, you may. Apparently they have much more powerful reaction jets." There was a long pause as both of them considered the problem.

"Most likely they have reprogrammed their ships for the hard maneuvering," the admiral said.

"Our programmers can't do anything that extensive," the staff officer pointed out.

"No, we can't," Admiral Zom said. Then an idea hit him.

"We cannot reprogram our ships, but we can use what we have," he said. "Staff Officer Number Seven, are there attachment points aft for engineers working outside on the engines?"

The staff officer inspector for engineering immediately answered from several meters away. "Yes, My Most Eminent Admiral."

He sounded quite surprised to be called upon but also excited.

"Are they on the spinning part of the hull or the stable part?"

"Stable," Most Eminent Admiral. "We cannot spin the hull well aft. There are too many engineering fixtures to risk it. That is why our sterns are so vulnerable."

"Good, good, good," Admiral Zom said, almost giddy with excitement.

"When I cut down to two gees or less, have every battlecruiser break out four of its longboats. Get them attached to the aft hull covering the cardinal points of the compass. Rig them into the directional jets. We'll see how that Longknife Human takes to that surprise."

"Very interesting, My Most Eminent Admiral," Number One said.

"There's one thing more," the admiral said. "An idea that flit across my mind, but it's just outside of reach. Let me think."

The bridge fell silent around him.

I was thinking about giving our maneuvering jets more power . . .. About how we attach the longboats to add their rocket motors to those jets . . .. If we attached them to our hull that spun it would make a mess of any vector we added to the ship . . .. They had to be attached to a stable part of the ship's hull.

"Computer, how long do our lasers fire before they empty their capacitors?"

"Six seconds, Admiral."

"So, we need our hulls to rotate fully in six seconds to distribute the heat from a hit."

"So it would seem," Number One staff officer said.

"Yes!" Admiral Zom shouted. "Yes! We have been rotating our hulls too slowly. Number One, send to all ships: 'When next we go into battle, all ships will rotate their hulls twenty times a minute'."

"To hear is to make it so," Number One staff officer said, and began to talk into his comm unit.

Admiral Zom relaxed into his high gee couch. He had done it. He had surprises for the Longknife Human that could put her in a fine fish stew.

"Number One," he said.

"Yes, My Most Eminent Admiral."

"What are our three most damaged ships?"

"Ah," he said, and glanced at his own board, "the *Emperor Boos 213*, *Emperor Donha 412*, and the *Warriors of Domm 387*. Why?"

"Pass them our observation that our ships need more reaction motors and how we're getting them. Surely they can do better. Also, that hull revolutions need to be at least twenty times a minute. If we are to take six seconds of laser hits, we need to distribute the energy quickly."

"At least 20 times a minute? If it's shorter won't that mean they are burning the same area?"

"No. Ships are moving. Lasers are moving. If the laser beam starts hitting at one place and that place comes back again, the beam will likely be hitting forward or aft of that place."

"Oh," Number One officer said.

Admiral Zom could almost see the light turning on behind his eyes.

"Yes, yes. Immediately, My Most Eminent and Thoughtful Admiral. I shall send the message immediately." He again began talking into his comm unit.

"One more thing, Number One," Admiral Zom said. "For the duration of this battle, please just respond to me as admiral. With lasers traveling at the speed of light, we can't afford for you to tie up so much time just saying 'Yes,' or something. Understand?"

"Yes, My Most . . . ah, Admiral." Number One staff officer sputtered.

"Good, now send your message to those three ships and order

them to make for three different jumps out of this system. That message must get back to Navy Clan Central. If we fail, someone else may succeed."

"Yes, Admiral, but we will not fail."

"Then three badly damaged ships will not matter that much."

While Number One staff officer sent his message and orders, Admiral Zom relaxed into his water-cushioned couch. He had done a very good job of examining what went wrong during his first encounter with the Longknife Human and her fleet of wonder ships. This truly was the best day of his life.

If he succeeded in winning this coming battle, songs would be sung about him for a thousand years. Even if he failed, he would be remembered in song as the admiral who discovered how the Human had been beating the ships of the true Emperor and helped the next admiral to victory.

He pulled another candied yam from the bag beside his couch and unwrapped it. Again, he chewed it carefully. He also drank plenty of water. A big battle was coming. He wanted nothing to detract from his performance when it did.

65

Kris Longknife balanced her time between her battle board and breaks in the loving clutches of her high gee egg. While gees of 1.75 on a human were not as bad as the equivalent two gees for an Iteeche, it was still no walk in the park.

The galley provided coffee, tea, and meatloaf sandwiches. They sent the rations around on a cart that drove itself and stepped over hatch combings. At this point, no one left their battle station.

Some did what maintenance needed doing. Some napped. There were a few that were actually able to persuade their chiefs that they were 4.0 in both their equipment and last drill. Now they played a video game from inside their eggs.

Kris had a hard time believing that any chief could get that soft, but she discovered that more gun crews were bringing their lasers up to 4.0 and maxing out their drills so they too could play the game of their choice.

Most of them were losing themselves in wild games of cartoon auto chasing with characters from their childhood tossing bombs at each other.

It kept the mind off of the coming murder and mayhem.

Kris wished she and Jack could lose themselves in one of the video games that their kids loved. Admirals could wish it, but admirals didn't often get what they wished.

"How do you think he's going to work it?" Kris asked Jack and Nelly. "Chase us with an acceleration of 3.5 gees, then flip and decelerate at 3.5 gees until he matches course with us? Then drop down to our deceleration and go at us with every laser he's got?"

"He could do that," Jack said, thoughtfully. "However, he'd be going into a shot with his crews exhausted from the heavy gees of the approach. I don't know what they're using for high gee stations, but they're never as good as the advertising from the company that manufactured them. If he's smart, he'll allow some time to fix and mend any gear that's come loose. If he hasn't tied his lasers down tight, all this high gee and other honking around has got to have worked all sorts of stuff loose."

Kris nodded. "We've had the last day to dial our gear in to damn near perfect. When have his crews been able to get out of their high gee stations to do any maintenance? He passed awfully close to that gas giant. The ride through the upper reaches of its atmosphere must have been bumpy as hell. It couldn't have been easy on gear or crews."

"Yep," Jack said. "They didn't do so good on their last shoot. What was our kill ratio, fifty-to-one?"

"Close enough that I will not correct you," Nelly said.

Her computer was learning to be a real girl, Kris thought, then said, "Thank you, Nelly."

"For telling Jack he was right, or for not correcting him to the thirteenth decimal?"

"Both," Kris said, but her focus was on her battle board. "What's he doing? What did he learn from all the casualties he suffered in that one-minute shoot? What surprise is the enemy thinking up?"

"Kris," Jack said, "I have no idea how to answer any of your questions. The ball is in his court. We've done about everything we can do for the coming fight. Now we just wait for him to come up, then blow him away. He decides where and when we fight. We decide how fast he dies."

Kris made a face, not easy to do when her body weighed three-quarters more than normal. "He's messing with me. If I want to make orbit, I have to correct my course to one aimed forward of our present course."

"That is obvious," Nelly said, and estimated the course to put them in orbit around their target planet if they changed it now."

"But when he comes up," Kris said, "he comes up close. Very close."

Nelly added a line showing that if the enemy continued on the course he was on presently, there would be a bit more than a hundred thousand kilometers between the two fleets when they heaved into range.

"Of course," Nelly said, "range for the 24-inch lasers is 270,000 kilometers. You could use his final approach to shoot up his stern and blow up reactors while he's on final approach. He'll be very vulnerable then."

Kris thought on that for a long moment.

"It seems to me," Jack said, "that we want to join battle as soon as we can. Shoot him up, then adjust course for Longnae 4 when he's out of the way."

"So, we stay to our present 1.75 gee deceleration and let him catch up," Kris said. "That way, after the shoot we'd have more time to decelerate. We could use something decent like 2.5 gees."

"It all depends on when he chooses to make contact," Nelly said.

"Or we could slam on the brakes and make him catch up with us sooner," Kris said. "Admiral Tong?"

"Yes, Admiral?" came immediately on net.

"Considering the quality of your high gee stations, could your crews bear a 4.5 gee deceleration?"

"We have tested it. It is very hard on our hips and shoulders."

"Still, you have done it. How long do you think you could tolerate it?"

"I would prefer that you don't go harder than four gees deceleration. Remember, our hips and shoulders evolved for one gee straight down, not four or more gees applied to our backs. Even if the back is cushioned so very well in one of the high gee stations you Humans have designed and spun out for us, it is hard on us."

"Understood," Kris said. "No more than four gees. You'd prefer we hold it to 3.5 gees."

"Very much prefer," Admiral Tong added.

"Okay. Thank you for your advice, Admiral," Kris said. "Nelly, remind me not to put on more than three Human gees."

"Yes, Kris."

However, Kris was already lost, meditating on the lines across her battle board. Several hundred of the cruisers had skidded around Longnae 5 and were now working hard to set a course for Longnae 7. They had all cut their acceleration down to one gee, Iteeche. Calculations showed them arriving at the ice giant well after Kris's troop ships swung around it and headed for Longnae 4. That was not a problem.

The problem was all the ships that had made it around the gas giant and were now accelerating for her fleet. Did she want to bring them to battle sooner or later? Sooner meant decelerating more now with less to do later.

Delaying battle meant continuing her light deceleration for as long as she dared, then going to high gee deceleration in order to make orbit around Longnae 4.

Which to choose?

Delaying heavy deceleration risked her getting close to the planet and having her need to make orbit dictate her course. Raising the deceleration now gave her more options for maneuvering her fleet in battle.

Really, there was only one option.

"Comm, get me Admiral Tong."

"Aye, aye, ma'am."

"Yes, Admiral," Tong said from the main screen.

"I've decided to join battle sooner rather than later. I'd like to take the fleet up to three gees, Iteeche, deceleration. Do you have any problem with that?"

"No, Admiral. We performed maintenance when you took us to two gees deceleration. We are ready now, ma'am."

"Very good, Admiral Tong. Take the fleet to 3.0 gees."

"Aye, aye, ma'am."

A few moments later, the 1MC announced, "All hands, prepare for 2.5 gees in five minutes. If you aren't in your egg, strip down and lock in. If you must, you can take your teddy bear."

The PA system closed down with an audible click. No doubt another boson's mate would not be making announcements for a while.

Still, it got the needed laugh from all hands on Kris's flag bridge. After the battle, she'd have to cautiously ask the skipper to go lenient on the miscreant if the chief brought her up at Captain's Mast.

Once again, Kris pulled off her shipsuit and slipped into her egg. It was tempting to take a moment to give Jack a hug and a kiss, but PDAs were discouraged, and a naked admiral had to provide some leadership.

He winked at her. Maybe they'd been married long enough for him to read her mind.

She winked back.

Surviving the way Kris fought battles took a lot of accommodation for the flesh and blood that did the fighting.

Settled into place, Kris again found herself staring at her battle board. Only now, the vision was projected onto the video screen in front of her egg. For now, she sat half up. As acceleration grew more brutal, she'd recline more and the screen would become the faceplate of her egg.

The high gee station doubled as a survival pod. If worse came to worse, the pod would become airtight and the ship would expel her pod and as many others as time allowed in the brief interval between the captain hitting the abandon ship button and the ship's destruction. If the reactors went wild and released their plasma, there would be little time.

Still, sailors fought harder when they felt they had a chance of surviving the battle.

Around her, watch standers watched dials and lights. These were not games being played in this workspace.

Now, rather, the most deadly game was afoot. The game of war that decided empires.

66

Admiral Zom scowled at his board. He was still accelerating at 3.5 gees, playing catch up with the Longknife Human's fleet.

Now, she had changed the game.

Before his eyes, the enemy fleet began to decelerate at three gees, slowing themselves down and shortening the amount of time it would take his fleet to catch up with her ships.

Was that what he wanted?

It did afford him more options for his approach. He could slow his deceleration down at some point to 1.5 gee. That would make it easier to rig out the longboats he intended to use to augment his maneuvering jets.

Still, should he do that sooner or later?

If he did it later, it could be combined with a last check of the battle efficiency of his lasers and gear. If he did it sooner, any repairs they made could be undone.

Clearly, he'd do it later.

But not too close to the enemy. If he slowed and set about making his ships more battle ready, she could slam on the breaks and commence firing when he was least ready for it. Or worse, he might have to begin dodging and dancing, leaving his longboats behind in his wake.

No, the low gee period would have to be close to the shoot, but not too close.

Zom found himself wondered about that young plebe that was him on his first day at the academy. If he had known then that his career choice would put him in this seat at this time with a battle breathing down his neck, would he have fled back to his Chooser's palace quarters? Would he have begged for another choice for his life?

He slowly shook his head. From the first time he'd heard the battle songs of old at the Palace of Learning, he'd wanted to pace a bridge under fire. For as long as he remembered, he'd dreamed of winning the fight that killed one dynasty and spawned another

Now, here he was. Of course, he wasn't pacing his flag bridge, but forced to recline under the brutal weight of 3.5 gees. Still, he was where he had always dreamed of being. This was his time. He would not fail.

For a long time, he gazed at his battle board. Finally, he hit the button and let the couch recline all the way. He set an alarm to make sure he was awake in an hour. That was when he would order the fleet to flip and begin deceleration. That deceleration would have to be at the same 3.5 gees that his acceleration had been. Then, an hour before he got in range of the enemy fleet, he'd slow to a workable deceleration and order maintenance and the launching of the longboats.

Admiral Zom had made his decision. He had his plan. He relaxed into his high gee couch a contented man.

67

Admiral Kris Longknife watched the vector of the enemy fleet as it extended. It held steady, reaching out for her ships as it put on more and more velocity at an acceleration of 3.5 gees, Iteeche. Now the distance between them narrowed at a much faster pace as she bled off velocity at three gees Iteeche.

That was the way she needed to think. Most of her fleet were Iteeche. It was their fragile shoulders and hips that limited her acceleration and deceleration. Strange, Kris had always considered the human backbone a weakness. It had certainly been a source of great discomfort when she was heavily pregnant with Ruthie.

Now, however, the human hip, backbone, and shoulder could more easily be cushioned against high gees. Interesting how evolutionary decisions made half a billion years ago when both species were little more than unicellular animals could come back to bite them on the ass now.

The enemy admiral had had an hour to respond to Kris's command to increase the rate of closure. To cut down on the amount of time before they came in range of each other and began slashing at one another with gigajoule lasers.

Apparently, he was content to hurry tens of thousands of intelligent lives out of this world.

Kris really wished she could find a way to persuade him to surrender. It would save a lot of pain and death. Of course, there was no way she would surrender to him, so she really could not expect him to haul down the colors and run up a white flag.

Indeed, if he broke off the attack and tried to run away now, she'd have to pursue him. She couldn't have a fleet this big joining with another fleet. She had this chunk of the rebel forces in her crosshairs, she had to destroy it now.

"Captain," she called to the head of the flag bridge watch.

"Yes, Admiral?"

"I may take a nap. The enemy fleet should flip over and begin deceleration soon. Don't wake me if that happens. However, if they change their acceleration or deceleration from 3.5 gees, Iteeche, make sure I'm awake and notice it. Understood?"

"Yes, ma'am."

Kris leaned back in her egg until she was on her back. Her battle board moved with her until it was directly above her. She continued to stare at it, mulling over options, alternatives, and potential disasters, both for her and him. She felt her mind entering a kind of meditative state.

Before long, she'd slipped away into rest.

68

Admiral Zom's alarm woke him in time to review the situation before his fleet flipped ships and began decelerating. The enemy fleet was still decelerating at three gees. If he didn't begin decelerating too, the two fleets would whiz by each other again.

Zom gave the order to flip ship at the appropriate time, but an idea would not quit niggling at his brain. There was a solid risk that the Longknife woman and her fleet would have a powerful position behind him as he approached her fleet. They could shoot straight up the vulnerable sterns of his ships.

"What if I was to cut deceleration just as we come in range of her guns?" he mused to himself. "We could whiz past them before slamming back on the deceleration. I might lose some ships, but I could get behind them and jam some lasers up their backside."

He liked that idea.

"Did you say something?" Number One staff officer asked.

"Just to myself. There is no need for a slug fest to be just a slug fest. We can be fast on our feet."

"Sir?"

"I will tell you about it later," Admiral Zom said.

Of course, two could play the same game. If he was too obvious, she might cut her deceleration just as quickly. Mentally, he examined the options. If he cut deceleration down to nothing, he'd have no weight on the ships as he sped by her fleet. There would be no dodging and dancing.

She could slaughter them. Still it would only be for a few seconds. Then she would be ahead of him and he would be slashing at her reactors.

Now he switched and examined her options. One was only too apparent. She could drop her deceleration just like him.

However, if she cut her deceleration, she would also have no weight on her ships. She would be no better able to dodge and dance than his ships could. It would turn the battle into a bloody massacre, but she would not have the advantage she used so often.

This might, indeed, turn the tables on that Longknife Human.

But would it be enough?

He eyed the fleets as they met. They would be little more than 100,000 kilometers apart. The gunnery on both sides would make bloody work of each other.

More importantly, the small gunboats would be in a position to charge the enemy fleet and get in range to use their powerful short-range weapons. They might be in a good position to get in between the battlecruisers and do their bloody work while being ignored by the other side's battlecruisers.

Zom closed his eyes and breathed as deeply as 3.5 gees allowed. He was planning a battle like no other battle had ever been fought in the long history of the Empire.

Yes, there had been auxiliary warships and smaller ones sailing in the wake of the larger ones. Still, using the gunboats and frigates as a strike force at the same time the battlecruisers did their best to blow each other apart. No, that had never been the way of the Iteeche.

Would this come as a shock to the Longknife Human? He thought back on what he could remember of Human Navy history. Yes, they had destroyers to help their cruisers and battleships. But they were assigned to keep the other side's destroyers from slipping in and firing missiles at the other side's big ships.

Admiral Zom had heard of no new destroyers being constructed. Everything the Humans built nowadays were battlecruisers, or so it seemed. How would this new admiral with such a short career react to his small gunboats? Had she ever faced small ships attacking her big battlecruisers?

It took the Iteeche admiral a moment to remember the Longknife woman's first battle. Oh, right. She had commanded small ships attacking huge battleships in the defense of her home world.

Admiral Zom grinned, though at 3.5 gees it was more of a grimace. Wouldn't it be interesting if he defeated her with some of the same tactics she used to win her first battle?

Contented that he had the situation well in hand, the Iteeche admiral reclined in his high gee couch and considered how he would get the little gunboats in range to do the most damage. It would be hours before it was time to reduce deceleration and make what preparations he could that would win this battle for him.

"Number One staff officer."

"Yes, Admiral?"

"I intend to slow when we come within a million kilometers of the enemy fleet. If I fall asleep on this couch, make sure I am woken."

"I find it hard to think that anyone could sleep on one of these couches," the staff officer said.

"This bouncing around at high gees is a young man's war, Number One. You would be amazed what I can do."

"Yes, Admiral."

Zom took one more long look at his board. Now his ships were slowing down, decelerating toward their planet and delaying the onrushing battle. Delaying it so they could make it last longer.

He let his couch recline all the way and stared at the overhead. He saw the lines of his board etched in his memory and projected above him. He tried to think of all the things he could do, and what she would do in response. It was like playing a solitaire game of chi. Here he moved a knight. There she moved a castle. Now he moved an

Imperial advisor. She countered with her war leader. Every move was aimed at capturing the Emperor.

He'd enjoyed many games of chi in his life aboard ship. He wondered if he'd ever want to play that game again. After living through this coming fight, the game would be very tame.

69

Kris came awake with a start. She hadn't really expected to nap, but apparently she had. The burden of high gees was tiring. That and the reality that she'd done about all she could do had let her mind drift off.

"Kris," Nelly announced, "the hostile fleet just cut its deceleration to 1.5 gees, Iteeche. They're a million klicks out."

Blinking sleep from her eyes, Kris studied the battle board above her face. Nothing was different from what she expected. Fine. She wanted to be well-rested and on her toes for the coming fight.

Of course, she'd likely be on her back for that fight. Ah, the vagaries of the language and Human behavior.

"Any idea what they're doing at that low gee? They've been at 3.5 gees since forever."

"Sorry, Kris, but a million klicks is a long way for even our fire control optics."

"See if the boffins don't have a telescope they can turn on his ships. I know if he's repairing and dialing in his lasers, we won't see anything. If he does anything we can see, I want eyeballs on it."

"I've alerted the science team. They are swinging their best optics on the enemy fleet. They'll get back to us in a few minutes."

"Fine," Kris said and turned her head to suck in some water. That made her mouth a lot happier.

"What's the fleet situation, Nelly?" Kris asked.

"We're still decelerating at three gees, Iteeche. No complaints from anyone. No ships are having any trouble holding this deceleration. Guns are at over 99 percent. Every once in a while a laser will hiccup, and the gun crew get to work on it. We're the closest we can come to perfect that Humans and Iteeche can hope to get."

Kris took another swig of water, then tried the nutritional paste a tube on the other side of her head was dispensing. It was promised to be tasty and low residue. Although the high gee stations were supposed to take care of all bodily needs, the bridge air blowers were on high. The place was starting to stink of sweat and worse.

Pictures of the enemy fleet began to fill the screen above Kris's head. Most showed a few dozen ships. The ships were little more than large, bright dots. Their rocket engines pointed at the cameras. There seemed to be something different about the hulls. They weren't perfect dots, but seemed blurred a bit.

"Nelly, ask the boffins if they can clear up the pictures any. Some of them seem to be a bit off."

The next batch of pictures to float across Kris's screen didn't look like dots. They'd been rasterized. Each tiny square had the brightness value of the ship's picture.

It was as you'd expect. The center of the dot was white. The pixels slipped into shades of gray before going black around the edges. However, there were stray squares that showed a brighter gray than those immediately around it. Most of those could be the reflection of a nearby ship's rocket motor or even the distant sun. However, they still puzzled Kris.

"Nelly, have the boffins concentrate on the stray pixels near the hull that have a different brightness from those around it."

"Will do."

A few minutes later, more pictures began to fill Kris's screen. These showed similar photos to the first batch. On serious review, some of those looked exactly like the first batch.

"Talk to me, Nelly."

"Kris, they took a second set of photos and compared them to the first. Most still have the stray bright pixel. However, in almost all cases, the stray has wandered to somewhere else in the photo."

"They still can't tell what they are?"

"No, Kris. All they've got is the raster map with various gradations of light and dark. We can't make anything else out."

"Okay, well tell our science team to stay on this. I think this guy is trying to pull a fast one on us and I'd like to know what it is, soonest."

"Aye, aye, Admiral."

For the next quarter hour, the enemy fleet cruised along at a much more comfortable deceleration. Still, the two forces closed as two irresistible forces moved into position to pummel each other.

"Let's reduce our deceleration," Kris said. "We're far enough out from our target that we can stay loose. Let's go to 1.5 gee, Iteeche, and see how our opposite number reacts to that."

"Aye, aye, Admiral," Nelly said, and passed the order to the comm officer.

Two minutes later, her fleet was at the same deceleration as the rebel fleet. They were at 800,000 klicks and holding as they hurried toward Longnae 4.

With the gees reduced, she ordered her egg to let her sit up.

"Let's get ready for this fight. Admiral Tong."

"Yes, Admiral."

"Bring the fleet back to Condition Zed. Apply sixty revolutions per minute to our outer skin. Bring us up to immediate readiness for a shoot."

"Aye, aye, Admiral. Will you hold for a moment while I issue the orders?"

"Of course, Admiral."

The screen blanked for a moment while Admiral Tong got his ships buttoned down. Then he was back.

"Admiral, we have noticed that the rebel ships have been doing something. Have you figured out what it is?"

"No, Admiral, we're just as puzzled as you are. I've had my scientific team on the *Princess Royal* go over the visuals with a fine-tooth comb. We'll have to get closer before we can make it out."

"It appears that almost every one of their battlecruisers has done whatever this is."

"Yeah. I figure our rebel admiral has come up with some trick that will make our life miserable."

"I fear so, too."

"Well, he certainly didn't come here to lose a battle," Kris pointed out.

"*I* most certainly did not."

"Then keep your high gee station loose and your ship ready to scoot when I say so."

"Scoot we will," the Iteeche admiral said, and cut the comm link.

Kris leaned forward in her egg, eyeing the forward screen. It showed the entire enemy fleet, but in a small window, it showed the ship nearest to her fleet. The visual was still the jagged image of a heavily pixelated point of light.

"What are you up to?" Kris muttered to herself. "And when the blazes are you going to get up to it?"

"Patience, dear admiral," Jack said.

Kris made a face. "Patience my ass. I want to kill something."

"Well, my dear vulture," Jack said, reminding Kris of the ancient cartoon she was quoting from, "You're just have to hang around on this dead tree like the rest of us dirty birds."

Kris stared at the screen. Nothing happened. More staring. Still nothing happened.

Then everything started to happen at once.

70

Admiral Zom watched as information flowed into his battle board. Availability of lasers had fallen to nearly 80% during the brutal approach. Now they were back up to almost 95%.

All the longboats were deployed. In fact, most of his battlecruisers had deployed eight long boats if they had them, six if they did not. The idea was to use the first four at the cardinal points of the compass. Then, when they were shot away, fall back to the four aimed at the ordinal points.

It was good that his crews were thinking on their feet, even if they did lie on a couch.

He was the first to notice that the distance between the two fleets was no longer closing.

"Oh, so the Longknife Human sees what I am up to. She has been reacting to my actions this entire battle. Now she gives over to me the decision for when we give battle. I thought she had more fight in her."

"She does not appear to be a very aggressive admiral. Could it be that being a woman, she cannot decide?" Number One staff officer said.

"Do not underestimate this woman," Zom said, as much to

himself as to his staff officer. "She did not win so many battles by accident. One? Maybe. Two? No. She knows what she is doing."

Number One staff officer did not reply.

This left Zom wondering just what she might be doing, giving him this important decision. Was she also bringing her lasers back up to 95 percent available? Did she have repairs to make to engines that had been worked too hard?

There were many questions, but few answers for him. His board showed that every admiral had reported that all their ships now had deployed their longboats.

It was time to take action.

"Communications, send to the fleet, on my execute command, battlecruisers will cease all deceleration. When that order is given the gunboats will accelerate at two gees at the enemy fleet. Battlecruisers will fire salvos by squadron as we pass within range of the enemy ships."

"The message is sent, Most Eminent Admiral.

Zom waited for half a minute, then said, "Execute."

In a moment his body went from weighing half-again more to nothing. On his battle board, the battlecruisers began to zoom toward the enemy. The gunboats followed the same plunge. However, with their engines now pointed away from the enemy, their acceleration toward the enemy rapidly closed the distance.

He had the Longknife woman. His one regret was that he could not see the look of shock on her face as she gaped open-mouthed at what he was doing to her.

Admiral Kris Longknife had devoted a tiny portion of her battle board to the range to the enemy fleet. So it was that her eyes spotted the numbers beginning to unwind even as Nelly said, calmly, "Kris, the enemy has cut all deceleration."

"So he has," Kris said then snapped. "All ships, fleet will make a hard left ninety degrees turn and accelerate to three gees, Iteeche, away from the enemy's base course." She paused for a moment to let her word get out to her fleet. There was no time for intermediate commands, she'd apologize to any offended junior admirals later.

She didn't wait for acknowledgments, but ordered, "Execute."

The ninety degree turn away was a bit ragged. The acceleration was also applied without the usual precision Kris expected of her fleet. Still, she was turning away from her present course, so there was little chance of collision and no problem with ships taking a bit longer to go to three gees.

Kris ignored the disarray in her wings and concentrated on the range. It was actually opening as her ships opened up the distance from her enemy's course and all the ships fell toward Longnae at the same general velocity.

Now, she began issuing targeting orders to her admirals. They would use the same firing order. Most ships would fire by divisions. The combat experienced Iteeche ships under Admiral Tong would fire in pairs as would the Human cruisers.

Once again, the target would be the lead ships that made up the advanced vanguards. They'd been hard hit by the last shoot. They'd be even harder hit by the second.

Kris knew that envelopment was at the heart of the rebel admiral's plan. She doubted she'd have much to worry about from the vanguard's quarter.

She spared a glance at the incoming cruisers. Their effort to close the range was negated by Kris's decision to open the range.

Kris could not hold this course for very long if she intended to reach orbit around Longnae 4. Still, for the moment, she had blocked the rebel admiral's move.

"Now, fine sir," Kris muttered, "what will you do?"

71

Admiral Zom gnashed his beak together. He should feel like he'd won a victory, but he didn't.

He had the Longknife woman on the run. She was fleeing ahead of his ships. She would never be able to make orbit around Longnae 4 if she stayed on this course. Likely, she'd never make any orbit around a planet with a space station. She'd run her ships dry and end up drifting in space forever.

Then the Iteeche admiral remembered that the battlecruisers could send off a pinnace to do a refueling dive into any handy gas or ice giant. No, he had not seen the last of the Longknife woman.

Which placed him on the horns of a dilemma.

His orders had been to save the Longnae system from invasion. However, he was also ordered to engage and destroy any major portion of the false Imperial fleet that he encountered. Fleeing from him was a major portion of that fleet led by its most victorious admiral.

Could he report that he merely chased her out of the system? Would that be acceptable, or would he be immediately cashiered from the service of his clan? Assuming he didn't have to make a Formal Apology.

Admiral Zom slanted his chair up to get a better look at his battle board. He might have no weight on him, but he wasn't about to leave the safety of the couch. He examined the lines and vectors. The board showed his ships dropping toward the distant planet. Her ships fled from him and would be well out of range before he came level with her.

She was presenting him with shots right up her stern.

If he pursued her, would she turn and engage him? How would she choose to meet him in battle?

There certainly was one advantage to chasing her. If she tried to change course to make orbit around Longnae 4, he'd be in a better position to block her and give battle.

"Number One, send to fleet: 'On my order we will execute a ninety degree turn and begin accelerating at three gees in the direction of the enemy fleet.' Send it and get acknowledgements."

Five minutes later, every admiral in the fleet had responded.

"Execute," he ordered.

His battlecruiser executed left turns, some smartly, others not so much. The accelerated 3.0 gees toward the enemy warships was also ragged. Still, it was done.

Zom leaned back as his couch reclined to level. That should leave the Longknife woman thinking. Would she keep running or turn to give him battle?

Admiral Kris Longknife smiled as the rebel commander turned his ships to pursue her. She hadn't been sure he had it in him.

Still, she'd expected that even a peace time admiral would not pass up a fleeing enemy. His class standing might put him out of touch with the lower decks, but it couldn't isolate him from the desire for victory.

Good.

"Remember, my admiral," Jack said, "you're fighting battlecruisers just like our own."

"Thank you, Jack, but the question is, how much are they like our own? We have more powerful reaction jets. From the looks of the last fight, they can't jink worth beans. We've trained our gunners and fire control people for hours on end. We killed over a thousand of his battlecruisers, he got less than forty of ours. Our fleet may be a scratch team hastily thrown together, but Admiral Tong has taken advantage of every minute to train. How much training did that snob have his subordinate admirals do with his fleet, which is likely also newly built?"

"All potentially true," Jack answered, "but also, potentially all wrong."

"Yes, there is that," Kris agreed. "We have only the sample of our one quick brush with him and the poor quality of many of his ships when they turned to give chase."

"That is true. What do you intend to do?" Jack asked.

"Slip up on him and see if his long range shooting has gotten any better. I'd prefer to plunk away at him from maximum range. See how he takes to it."

"So?"

"Nelly, get me Admiral Tong."

A moment later, a small window on the screen of her egg showed the Iteeche admiral. He was flat on his back as well, in one of the high gee eggs that Nelly had designed for Iteeche use.

"Yes, My Admiral," he said.

"What are your thoughts on the rebel admiral giving chase?"

"He may be an ignorant clan spawn, but he does appear to have a fighter's heart. It will be interesting to see how long it beats like a warrior's."

"I would like to steer closer to the rebels, but not too quickly. Can we keep up that three gees?"

"For however long you want. We will not lose our fighting edge, My Admiral."

"Very good. I'd like to hold at three gees, Tong, but I want to swing the sterns down fifteen degrees. That will give us a vector of 2.5 gees away from the rebels and half a gee slowing down our dive toward Longnae 4."

The Iteeche closed his eyes to think. "That will allow the rebels to slowly catch up with us while we also climb up to them."

"Yes," Kris said. "If they keep on the course they're on right now, they'd still be 600,000 kilometers distant when they came even with us on our own course."

"Let them close on one vector while we slowly close on another. It will still give us a shot at their sterns."

"I wouldn't count on that," Kris said. "All it takes is for them to keep zero vectors away from the planet and they zip by us and start shooting up our sterns."

"I foresee that there will be much jockeying for position in this battle."

"Yes. We'll need to stay ready to adjust vectors and gees at a moment's notice."

"No problem, My Admiral. We are ready for this."

"Good, then order the change in vector and let's see how our opposite number responds to us offering battle, but slowly."

A moment later, the *Princess Royal* did something that Kris only felt in her inner ear. A few minutes later, Kris could see the results. Her fleet still fled the rebel force. However, they were now closing on her along one vector. Meanwhile, along a perpendicular vector, she was closing on them.

Battle was still a long way off. However, both she and her opposite number now knew that they had made the decision for battle.

There would be a bloody and possibly decisive battle here today.

Kris relaxed back into her egg and took a swig of water. How would the rebel admiral react to her move on this deadly chess board?

72

"My Most, ah . . . Admiral, the Longknife Human's fleet has changed course."

With a groan, Admiral Zom pushed the button and his couch began to angle up. The servos raising his high gee couch protested against raising the tripled weight of his body to where he could see the battle board.

"Number One, send to the ships carrying messages back to headquarters. Battle board must be rigged so that they can be seen when the person in the couch next to them is flat on their back. Also, strengthen the power and endurance of the servo motors on the couches. Three gees taxes them."

"Yes, Admiral."

"Oh, and tell them the water couches need to have a thicker skin. My couch is being held together by that incredible Human product, duct tape." While they were at 1.5 gees, they'd checked all the cushions and found many that were wearing thin. Two corners on his own couch had to be reinforced.

Zom closed his eyes and sighed. If an eager Human merchant had not brought a ton of the stuff and sold it to a rebel agent, way too many of his men would be zonked on pain suppressants. He might be one of them.

"Both messages are sent," Number One staff officer said.

"Good, now let me look at this board," Zom snapped. Every joint in his body seemed to be aching. Every move at 3.0 or 3.5 gees had been a struggle and was only getting worse.

Maybe I should cut my acceleration and see if she will slow her flight?

Zom considered that, then put it aside for later. She had just turned into him. He would not want to show her any sign of weakness. No. Let them close for an hour. The Iteeche admiral set his alarm and lowered his couch to the full horizontal.

"Admiral, what are you doing?"

"I am doing nothing, Number One. I like the way the battle is developing. Let's see if she will keep on this course for a while. If I fall asleep, wake me in an hour."

"Yes, My Admiral."

Well, at least he got his Number One to shorten the time it took him to say anything to him. Still, the staff officer had sounded incredulous. Whether that was for his decision, or his mentioning he might fall asleep, Zom could not tell.

Maybe for the younger officer it was easy to bear up under the feeling of having a dozen denizens of the deep, dark abyss jumping up and down on his chest. For the admiral, it was exhausting . . . and getting worse. He might well need to rest. Maybe even close his eyes.

He did. Behind his eyelids he contemplated his coming battle. The Human was coming back at him, slowing her ships to let him catch up with her. He was closing the range from another vector. He would come under fire from her at maximum range. However, if he changed his vector and charged toward the planet, that would put him in much closer range of her fleet very quickly.

There was another thought that lurked in the back of his mind. He relaxed and let his mind go blank.

And so he fell asleep. However, just before he drifted off, the thought came at him. *Yes.* There was something he could do that would totally ruin that Longknife woman's day . . . and likely end her charmed life.

An hour later, Number One woke him before his alarm.

"Has anything changed?" Admiral Zom asked.

"Nothing, My Admiral. Both fleets are still on the same vectors and accelerations."

"Very good. Now, let's play with our hooked fish. We know she's willing to give battle. Let's see how willing. Number One, order the fleet to reduce acceleration to 2.5 gees. Let's see how she reacts to that."

Admiral Kris Longknife was about ready to break out a video game. Watching this battle develop had all the excitement of watching paint dry. Worse, yawning at three gees was agony on the jaw muscles.

Nelly, as usual, was the first to identify the rebel's change in acceleration. "Kris, the enemy fleet has lowered its deceleration to 2.5 gees."

Kris eyed her board and waited for it to show any change. It took it half a minute to switch the acceleration next to the rebel fleet's vector. That didn't change. He was still pursuing her, just at an acceleration that would never catch her.

"Do you think he's gotten cold feet?" Jack asked.

"Cold feet would be switching his vector to slow him down so he could make orbit on Longnae 4. No, he's still chasing us, but I bet he's tired of three gees and would like to take some of the weight off."

"So he goes to 2.5 gees for a diet?" Jack said, with a bit of a chuckle. "Do you want to take some gees off the fleet? The Iteeche might like it."

"Nelly, get me Admiral Tong."

"She already has me," the Iteeche admiral said. "I've been listening in on your conversation since our rebel friend went to 2.5 gees."

"Any ideas?"

"I have plenty of them. I just don't know which of them relate to reality. Their high gee stations are very likely not as good as ours. I would expect that his sailors, maybe even the admiral himself, are all tired of all the extra weight. Remember, you asked for younger officers and sailors. You wanted crews with strong backs. I wonder how many of his people are lost in drugged dreams."

"I thought about that," Kris said. "What are the chances he just wants me to come to him?"

"That is also a fact. You must have noted how poor their gunnery was during that very brief shoot. If you approach him on a slat range, he could flip ship and accelerate toward the planet. That would get him into moderate range very quickly."

"Yes," Kris said. "I do like to keep my battles at long range for as long as I can manage it."

"Might we also dive toward the planet?" Jack asked.

"We'd have to," Kris said. She then changed the subject. "Admiral, how are your Iteeche taking to three gees?"

"About as good as can be expected. I can't say that these high gee stations make it fun, but it is certainly survivable."

"How many officers and men have reported for sick call?" Jack asked.

"Jack, your Sal offered to keep track of that for me."

"Sal, are you freelancing again?" Jack drawled.

"More like looking for something to do, General," his computer answered back, not quite as insubordinate as Nelly.

"Admiral," Jack said, "when things are slow, feel free to keep Sal as busy as you want to."

"It is nice being on Nelly Net and getting access to her kids," Admiral Tong said. "Anyway, on average less than one percent, say ten out of a thousand in the crew, have suffered muscle tears and sprains since we jacked up acceleration. If you plan to keep this up for a week, I might have a mutiny on my hands, but the next day or so, no problem."

"Good, because I'd like to use the extra half gee to slow down our approach to the planet."

"So," Tong said, "you want to spend one third of our vector to slow us down and the other two thirds to let the rebel slowly creep up on us."

"Yes. We'll still be letting him approach us using the two gees. He's not slowing his velocity at all toward the planet. We'll let him accelerate at half a gee toward us.

"I will issue the orders. Anything else?"

"What do you think of going back to Condition Charlie so the cooks can get a hot meal into the crew?" Kris asked.

"I would not object to that. It would have to be soup or something that could be eaten at their battle stations and in their eggs."

"Let's do that. Tell every captain that they are free to go back to Condition Zed on their own authority if things start developing fast. Also keep the hulls rotating at twenty revolutions a minute. I don't want us to slip into battle without that defense up and working."

"It will all be done, My Admiral."

They ended the call. After a minute, Kris again felt that strange sensation in her inner ear. She still weighed a bit more than two and a half times her normal weight, but this was three gees for an Iteeche, not her.

She relaxed back into her egg and eyed the screen above her. Her fleet slowly approached from below the rebels. They slowly approached from behind. Kris would have to watch the rate of closure carefully, as well as the velocity of the two forces. If the rebels picked up too much velocity, she might lose control of choosing the range.

She couldn't let them barge in with enough velocity to rapidly close the range so that even poor gunnery could win the battle.

Kris knew the battle was only an hour away. It both terrified and excited her. She knew the feeling well, now, having felt it so often in her time in the Navy.

She sighed. She was in that awful time when everything had been done and all she could do was wait upon the outcome. She eyed the enemy fleet and waited for the rebel commander's next move.

If he tried to pull a fast one on her, she'd have to be ready to respond immediately.

Hot soup in a plastic bag with a long straw was delivered to her egg by a mechanical arm. She sucked on it. It was a nice fish chowder with the fish reduced to tiny slivers that would not block the straw.

"Tasty," Jack said, beside her.

"Warm and filling," Kris added. "Just what I like while I wait for something to happen."

"Yeah," Jack said.

Together, they talked about the kids while both kept their eyes on their boards. The fight would come soon enough.

73

"The Longknife Human has reacted to your decreasing acceleration to 2.5 gees, My Admiral," Number One reported.

Once again, Admiral Zom forced his high gee couch to bring his head up above the lip of his battle board. He raised it only as high as he needed to. The weight was taking more out of him than he wanted to admit.

More than that, he feared that the gears raising and lowering his couch would fail with him not high enough up to see his board, but not low enough down to keep the blood from flowing to his feet.

"We should have tested these high gee stations in a long high gee cruise," he muttered to himself.

"Who would have thought that we would be in such a grueling high gee battle?" Number One said.

"We have read the battle reports," Admiral Zom shot back. "This Longknife Human luxuriates in her youth and fights like an eel, striking fast, but never there when you try to spear it."

"You have sent back reports. The next fleet will be better prepared," his senior staff officer answered.

"Hopefully, we will live long enough to make our own report to headquarters," the admiral said ruefully. "Now let's see what she has done."

The board showed her closing faster than she had been.

"What did she do?"

"My Admiral, she did not reduce the gees she's forcing her Iteeche allies to take," Number One said. "Instead she has divided the vector of her three gees so that two gees add acceleration to her flight from us and the third gee decelerates her on her approach to the planet."

"She keeps her own Iteeche under three gees?" the admiral muttered.

"She has only recently put her sailors under such a punishing acceleration, Sir. Certainly, they can survive this."

"Yes, yes, they did not spend almost half a day at 3.5 gees to get where they are," the admiral grumbled. So, she was slowing as he slowed. *How far would she slow down if he kept sliding down the gee scale?* He'd love to settle the fleet at 1.5 gees.

Over the next quarter hour, he did just that. First he slowed to 2.0 gees, then to 1.5 gees, and finally settled finally at 1.25 gees. One gee decelerated toward the planet. The other .25 gee slowly let him catch up with this Human.

He had his board do some alternate courses. The way this was going, they'd be at nearly the same velocity when his fleet came in range. She would have a very slight angle on his stern, so shots at his reactors were unlikely.

Still, if he hiked up his gees to close with her, there would be little gained by diving down on her. Even if he dropped straight down, he couldn't get a better range than 250,000 kilometers on her.

That was still extremely long range for his ships.

Admiral Zom eyed the amount of time he had before the two fleets came in range. He also studied the enemy ships. "Number One, are they at Condition Charlie?"

"Yes, My Admiral, they do appear to have expanded their ship to that size. I imagine that is to allow some hands to get meals just before the fight begins."

"Let us do the same, alert the fleet that they may go to Condition

Charlie and dismiss one quarter of the crew at a time to the mess deck and washtubs. Let us try to loosen up. Also, check the high gee couches again. I don't want any cushions going flat if I have to ask for 3.5 gees again."

"Yes, My Admiral," and Number One began talking on his comm link. A few minutes later, Zom's flagship spread out. Runners were sent to the wardroom to draw tea and biscuits.

"Will some mechanic look at the workings of my couch? Its gears seem to be grinding."

A chief and two ratings soon had the cover off and were looking inside.

"There is definitely something wrong, Admiral," the chief reported. "There is an oil leak with what looks like small metal filings in the oil. I think your couch is in failure mode."

"Can you repair it?" the admiral asked.

"No, sir. We did not get a supply of spare parts before we sailed. They were on order. They didn't arrive."

"Hmm, Number One, do we have a spare couch?" Admiral Zom demanded.

"No, My Admiral. When we sailed, we were short by several hundred thousand high gee couches. Some sailors that don't need to move around much just have water or air mattresses."

"Number One, swap my couch out for someone who doesn't always have to go up to see and down his battle board."

"Yes, My Admiral."

A few minutes later, one of the Marines pushed his couch up beside the admiral and helped the admiral move to it. Then he pushed the failing one back against the wall.

Only now did the admiral realize that a dozen runners now sat on couches that lay along the wall. They talked quietly among themselves. Doubtlessly, they'd recline if the gees got too high.

Zom realized he should have been more observant, but then dismissed the matter. Runners hardly mattered in a battle as complex as this. He could ignore them.

Now in a high gee station he trusted, Admiral Zom studied the map in front of him. He fell toward the planet, and closed on the Longknife woman. She pushed against the planet's gravity and built up her velocity as the two of them closed inescapably.

He estimated an hour before they came in range. He hunched over his board and waited to see if anything would happen in that time.

Admiral Kris Longknife was not surprised when the rebel commander slowed his fleet to 1.5 gees. After the day they'd had, she imagined all of them needed a break.

Kris also wasn't surprised when he chose to go to Condition Charlie. Again, he'd put his crews through a brutal approach. The question was, should she do anything to mess with him.

Her fleet was also at Condition Charlie. Her Iteeche crews were enjoying a mere 2.25 times their normal weight. For her Human crews it was slightly less than two gees.

"Kris, you were wondering what the rebel admiral was doing a while back."

"Yeah. He seemed to be messing around somewhere aft."

"I have a picture now. It appears that his ships have four, six, or eight longboats attached just forward of the rocket motors."

"He's trying to jack up his maneuvering."

"It looks like that, Kris," Nelly said.

Kris eyed the picture that Nelly projected onto her screen. Yep, those sure looked like longboats with their bows up against the stern, ready to push the ship around harder as it maneuvered.

It was time to give him a surprise.

"Nelly, get me Admiral Tong again."

"Yes, Admiral," came back in a moment.

"How do you think our crews would take to me cutting back on their rest and relaxing time?"

"What do you have in mind, My Admiral?"

So, Kris told him.

The Iteeche coughed up a laugh.

"We'd need to go to full battle stations and Condition Zed, but we'll be ready for action as soon as we've got him in range."

"Give the order, Admiral. I think our crews are tired of the wait. Let's get this battle going."

"Aye, aye, My Admiral," and he closed down the call.

Less than thirty seconds later, the *Princess Royal* announced. "Battle Stations, Battle Stations. The ship will go to Condition Zed in five minutes. The ship will put on 3.5 gees Iteeche, 3.0 gees Human, in five minutes." The message repeated itself with the time shortening with each repetition.

By the time the *Princess Royal* began to shrink itself and take on three gees, Kris was ready for it.

Her inner ear did the little flip it did when the ship changed directions. From a blended vector, 2.0 gees down and 1.5 gees away, her flag jacked up its acceleration to nearly 3.5 gees, Iteeche. Most of it was directed down to slow the fleet's course toward the target planet. That also jacked up the rate of closure between the two fleets.

Kris's fleet flipped as one. Now their 1.5 gees were directed right at the rebel fleet. Suddenly their 1.5 gee acceleration chasing *after* Kris's fleet was met with her likewise accelerating at 1.5 gees directly *at* him.

Kris waited to see how long it would take the rebel admiral to respond to her gambit. He wouldn't have a lot of time. The rate of closure was fast and getting faster.

Meanwhile, all around Kris, the *Princess Royal* prepared for war. Again, the ship shrank to Condition Zed. Again, the honeycomb under the crystal armor filled with cooling reaction mass.

Kris smiled. Someone had forgotten who he was fighting. That was never good.

74

Admiral Zom was enjoying the blessed feeling of only half again his weight. A strong mess hand was pushing a large container of soup around the bridge. He stopped at each station, filled a drinking bottle with steaming soup and handed it off to the crewman or officer, then went on to the next.

Admiral Zom had just taking his first sip of the soup. It was too hot to drink; he would have to let it cool.

"Admiral, something is happening. The range to the Longknife Human's fleet is drastically changing," Number One officer said.

"I don't see it on my board," Zom snapped.

"It is just starting to change," he insisted.

Zom eyed his board as the enemy fleet's vector began to change directions and lengthen. "Cold and bleak abyss, the woman has changed her mind. Number One, send to fleet. Go to Condition Zed immediately. Stand by to open fire."

He paused for a moment. He had more orders to give, but it would not help the fleet if he befuddled his captains with too many orders, too fast.

Around him, the flag bridge began to shrink. The mess hand

retreated away from the closing walls; his soup wagon skated away from his hands.

"Get that soup away from my battle board!" the admiral shouted as the container of steaming soup bore down on his high gee station.

The Sailor struggled to pull the wagon back toward the rear of the bridge where the Marine guards and the runners huddled, waiting for orders. There was no extra room, and the wagon toppled over. The soup container spilt hot soup all over the deck and on a pair of runners. Their screams added to the cacophony of Condition Zed.

With the smell of vegetable soup in his beak, Admiral Zom turned his attention back to the rapidly developing battle. He watched vectors of the two fleets draw closer.

"Execute," he ordered.

"Sir, I issued the last order as an order. It is already being executed."

"Of course it is," Zom reminded himself. The skipper of his flag ship had gone to Condition Zed without any announcement.

He took two deep breaths. That Longknife woman had flustered him. He could not let that happen again.

She clearly had taken the initiative. *Did he want to accept battle now?* Her deceleration was not only slowing her course toward the distant planet, but also sending her hurtling toward his ships as they fell toward it with no braking.

Laterally, she now closed with him as he raced toward her. The rate of closure was so high that they'd be in range of each other in only a matter of minutes.

"Do we change our course, Admiral?" Number One asked.

"No. I like this course and speed," Admiral Zom said. "Let her charge us. With any luck, her inertia will carry her deep within our laser range before she can do anything about it."

"Very well, Admiral."

"Now, Number One, let us see what we can do to win this battle. Order all ships to rotate their outer hulls at twenty revolutions per minute. Prepare to execute Dodging Plan 3 on my order."

"It will be done, My Admiral," and the staff officer began issuing orders.

Zom studied his board. Would the Longknife woman make the mistake of charging right into his range? All reports said she insisted on fighting at long range where she could dodge in and out of range at her own choosing. *How were her ships and crew taking to 3.5 gees? How long could they bear it?*

The reports were that the Human high gee stations were very good and that the Iteeche in her fleet enjoyed better couches than his crew. Zom found that hard to believe, although he no longer had the boundless confidence in his station after seeing water couches sprout leaks and machinery fail.

There were no reports of any manufacturing concern in the false Emperor's area who had delivered high gee couches to her fleet. No one wanted to say it, but it seemed likely that the Humans were again making things out of their magic metal. That puzzled Zom. He looked at the bulkheads of the flag bridge. They were hard as any stone wall. Harder. How could something this hard be a cushion?

Once again, Zom wished that the Iteeche programmers had asked more questions before expelling the Human ship spinners and programmers.

The Iteeche admiral shook his head. Now was no time to consider past mistakes. He had to avoid making any new ones.

It was good that he returned his attention back to the battle board. The Longknife woman was making her move, and it was the one he had hoped he would not see.

The vector of the enemy fleet was changing again. Now she was veering away from him, slowing down her approach. It was a good move, just not one he wanted to see. Now their rate of closure slowed; it was still a rush, just not a mad rush.

Admiral Zom ordered his battle board to track the range and rate of closure in the space between the two forces. He probably should have done that sooner, but, not being one of those officers who enjoyed war gaming against others, he wasn't that sharp about using the board. It was hard to find anyone to war game with that was of his station. It would be embarrassing to lose against an officer of a lower rank, so they would likely let him win. At least, he had won every time he war gamed with officers of only a single name.

One had to maintain one's status.

By the time to two fleets had closed to 400,000 kilometers, it was clear that the enemy would be pulling in range first of the much weakened vanguards. Zom did not want them put to the torch again.

He did, however, have his own idea of how he wanted to join battle with the Human admiral.

"Number One, order the remnants of the vanguards to the rear. Let's see how she likes facing all five of our middle wings. Also, order the two rear guard wings to come up and form a line directly behind the main body. I want both of them, along with what's left of the vanguard, to tuck themselves right in behind the main body. That way, we will bring five wings to bear on her rear guard. Let's see how she likes that."

"My Admiral, may I point out that five wings may be too wide? Many of the ships in the top and bottom-most wings might not be in range."

"Your suggestion?"

"Have the top-most center wing fall back to be included in the second wave of ships. We should charge them with four wings aimed directly at their rear guard, and three more, plus the remnants of the vanguard right behind them. If she tries to dance in and out of range, let her wing of twelve hundred dance in front of our wings of more than seventeen hundred."

"Very good idea, Number One. Make it so."

The staff officer began issuing orders. As Zom watched, the juggling of wings began. The two rear guards came up to form a line behind the main battle line main body. The topmost wing fell back to fall in line beside the rear guard. The much attuited vanguards fell in behind the main line.

The five forward wings now formed a T with a much shorter line behind them.

Almost as an afterthought, the four blocks of gunboats formed two above and two below the four leading wings of battlecruisers. If they got a chance, their admirals were ordered to charge in and do as much damage as they could.

Beyond that, Zom would ignore them. It was his battlecruisers that would decide this battle.

Zom remembered his ancient history. Back before the days of sharp steel, the Iteeche armies had fought with long bronze-tipped spears and shields made of wood and animal hides. Then, they had fought shoulder-to-shoulder as they slammed into each other. The formation was called a phalanx.

He had formed his fleet into a phalanx, four wide and two deep.

Zom waited to see how the Human would react to this. Did they even know what a phalanx was? Had Humans ever dared to face cold, sharp bronze spearpoints?

The Iteeche admiral looked upon what he had done and found it good. He doubted the Longknife woman did.

Admiral Kris Longknife watched with fascination as the rebel Iteeche admiral reformed his fleet into a phalanx. She hadn't expected something that creative from one of the hide-bound clan lordlings. He'd certainly waited until the last minute to pop this surprise on her.

It was a good battle array for what they faced. In effect, he would cross her T-shape like wet Navy admirals had dreamed of doing since the age of sailing ships.

The rebel ships were having some trouble following their orders. Unfortunately for Kris, the four wings that were likely to come into range first didn't have to make any changes. They stayed rock solid as the range closed.

"It looks like we're dealing with a maverick," Jack observed.

"One smart move out of the ordinary does not make a maverick," Kris said, thinking hard on her response.

"Nelly, Admiral Tong."

"Yes, My Admiral."

"What do you make of this?" she asked.

"He's forming a phalanx," the Iteeche admiral said.

"Is that part of your military history?" she asked.

"Very much, although we are talking over five thousand years in our past. Maybe all the way back to before the first Emperor."

"Very good. I like someone who knows his history. Admiral, please order the rear guard to move to alongside the lower wing. Have the vanguard come in line above the top wing. No reason why we can't meet him, phalanx to phalanx."

"You want to concentrate all five of our wings against his leading four?"

"Yes. Nelly, what kind of odds will that give us?"

"We have six thousand battlecruisers all told. Four of their wings have about seven thousand."

"I don't think he's going to be happy with those odds," Jack said. "I sure wouldn't be."

"Admiral Tong, reorganize the fleet and see how he reacts."

"To hear is to obey, My Admiral," and Tong cut the comm to give orders.

A few moments later, the forward and aft wings began to maneuver to lengthen the line formed by the main body and the top and bottom wings. The wing movements were sloppier than Kris wanted, but considering how long her fleet had been drilling and that this was not a drill they had practiced, it looked good enough.

Even before the maneuver was complete, the rebel admiral had realized the mistake he'd made. While depth might allow him to bring up fresh ships when she decimated a wing, it just meant that Kris could knock them out in order, one after the other.

The four rear rebel wings had not yet finished settling into place and smoothing out problems before they got new orders. The topmost wing now reversed course and headed back where it had come from. The aft rearguard was not yet in place before it also was ordered to lengthen the line.

However, there was a problem with that. The much-battered

vanguards were between the rear wing and bottom of the phalanx. It had to accelerate itself away from the line, turn, then turn again and hurry to catch up with its place in line.

With each turn, that wing lost ships as they wondered off, fell out of ranks and, on occasion, collided with each other. No ships exploded, but several got seriously dinged.

The Human admiral grinned. Dented hulls would have a hard time putting revolutions on their outer hull. Kris watched to see how the rebel admiral responded to this.

Kris would have ordered the damaged ship out of the battle array. There was little reason to take a doomed ship into battle.

Unfortunately for the rebel skippers, their orders were to get back in line and follow their squadron commanders. Kris shook her head; someone was desperate.

Her fleet was now in a line, five wings long. The rebel fleet was five long and struggling to add a sixth. However, her wings were thinner than his. That offered her an idea.

However, time ran out.

The rangefinder on Kris's board showed they were coming up on the maximum range of the 24-inch lasers. It was time to go to work.

"Comm, order all ships to Evasion Plan 4. Set course at thirty degrees off enemy base course, outward bound. Admiral Tong, assign enemy targets by wings of Iteeche ships, fire by divisions. Human ships, fire by sections of two. Admiral Tong select whether your ships fire by division or sections. Fire as the enemy fleet comes into range."

She was giving up the option of firing one huge salvo, but she was also arranging it so her ships would not all be turning their sterns toward the enemy fleet at the same time.

Apparently, Admiral Tong saw the advantage of his fleet taking the first salvo on their bows. He swung his ships' bows around, cut acceleration to one gee, and fired each wing as it came in range of its opposite number.

So it was that 224 Human battlecruisers reached out at extreme range. They aimed at 112 radically maneuvering rebel ships. Over 50 of them ceased to exist. Some vanished in huge explosions. Others went out with more class, shedding parts of their hull, or containing an explosion forward that left the ship missing its bow.

Nearly 1,500 divisions of loyal Iteeche battlecruisers reached out for their rebel opposite, per Kris's order. Each division leader had assigned a quadrant around the rebel ship to one of his own. Some fired high and to the right or left. The other two fired low and covered those two quadrants. The rebel ships were more lively this time in their evasion, but the box widened up to assure that they didn't dodge out of their role as a target.

Over 400 of the warships across from them vanished. Others took off on wild courses when their rocket motors were damaged. Still, others blew out this or that part of the hull and began to cartwheel or roll through space.

The opposite side of the battlefield was not inactive. Eleven hundred rebel squadrons opened up with all twelve of the 24-inch lasers in the bows of eight battlecruisers. The squadron commanders, however, only assigned a single target. They did not make any effort to guide the fire of their subordinate ships.

Each battlecruiser followed its own firing solution and fired where it expected the jitterbugging battlecruiser to be. Few got lucky. Even fewer actually guessed where their target might be. Only 53 of Kris's ships suffered major damage.

With all forward batteries exhausted, both fleets flipped ship and fired their aft eight 24-inch lasers. Some aimed at new targets. Others chose to fire again at a ship they may or may not have damage.

By the time the two fleets had emptied both fore and aft batteries, the rebels were down 900 nine hundred ships and the Emperor's forces were missing 90.

Kris raised her eyebrows at the rate of exchange. With all the advantages her ships had in more accurate lasers, faster fire control and better high gee stations that allowed wilder jinking, she was not surprised.

With her fleet back on the same base course at 1.5 gees accelerating to keep herself steady off the enemy fleet's planet-ward flank, she waited to see what her opponent's next move would be.

75

Admiral Zom stared at the list of ships under his command. It was organized by wing. Before he entered this second engagement, he'd already lost 1,300 of the 3,500 in his two vanguard wings.

Now, as his fleet returned to its base course and acceleration of 1.5 gees, the names of more and more of his ships vanished from the list.

"Computer, tally our losses," he ordered.

He watched as the missing spaces in the five wings presently engaging the enemy lit up as ships were being counted. The order to reload the bow guns came before the count finished.

Zom's ships were already pointed at the Longknife Human's fleet. As soon as the forward battery finished reloading, they fired.

The enemy did the same, and more blank spaces opened up on his main screen. The computer could not count their casualties in the time it took to reload and for more casualties to start appearing on his board.

"The tally was nine hundred and three ships destroyed," the computer answered. "I am starting the count again."

"Do," Admiral Zom snapped. He was pretty sure that another thousand of his ships would miss the next roll call.

"Number One, have your battle board count the enemy battle-cruisers destroyed."

"There is something wrong with my board, Admiral. It is only showing a count of less than a hundred. It must be in failure mode."

"No. The problem isn't with the board, it is with our shooting. Six thousand of her ships fired, and a thousand of our ships are destroyed. Seven thousand of our ships fired, and a hundred of hers exploded. This is not an exchange rate we can bear. Order the fleet to maximum dodging effort."

"The order is sent."

It would not help the thousand ships that the Longknife woman blew away during this exchange of salvos, but it would help the remainder of his force.

"Reduce acceleration to 1.0 gee," the admiral snapped, then snarled, "Order the gunboats to 3.5 gees. Let's see what the survivors can do."

The third salvo in hardly more than a minute showed the impact of the change. His fleet reduced its losses to only 284, however, they destroyed only 22 more of the enemy.

"Admiral, reports are coming in that our ships cannot get a good firing solution when they are dancing so wildly."

"Then how does that Longknife woman keep killing us? Her ships are jiggling about like terrified fingerlings. Still, they hit our ships."

"They hit less," Number One pointed out.

"Flip the ships and go to 3.5 gees acceleration," Admiral Zom ordered and Number One obeyed.

The range began to open up. Zom breathed a sigh of relief as his ships fell farther behind the enemy fleet and crossed the invisible line that was the maximum range of the 24-inch lasers. It was still possible to reach out with those massive guns; it was just less likely that they could do any significant damage.

Zom would have to decide whether to give his ships time to recover or return to the fight. Meanwhile, the gunboats charged into the space between the fleets. He still had 7,500 of the heavy gunboats. Of the lightly equipped vessels, 5,000 frigates that didn't blow up were joined by another 3,000 of questionable reactor status: they had captains who had risked reactor failure in order to stay in the fight.

Admiral Zom would have to mention those courageous men in his report and recommend that they be first in line for battlecruisers.

For now, all the gunboat skippers showed tremendous courage and élan as they charged into the empty space between the two fleets of combatants.

Admiral Zom leaned forward in his high gee couch to rest his front elbows on his battle board. *How would the Longknife woman respond? Would she run from the gunboats or ignore them and also hit the brakes on her deceleration so that she could keep shooting up his battlecruisers?*

He had not long to wait.

Admiral Kris Longknife immediately knew the battle had changed. The ranging report on her battle board suddenly began to climb again. Even as she watched, the enemy fleet slipped out of range.

"Somebody can't stand the heat," Jack muttered beside her.

"Yeah," she said, "but he's aimed an entirely new bonfire at us. Look at those little boys charging at us."

"Hard not to notice. So, do you run away from them, and let the battlecruisers wander off unsupervised? Idle hands are the devil's workshop."

"Or do I charge in to catch up with the battlecruisers and ignore these mischief makers?"

"Some of those little boys as you call them, dear Admiral, carry 22-inch lasers."

"And 20-inch and 18-inch lasers. Yes, dear General, I have not forgotten."

Kris eyed her board. She'd have to make her call quickly. She was fleeing them at an effective vector of 1.25 gees while they put on 3.5 gees in pursuit.

"Admiral Tong," Kris said.

"Yes, My Admiral," he immediately answered.

"I want you to please target the small ships charging us. However, I don't want to let the battlecruisers get too far behind us. Let's pursue the rebel battlecruisers while we wipe out these nuisances."

"I fear they may be more of a nuisance than you want, My Admiral."

"Ruin my day," Kris told her Iteeche subordinate.

"We have only one fire control system on each battlecruiser. There are other systems to support the small secondary batteries, but they don't have the range for these targets. Thus, our ships are capable of targeting only one of the small ships at a time."

"Then we better start as soon as we can," Kris snapped.

"To hear is to make it so, My Admiral," and the Iteeche closed the call.

In a few moments, the fleet accelerated to 3.5 gees, Iteeche. Three gees pursued the enemy battlecruisers while the other 0.5 gee vector still slowed down their rush toward the planet ahead of them.

The onrushing cruisers began to vanish.

The battlecruisers brought their forward batteries to bear. Kris had Nelly follow the action of the *Princess Royal*.

Kris's flag fired only four lasers at her first target. Each one put out a quick staccato of six one-second bursts over nine seconds. Twenty-four massive bursts of power sped downrange at the speed of light.

In a moment, a 15,000-ton cruiser exploded. It had no armor, just its ability to zig and zag. However, with 24 laser blasts filling the space ahead of it, it was inevitable that she collided with one of them.

One hit was enough.

Another ten seconds later, the next four lasers in the forward battery fired, and another rebel cruiser died.

"What's taking so long?" Kris asked Nelly.

"The fire control computer can have a solution in two seconds and fire in three," her computer said, "however, it's more likely to miss than if the sensors track the ship for an extra seven seconds so it can better calculate how hard it is jinking and how radically it is changing course."

"How are the other ships handling this shoot?" Jack asked.

"The Iteeche battlecruisers are firing six of their forward lasers, so there are thirty-six laser bursts reaching for a particular cruiser. By the time they fire the second half, the first half are recharged and they have a new firing solution ready."

"How's our shooting?" Jack asked.

"About fifty-fifty," Nelly said, "These cruisers are pretty small targets and they're evading hard. Still, every twenty seconds, somewhere between two and three thousand of them die."

Kris winced at the slaughter. What did the rebel admiral expect to get from this?

She found out before the fourth salvo of short blasts headed for the surviving 9,000 cruisers.

The rebel admiral had brought his battlecruisers back into the battle. At 3.5 gees, they were jinking mildly. They got off their first salvo while Kris's ships were still fixated on the cruisers.

A snap order from Admiral Tong ordered the fleet to Evasion Plan 6. This not only got the ships jitterbugging wildly, but presented their loaded bow lasers and bow armor to the enemy.

Unfortunately, 300 of Kris's ships were slow to go into evasion. In the blink of an eye, loyal Iteeche ships took four or five laser blasts on their bows. Some broke through the laser ports and slashed into the capacitors. They blossomed as horrid flowers of red, gold, and yellow before vanishing away to just an expanding ball of hot gas.

The *Princess Royal*'s skipper had not needed the order start jinking. He had his own range-to-target report on his board. Two range-to-target windows were prominent on his forward screen. One tracked the rapidly closing cruisers, the other tracked the fleeing battlecruisers.

The skipper might not have spotted the sudden change in range before Kris and Nelly, but he wasn't far behind. He had the *P. Royal* flipping before Admiral Tong's order got out of his mouth.

That was a good thing. They took a hit square on the bow on the rapidly rotating skin. The crystal armor slowed down the light and spread it over most of the hull where it harmlessly radiated back into space. It operated on the same theory as quantum computers, only at a much larger scale.

Sadly, only the Human battlecruisers had this protection. Back in Human space, the various governments still refused to make it available to the Iteeche Empire. At last report, several Iteeche and Human spies had been convicted of espionage. The debate was whether to bury them deep on a penal planet or bring back the firing squad.

Kris ignored that bit of news.

What it meant at this moment was that three hundred of her Iteeche allies' battlecruisers blew up and none of the Human battlecruisers did.

"Target the battlecruisers," Kris ordered on net. She probably should have waited for Admiral Tong to take a breath, but she wasn't about to.

However, her order had no effect immediately. The same seven seconds was needed to track a target, whether it be a battlecruiser or a thin-skinned cruiser. Ten unbearable seconds later, her fleet responded in a ragged series of salvos.

This did bring her fleet a minor bit of luck. The rebels had flipped ship and were bringing their stern lasers to bear as Kris's ships fired.

The rebels presented vulnerable sterns with unarmored reactors to their enemy. Over 1,200 hundred ships were blown to gas or wreckage in one rolling crescendo of destruction.

Throughout Kris's fleet, over 1,600 divisions of Iteeche aimed for the same ship. The Human battle cruisers fired in pairs, 112 of them. Of the nearly 1,800 groups, 1,200 had found a rebel battlecruiser's reactors.

It was fantastic shooting.

"Admiral Tong, I suggest we keep our bow to the rebels."

"I totally agree, Admiral. I will make it so."

Now her fleet was prepared for the next salvo. Thick nose armor on, Kris's fleet advancing on the charging rebels at 1.5 gees Iteeche, 1.3

s Human. The Emperor's battlecruisers had plenty of weight on to zig and zag according to their most energetic evasion plan.

While Kris's fleet was reorganizing, the rebels finished firing their aft batteries of lasers and flipped back over, bow on, as they rushed at her at 3.5 gees. Now they went to their own most evasive pattern of dodging and bobbing.

It did not help them a lot.

Nelly had kept an eye on them when they were last at their wildest dodging plan; she and her kids had begun to spot a pattern. Not much of one, but something that she thought might help reduce the chances of the rebel battlecruisers dancing out of the incoming salvos.

Nelly and her kids fed their assessment to all the fire control computers in the fleet, now reduced to about 5,500 warships. Again, Kris's battlecruisers fired their forward batteries for a full six seconds. This time, some 500 rebel ships vanished or crumbled.

The rebels return volley destroyed only 23 Imperial battlecruisers.

The exchange rate was again brutal.

Still, the rebel commander kept up the charge. Eight thousand cruisers continued to close at 3.5 gees as did some 12,000 battlecruisers. If Kris didn't do something quickly, she would have some 20, 000 rebel ships sitting right on her lap.

"Admiral Tong?" she said.

"Yes, My Admiral."

"I think it would be a good idea if we opened the range a bit."

"If we set a course thirty degrees off the rebel's base course, they likely would not be able to get a direct hit on our reactors."

"Let's go to 3.5 gees Iteeche, on that course and see what our aft batteries can do. We can wear ship left and right each time they fire themselves dry."

"I will make it so, My Admiral." Half a minute later, the *Princess Royal* was on a new course and Kris weighed three times what she saw every morning when she checked the scales.

The next salvo, from the Imperial force used only the aft battery. Still, it destroyed nearly 300 hundred rebel ships with only 27 lost.

Kris's fleet was keeping up the ten-to-one exchange rate, even if it was slower.

Thus the battle proceeded. The rebels accelerated after the Imperials at 3.5 gees, Iteeche. Kris's fleet ran ahead of them, also at 3.5 gees. Only this time, their vector was only slightly divided. Now, little went to slow her toward the planet they were fighting over. Most of her vector pushed her ahead of the warships bent on their destruction.

Slowly, the rebels closed the range on her ships, but not nearly fast enough in the face of this murderous exchange rate.

Then one of the larger cruisers got Kris's attention.

It had managed to get in range and release three 22-inch lasers. It was close enough to nip a battlecruiser's rocket motor bell. That set the loyalist ship spinning out of formation. It, however, quickly recovered and repaired the damage.

"Target the larger cruisers," Kris told Admiral Tong.

"Yes, I think we should," he agreed.

While her fleet dodged the next salvo from the rebel battlecruisers, they themselves took aim with their aft batteries for the remaining large cruisers with hand-me-down battleship lasers.

Few of the large cruisers survived the next salvo from the aft batteries of Kris's ships. What was left was vaporized ten seconds later.

The remaining cruisers chasing after Kris's fleet were ships of less than 10,000 tons with powerful lasers that had a range of only 80,000 kilometers.

It would take them a long time to close to that range.

While the Imperial ships had been annihilating the large cruisers with the cast-off cannons, the rebel battlecruisers had continued their own campaign against Kris's fleet. She lost 47 battlecruisers to their two pairs of salvos.

Now the Imperial fleet turned its attention totally on the remaining rebel battlecruisers. The attention was brutal. In 67 seconds, three salvos left both the forward and aft batteries of 5,400 loyalist ships.

By the time the aft batteries fell silent after the third salvo, the rebels were missing another 1,300 battlecruisers and had only the destruction of 72 Imperial ships to show for it.

The exchange rate was getting worse, not better.

Kris wondered how long her opposite number could stand the heat.

Then everything changed.

A wing of battlecruisers at the end of the forward line, flipped ship and kept to 3.5 gees. Now, however, all the gees were spent opening the range between that wing and the Imperials.

"What the hell?" Kris muttered.

76

"Get back in the battle line, you no-name, last-chosen piece of slime!" Admiral Zom shouted.

"My pedigree is as long and ancient as yours Zom. My clan entrusted these ships to me and I will not have them wasted in your vain attempt to win a battle that is lost already. I'm not the only one who has had it with you and your mindless orders. There is no honor in standing up to be slaughtered and cut into chum," an admiral commanding a lower vanguard wing cried.

To Zom's dismay, the much-hammered vanguard wing at the bottom of the line joined the top wing in turning to flee. The remnants of the forward vanguard were not long in joining the flight.

The next Imperial salvos were aimed solely at the ships in the four wings still in the battle line. A thousand of them vanished like water on a hot skillet.

The two rear wings broke. They did an uncoordinated flip and went 3.5 gees away from the Imperials. Immediately, as Zom watched in shock, the other four wings did a ragged flip and took off running as well.

Even his own flagship had turned with the rest of the middle wing and was running.

Beside his admiral, Number One staff officer offered no thought on how to avert this disaster.

Zom reclined, smoldering with anger as the Imperial commander Admiral Kris Longknife flipped her ships and took off in a 3.5 gee pursuit of those fleeing her guns.

Zom would have shaken his head at the folly, but 3.5 gees did not recommend such activity. His traitorous subordinates were fleeing, but without the brains destiny gave a sand gnat. Every ship in the rebel fleet was accelerating as much as it could on a single vector – directly away from the enemy ships that were even now blowing several hundred of them into dust.

"If you must run, scatter," Zom shouted on net. "Go to thirty or forty degrees from our base course. Break up into single ships or pairs and run for your lives. Maybe some of you will escape but none of you will if you stay clumped together like a dumb school of lollarm."

Zom felt his flagship swerve as it changed its course to head for the depths of the outer system. Maybe it could refuel at one of the major gas giants and sneak through a jump and get out of here.

It would likely take time, and they'd be on short rations of bitter yams by the time they straggled home. Still, they might survive this disaster.

"Oh, monsters from the deepest, darkest abyss," he heard his number one mutter. "Look."

Zom looked at his board. His fleet, indeed, had no hope. The Longknife Admiral separated her wings into smaller groups and sent them after his dispersing fleet.

"Regroup, regroup!" the rebel admiral screamed, but the panic had caught hold of every heart. No one was listening to him. His former command fled as fast as they could. Some even put on 3.6 or 3.7 gees as they strove to outdistance their pursuers.

They had no chance, but they ran because there was nothing else to do.

"What will you do, Human, with my fleet? What poison will you have me take?"

He could only wait helplessly while the last of this tragedy played itself out.

Admiral Kris Longknife could almost feel sorry for the poor dumb bastard commanding the rebel fleet. Correction, who *had* commanded the rebel fleet.

From the looks of it, no one commanded there now. It was every man for himself and devil take the hindmost.

Admiral Tong had flipped his fleet and now was in hot pursuit. One wing admiral was negotiating the surrender of the cruisers. Most now drifted as they emptied their lasers into empty space and smashed their main armament bus bars.

They had no other choice. The fleet would be passing close among them as they pursued their larger brethren. If they didn't surrender and become harmless, they'd have to die.

Even as she looked, one of the few surviving large cruisers, one with castoff battleship lasers, went to nearly 4.0 gees, charging her fleet.

A battlecruiser blew it to dust.

In a moment, no other cruisers had a charge on their laser capacitors as they drifted silently in blackest space. Admiral Tong peeled off a dozen of his most damaged battlecruisers to ride herd on them, and led the rest of his battlecruisers after the fleeing battle fleet.

Kris took in the entire wreckage of the enemy's forces and knew that the rebel admiral had put her on the horns of a dilemma.

His ships were running helter-skelter for the exits. If she wanted to force all of them to surrender, she'd have to scatter her fleet after them.

That, of course, meant dividing up her forces. Every boot ensign who ever dreamed of commanding a fleet knew that you didn't divide your force. That allowed the enemy to concentrate and defeat you in detail.

If Kris scattered her ships to chase the running rebel ships, she risked some of them concentrating back together. Then they could overpower a small detachment of her ships.

However, if she didn't release her battlecruisers to chase the fleeing rebels, she risked letting most of them get away.

Kris very much wanted those ships. She could add them to her fleet without having to worry about clan connections. They were in rebellion against their Emperor. Once captured, they had no further allegiance to any clan, rebellious or otherwise.

Kris liked ships that came with no strings attached.

She settled on a middle road.

"Admiral Tong, Admiral Kitano, may I have your attention?"

Both immediately appeared on her forward screen.

"I want to capture all or at least most of those rebel ships."

"Yes, My Admiral," Tong quickly replied.

"However, I don't want them picking off my ships, so I propose to order your five wings, Admiral Tong, to pursue the six rebel wings that are closest to us. Admiral Tong, please order the wing commanders to pursue the ships of their assigned wing. Spread out as much as may be necessary, however, have the wing commanders keep an eye out for any effort to pick off some of our ships."

"Yes, Admiral," Tong said, "I will have each wing commander open up the intervals between ships and flotillas. That should spread us out enough to chase down most of the fleeting rebels. It will also keep our ships close enough to support each other if the rebels try to lure them into a trap."

"Very good. One of your wings will have to chase two of theirs."

"Yes, our rear guard has suffered less. I will divide it and send it after the two top wings."

"Very good. Now, Admiral Kitano, I want you to operate independently. The three wings pulling up the rear and now in the lead of the flight look to me to be perfect targets for the Human battlecruisers. You have seven flotillas. Split them up to chase down the two on either end of the reserve line. We'll leave the middle wing for later. No doubt, if you collect the two flank wings, the guy in the middle will be comfortable being collected later."

"Hmm," Kitano mused. "Twenty-five hundred surviving rebel ships in those two wings, two hundred twenty-four Human battlecruisers. As the guy said, 'One riot, one ranger, even odds.' Yeah, I think we can handle that."

"If you can't, there's nothing dishonorable about flipping ship and pulling out of range."

"No doubt. Now they're running, and it looks to me like we'll be gunning for their sterns. How many of those ships am I permitted to blow to atoms, Admiral?" Kitano asked.

"Nelly, how much laser power would it take to slice a part of a rocket motor's bell off of a battlecruiser at near maximum range?"

"Five percent will likely do damage without burning through to the reactors. There's no guarantee you won't slice and dice a few reactors, but the odds are better that you don't."

"Okay," Kris said, "Tong, Kitano, have your ships reduce power on their lasers to five percent. That should keep the capacitors pretty full if some problem raises its miserable head. Any questions?"

"No, ma'am." "I will make it so," and the faces vanished.

Moments later, Kris knew her orders were being carried out. The Human battleships were not in range of the three distant reserve wings. Apparently, Admiral Kitano ordered the Human warships under her command to 4.3 gees in pursuit of the distant rebels.

Kris's weight grew until she could only breathe with effort. She'd known this would happen when she gave the order.

As luck would have it, the Human ships were in the vanguard. That put half of them in a good position to pursue one of the fleeing reserve wings. However, the other wing was on the other side of the line. It seemed that Kris's flag was one of the ships that drew the short straw. Now it headed up to clear the forward part of the battle line while also taking a diagonal course to chase down the distant wing and capture it.

Kris took the measure of the battle.

Most of the rebel wings in the forward battle line had suffered badly. The six wings each numbered approximately 900 fleeing battlecruisers.

Tong was in the process of detaching Kitano's seven Human flotillas and shuffling five of his wings into six. Each would have some number of battlecruisers. For once, he would be fighting against even odds.

Pity the rebels.

Admiral Kitano split her seven flotillas unevenly. What was left of the rebel vanguard was dispirited and down to barely a thousand warships. With luck, her 128 ships would roll them up quickly. After all, the Human battle cruisers had the crystal armor.

Kris was in the smaller force of 96. They headed for a wing that had been out of the fight. It still had over 1,700 ships.

"How do you eat an elephant?" Kris muttered to herself.

Jack provided the advice they regularly gave the kids, "One bite at a time."

Kris considered taking command of her small task group, but a check showed that Admiral Ajax from her flagship *Intrepid* had assumed command.

With a blink of her eye, no way could she shrug at 4.5 gees, Kris gave over the smaller battle to her junior officers and concentrated on keeping an eye on the big picture.

Many of the rebel battlecruisers were so desperate to escape that they failed to keep up their dodge and duck routine. They headed off in the straightest line that put the most distance between themselves and their pursuer.

The first time Admiral Tong's battlecruisers fired their underpowered salvos, they hit over a thousand rebel battlecruisers. A handful exploded, but the vast majority took off in wild aerobatics as one or more of their rocket motors were damaged. A hole in the huge bell of the motor or, better yet, slicing a chunk of it off, left plasma going in all the wrong places.

All but a few of those thousand immediately begged to surrender. Several hundred that weren't hit decided to throw in the towel as well.

Kris's fleet now had 1,500 prizes and the enemy had 30,000 fewer high energy lasers.

The capacitors of the loyalist battlecruisers were topped off by the time the fire control computers spit out another target. Another 800 suffered some damage to their engines and cut power.

"Kris, we have a problem," Nelly said from Kris's neck.

"I see it too, Nelly," Kris answered.

Her situation had just changed . . . drastically.

77

The rebel fleet had flipped and put on 3.5 gees. The former vanguard continued to flee, drawing Admiral Kitano after it.

Two of the rebels' reserve wings had taken advantage of being out of range. They had put all their speed into increasing the distance between them and their pursuers. The two undamaged wings now aimed for fifteen degrees to the right or left, up or down of the base course. They'd opened the distance between their flotillas, but not between ships.

Kris thought they were running.

That may have been correct a moment ago. It wasn't now. The two undamaged wings leading the flight of the rebel battlecruisers were now steering a course to concentrate again.

Ninety-six Human battlecruisers now faced a potential rebel force of 3,500 ships. Suddenly, that was one huge elephant that Kris would be taking very small bites out of.

Before Kris could open her mouth, Admiral Ajax ordered her three flotillas to edge their course back toward Admiral Kitano's four. Kris had fought battle before where a small, concentrated force had nibbled at the edges of a larger force until there was nothing left. It was a delicate dance, but survivable.

She had not, however, taken 200 warships up against nearly 5,000 charging down her throat.

"Are you having second thoughts?" Jack asked from beside her.

"Sort of," Kris admitted.

"Admiral Kitano shared with me a bit of poetry from way back during the European Imperial times of old Earth."

"Yeah?"

"Something like 'the single man, he fights for one. The married soldier fights for him and her and them.' Or something like that."

"Yeah," Kris said, then realized that Jack had nailed exactly what was racing through the back of her mind. It wasn't just Ruth and Johnnie she was seeing, but Amber Kitano's two darling girls as well. *How many other men and women of her battlecruisers had left their kids behind in the care of Abby and the embassy?*

"Yeah," Kris repeated.

"It's not so easy to throw the dice when you want to see two young lives blossom and unfold."

"Nope," Kris said, then folded those thoughts up and saved them for later.

"Admiral Kitano, may I suggest that we concentrate the Human battlecruisers against the far flank of what's left of the rebel vanguard? There are more of them, but their morale has to be shaken."

"That's what I'm aiming for. Admiral Ajax, keep your distance from the ships of the main body as you come up on my flank."

"Already tiptoeing around the rear of those bad boys. I'm cutting gees to 3.8 while I cross their rear."

Two more salvos from Admiral Tong's ships had reduced the main body by another 2,000 battlecruisers... some destroyed but most surrendered. What was left were few and scattering desperately. Admiral Tong ordered his ships to scatter by files of flotillas. That kept approximately 150 together as they hunted down the remnants for the rebel force.

Kris weighed letting the 5,000 ships fleeing ahead of the Human battlecruisers go on their way, but quickly gave up that idea. Five thousand warships was too large a force for her to leave wandering around this system. She had two planets on opposite sides of its sun to occupy; she could not have 5,000 ships show up at the wrong time and place.

No, these loose cannons had to be destroyed or captured.

While Ajax and her three flotillas slipped back across the rear of the new main force, Kitano began to nip at the heels of the fleeing rebel battlecruisers. Many of the Human admirals commanding task groups of flotillas had one of Nelly's kids at their throat. That jacked up both the speed of their fire control computers as well as the accuracy of the results.

Every ten seconds or less, two ship sections would send out a series of short, sharp jabs and 50 or so battlecruisers would flip out of control. Most immediately pleaded for surrender. Those that didn't discovered that they were on a highly erratic, but predictable course.

If they didn't surrender, they were dust ten seconds later.

Sixty seconds, and 200 battlecruisers among the former vanguards had killed their acceleration, emptied their capacitors, and smashed the main bus to those capacitors. No more work for those lasers today. Those who were either unlucky or foolish were dust.

Over the next minute, the process repeated itself.

Now it was the rebels who found themselves on the horns of a dilemma. Having foresworn all allegiance to a central command, the three admirals commanding the wings could find no one that they were willing to subordinate themselves to.

While the vanguard screamed for help, the other two wings began to wear away from it and upped their acceleration to 3.6, then 3.7 gees.

Confronted by open abandonment, the remnants of the vanguard wings flew to pieces. Many put on as many gees as they could and tried to catch up with the other two wings. Others split up, some going off to the right, others up, still others down, distancing themselves from each other and the implacable pursuit.

Admiral Kitano ordered one flotilla to scatter, first by squadrons, then by divisions, and finally, by pairs or even single ships as they chased down the fleeing rebels. Few ships from the vanguards succeeded in their escape.

That left Ajax picking off 40 or so with her remaining three flotillas even as Kitano's force came up.

Now rebel ships that had spent too much time at 3.5 gees or worse began to suffer the consequences. Here and there, a battlecruiser vanished in a huge ball of gas. After a few of those, other ships began to fall out of line as their reactors overheated and they had to reduce the acceleration of their flight to 3.3, then 3.0, then fewer gees.

A few tried to go out in a blaze of glory, charging the loyalists. Only one or two succeeded in getting themselves killed. Kris's old friend, mutiny, hopped and skipped through the fleet as crews took it upon themselves to choose that surrender was better than annihilation.

Admiral Tong's Iteeche battlecruisers continued to cut their way through the routed rebels of the main battle line. There were few ships left, and they were widely dispersed. Tong detached pairs of his own ships to chase them down, but kept most of his wings together. Now, he was clearly aiming for the two wings retreating as fast as they could.

More ships had to be detached. A few of the ships that were the first to surrender took it upon themselves to bring their reactors back online and take off at 3.5 gees in the opposite direction from Tong's battle line.

A strong warning went out to all those who had surrendered that if they violated their parole, they would be blown out of space. Six of the battlecruisers left behind to guard the cruisers headed for the deceitful.

After two were blown out of space, the crews of the others decided to lock up their captains and bring the ship back again to drifting in space.

Still, Tong kept a flotilla of ships scattered among the white flag fleet to remind them that he hadn't forgotten them.

Meanwhile, the white flag fleet grew minute by minute as rebel ships were chased down and either surrendered or were nipped in their rocket motors and then chose to surrender.

While the Admiral Tong herded and chivvied the wreckage of the rebel battle line into surrendering, there were still two wings left with some 3,500 battlecruisers. They represented a force not that much smaller than the strength of loyalists had in the system.

As it turned out, they had more fight left in them than smarts.

While a few of Admiral Kitano's ships mopped up the fleeing ships of the vanguard, six flotillas of her and Admiral Ajax's force started taking small bites out of the middle nearest wing.

Four quick, low power salvoes in one minute clipped the rocket motors on nearly over 200 warships. Tagged and sent spinning out of line, they reduced their reactors to the minimum level, smashed the bus bars to their capacitors, and waited for collection.

It looked like Admiral Kitano was about to eat up another wing one bite at a time.

That was when the rebel fleet showed it still had fight in it. While the most advanced half of each wing continued its headlong flight, the rear half of each one flipped ship and charged directly for the three closest flotillas – under Commander Ajax's command.

Suddenly, the 96 Human battlecruisers faced the fire from the 24-inch lasers of several hundred rebel warships. Some admiral among the charging ships ordered them to concentrate on the top squadron of the top flotilla.

They did.

Fire was unevenly spread over the eight ships of the squadron. Apparently most concentrated on the flagship, *USS Royalist*. It glowed bright as it took hit after hit. Some beams caught her. Other hits she ran into as she zigged and zagged to try and get out of the laser fire.

When the enemy laser salvo ended, it looked like the *Royalist* might survive the blazing heat it was wrapped in. However, over the next few seconds, it became apparent that the ship was being boiled from the outside-in. It maintained its crumbling front, but then the attacking rebel battlecruisers finished their flipping of ship. Now every gun in the fleet's aft batteries concentrated on that one glowing hull.

It didn't have a chance.

Meanwhile, the rest of Ajax's ships had flipped ship and could bring their rear batteries to bear on the enemy's fantails. Another 40 ships spun out of control even as the *Loyalist* blew itself into a thin cloud of hot gasses.

Ajax chose to keep her ships headed away from the rebels until just before she expected them to fire their next salvo. Then she ordered them to flip ship and to execute Evasion Plan 6. The enemy still concentrated on the top squadron.

However, the time it had taken them to ravage the *Loyalist* had given the other ships time to shed much of their heat.

Now, having directed all ships to increase from 3.5 to 3.7 gees toward Ajax's fleet, more rebel ships were pulling in range. The next salvo came from nearly a thousand battlecruisers.

Again, the top squadron with its seven ships was the target, and again the targeting was left up to the flotilla commander or even ship skippers. All of the seven took heat, however, the *Stalwart* and *Valor* took a major portion of the fire.

The *Stalwart* heated up, going from glowing a warm yellow-white right into red before it blew itself to dust. The *Valor* held together longer, but did not survive the salvo from the aft batteries.

By the end of those volleys, all of the five remaining ships of the top squadron were glowing hot. They flipped ship and put on 4.5 to 4.7 gees as soon as the enemy lasers fell silent.

Ajax ordered the rest of the task group to go to 4.2 gees and cover their withdrawal. Again, they clipped the rocket motors of 40 battle-cruisers, but the exchange rate was higher than the Human fleet liked.

The next salvo from the rebels attacked the front of Ajax's ships. Many of the rebel ships had fallen behind and out of range as the Human battlecruisers applied the highest gees possible. Quite a few of them fired anyway. This time, the next highest squadron was the target, but the fire was much less concentrated and, while many ships glowed white hot, all were able to go to 4.5 gees and pull away from the fight.

This time, 66 rebel ships were knocked out of line. Ajax had ordered her flotillas to each put a maximum effort in scattering low power bursts all around the ships which were also doing a poorer job of dodging themselves. Apparently they needed a reminder that while their own aim got better when they dodged less, they also became better targets.

With Ajax conducting a measured withdrawal, half the charging enemy ships were again out of range. Many of them chose to flip ship and head for greener, or at least more open, pastures.

Admiral Kitano, for her part, ordered three of her flotillas to hasten to Ajax's aid.

Again, the enemy fire was not directed at any one ship. However, having focused on the lead ships in the last several attacks, the middle ships came in for hard handling this time.

The *Princess Royal* was the fourth ship in the squadron of eight.

78

The first Kris knew that the *P. Royal* had drawn the short straw was when the air in the flag bridge began to get warm, then hot.

She had kept her flag bridge amidships, right at the point where the hull was widest, and began to taper going either fore or aft. If the rebel fire control systems were aiming for the center of mass, the bridge shouldn't have gotten the worst of the hits.

That, however, only worked for those ships that were directly across from them. Ships to the right or left, up or down, could aim for the center and miss wide. Many of them hit the wide part of the hull.

The temperature on the bridge went from comfortable to blazing hot in the amount of time it took the heat to diffuse through the 10 centimeters of crystal armor, into the 30 centimeters of super chilled Smart Metal™ and down to the meter of honeycombed armor that was cooled by the rapid flow of moist reaction mass.

In theory, the spinning outer hull should have moved the heated crystal away from the slashing laser beams. This moment, too much heat was hitting the whirling hull from too many directions for any of that to matter.

Normally, the reaction mass circulated freely through a meter of honeycomb. However, reaction mass expanded explosively as the lasers raised the temperature of the armor to the near boiling point of Smart Metal. Valves at the aft end of each pipe run were specifically designed to open and vent the superheated gas into space. They didn't just open but blew out and tumbled into space.

In the bow, fresh, cool reaction mass flowed into the pipes. It quickly overheated and blew out the aft end.

All this was supposed to keep the *Princess Royal* from being blown apart by hits from 24-inch lasers. However, Kris's flagship was the focus of a hundred or more rebel battlecruisers, intent on getting some revenge for their slaughtered shipmates.

Instantaneously, Kris's high gee station locked itself down as a survival pod. Launching a pod through the superheated armor was suicide. Still, the pod did what it could to protect Kris's all too fragile life.

"Jack!" she cried through gritted teeth.

"I'm here!" was strangled and weak, but it was there.

"Hold on!" Kris half-commanded, half-begged.

Inside her pod, a fine mist of water tried to cool her and the walls that held her body close. The water all too soon flashed to steam. It would have boiled Kris like a lobster, but the pod sucked the heated air out of her tiny compartment, cooled what it could, and vented the rest into the flag bridge.

Quickly, the place came to look like the inside of a steaming fog. The air recirculation system struggled to suck the mist out, vent it to space, and fill the room with fresh air.

However, Nelly was making nearly instantaneous changes to the ship. All equipment not essential to survival vanished. Around the flag bridge, screens, workstations, and battle boards all melted into the heating deck. Now the survival pods had their own access to the ship's water supply, and more fine mist struggled to cool each of the crew before it overheated and had to be flung into space.

The overheated, meter thick honeycomb of cooling reaction mass grew thicker until a good half-meter had been added to it.

A blood curdling scream filled the net for a moment before it was cut short, either by a grateful death or a chief taking that pod off net. Someone's survival pod had failed.

Kris knew that the same death awaited all of them if they couldn't shed the concentrated laser beams holding them like moths pinned poorly to a board for a primary school report.

"I have the con," Nelly said on net. No one argued with her.

Kris found the weight on her chest dropping while she was slammed harder against the hot sides of her pod. She gritted her teeth and fought to hold in the scream of pain that clogged her throat.

Admirals did not scream.

Around her, the bulkheads, overhead, and deck began to glow with heat. Kris felt like she was being baked in an oven, bombarded by a vicious heat. It would have boiled her blood and roasted her flesh if the pod wasn't struggling to keep her barely among the living.

The heat was unbearable. Still, it went on and on, not giving way to blessed oblivion. Kris struggled to breathe in as little of the hot, steaming air as she could. She waited for the agony to end, begging any listening God to bring her back safe to her children.

Will you never go out again? The question came unbidden to her mind.

Kris scowled. Even in this extremis, she did not believe in a god that bargained for Her blessings. Kris would live or die the way she had lived: fighting and willing to keep fighting for what needed to be done.

She firmly believed that the survival of that poor kid on the throne was important for both humanity and every Iteeche alive.

No. She was satisfied with what she had done with her life, and in this battle. She wanted with all her being to return to her kids, but she and they knew she'd go back out when the mission required it.

That was her bequest to her children. If the mission was critical, you gave it your all.

Somewhere in Kris's dialogue with herself or her God, she noticed that the temperature was beginning to cool. It was still painfully hot, but it was a bit shyer of scalding.

"You okay, Honey?" Jack asked.

"I think we're going to make it," Kris breathed

The ship computer announced, "Maintaining survival pod integrity. We are venting the ship's atmosphere to space."

The steaming air on the flag bridge was sucked away. For a long minute, nothing replaced it. The overheated structure of the bridge was allowed to radiate much of its heat into the open space that surrounded Kris. A slow hiss of air and reaction mass blew through the bridge as it collected the heat and was quickly swept out.

Now Kris was again under 4.5 gees, maybe more, as the *Princess Royal* opened the distance between it and the rebel fleet that was defeated, but still deadly.

"Nelly, can you show me the battle?"

"Sorry, Kris, but we lost all our sensors. I'm afraid the *Princess Royal* is deaf, dumb, and blind. Once we bleed off more of this heat I will try to reestablish the basic sensor and comm suite, but for now, Admiral, this battle goes on without us."

"That's fine, Nelly. I trust my admirals. I just hope we don't crash into anything."

"So do I, Kris. So do I."

Even blind, Nelly began to take some of the killing gees off of the flagship. Slowly Kris felt her weight go from deadly to merely oppressive. The brutal heat slowly bled away to merely painful.

A small shape dangling from the overhead formed where everyone that was flat on their back in their survival pod could see. It soon morphed into a screen that showed the immediate million kilometers around Kris's flagship.

Admiral Ajax had broken off contact with the enemy fleet and they had flipped ship and taken off after their erstwhile associates. Now, the rebel wings were scattered across space in six contingents. The farthest two were the largest, the closest ones the smallest.

Admirals Kitano and Ajax were back at the chase. They'd close just in range and take out the rearmost rebel ships, then lower their gees to avoid overtaking the next batch while they reloaded.

Lasers charged, they'd again closed with the rebels. Some of the enemy tried to flip ship and take on their attackers. They got a full-strength salvo and either blew up or went tumbling out of control, a shattered wreck. Those that kept running usually ended up twisting about in space with damaged rocket motors and begging to surrender.

Admiral Tong's Iteeche wings were now coming up. They took over guarding the surrendered rebel warships. After sending over a boarding party to take possession of the ship and assure it could not become a threat, they were left behind to begin decelerating into orbit around Longnae 4. The sooner they did that, the fewer gees they had to suffer.

More and more of the rebel Iteeche fell out of the two fleeing wings.

"Nelly, are any of the ships we're chasing going to be able to make orbit?"

"Not with the high velocity and course they are on now. I think they may be able to steer for Longnae 9. Depending on their fuel state, they may be able to make orbit around that gas giant and refuel. If not, they are quite likely going to starve before they can make any orbit. It may be that they've put too much energy on their ships to slow down for any planet."

"Nelly, are you monitoring the main guard channel?"

"I am now."

"Get me a hookup to that channel."

"You have it now, Kris."

"This is Imperial Admiral of the First Order of Steel, Her Royal Highness Kris Longknife of the United Society. The Emperor of the Iteeche Empire has given me directly from his hand the honor of commanding the Imperial Combined Fleets. I address this to all Iteeche sailors and officers presently in rebellion against their Emperor and sailing in warships in the Longnae system."

Kris paused to carefully take a breath. The air in the pod was still scorching hot.

"Throw down your weapons. Take all acceleration off your ships, empty your lasers into empty space, and destroy the bus bars between the capacitors and your reactors. Do this and you will live. Many senior officers may need to be reassigned or demoted. However, I pledge on my honor that you will be treated as Prisoners of War under the Laws of War practiced by my people."

She'd offered them the carrot. Hopefully, they would believe that Humans were alien enough to them that her laws might just be survivable.

"If you do not surrender, I intend to stop chasing you. By my best estimate, most of you are near to exhausting your reaction mass. You are headed on a high velocity course to nowhere. If you stay this course, you will end up deep in interstellar space as your ships grow cold and your air grows bad. Maybe you will starve to death before you freeze or asphyxiate. It doesn't matter which, only death lies ahead of you.

Again, Kris paused, both to catch her breath and to let that thought sink in. She'd been on such a nightmare ride. She'd risked it because she had no other choice but certain death. *What would they decide?*

"Consider your next move carefully. Many sailors aboard ships in the last few hours have locked up captains that insisted on sending them on a death ride. The choice is yours. Choose quickly and wisely. You do not have a lot of time."

Kris paused for a moment then finished. "Admiral Longknife out."

"Nelly, get me Admirals Tong and Kitano."

The tiny screen above her had expanded by several centimeters as more metal could be pulled from the hull. The two admirals appeared above her head.

"Did you copy my last message?" she asked.

Both nodded.

"Break off the chase," Kris ordered, " and make for Longnae 4."

"Some of our ships may need to try for Longnae 5 to refuel," Nelly put in.

"Or Longnae 5," Kris added.

"Admiral Longknife, some of my ships have enough reaction mass to continue the pursuit for another hour, assuming the rebels cut their acceleration."

"Proceed cautiously, Admiral Tong, but I'd prefer to have ships surrender rather than head off into the void."

"Is that really their course?" Admiral Tong asked. "I tried to get my flag computer to calculate their course, but it insisted it had insufficient information."

"I assumed a slightly larger than standard reaction mass load out," Nelly said. "When I looked at all their heavy accelerations, decelerations and then going back to a hard charge with a lot of adjusting, I estimated that they are only hours away from the point of no return. I could be wrong on the basic assumption of their initial load, but I think I have measured their fuel usage accurately."

"Thank you, Nelly," Kris said.

"What was that admiral thinking?" Tong muttered.

"He was thinking he could win a fight, then work it out later, I imagine," Kris said.

"The fool."

"Admirals," Kris said, changing the topic to survival. "I am ordering all damaged ships to make for Longnae 4. I don't know how much reaction mass the Princess Royal has left after losing so much to cooling. I hope we can make it."

"I have checked the tanks, Kris. I think we have enough. We may have to be careful flushing toilets and taking baths or showers, but we should be able to make it."

Kris could have killed for a shower, but it was clearly days away.

On screen, Kris watched as her flag, and the rest of the crippled ships began the long, slow braking that would take them to their target planet. They each followed their own course. They had no spare fuel to waste for forming up.

While the rest of the fleet waited to see which among the rebel ships would choose to live or to die, the *Princess Royal* began the careful journey toward a desperately needed pier.

79

Most of the damaged battlecruisers barely made it. They ended up in high elliptical orbits. With the remaining fuel aboard, it took them time to regulate and lower themselves to match orbit with a space station.

That was when the next problem raised its ugly head.

The managers of the four space stations above Longnae 4 refused to let the crippled battlecruisers dock. Two, then four, then seven badly damaged warships ended up trailing the stations as their crews suffered in zero gee.

As the wrecked *Princess Royal* made its final approach to Longnae 4, Kris put on her dress whites and took an angry stance before the main screen in her flag bridge. It was barely half the size of normal, but the camera above it was at full power.

"This is Grand Admiral, Her Royal Highness Kristine Longknife of the United Society, Imperial Admiral of the First Order of Steel. I personally received from the Emperor's hand a mandate to command the Imperial Combined Fleet. I commanded the fleet that just beat the rebel warships in this system like a drum. Thousands of battlecruisers were blown to dust in the blink of an eye. Thousands more chose to accept the offered surrender. It is now your turn."

Kris paused to let their plight sink into any thick heads that were still unpersuaded that surrender was the only acceptable option. When she went on, Kris made sure that those hold-outs didn't want to try her fury.

"Know this, those of you who administer Longnae 3, 4, and 5. If you do not accept the offer to surrender, the battlecruisers presently in orbit will begin the destruction of your planet. By the time my fleet is done with your two planets, they will be balls of molten rock, unfit for any life for the next billion years."

Kris gave the screen a scowl of biblical proportions before telling Nelly to cut the line.

Fifteen minutes later, the USS *Dominant* was invited to come alongside the space station high above the planet's capital. Fortunately, she still had a full company of Marines.

The troopers were immediately offered guides and led to the command center and the reactor control rooms. Once those were secure, the rest of the damaged ships caught the hooks and were quickly pulled into their assigned piers. The *Princess Royal* was the twelfth to tie up.

Her flagship was no sooner docked than the skipper ran blowers to empty the ship of the air that had gotten stale and thick. A watch was set, and half the crew was released from stations to clean up. An hour later, they relieved the rest, and within two hours, everyone was almost feeling human again.

Everyone who was still alive.

The *Princess Royal* would likely never fight again. Launched at 5,000 tons over the normal 75,000 tons of her class, she now displaced barely 65,000 tons. The rest had boiled away to space.

Along with it had gone half of the forward battery. The port side guns were hit so hard and often that burn-through could not even be prevented by the crystal armor. Thanks to Nelly's quick action, the capacitors behind the guns had contained only a fraction of a charge. When several blew up, they damaged the immediate area, but did not blow out the rest of the ship.

Nelly may also have had something to do with that. She isolated the forward port battery behind a thickened bulkhead. When the explosions came, they were blocked from going inward. Instead, they blew outward into space.

Unfortunately, that assured that there were no survivors from half the forward gun crews.

There were other hull breaches. Under the intense focus of so many lasers, there was no way to avoid them. Nearly a quarter of the flagship's crystal armor was vaporized when it had been hard hit over ten seconds. Along with it went 15,000 tons of hull structure.

The Marines' quarters had the misfortune to catch the attention of too many laser beams all at the same time. Nearly half of the company died in less than a second. Many of those that survived were in pods that were splashed with failing liquid Smart Metal™ and had to be cut out.

Other compartments forward of the flag bridge suffered casualties when lasers broke through them. While some contained crew at their battle stations, most of those compartments did not.

When the *Princess Royal* went to Condition Zed, most of the supply spaces were shuffled around until they lay next to the hull armor. A lot of those were freezers for frozen meat, fruits, and vegetables.

Most of the meat aboard was parboiled when the ship structures were red hot and the atmosphere steamy. With three weeks of frozen rations on board, the crew ate a lot of meat during the hard trip down to the planet, even if it was lacking in taste.

Most of the vegetables were gone. Fortunately, the first compartment opened had contained salad fixings. The lettuce and tomatoes had wilted in the heat, as had most of the rest. However, a glance in the storage cooler showed the walls to be seriously dished in.

That led to an investigation of storage compartments forward of that one. Inventory discovered it had stored several tons of dried beans. Between the heat and the steam, they had been thoroughly cooked. In the process, they had done what dried beans are wont to do. They expanded.

Fortunately, before anyone opened that hatch, Nelly ran a probe into the room. Not only had the beans expanded, but the room was a mush of lima beans, kidney beans, and navy beans. Every type of bean stowed aboard was now mixed into the most revolting mass possible.

Most of the specially encrypted hull metal around those storage spaces had boiled away. Nelly had hastily filled the gaping holes in the hull with any Smart Metal™ handy. That made it easy to vent the compartment to space. Rather than lose air they couldn't afford, Nelly used the walls to push the ugly mess out into space.

That, however, brought its own problems. Suddenly, the *Princess Royal* was surrounded by a halo of bean mush: large chunks, small clumps, and here or there, an actual solitary bean.

Now frozen in space's vacuum, they became a threat to navigation or a shotgun blast headed for Longnae 4. That could not be allowed.

The 5-inch secondary guns had not had an active role in the battle so far. Now, they were unlimbered and given the job of cleaning up the space around the *Princess Royal*.

It became a humorous pastime for the off-duty sailors and officers to spend time as part of a 5-inch gun crew blasting beans out of space.

The beans weren't the only target. The compartment on the other side of the salad locker held the popcorn stash for movie night. Hit with extreme temperatures, it cooked and expanded. The *Princess Royal* had an entire compartment stuffed with popcorn!

Worse, Nelly had noticed the pressure building up and had opened that space to the next one over. It held mops, brooms, and cleaning supplies.

When Nelly vented the popcorn to space, the cleaning gear went with it.

The sailors came up with a game where mops and brooms had double the value of cleaning supplies. Corn earned fewer points than the beans because there was so much of it and it was mostly single kernels.

It was a silly game, but it helped the crew keep their minds off of the other compartments that had to be emptied. Compartments with crew members whose survival pods had failed.

Every day, there was another set of funerals. The battlecruiser had lost almost a quarter of the 500 souls aboard.

Thus, the ship that the space station pulled alongside the pier was a somber affair. The crew went about their duties in a much-enlarged battlecruiser now in Condition Able+. The extra included several small chapels where the crew could spend a few moments alone with their thoughts and memories.

There was no way to avoid the painful fact that many quarters that had been shared were now single occupancy. Kris felt almost guilty that none of the people who moved in her orbit had died. Both her and the captain's bridge had not taken direct hits or lost those standing watch.

Of course, the Marines standing guard at the rear of the bridge were often strangers.

Kris refused to allow herself to dwell on the thought of how close she had come to making Ruth and Johnnie orphans. Instead, she set herself to do what she'd come to do.

80

Admiral Kris Longknife informed the Overlord of Longnae 4 that she would meet with him or a fully empowered representative to discuss the unconditional surrender of the planet.

Two hours later, she, Jack, and Megan sat across a large wooden table from eight very nervous Iteeche. Kris had eight Marines in full battle rattle behind her. No one stood behind the Iteeche.

Kris did not like the situation across from her. The head of the Iteeche delegation was a deputy assistant to the Planetary Overlord. That sounded too far down the food chain for her taste. That there were eight of them hinted strongly that any four of them could veto anything the other four were willing to accept. Worse, eight people talking very likely meant nine opinions on everything and no agreement on anything.

The silence went long. She could hear feet shuffling under the table. Wordlessly, Kris reached out to Megan. The *aide de camp* just as wordlessly handed her admiral a large, sealed parchment scroll with magnificent calligraphy. After glancing at it as if she hadn't seen it before, Kris waved casually to Megan and the commander retrieved the document and carried it around the table.

She sat the scroll before the deputy assist to the Planetary Overlord and withdrew. All seven of the other Iteeche gathered around him to look over his shoulders.

Iteeche skin appeared to Humans as doughy by nature. These eight were now ashen pale.

"Wh- wh- where is the rest of the surrender document?" the deputy assistant sputtered.

"There is nothing more to be said. You surrender the Longnae system to the Imperium unconditionally. You will surrender all weapons. None will be destroyed. Neither shall the warships and naval stores on either planet be harmed. They are now the property of the Imperial Combined Fleets to do with as I shall chose. There is no need for anything else to be said."

The eight Iteeche slowly returned to their seats. Where Kris had expected a tsunami of words, she was met by abject silence as all eight of them stared at the table in front of them. They neither met her eyes, nor each other's.

"There is a place for the Planetary Overlords' representative to sign," Kris snapped before the silence grew malignant. "There is a place for me. There is also a place for the Planetary Overlord to personally sign the surrender instrument for Longnae 4. I expect him up here in six hours or less to sign in his place."

That drew no reaction from those across from her. They continued to avoid meeting anyone's eyes.

Finally, the deputy assistant whispered so softly that it took Nelly's hearing to catch his words, "We had hoped for better terms. Balan received better terms."

Kris cut him off. "Balan received better terms because Balan surrendered without a fight. Ten thousand rebel ships have been blown to bits in the recent battle in your system. Over ten thousand ships have surrendered. Over a thousand of my ships were destroyed with their crews. I was almost burned alive. No, you don't get easy terms. Surrender now, or the ships I have here will begin to burn the planet down to lifeless slag."

Now the eight did exchange worried glances.

"Yes. Yes, of course," the deputy assistant said and hastily reached for a pen to sign his name.

"Nelly, will you open a circuit to the Planetary Overlord so this underling can report what he has done and what he has committed the Overlord to do?"

"The circuit is open," Nelly said from Kris's neck.

The deputy assistant looked startled when the Overlord's startled voice came from no place in particular around the room.

The Planetary Overlord had apparently been in the middle of a call when Nelly cut in. Now a small holographic figure of a very shocked politician was projected onto the middle of the conference table. From the way the image twisted around to stare up at Kris and his delegation, she had the strong impression that Nelly was somehow projecting their holographic images to surround the Overlord in a similar scale to their appearance in the room.

The Iteeche negotiator stammered out a recapitulation of the negotiations. The Overlord bellowed his objection to the unconditional surrender. His negotiator stuttered as he explained the pressure Kris had brought to bear.

That resulted in the Overlord whirling around to look up at Kris.

"I can begin the destruction of your planet immediately, starting with your capital. When the rest of my fleet arrives, I'm sure we can slag the planet down to bedrock."

The Overlord's mouth dropped open. When he got control of his vocal cords again, it was his turn to stammer, "Let's not be hasty. I'm sure I can arrange to be up to sign the document some time tomorrow."

Kris noticed that he said document rather than instrument of surrender. She also didn't like the vagueness of his time commitment.

"Now that I have your attention," Kris said. "There is no reason to wait six hours. If you have not affixed your signature to the instrument of surrender in three hours, I will order the destruction of your capital. We can start with the government district."

The Overlord allowed that he might be there in four hours. Kris agreed to let him have the extra hour, but assured him that she would be following him and would know exactly where to aim laser batteries to destroy the kilometer around his location if he wasn't in this room in four hours.

A very humbled and crestfallen Planetary Overlord agreed to Kris's demands and the line was broken.

Kris left the eight defeated and subdued negotiators at the table, guarded by four of her Marines. Her team, escorted by the other four Marines, went back to the *Princess Royal* for lunch. There, the cooks had thrown together a stew of questionable origin.

As luck would have it, the ship's spud locker had survived the battle undamaged. They'd swapped a ton of potatoes for a half ton of carrots and a few other odds and ends with other ships that resulted in the crew of all twelve of the damaged ships having a decent lunch with garlic bread and a low-alcohol ale.

Kris suspected and wouldn't mind that she'd have leftovers for supper.

Three hours later, Kris was alerted that the Planetary Overlord and his entourage were coming up the beanstalk.

Admiral Kris Longknife ordered a Marine platoon to greet the Planetary Overlord at the ferry and inform him that he could bring a military honor guard of a dozen soldiers. No more.

Several damaged Iteeche-crewed battlecruisers had made port in the last several hours. She drew another Marine platoon and a company of armed sailors to reinforce her Human Marines. Kris did not want snakes or axes anywhere near the surrender site.

The Overlord had to accept before signing that his days of power and authority were gone. They'd vanished with the fleet he called to his defense.

Kris also included in the reception committee the only Iteeche admiral she had on hand. Her suspicions were confirmed via spy bot that the admiral brought along most of his staff. The officers certainly showed their delight at meeting a much humbled Clan Lord and blocking most of his retinue from exiting the ferry.

With his small guard buried in the column of Human and Iteeche

Marines and sailors, it was rather hard to tell if they were his honor guard... or arresting officers.

Kris chose to meet the outgoing Planetary Overlord at a large wooden table on A deck. There was plenty of room for onlookers and many sailors from the ships in port as well as station workers made time to be there to see a Planetary Overlord eat humble pie before an admiral, even if that admiral was a Human.

He stood on one side of the table with his eight-member negotiation team. They were backed up by the twelve guards that he'd been allowed to bring. They and the table were surrounded by sailors and Marines in ranks.

Kris and her staff invited the Planetary Overlord to sign the instrument of surrender. He insisted on reading it; it didn't take him very long. With a sour face, he bent over and signed his name.

Kris came forward, settled into the available chair, and checked to make sure that everything was in order. Nelly had done her usual officious best. Kris signed with a flourish.

She stood. "These ceremonies are over." She turned to the deputy assistant and said, "You and your team may return to the ferry with these soldiers." Then she turned to the former Planetary Overlord. "Will you please come with me?"

"No," the former lord snapped. "I will not!"

"I wish you had not said that," Kris said and turned to the senior Iteeche officer present. "Admiral, please detain this man and house him in the brig of my flagship."

"Aye, aye, Admiral. Major," he snapped.

An Iteeche Marine officer snapped to attention, issued several terse orders, and a dozen Marines moved on the double to surround and apprehend the fallen lord.

"Soldiers," the now deposed Planetary Overlord screamed, "save me!"

The captain commanding the small honor guard glanced around and took the measure of the odds against him.

"Stand fast," he ordered in a voice that only cracked a little bit. He cautiously removed his pistol from the holster at his side, then lowered it to the deck. Behind him, his troops did likewise.

The ex-clan lord was screaming as Iteeche Marines bore him away to his new quarters in the *Princess Royal*. No doubt, they would not be as big as the mating pool in his palace.

With the surrender done, Kris dispatched her admiral down the beanstalk with Marines and armed sailors to assure that the minimum instructions in the surrender were obeyed. No military equipment or supplies were destroyed. Even the battlecruisers under construction in the space stations' yard were left in their partially completed stages.

Apparently, watching such a large fleet be beaten by such a smaller one was enough to petrify the people of the two planets. Of the clan lordlings, they were too frozen in place to issue orders for the destruction of anything. Alternately, those who received such orders misplaced them and then forgot to carry them out.

However it was, Kris found herself in possession of two million Iteeche armies, one was on one planet, the other on the second. They were fully equipped for mobile warfare, even if the tanks and vehicles were made of traditional metal.

The situation out in space continued to sort itself out. The cruisers and gunboats sought to surrender. They all needed refueling to stagger back to Longnae 4. Admiral Tong detached a flotilla of his loyalists along with a dozen flotillas of recently surrendered battlecruisers to refuel at either Longnae 5 or 7. From there, they ran down ships that had spent their reaction mass.

Some were so damaged that they took the crew off and reduced the rest to dust. Others had their weapons rendered harmless and were sent on their way toward Longnae 4.

The same was done to help the battlecruisers that found themselves low on fuel. Some of them had to aim for Longnae 8. That meant a long voyage. Fortunately, ten flotillas of mixed loyalists and recent rebels could reach the gas planet before them, refuel, and match orbit with them. With help refueling, the former rebels managed to swing around the gas giant and make for Longnae 4.

It would be a long, slow voyage.

The troop ships broke into two task groups. Two-thirds headed for Longnae 4 with six of the Battleships of State and the politicians that occupied them. The remaining troopers and politicians set course for Longnae 3 with the clear desire to take it over, supervise its return to loyalty to the Emperor, and profit from the process. They were soon joined on the long voyage by 20 flotillas of battlecruisers to reinforce the 5 protecting them.

More ships, most damaged, continued to straggle in. They provided sailors to guard the key installations on the planet and technicians to assure that key services continued like power, water, sewage, and communications. Although, not necessarily in that order.

The occupants of the planet below seemed to be holding their breath, waiting to see what was in store.

Kris decided to resolve some of the tension. She had her senior Iteeche admiral begin to assign rooms on the Battleships of State for the clan lordlings that would be leaving.

The feeling of relief was palpable as more of the minor and major officials got their tickets home. Moreover, they got them in a stateroom rather than a jail cell. Kris personally gave the former Planetary Overlord his ticket.

"Why are you giving me the largest suite on the *Golden Emperor of the Stars*? he asked, incredulously.

"You surrendered," she answered. "I have asked for and received from the Emperor authority to grant pardons to rebel officials. That assumes that they surrender and do not wreck their planet in a senseless battle of resistance. You surrendered, so you get a ride back. You will likely be assigned a much less prestigious job by your clan, but there will be no snakes."

Mentally, Kris added, *that is, unless we lose control of our side.*

81

During the next week nothing happened, which was exactly the way Kris wanted it to be. The yards at the four space stations commissioned twenty new battlecruisers and laid down another twenty. *What was there to complain about?*

The prospective captains who had overseen their fitting out stood aside while an XO from one of the newly arrived Imperial fleet ordered the raising of the commissioning pennant, or whatever it was the Iteeche did. The ships then entered Kris's fleet and began working up under a loyalist captain who would become their flotilla commander.

All over Longnae 4 matters progressed as normal.

Then, over the course of a morning, the fleet arrived.

The Battleships of State insisted on docking ahead of the troopships. They took the three piers next to the *Princess Royal*. Meanwhile, the troopers divided and docked one quarter of their army at each of the four space stations.

The space elevators at each station would be very busy most of the morning moving troops down and returning with Longnae troops to fill the troopships back up. Hopefully, the only problems would be traffic jams at the dirtside stations.

Kris and Jack were hardly back from breakfast when Nelly informed them that the new Planetary Overlord for Longnae 4 demanded they visit him in his suite aboard the *Golden Emperor of the Stars*.

"Tell him we can see him at ten in my flag quarters," Kris snapped back.

"He insists you go to him," Nelly said a moment later. "He is, he reminds you, a Planetary Overlord and Clan Chief."

"How's his blood pressure holding up?" Jack asked.

"If Kris aims to give him a stroke, I'd say he's borderline already."

"Nelly, remind the jerk that I am the admiral that made him overlord of a planet. If he doesn't like matters, I have another Planetary Overlord in waiting on this station. I'll appoint him overlord for this planet."

Nelly was a bit delayed in passing along the answer to Kris's blunt statement. "Sorry for the delay, but it took a bit of time for his staff to talk him down from ordering the soldiers on the troop ships docked here to march over and take you captive."

"You're kidding." Jack said.

"Not a bit."

"We seem to have ourselves a two-bit dictator here," Kris mused. "Maybe I should find someone to take his place."

"Well, Kris, he now says he will be here for the ten o'clock meeting."

"With a division of soldiers to lock me in my own brig?" Kris said.

"I will monitor the net to let you know if he tries any such thing."

"Good, Nelly. Jack, I still feel the need for a long soak in a nice warm tub. Will you join me?"

"Don't you have some paperwork to sign? Maybe even read."

"Not that I want to."

"How about planning what we do next?" he asked.

"I can do that in the tub."

"Oh. So, you don't want me to bother you."

"I'm sure I can think while you bother me."

"Don't be so sure."

Despite Jack joining her in the tub, both of them were ready an hour later in full dress uniforms, sporting enough medals to sink a small battleship. Kris did not, however, have Nelly bother with remaking the ship into an Imperial bordello. The *Princess Royal* had fought hard to get this bozo his planet. He should know the price paid.

As it turned out, Nelly had her own idea of what Kris's flag should look like. She noticed as she strode onto the quarterdeck to greet the pain in the neck that the quarterdeck showed warped plates on the deck, bulkheads and overhead. Their "paint" was also scorched and flaking.

Kris greeted the future Planetary Overlord for Longnae 4 with the proper bland political smile she'd learned at her father's knee.

As they turned toward her quarters, the new Overlord glanced around. "Can't your computer clean up your ship? This looks disgusting. Totally inappropriate for a meeting with a Planetary Overlord."

"Sorry, Clan Chief," Kris said, using his present title rather than his not quite yet title. "My flagship was the center of attention for a major portion of the rebel fleet. Over fifteen thousand tons of her hull were burned away. We're not sure that part of the ship's Smart Metal wasn't overstressed by the heat and fear that it may have lost part of its programming. We don't want to order it to move and discover that it can't hold together."

"Oh," the civilian glanced around. "Is it safe to be on this ship?" he whispered, assuming this secret was for high clan ears only.

"That is why we aren't changing the ship around. To keep it safe."

"Good. Very good," he said, then stumbled over the uneven deck.

Kris offered him a hand as she ushered him into her day quarters. They now looked like they'd been through a hot fire. Even the wood of the conference table they sat at was charred around the edges.

After they sat, Kris asked, "Would you like coffee, tea, or hot chocolate?"

"Hot chocolate," the Clan Chief answered.

A mess steward wheeled a cart over from the wall to Kris's elbow and she served him hot chocolate, then added a dollop of rum to spice it up as he was wont to have it. She also offered him a bowl of fresh lollarm which she'd ordered up from the planet this morning.

"Very good," he said as he crushed the first one between his teeth. He swallowed the small crustacean, shell and all.

"It's from Landnae 4. I think you will find plenty of good food waiting for you in the Overlord's palace."

"Yes. How soon will my enthronement take place? How many rebel lords and lordlings will make a Most Sincere and Very Complete Apology to Me as the Embodiment of the Emperor?"

Kris opened her mouth, but the Clan Chief rushed on past his question.

"I only brought twenty Red-robed Ones. However, we can have two installments. There are a lot of people on my new staff who have bones to pick with some of the clans running this place. Some even by name. We made a game of deciding who got to choose someone. For a thousand gold gildons you got to put a name into the pot. I'll draw the names today at a grand banquet with my senior lords and lordlings. I'll definitely draw forty names. Maybe sixty."

No doubt if they got drunk enough, he'd just empty the bucket. Kris wondered who got to keep all the gold gildons the lottery brought in.

She let the fool run down. It took him a while to notice that neither Kris nor Jack were joining in his glee at the fulfillment of so many vendettas for so many enemies.

"Maybe I'll only draw twenty," he said, winding down like a child's toy with a dying battery.

"There will be no executions of the rebel administration on Longnae 4," Kris said.

"And why not?" the future overlord demanded.

"Because the Emperor has given me the power to award amnesties to officials who surrender their planets. The overlord surrendered this planet. I have given him and all those under him a pardon. They will be returning to the capital where their loyal clan chiefs will determine their punishment before assigning them to less prestigious jobs."

The new Planetary Overlord didn't look at all happy for the chance at long life that his predecessor now had.

"You are too easy on the traitors. Look, your ship bears damage from the resistance of the rebel fleet. Certainly, these rebels deserve no such mercy."

"The rebel fleet did not fight under the command of this Planetary Overlord," Kris shot back, "any more than my fleet fights for you. They were from the combined rebel fleets as I command the Imperial Combined Fleet."

The new overlord opened his beak, but Kris cut him off. "Positions will be exchanged on a one-for-one basis. As one administrator exits the ferry, his replacement may board the ferry for the trip down. Do you understand?"

"An admiral cannot command a Planetary Overlord and Clan Chief with the brazen arrogance you do. You promised me a system to rule over. Now you give me half a system. I demand what my clan ships fought for."

"You mean half a flotilla out of six thousand battlecruisers?"

The not-yet and maybe-never overlord blanched and said nothing.

"If you want, we have another Planetary Overlord waiting on another Battleship of State. He's Lista, the one that was promoted when Sam screwed up at the Balan system and earned a ride in my brig. If you don't want Landnae 4, I can give this planet to him and give you the next one we capture."

"What next one?" The whiner jumped at that thought.

"I told everyone I planned on capturing three planetary systems from the rebels. I still haven't decided which system to invade next."

"Will it have two planets?" he demanded.

"I don't know. It might. It might not. I'm not sure we have the forces to tackle another assault. I've got to talk to my admirals and find out the status of my fleet."

Kris had never seen such a sneer on the face of an Iteeche. "I'll take the planet below us," he snapped.

"We have such words of wisdom. 'The bird in the hand is worth two in the bush'," Kris said.

"Yeah. Are we done here?"

"If you have nothing else to discuss with me."

"I don't."

"Then I will see you when next we come this way. Your dockyards are yielding eighty battlecruisers a month. I expect you'll continue to deliver them to the Combined Fleets."

"Maybe I'll build my own Clan fleet."

"I wouldn't suggest it," Kris said, softly.

"Or what?" he half-shouted back.

"I just would not suggest it."

Kris left it at that, and the new Planetary Overlord stomped straight from the *Princess Royal* to meet his retinue at the ferry station. They commandeered seats on the next ferry to drop and the station air suddenly became less oppressive.

Kris and Jack went off to the wardroom for lunch. They definitely needed to get that bad taste out of their mouths.

82

That afternoon, Kris scheduled a conference to determine what her fleet could do next. Soon, she, Jack, and Megan were seated around her conference table in her day quarters with Admirals Tong and Kitano. Her quarters no longer looked scorched and burned, but they were a tad smaller.

She left it to Admiral Tong to report the status of the fleet.

"We finished this battle with nearly 500 loyal Iteeche battlecruisers that were battle worthy. A few of those may need a few days to mend the damage. Several hundred more will require some serious yard time and a good dose of your magic metal to bring them up to battle readiness."

He paused for a moment to consult his commlink. "A bit over seven thousand rebel battlecruisers surrendered in or are close enough to fighting condition. They have docked and should be combat ready in a week, two at most. Another thousand or so will need serious yard time and magic metal to restore them to combat status. A thousand more are still headed for Longnae 8 and won't be here sooner than a month from now. Five hundred are too battle damaged. We'll have to write them off. Maybe we can convert them to fast attack transports for your army."

"Very good," Kris said. "Will you please pick out the best for my prize money? Assign them your best XO's who are ready for command. I may need some of them very soon."

"Of course, My Most Eminent Admiral," Tong replied.

"Admiral Kitano, what of my Human task fleet?"

"I'm down half a flotilla," she answered quickly. "Four battlecruisers were lost. Six more, including the *Princess Royal*, are too badly damaged to be brought up to battle ready condition. Sorry, Kris, but your flagship will have to be sent back to Human space. No doubt she'll be decommissioned. At best, her metal might be used to form two fast attack cargo ships. I wouldn't chance them as fast attack transports. They've got too much over-stressed metal in them for us to risk a large number of troops and personnel. I wouldn't trust my kids on them."

Kris glanced around at the four bulkheads of her day quarters, then the overhead. "No. I wouldn't either. Okay, six battlecruisers headed back to Wardhaven."

"Twelve, Kris. The other six are too badly damaged to be repaired this side of Human space."

"Okay, so you are down half a flotilla."

"Also, I've got a flotilla detached to bring the lost lambs from Longnae 8 back in."

"So, you're down to five and a half flotillas, huh?"

"Pretty much."

"How soon before you'd be ready to sail?" Kris asked.

"As soon as I can resupply, I'll be ready, but . . ."

Kris cut her off. "The ships with Human provisions will be coming in with the army cargo ships later today. Good. Admirals, I'd like to sail a mixed force of five thousand loyal and formerly rebel battlecruisers as well as the Human flotillas in no less than seven days."

"You intend to go ahead with the next invasion?" Kitano said, incredulously.

Tong looked like it took only years of carefully nurtured obedience to absurd orders kept his beak shut.

"Of course," Kris said, knowing that she was once again expecting agreement where no sane Human being would give it. "Admiral Tong reports that he has eleven thousand ships already docked that are available to sail. He has several thousand more that should become available over the next several weeks. More in the next month."

Kris paused but her subordinates did not respond with the expected acceptance of her logic. So, she continued.

"Admiral Tong, do you have a subordinate that you would trust with the defense of the Longnae System with the forces available?"

"I imagine so," still wasn't as enthusiastic as Kris was hoping for.

"Good. I'd prefer to have you in command of my fleet if we run into another fight."

"Are you expecting one?" Kitano asked.

"Not really. I think the rebellion will need some time to put together another major battle fleet. They'll also need time to figure out how to respond to this defeat. I didn't miss the four battlecruisers boosting for the jumps out of here. This time, they'll have a very accurate after-action report to examine. Our next fight is going to be a whole lot tougher."

"Really?" Tong asked.

"Either that or they won't figure out how we keep beating them and they'll throw in the towel," Kris said. "What do you think are the chances of that?"

Tong shook his head, which involved shaking his entire body. "Not bloody likely, as you Humans like to put it. No. Whatever they figure out, they'll be absolutely sure it solves their problems. They'll have to try at least one more roll of the die."

"I was afraid you'd say that. Still, I think we've stripped them of all available forces on this side of the Empire. We're leaving over seven thousand ships here. Five thousand should be enough to take on whatever is hanging around the Progsus system. Remember, there were only a thousand battlecruisers defending the Balan System. The rebels had to strip all the other systems to amass a defending force like they had here."

The two looked like they couldn't think of any argument to throw at Kris, though neither of them was happy with her proposed course of action.

She turned to Jack. "You going to lock me in my room?" she said, getting a smile from everyone but Admiral Tong.

The Humans knew that her Grandpa Trouble and King Ray, also a grandpa, had tricked Kris into commissioning Jack as a Marine and her subordinate security chief. Meanwhile, the old bastards had slipped in a new law authorizing the head of any security detail serving a member of the blood family to detain him or her if they proposed a course of action outrageously dangerous.

The law was clearly aimed at Kris. She was the only member of the royal blood on active duty in the Wardhaven military.

Jack had never actually locked up Kris, but it had been a close thing a few times.

Now Kris raised a questioning eyebrow at her husband and father of her children who still commanded her security detail.

"If you were anything less than a Grand Admiral," Jack said with a serious face, "I'd likely do just that. However, my beloved, you have pulled too many jackrabbits out of your cover for me to object to you rummaging around in it once again. Sorry, guys," he said, glancing at the two admirals around the table. "I'm not going to veto this lame brain Longknife crazy stunt."

"Thank you, hon. You say the nicest things," Kris said, then switched back to formal, iron-assed grand admiral. "Let me know if you come across anything that needs fixing before we sail."

"I most certainly will," Admiral Kitano said. She'd been with Kris through too many of crazy operations not to. Of course, she was still alive despite Kris's devotion to getting them all killed, so she really had nothing to complain about.

The meeting soon ended.

During the next week, Kris only had to make two trips down to the surface, neither of which she wanted to make.

The first was to have the new Planetary Overlord officially sign a commitment to the Emperor to provide 80 battlecruisers a month to the Imperial Combined Fleet. She had to hold his feet to the fire, but her officers now commanded the planetary ground forces and Kris made it clear to the new guy that those forces were Imperial forces, not clan forces.

She said the same to the generals commanding the Army. They were delighted to receive the Imperial title and quickly had it sewn to the left arm of all their uniforms.

The second problem related to several hundred lordlings. There were more minor administrators on the planet than had been brought on the Battleships of State. The new overlord decided that meant these last lordlings had no one to be exchanged for.

He clapped them in some pretty dank jails. There was talk of formal apologies. Kris made the second trip down and returned with the lordlings.

They were delighted to see her and desperate for a bath. She sent them off to a Battleship of State and returned to her new flagship, the *USS Stalwart*, to issue the final orders to her fleet. They would sortie the next day.

Most of the fleet stayed at Longnae. They not only continued repairs, but also kept an eye on the new ten-penny dictator. Ready, Kris boosted her smaller fleet for the jump.

With her 5,000 battle cruisers were the fastest troopships in the invasion fleet. Any that couldn't maintain 3.0 gees Iteeche, got left behind. There were only 300,000 troops, but that was enough for Kris.

Also riding along with them as far as the jump out were the 12 crippled Human battlecruisers, 20 more fully combat ready Iteeche battle cruisers to round out a flotilla, and 3 Battleships of State. This force was headed for the Imperial Capital.

For the Human ships, Wardhaven was likely their next stop.

Kris intended to take the fleet through the jump at 49,000 kilometers an hour. That would put them on a fast course for the Progsus System.

As she was about to send the jump buoy through to warn all incoming traffic of a battle fleet coming through fast, a tiny currier ship jumped through instead.

"I have news for Imperial Admiral of the First Order of Steel Kris Longknife," the Iteeche captain of the messenger ship immediately announced.

This close to the jump, there was no time delay.

"I am Admiral Kris Longknife."

"My Most Eminent Admiral. I bear ill tidings," the Iteeche announced on the main screen, then hastily continued.

"The fleet of the oldest and wisest clans went forth to conquer and conquer they did. The Golden Flying Fish System easily fell to them."

"So far, so good," Jack muttered from beside Kris.

"Umm," she murmured.

"Since they faced no enemy fleet for that conquest, they went forth to conquer the Golden Giant Squid System and there they fell in with a major rebel force. They were badly defeated. The Rebels then went forth to reconquer the Golden Flying Fish System. That they did regain. It is feared by those in the Capital that the Rebels may come forth to conquer the Imperial Capital."

"Well, that puts an end to this," Kris snapped. "Admiral Tong."

"I copied the message traffic."

"Good. Order the troopships back to Longnae 4. Order the admiral commanding the Longnae 4 fleet to sortie three thousand ships for the Imperial capital. Admiral Kitano?"

"Yes, Admiral?"

"You have one and a half flotillas still here in the system, right?"

"Yes, Admiral."

"Have them set course for the Imperial Capital. They are to lead the Longnae three thousand warships through the advanced jump points. We're going to need them fast."

"Aye, aye, Admiral. I'll issue the orders."

"I do remember you telling them to keep a battle fleet at the capital," Jack muttered softly from where he stood beside Kris.

"Yes, I do remember some such thing. Now I'm just hoping we can provide that Navy fast enough to save our kids," Kris whispered softly, then her voice firmed.

"Admiral Tong, take the fleet through the jump point smartly. Nelly will provide you with the fastest course for the Imperial Capital."

"Aye, aye, My Admiral."

Quick as that, Grand Admiral Kris Longknife switched from conqueror of the rebel fleet to defender of the Iteeche system.

ABOUT THE AUTHOR

Mike Shepherd is the National best-selling author of the Kris Longknife saga. Mike Moscoe is the award-nominated short story writer who has also written several novels, most of which were, until recently, out of print. Though the two have never been seen in the same room at the same time, they are reported to be good friends.

Mike Shepherd grew up Navy. It taught him early about change and the chain of command. He's worked as a bartender and cab driver, personnel advisor and labor negotiator. Now retired from building databases about the endangered critters of the Northwest, he looks forward to some fun reading and writing.

Mike lives in Vancouver, Washington, with his wife Ellen, and not too far from his daughter and grandkids. He enjoys reading, writing, dreaming, watching grandchildren for story ideas and upgrading his computer – all are never ending.

For more information:
https://krislongknife.com
mikeshepherd@krislongknife.com

2019 RELEASES

In 2016, I amicably ended my twenty-year publishing relationship with Ace, part of Penguin Random House.

In 2017, I began publishing through my own independent press, KL & MM Books. We produced six e-books and a short story collection. We also brought the books out in paperback and audio.

In 2018, we began the year with Kris Longknife's Successor, followed by Kris Longknife: Commanding, and Vicky Peterwald: Dominator.

In 2019, we published Kris Longknife: Indomitable, Vicky Peterwald: Implacable, and ended the year with Kris Longknife: Stalwart.

2020 will be an adventure! I'm anticipating another Kris novel, a Vicky novel, and perhaps a book involving Sandy Santiago or Grandma Rita, and or interim novella or two.

Stay in touch to follow developments by friending Kris Longknife and follow Mike Shepherd on Facebook or check in at my website https://krislongknife.com

MORE BOOKS BY MIKE SHEPHERD

If you enjoyed this book, here is a list of more books by Mike Shepherd, including some of his early works and short story collections. All have hyperlinks. Enjoy!

Published by KL & MM Books

Kris Longknife: Emissary

Kris Longknife: Admiral

Kris Longknife: Commanding

Kris Longknife: Indomitable

Kris Longknife: Stalwart

Kris Longknife's Relief

Kris Longknife's Replacement

Kris Longknife's Successor

Rita Longknife: Enemy Unknown

Rita Longknife: Enemy in Sight

Vicky Peterwald: Dominator

Short Stories from KL & MM Books

Kris Longknife's Maid Goes on Strike & Other Short Stories

Kris Longknife's Maid Goes On Strike

Kris Longknife's Bad Day

Ruth Longknife's First Christmas

Kris Longknife: Among the Kicking Birds

Ace Science Fiction Books by Mike Shepherd

Kris Longknife: Mutineer

Kris Longknife: Deserter

Kris Longknife: Defiant

Kris Longknife: Resolute

Kris Longknife: Audacious

Kris Longknife: Intrepid

Kris Longknife: Undaunted

Kris Longknife: Redoubtable

Kris Longknife: Daring

Kris Longknife: Furious

Kris Longknife: Defender

Kris Longknife: Tenacious

Kris Longknife: Unrelenting

Kris Longknife: Bold

Vicky Peterwald: Target

Vicky Peterwald: Survivor

Vicky Peterwald: Rebel

Mike Shepherd writing as Mike Moscoe in the Jump Point Universe

First Casualty

The Price of Peace

They Also Serve

Rita Longknife: To Do or Die

Ace Science Fiction Short Specials

Kris Longknife: Training Daze

Kris Longknife: Welcome Home, Go Away

Kris Longknife's Bloodhound

Kris Longknife's Assassin

The Lost Millennium Trilogy by Mike Shepherd, published by KL & MM Books

Lost Dawns: Prequel

First Dawn

Second Fire

Lost Days

Award-Nominated Short Story Collections by Mike Shepherd, published by KL & MM Books

A Day's Work on the Moon

The Job Interview

The Strange Redemption of Sister MaryAnn

Printed in Great Britain
by Amazon